The Dragon of Two Hearts

Book Two

of

The Star Trilogy

by
Donald Samson

Illustrated by
Adam Agee

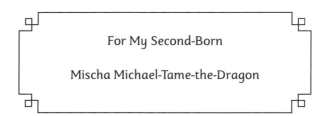

For My Second-Born

Mischa Michael-Tame-the-Dragon

Printed with support from the Waldorf Curriculum Fund

Published by:
The Association of Waldorf Schools
of North America
Publications Office
65-2 Fern Hill Road
Ghent, NY 12075

Title: *The Dragon of Two Hearts*
Author: Donald Samson
Illustrator: Adam Agee
Proofreader: Ann Erwin
Layout: David Mitchell
Cover: Adam Agee
© 2009 by Donald Samson
ISBN # 978-1-888365-93-1

CONTENTS

Part III Michael and the Dragon

Part IV To Seed the World

PROLOGUE

A haze hovered over the ruined land and the stench of burnt earth filled the air. The rolling hills were ringed by cold shadows, and the stubble of scorched trees cast eerie shapes in the stark light of the moon. A small figure crept furtively from shadow to shadow. A fox from the nearby forest had stolen into this forbidding landscape, hoping to find unsuspecting prey. Suddenly, his hackles stood on end. A nearby hillside had shifted. Was that a trick of the odd light on the desolate landscape? Out here even the shadows seemed alive. The night-hunter raised his nose to pick up some scent, but all he could smell was the burn of the land. He eyed the distant line of trees where there were bushes he could hide in. The fox was spooked and every instinct called him to abandon his hunt. He turned his nose back towards the forest, towards his den, towards the safety of thick undergrowth. Crouching low to the ground, he started trotting along the line of the shadow. Then, without the slightest warning to his keen senses, his small life was abruptly and violently snuffed out.

The great beast sniffed at his quarry and was satisfied. He picked up the limp body of the fox in his immense mouth and carried it back to his lair. He cast it onto the stinking pile where its bones over time would mix with the remains of all of his other victims. He gazed up at the moon, spread his cavernous jaws and bellowed loudly. Let it be known that he was the master of this ruination. He returned to patrolling his land.

He approached the line of trees where the fox had sought refuge, the barrier between his devastation and the lands beyond. He stopped in the open, away from all shadows, allowing the harsh light of the moon to shine ghostlike upon the massive length of his body. He lifted his long snout to the air and sniffed. The burn did not dull his sharp sense of smell. He detected that there was someone watching him from the cover of the trees. He recognized her scent. She had come before, and something in him was confident this would not be the last time.

He raised himself up to his full height, as if to show off his glory in the moonlight. He flexed his horns and spikes and thrashed his long tail. It would be a simple matter to pounce on her and add her bones to the pile in his lair, yet he did not. He would let her come as often as she needed until she had seen her fill. He raised his head to the moon and bellowed. He could smell her fear. He smelled her agitation and anger. But most of all, he sensed her irrational attraction to him. He bellowed again.

A day's ride away, a knight awoke from a disturbing dream. He shook his head as if he could shake off the images that still lingered before his eyes. Then he looked up at the sky, well-lit by the waxing moon. He groggily acknowledged that morning was still far away. He glanced about and was satisfied that there was nothing in the night to match the terror he had seen in his dreams. He pulled the covers over his head, turned on his side, and forced himself back to sleep.

Part I

The Knight Errant

Chapter One

Thief in the Night

There you go again," the boy said, looking up sharply. "Star, why did you say that?"

"Say what?" asked the dragon.

"That one day you will have to leave the Dragon Compound, leave Nogardia. I don't like it when you say that."

"It is what will happen," the dragon calmly responded. "It matters very little if we like it or not."

"But I don't want you to leave."

The dragon chuckled with chime-like tones. "Maybe it will be the other way around."

"What do you mean?"

"That you will be the first to leave."

"That frightens me even more!" Straw exclaimed, a surprised look on his face. "Why would I do that? I don't ever want to leave you."

"You will leave because that is simply what has to happen," the dragon said cryptically. "When there are things waiting for us, we sometimes just have to be nudged along to go meet them."

"Every once in a while you tell me things I just don't understand," the boy complained. He picked up a stone and threw it from where he sat into

the river. It landed with a cracking noise, like a dry branch breaking underfoot. He looked up with surprise and studied the water. Why would it make a noise like that?

The knight's eyes abruptly shot open. Something had woken him up. He listened to the sounds of the night closing in darkly around him. He could hear the wind gently rustling the leaves in the topmost branches of the surrounding trees. Faintly, he could hear the mumbling of the brook as it dropped from higher ground. Had the noise come from the stream? No, it had been in his dream. But the stone had made the wrong sound when it landed in the water.

Closer by, he heard a soft thump, as Storm shifted her weight from one leg to another. Storm's own calmness quieted him. She was his vigilant guardian in the night. Her keen senses were always ready to react to anything out of the ordinary. If she could continue quietly sleeping, all was well. It had been just a dream.

He looked up to a sky stretching endlessly above him. The moon had set, leaving the stars alone to guard the night. They glistened with a ferocity that made him blink. He sought out familiar bearings, and saw that first light was near. He closed his eyes, hoping to drift back to sleep, and became aware how uncomfortable he was. He could feel every stone that he had neglected to move away from underneath him the evening before. The bumpy irregularity of the ground irritated him. This sort of thing did not usually bother him. What had changed?

He sighed and opened his eyes. A place of light in his mind had woken up. He knew that it was fruitless to try and fall back to sleep. It would be a frustrating battle, and he would end up more exhausted than rested. He gave in to wakefulness and allowed all the thoughts he had banished the night before to flood him now.

He returned his gaze to the stars, a field of radiant flowers in the meadow of the night. He had heard a bard once sing of the night sky in those words, and he had liked the description. He had become intimate with that meadow of flowers. While others fled the night to hide beneath roofs and between walls, Michael was always comforted by the subtle, powerful strength in those sparkling lights. That's where dragons come from. That's where Star came from.

Star. Gazing at the sparkling heavens always reminded him of his beloved Star. How many years had it been now since he had left him behind in the Dragon Compound? How long had he been traveling, an errant knight on no one's errand but his own? Ten years? Twelve? Nay, more like fifteen years. He shifted his position at the thought. No wonder the ground felt so hard and unwelcoming. He had been on the road a long time.

He stared at the sky again, looking for the Great Hunter. Follow the line of his belt, he knew, and it would lead him back to the only home he had ever known. How far away was he? Three day's journey? A week? A full month away? He made a point of never finding out, since it would be too much of a temptation to return. Would they remember him? Would they have forgiven him? But then, did it matter? Without Star, it would not be home.

He had repeatedly heard rumor that there was a kingdom far to the south that was living in remarkable prosperity. The rumor hinted that they were blessed by a Luck Dragon. Was it possible that Star had gone and settled there? Or was the rumor only using the common phrase, blessed by a Luck Dragon, to explain their unusual good fortune. He often intended to go find out, but some new adventure always distracted him.

He sighed, and followed up the sigh with a laugh. The noise he made woke up Storm, and he could sense her in the darkness lifting her head in his direction.

"It's all right, Storm, my lass," he whispered into the night, more to himself than to his horse. "I'm just laughing at how easy it is to feel sorry for myself."

This was the life he had longed for. This was the life for which Star had prepared him. It was a little late to begin reconsidering his choices simply because the ground was harder than it had been when he first began his wanderings. Storm snorted and the unexpected noise startled him, and he smiled at his own foolishness.

It's time, he decided with resolve. Time to find a new way of life, whatever that may be. He shifted his weight again, trying to smooth the bumpiness that troubled his hips. Was it time, or was he spooked by what he feared he would find by sunset of the next day when he reached his destination?

Well, perhaps both were true. He did not look forward to this new venture, and that in itself was a first. Over the past ten, twelve, fifteen years there was not an adventure from which he had turned away. No adversary had ever caused him pause. He had entered every new situation, every confrontation, every battle with a sense of confidence that he was stronger, faster, more skilled, and better trained than any opponent he could meet. Now, for the first time, it was different.

He heard Storm continue to stir, and then she snorted again. She had also not gone back to sleep. She, too, was getting on in years. How many campaigns had she carried him on? How much more could he ask of her before it would be only fair to reward her with a grassy field to roll in to her heart's content? She had served him faithfully and he owed her a peaceful old age.

He heard her fidget again, stamping her hooves, and then she let out a warning whinny. What was up with her? Had a prowling night animal spooked her? It had been ages since he had met a lion; he had thought that the hills were too distant for them to roam this far into the woods and fields. Besides, they roar when they begin their hunt, and he would have heard it. Just the same, as long as he was awake, he might as well check.

He reached underneath the pack he used for a pillow and quickly found his battle knife, well weighted for wielding or throwing. The haft was cold in his hand and it woke him up even more. Storm whinnied again, stomping the ground. The knight shifted silently under his blankets to look over his shoulder. He was startled to see the cause of her distress. She was not alone! Silhouetted against the sky, barely visible between the backdrop of the trees, a man was trying, with obvious difficulty, to quietly lead a reluctant Storm away.

Suddenly all soreness of muscles was forgotten. As stealthily as a cat, the knight rose silently from his bedding, careful to keep low to the ground. He paused to assess the situation. Was this horse thief working alone? He looked quickly in all directions and satisfied himself that if there were others, they were keeping well hidden. So much for reconnaissance. It was time to act.

He did not want to give this thief any chance to hear him coming and gave up the idea of slipping on his boots. The size of this thief concerned him. He was uncommonly small. The knight had fought small-statured men before. He himself was shorter than most. He knew small men to be uncommonly strong, quick and agile.

Covering the distance with a quiet sprint, the knight sprang unexpectedly upon the dark figure next to Storm. He took the prowler totally by surprise and rammed into him from behind, knocking him off of his feet. The man sprawled on his face with a cry of surprise. In an instant, Michael was sitting heavily on the man's back, pinning his shoulders to the ground beneath his knees, his knife ready. The thief let out a grunt which made the knight very curious. He began to doubt whether he was dealing with a man at all.

Kneeling just below the shoulders, he snatched the hat off the thief's head and let it drop beside them. He took a firm handful of hair and pulled the man's head back towards him.

"Mercy!" squeaked a voice. "Mercy on my life!"

"Well, do tell," purred the knight, "if I haven't caught a boy."

"Please don't kill me!" the voice continued to squeak. "'Tis no honor to kill a whiff of a boy."

The knight chuckled and lowered the boy's head to the ground, but did not give up his handhold. "'Tis also no honor to steal a knight's horse while he sleeps," he countered. "Whiff of boy or no."

The thief was tongue-tied for a moment, and then stammered, "Did not know you were a knight. I meant no harm."

"No harm?" Michael snorted. "To leave a knight on foot as he rides on a call of mercy?" He took the blade of his knife now and laid it along the boy's cheek. He scanned what he could of the horizon in search of moving shadows as he listened carefully for any sounds behind him.

"Feel my blade?" he whispered as he bent over.

The boy nodded his head.

"Then tell me, as quick as your life, the truth. What I do with this blade depends upon it. How many others have come with you?"

"I'm alone," the boy said quickly. Michael listened intensely a moment longer to the sounds in the night. He only heard Storm shaking her mane. He decided to believe the boy.

"Then give me as quick your name."

"Sounder, sire," the boy said miserably.

"So you're the lookout."

"Yes, sire. How did you know?"

"Your name is somewhat of a giveaway, Master Sound-the-Alarm."

"Yes, sire," the boy mumbled.

There was quiet, as the knight sat there considering. Did this mean that the lookout was doing the stealing? He glanced at the sky and realized that at least this little adventure had helped to close in the time before first light. The boy interrupted him in his musings.

"Sire? Uh, could I go now?"

"Go?" the knight laughed.

"I didn't think so," the boy sighed. "Perhaps, then, you could let me up? You're mighty heavy on my back."

The boy had pluck, Michael thought to himself. He liked that. He lifted himself off the boy's back. In the shadowy light he watched as the small figure raised himself onto his hands and knees, and then pulled his feet underneath him. The knight observed this, though, and was ready. When the boy sprang from his crouching position with the intent to run away, the knight was on him in a moment, snagging him firmly by the ankle. The boy once again fell heavily to the ground with a loud grunt.

"Ah, I didn't think it would work," he mumbled to himself. Then he called out louder, "Mercy, mercy on me but a whiff of a boy!"

"Mercy?" spat out Michael, now somewhat irritated. "What sort of excuse is that for a lack of honor? You come out in the night to do a man's deed to steal a knight's horse, and you want mercy shown you because you are but a whiff of a boy? And what if you had succeeded? You'd crow loudly what a fine man you'd become. What if I offer you a man's punishment?"

"No!" squeaked the boy. He was sitting now, facing the knight, his leg pinioned underneath Michael's strong hand.

"Perhaps I should take an ear, assuming you've one left. Or maybe your nose would do as well."

In the gloaming of the coming day, the knight could see the boy quickly raising his hands protectively to his face. "Please, no! Mercy!"

"Now, Master Sound-the-Alarm, no more tricks. Understand?" He punctuated this question with a shake of the boy's leg. The boy silently nodded his agreement into the darkness.

"Since you've come out to do a man's deed, I want your man's honor that you will acknowledge yourself my prisoner and no longer attempt to escape. Will you give it?"

The boy cleared his throat and hesitated. Michael shook the leg again and pulled him bodily closer towards him.

"I give my word," the boy squeaked.

"Good," the knight said decisively, and removed his hand from the boy's ankle. "No more nonsense." He stood up and turned his back, stretching his arms over his head into what was left of the night.

"'Tis not the way we like to wake up on a morning, eh, Storm?" Hearing her name called, Storm nickered softly and walked the few steps to nuzzle his shoulder. He reached up to rub her soft muzzle and felt the heat of her breath on his face. He turned now and looked back to where he had left the boy. He half expected to find him gone, swallowed up by the fading darkness. He was actually surprised to see that the boy was still there where he had left him. He liked that. The boy had been raised well. Not only courageous, but also honest. He was no common thief.

"So tell me, Master Sound-the-Alarm, for whom are you watching, and what are you watching for?"

The boy was silent. For a moment, the knight questioned whether he had mistaken the shadows for substance and that the boy had slipped away after all. Finally the knight heard him clear his throat.

"I don't think I'm allowed to tell, sire."

"Well, this is intriguing," the knight mused. "You realize that you've no choice but to take me to where you live?" He was moving around now. There was the barest smudge of light on the horizon, and he could see just enough to begin packing up his camp.

"What if I refuse?" the boy wanted to know. He was asking out of curiosity, to find out if defiance was worth the effort.

"Ah, well, if you refuse, then you become my servant and join me on my journey. Eventually, if you merit the honor, I will make you my page. Remember, you've given me your word not to try to escape until I release you."

"Your page? A knight's page?" The boy was interested. "And to where do you journey?"

"By my reckoning, I should be a day's distance from the king of these woods. I am headed to Gladur Nock."

"Oh," was Sounder's disappointed reply. The knight stopped rolling up his blankets to look over at the boy. He looked well enough dressed, though he guessed the full morning light would reveal that the boy was somewhat ragged around the edges. He based this upon the boy's hair, which was long and unkempt, tied back loosely.

"We are in the woods of the king of Gladur Nock, are we not?"

"We are."

"Do you not owe fealty to the king?"

"No, sire," said the boy with defiance in his voice, sitting up straight as if he might have to defend himself.

"Curious," mused the knight. "And would you not want to accompany me to the king?"

"No, sire," the boy repeated, with vehemence.

"Well then, that leaves us only one choice," the knight said. "You must take me to the others. We've enough light now to find our way. I am soon packed and I'm hungry as a bear for his breakfast. Lead on, Master Sound-the-Alarm. Where our eyes fail to find the path, let our noses lead us. I want breakfast for my troubles of returning you safely home. Show the way."

The boy stood, but hesitated, trying to decide on the right thing to do. Michael finished tying his sleeping roll and packs onto Storm. He secured her saddle and fastened her harness. She shook her head and little silver bells jangled merrily. Then he took Storm's reins and thrust them into the boy's hand.

"Come, page, lead my charger. You've caught yourself not only a superb horse, but a knight as well. Fine harvest for one night's thievery, I'd say. I permit you bragging rights once we arrive. I hope it's not too far. Lead on."

The boy opened his mouth to say something, then closed it again. The knight was too compelling for him to resist. Resigned to his fate, he turned and, leading the knight and his horse, walked silently through the woods.

Chapter Two

The Village in the Woods

*T*hey walked for some time through ever-deepening woods. The sun rose splendidly, but the cover of trees was thick and kept out the full benefit of its light and warmth. The knight pulled his cloak tighter around his back to keep out the chill of dawn, more bone-chilling among the shadows of the trees than it would have been in the open fields. He wondered how the boy in his tunic could take the cold, and then memories of his own life before entering the Dragon Compound flooded him. The boy could take it because he had no options. It was that simple.

They walked for so long that Michael began to wonder if Sounder was leading him around in circles. Then his nose noticed that they were soon at their destination. He could smell the smokiness of a morning fire lightly mixed with a tease of roasted meat.

"Make yourself known, Master Sound-the-Alarm," the knight said quietly. "I don't want to take anyone by surprise and cause misunderstandings. I'm terribly shy of arrows I can't see until they've found their mark. I have a feeling your friends are somewhat skittish."

The boy stopped in his tracks and, glancing at the knight, raised his cupped hands to his mouth. He cooed like a wood dove three times and waited. After a few moments, the coos were returned.

"It's safe," he mumbled. "They're expecting us now."

"Well, I hope they put out the welcome mat," the knight said cheerfully. "Walk on."

It was not long before they saw a figure coming towards them through the trees. It was also a boy; he carried a bow and a quiver on his back. When he got close enough to get a good look at them, he stopped in his tracks. He looked like he might bolt, when the knight's companion waved and called out,

"Liam! It's all right. We're together."

With this the boy came trotting up to meet them.

"Sounder, you've got everyone worried. Where did you disappear to yesterday?" And then more urgently, indicating the knight, "Who's he?"

Michael spoke in answer, "Your friend noticed an errant knight hungry for a solid breakfast and good conversation. He kindly invited me to join you for both."

Sounder glanced up at Michael with a look of gratitude. His failed exploits would be kept a secret between the two of them. Liam looked at the knight suspiciously, nodded his head as if in greeting, but said nothing. He walked next to Sounder, whispered something in his ear, to which he got only a shake of the head as answer. The three of them continued on in silence.

They soon broke through the thick tree cover into a pleasant open glade. The knight had expected a camp of some sort, but what he found was far larger than what he had imagined. Many tents of different sizes filled the meadow and there were so many people bustling about in the haze of the many cook fires and the dim forest light that it had all the commotion of a village. The knight stopped in his tracks and just looked.

It took but a moment for him to be noticed. Women and children stood where they were and stared at him. A number of men began approaching him cautiously, not sure whether to receive him as a friend or foe. He saw several of them take up thick staffs and a few had picked up swords. Sounder suddenly slipped away with Liam, so the knight knew that he was on his own.

"Greetings and good morrow to you all," he said, wanting to keep things friendly. He was by now ringed on three sides by men who looked like they did not take kindly to uninvited guests. They blocked his view of the rest of the camp, which had grown uncommonly quiet. One of them motioned towards the forest from the direction that the knight had just come and said brusquely, "Check for others." Three men slipped silently into the trees, carrying bows.

"I come in peace and friendship," the knight spoke, holding up his empty hands. "And alone," he added.

"What's your business?" one of them asked suspiciously. "Why do you seek us out in the forest?"

"Why don't you just go back on your way?" a rough-looking man spoke up. "We don't want you here."

The ring of men began to close in on him. The knight had taken them by surprise, and it was obvious they were not used to visitors.

"Forgive me if I've come unannounced. I was returning a boy who had gone astray."

"Likely story," a man missing several teeth spat out. "Sounder don't get lost."

"Well, I can see that my coming is not welcome," he observed.

"Then just be on your way," one of the men said. "Sooner the better."

"I accept your friendly invitation to leave," the knight sighed. He was just turning to Storm when another man joined the circle.

"It would be most inhospitable of us to turn away a stranger," the newcomer spoke breathlessly. Michael looked up to see the owner of the voice. He was a middle aged man with a very pleasant face and a warm glow in his eye. He had just pushed himself between three men, two with drawn knives and one who had raised a short sword.

Michael realized that when he had turned his back on them, they had advanced on him. They had no intention of letting him go his way. This newcomer had stepped between them.

A shock shot through the knight that had this man not arrived, they would have cut him down. That was why the man was breathless; he had run full out. The three men lowered their weapons and stepped back. This new fellow obviously commanded some respect. Michael saw a glimpse of Sounder behind the circle around him. He must have run off to fetch this man.

"You must be hungry," the newcomer continued. "Please, allow me to welcome you to our small encampment. My name is Will. Please stay and take a bite with us?"

"I would most gladly," the knight said graciously with a small bow. "It certainly seems safer than taking my leave. At least for the moment." Sounder ran up and took the reins from his hand.

"I'll take your horse and look after her," he said with a big grin. "I'll bring her when you're ready to go. Honest." And without waiting to hear how the knight might answer, he walked off with Storm, who followed his lead willingly.

The men who had been crowding around him disbanded and went about their business. The man named Will led the way through the camp. "Please excuse the gruffness of our greeting," he began. "We're not used to strangers here. Few seek us out, and those who do mean no good. We've never been visited by anyone as honorable as a knight."

"And it seems to me that few who find you return to tell the tale."

"Ah," he sighed. "Forgive their rashness. Truth to tell, there is great fear among us that we be found. Come, if you give me ear, I shall willingly share with you why we are so cautious."

Together they walked through the camp. There were many cook fires tended by women, a number of whom had toddlers in tow. He saw a group of young women sitting in the shade of a tree happily gossiping as they wove baskets. Children romped freely at their play.

The men he saw were engaged in some handcraft, working leather, building with wood, or mending weapons. They looked up from their work and eyed him suspiciously.

Will led him to a stand of low trees. Cloths had been spread between their low hanging branches to create a canopy of shade. In that space stood several rough-hewn tables and makeshift benches. Several men and women were sitting at the tables eating and chatting, but they grew silent as the knight joined them. "Now be sociable," Will warned them. "He's not come taking sides."

"The side he takes is already clear," a woman with golden hair loosely tied up said. "By his looks, he's a knight, is he not?"

"Give him a chance," Will insisted. "Let's hear him out."

"Give him breakfast first," a big burly man said. He had black, curly hair and a bushy beard. He had merry eyes. He handed the knight a plate piled with food. "Living outdoors can make a man powerful hungry. Eat first, talk later."

The knight received the plate. "I'm grateful for the hospitality," he nodded in thanks. He sat himself at the table with those who had spoken and Will joined him. The food was simple, yet good. Much better than anything he made for himself while on the move. They ate for a few minutes in silence. Sounder appeared beside the woman and whispered something in her ear. Michael watched her pensively. Something about this woman looked vaguely familiar. But he had never been near here before, so he figured she reminded him of any of the countless people he had met over the years. The woman responded to Sounder sternly in a low voice. The boy went away looking discouraged.

"You are discontent with your king, it seems," Michael commented after he had stayed his hunger.

"That's putting it mildly," chuckled the fellow who had served him the food.

"The king of Gladur Nock is cruel, greedy and mean-spirited," the woman spat out impulsively. "He does not care for the well-being of his people. He tramples on us and uses us as if we were his livestock."

"Maisy, that's enough," Will said holding up his hand to stop her.

"Maisy?" Michael said astonished. Now he knew why she looked familiar. "Now, you wouldn't be the same Maisy who once lured an untried knight into the forest to be tied up like a pig ready for slaughter on his very first adventure, would you?"

Maisy stopped chewing and stared at him. She turned pale and her mouth fell open. "Oh, my," she said, covering her mouth quickly with her hand. "It's you. The young knight, hardly more than a boy."

"At your service," he said with a small bow from where he sat.

"Oh my," she repeated, still astonished. Then she added quickly, "I never meant you any harm. I was doing what my Pa told me."

"That's true enough," the knight said. "If my memory serves me, I believe you even wanted to marry me."

"I was just a silly girl," she protested. "There was no way I could have stopped them."

"Which is why I stopped them myself," the knight said with a shrug.

"Well, it sounds like there's a story here," the burly man was interested.

"Maisy and I met once many years ago," the knight explained. "It was a brief encounter, but it left a lasting impression on me. I was newly on the road and hungry. She provided me with a hearty meal." He did not add that her family had taken his horse and was prepared to slit his throat in the bargain. They called it giving him "the smiley."

"I left that life behind," Maisy said. She fidgeted and smoothed out her skirts.

"Living in the woods still holds an appeal for you, I see," Michael commented.

"Not by choice," she protested. "I had a proper life. I had a city life and I married a good man."

"That would be me," the burly man said with a smile. "My name is Benick."

"Raised our sons," Maisy continued. "But we couldn't live a decent life under the king. Any gain we had, he stole. He wanted the boys for his army for senseless skirmishes with neighboring lands that have never done us any harm. Anyone who disagrees with him just disappears. Good neighbors would vanish overnight."

"That's about when the dragon came," Will said.

"The dragon," the knight repeated. "So there really is one." He had hoped that it was only a rumor, that the story he had heard was a fantasy, an exaggeration.

"Oh, Scorch is a dragon, all right," Will said. "And every bit as greedy and mean-spirited as the king."

"Tell me about it," the knight said gravely.

Will told their tale of woe. "At a time when we thought we could be no more deeply oppressed, a shadow fell over Gladur. We looked up to see a fearsome dragon circling over our houses. For three days it circled, and finally settled in a nearby forest. Hysteria and fear spread through the city. The dragon burned up the trees. It made forays into the fields, destroying our crops."

"We appealed to the king," Benick continued. "He sent out forces to drive the hated worm away. Not a horse or man of the army ever returned. All the townsfolk shook in their homes for fear."

"The day came when the dragon stood at the gates of Gladur Nock," Will recounted. "We knew the city walls weren't going to hold it back. It could fly, after all. It breathed fire and could easily burn down the gates and all our homes. It wasn't sitting there out of fear. It wanted something from us. The king's counselor told us that the dragon was waiting for us to make it an offering. We took out a wagonload from our store of crops. The dragon was satisfied. But a week later, it was back.

"This went on until we began running out of food. Then the king sent out a proclamation that we were to gather together everything that was precious to us: cloth, gold, silver, even the plates we ate off. Each wagonload bought us another week."

"But even this couldn't last forever," Benick continued. "We implored the king to make an offering from the riches he had taxed from us. He made a showing of giving some, and then insisted he had given it all. We know how much he has taken. He's no better than the dragon. He was hoarding his own piles of treasure."

"Where did it go from there?" the knight asked.

"That was when the king started taking our children," Maisy said grimly.

"We thought he must be joking at first," her husband quickly added. "But then, once each moon, his soldiers came to a different borough and rounded up the children. Then they had to draw straws. The one who drew the short one...." He left the rest unspoken, but the knight could well imagine what happened to that child.

"We lost our eldest that way," Maisy said with tears in her eyes. "I swore I'd lose no other."

"So all these families have lost children?" Michael asked, indicating the camp.

"Either lost one or not waiting for it to happen," Will said. "At first folk feared that the dragon would pick us off as we fled the city. That hasn't been the case. The dragon allows safe passage to each family."

"And so the carnage goes on?" Michael asked.

"It's taken a new turn," said Benick. "Now the king has set up a warrior's camp."

"What's that?"

"Every boy, when he comes of age, has to go into it."

"What do they do with him?"

"He's trained," Will explained. "The boys are trained in fighting. At a certain point, most are taken into the army. The king has built a new one since then, but he won't send it out against the dragon."

"What about those who don't go into the army?"

"They're sent, one at a time, to go fight the dragon."

The knight could see that he had found more than he had reckoned for. "Tell me about this king," Michael said.

"Well, let's see," Benick began. "His name is Worrah."

"How old is this Worrah?"

"No longer young, but still able to swing a sword," Will said.

"And has he a queen?" the knight asked.

"Had," Maisy said. "We all loved her. But she died."

"There is a princess," Benick said. "Aina is her name. While her mother lived, she was as kind and generous as the queen. But now she has become an evil shadow of the king."

"In what way?" Michael asked.

"She takes pleasure in overseeing the Warriors' Compound. They're kept there like prisoners. She's the one who sends them out to their deaths."

"Not true," Will countered. "It's said that Princess Aina looks after them out of a sense of caring."

"Odd way to care for men, who sends them off to certain death," Benick responded.

"As you can see," Will said with a faint smile, "we are divided in our opinions."

"This is a gruesome picture you paint," the knight said.

"Aye, gruesome it is," said Will. "You can understand why we live here in fear of discovery."

"I won't be the one to betray you," the knight said. "Maybe I can bring you some relief."

"That would take a miracle," Maisy said.

"What sort of help are you thinking of?" her husband asked.

"I came this way because I heard of the dragon," Michael said slowly.

"Certainly you're not thinking of challenging the dragon? That would be death for you and your horse," Will exclaimed.

"Maybe," Michael said thoughtfully. "But I've had my share of encounters with a dragon. If anyone could help, I figure I could."

"You're a fool if you think that," Benick said, shaking his head. "That dragon can overwhelm a whole army and will show no mercy."

"I believe you," Michael said. "Still, it's what I've come to try. If nothing else, it will mean one less of your town's young men to march into the dragon's jaws."

"It'll mean one more month of living and nothing more," said Benick with disgust. "Why go throwing your life away?"

"Well, I certainly don't plan to," Michael said. "And I thank you for your concern and the food. I'd best be on my way." He placed his plate on the table and stood up. The others stood as well and stared at the ground awkwardly, not knowing what to say next.

"We thank you for your desire to help," Will finally said. "If we can assist you somehow...."

"First of all," the knight said. "You can give me directions and set me on my way. And then you can tell me how I can send word to you if I ever want to take you up on your offer of help."

Will looked at the others, as if seeking their approval. Both Maisy and her husband gave a quick nod. "There's a gate into town on the south side. The captain of the postern, he's a crusty old soldier by the name of Hands, because he's got big ones."

"What about him?"

"He's our contact with the town. He's got no children to lose. He knows how to get a message to us. It would cost him his life, though, if the king knew about him."

"I'll not breathe a word of it. And I'll only contact him if I want to get in touch with you," Michael assured them. Then he looked around. "Now where's that boy with my horse?"

Even as the knight spoke, Sounder was already approaching, leading Storm. Michael took the reins from him and lifted himself into the saddle. "Might I borrow the boy to show me the way?" he asked. "He still owes me a favor, and this would make things even between us."

Maisy looked at her son for an explanation. Not receiving any, she looked up at the knight. She stepped over to stand at his stirrup. "I would have stopped them if I could," she said earnestly, looking up at him. "I swear to you, I meant you no harm."

The knight saw the concern in her face. "Nor do I mean any harm to your son. I'm already fond of him. I promise to send him back."

"All right," Maisy said with a shaky voice. "Sounder, I want you right back, you hear? No more adventures today."

"Yes'm," Sounder said. The knight offered his hand and pulled Sounder up onto the saddle in front of him. He gave Storm a gentle kick with his heels, and off they rode away from the camp.

Chapter Three

Expect the Uexpected

"Nice horse," Sounder commented as they trotted along. "Though she is a bit on the small side. 'Course, she's a mare."

"Storm is more than a nice horse," the knight laughed.

"I mean, I like the way she rides. I meant no harm about her size. She's also very beautiful. And I bet she's smart," the boy said.

"Yes, she is all of that," Michael replied. "And don't let her size fool you. She is quick and agile and can make a turn tighter than any other horse I've seen. That's a great advantage when you have to make a lot of quick decisions during a fight. She is also an excellent companion."

"Will you take me with you?" The knight was startled by the suddenness of the boy's request. Obviously, Sounder had been thinking about the offer to become his page. "I want to be a knight like you."

Michael winced at these words. Years before, Mixer had said something similar.

It had been nearly a week after he had been exiled from the Dragon Compound and two days following his narrow escape from Sounder's mother, Maisy, when he had nearly lost both his horse and his life. He had been roused from sleep by someone pulling on his feet. "Come, on, Straw, you sleepy head, wake up!"

He opened his eyes to see Mixer's face smiling down at him. "Mixer!" he exclaimed, jumping up from his blankets, giving his friend an excited embrace. "What are you doing here? Where did you come from? How did you find me?" He was bewildered, yet delighted to see him.

"I followed you," Mixer explained, as if it had been that simple. "Your horse, you know, did leave something of a blazed trail as you cut across just any old field. And when I was uncertain, there was always a shepherd or goat boy who had seen you pass. You do sort of stick out, you know." Mixer was dressed in a leather jerkin much like Michael's. His own horse stood nearby, nuzzling Storm.

"Where did you get the horse?" the young knight had asked. "You never had a horse while we were living in the compound."

"You're forgetting that we all come from noble families. My father owns many horses."

"Your father gave you a horse to follow after me?" Michael asked incredulously. He looked to see if there were others who were about to ride up and join them.

"Well, not exactly," Mixer looked slightly embarrassed. "I sort of borrowed this one."

"You stole a horse?" Michael could not decide if he was shocked or tickled by the scandal.

"Look," Mixer said seriously, "I didn't leave Mali in peace until he told me what he knew. Garth let some things slip and Mali figured out that you had been sent away as a wandering knight. From the looks of it, he had guessed right." Mixer gestured to the armor lying next to Storm's saddle.

"When I heard that, nothing was going to hold me back. I had always planned to be a knight, you know. The clothes are mine and so is the sword," he said grabbing the pommel at his side, "though I don't have much training yet. I figured we'd pick that up on the road. You know, together." Then he laughed, and Michael could not help laughing with him. He had been feeling so homesick and Mixer's arrival was exactly the tonic he needed.

"But Mixer, I don't know where I'm going."

"Sounds good to me," Mixer said with a big smile. "Let's go there together. If there are two of us, then we can't ever be lost."

Mixer was the answer to Michael's thirst for companionship. Over the next few days they laughed and whooped and joked, making something to yell about out of every moment. They merrily trotted along the highways and the byways, occasionally raced their horses just to break up the monotony of the wilderness, and shared everything, both the lean and the fat of the fortunes and adventures of the road. When they passed a town, Mixer would boldly ride in and return with enough supplies so they could both dine like kings of the road.

"How did you afford so much?" Michael once asked while they were roasting a chicken.

"Ah, well, I didn't exactly come empty-handed," Mixer said with a smile and jostled the money pouch at his belt. "But the chicken, to say truthfully, was a gift from a barnyard I passed by." When he saw Michael's shocked look, he said, "Look, Straw, on the road, we do good where good is needed, and we don't do harm. But we can't do good if we're hungry. And I did take the scraggiest one I could find."

There were days when they saw very little other than one another, and they often spoke about how marvelous was the life of a wandering knight.

"It sure beats sweeping out a stall," Mixer once said. Michael did not answer, and Mixer must have noticed his mood darken as his thoughts turned to losing Star. "Sorry, Straw," Mixer quickly said. "I didn't mean it that way." It was the last time he mentioned the life they had both left behind.

On their ninth day together, Aga's prediction that adventure would find him once again surfaced. Their path across the open countryside had brought them to a road, and they agreed to follow it and see where it might lead them. They were once again low on food and were in search of the next village. The fields around them showed signs of cultivation, so they knew they were not far from some sort of settlement.

They saw the figures on the road ahead of them about the same time as they heard the sounds. They pulled up their horses to listen. "That's a woman shrieking," Mixer said. "Look, I think there are some people in distress."

They spurred their horses and, as they neared, quickly sorted out what was happening. Several agitated horses without riders were milling about a laden cart pulled by an ox. A woman, clutching a baby to her chest, was standing in the field beside the road shrieking for help. Next to the cart, three men were beating a fourth man with clubs.

"We've go to stop this," Michael said and pulling his sword bore down on the men with the clubs. Mixer was not far behind him. The pounding of their horses' hoofs alerted the men to their arrival. They dropped their clubs and pulled out the swords hanging at their sides.

Michael was off Storm even before she had come to a halt. Immediately he engaged two of the brigands who were visibly surprised and alarmed by the sudden appearance of the two riders. Out of the corner of his eye he noticed Mixer fighting with the third and then gave his full attention to the two men before him. They were not skilled swordsmen, and Michael disarmed one, who quickly retreated from the fight and a moment later was riding off on his horse. Once the second man realized that he was no match for the knight, he threw his sword at him, sprinted to his horse and also dashed away.

It was fortunate for Michael that he turned at that moment to see how Mixer was doing, because he was able to parry the sword thrust that would have otherwise cut him down. His powerful return stroke, however, disarmed and injured his far less experienced opponent. Clutching his bleeding hand, the man sprinted to his waiting horse and, clinging to his saddle, rode away to join his companions. Michael glanced at the woman, who by now had stopped screaming and was tending to her husband, sitting up with his back against the cart. Then he looked around for Mixer.

"No-o-o-o!" the young knight wailed at what he saw. His sword fell from his hands.

Mixer lay very still, sprawled on his back. Terror gripped Michael's heart when he saw the handle of a knife sticking out of his friend's chest. He hurried over to him and crouched beside him.

"Mixer!" he called out. "No! Mixer!" His friend's eyes were staring vacantly at the sky. As Michael huddled over him, the eyes flickered and settled briefly on his face. "You're alive," Michael breathed in relief.

Mixer's voice was as weak as a breeze that barely ruffles the leaves on a sultry summer's day. "Pull...it...out...," he spoke haltingly. The words were hardly audible, but their meaning was clear. Then his eyes turned again to the sky above.

Michael understood what he had to do, and he grasped the handle of the knife. With a decisive upward movement, he drew the blade out of his friend's chest. Mixer's eyes grew big and he heaved a long deep sigh. But it was not followed by an in-breath. His eyes remained staring vacantly at the sky.

"So what do you say?" the boy asked again. "Can I go with you?"

Michael was jarred back from his memories. For a long time he had blamed himself for allowing Mixer to join him. What had he been thinking? Mixer was untrained and untried. He had spent his youth looking after the needs of a Luck Dragon. He was experienced at wielding a broom, not a sword. Michael had been trained by the dragon to fight. He could have handled all three of the brigands alone. Mixer could not handle even one of them. The young knight had made a promise to himself after that day.

"Sorry, Sounder, but I travel alone. It's enough for me to look after myself." He was never going to make the same mistake again.

The boy pursed his lips and looked disappointed. Then he said what he really wanted. "Maybe you'd let me take her out for a ride." He patted Storm's neck. "You know, just to see how she handles."

"I bet you would like that," the knight laughed, relieved that the boy was not going to insist on joining him. "I'll tell you what, I will keep your wish in mind. Perhaps the day will come when I let you ride her full-out and see what she can do. That is, assuming you can stay in the saddle. Would you like that?"

"Oh, indeed, very much." If he could not become a knight, at least this promise was something to look forward to.

They rode until near midday before they came to a trail that was not much more than a path. "You can let me off here," the boy said. Michael halted Storm, and the boy slid down to the ground.

"If you follow this trail, it will lead you to a river. Follow up-river and you will find a road that crosses the water. Ford the river and follow the road. That will take you to Gladur Nock."

"You keep yourself well hidden," Michael warned.

"I have to. They are always hunting for us."

"Will you be all right?" the knight asked. He had promised the boy would return safely.

"I know my way around. You only caught me because I thought you were asleep."

The knight laughed. "Well, don't let anyone else catch you while he's sleeping."

"Not a chance," the boy smiled broadly. "Have a care, though. The king's guards snatch up any passing stranger for their training camp. Not that many strangers pass through here any longer. Just the same, have a care."

"Thank you for the warning," Michael said with a nod. "I look forward to our next meeting, Master Sound-the-Alarm."

"Farewell, Sir Knight. I look forward to that ride you will let me have." The boy slipped between the trees and disappeared.

The knight followed the trail as it wound through meadows and pine forests. As peaceful as his surroundings were, he had the nagging feeling that he was being watched. He turned around on occasion to see if he could spy someone. He began to wonder if Sounder was tracking him. As the day wore on, he had to assume he was imagining things.

Late in the afternoon Storm perked her ears and tossed her head. She smelled the promised river. It was slow-flowing, the water a mixed brown-green. He stopped in the shade of some trees, took a bite to eat out of his saddlebags and let Storm drink deeply.

He remounted Storm and although not yet at the ford, they waded across. The water rose higher than the horse could stand, and she had to swim a short distance. The current was slow, so it was an easy crossing. In the middle, though, Michael felt his left stirrup give way. When they had cleared the water, he saw that a strap had broken. He did not like to ride with broken gear, so he made an early camp under the trees near to the water's edge. He found the singing of the current pleasing. It reminded him of the happy days of his youth when he walked his beloved Star down to the river every day and scrubbed him down. He whistled to himself as he repaired the broken strap.

He fell asleep that evening thinking about what he had learned in the forest. He knew every truth had at least two sides to it. He wondered what he would find when he arrived at his destination.   At least one thing seemed certain: There was a dragon, and it was wild and hungry. He fell asleep imagining himself scrubbing Star's scales.

"How's your wrist?" the dragon asked, sniffing at the boy's arm.

"It's a bit sore," Straw said, carefully rotating his hand. "I fell on top of it and got it caught in a bad position. Should we stop?"

"Take up the sword in your other hand," Star suggested. "In a fight, if you injure one hand, you have to be ready to keep going with the other."

Straw picked up the sword in his left hand. "How does it feel?" Star asked.

"Strange," the boy admitted, swinging the sword through the air. "I never thought about trying to use my left hand. But I can get used to it."

"That's good," the dragon said. "On the road, you will have to get used to a lot of things you never imagined doing. Expect the unexpected. Quick thinking and dealing with odd circumstances will be your daily bread."

"You really think I am going to be a knight one day, don't you?"

"That's why I'm training you, boy," the dragon responded. "And I am more than satisfied with your progress. You will make a fine knight, I have no doubt. Now, prepare yourself for my attack. Are you ready? Pay attention, boy! Are you ready? Boy, are you listening to me? Boy! Get ready!"

The knight awoke with a start and stared into the night sky. Instinctively, he reached for his wrist and rotated his hand. There was no hint of soreness. Now what had all that been about?

He could see the darkness beginning to pale before the inevitable onslaught of light. It was always a breathtaking moment for him. He watched the great cosmic tug-of-war as the balance shifted. For a brief span of time, the blackness of the sky turned the most comforting blue.

It never ceased to comfort him, how the morning light gained this victory over darkness. It was a daily reminder of what he had dedicated his life to. He felt hope and strength surging into him, and sitting up, he threw off his blankets.

He got up nimbly and walked the few steps to where Storm stood and caressed her soft muzzle. She smelled him deeply and nickered softly. Then he turned happily to rolling up his blankets and getting ready to move on. A bright new day promised new adventure, and one never knew what new adventure might come. Perhaps that was Star's reminder: Expect the unexpected. He stretched sore muscles into pliancy and then led Storm down to the water for a drink and for himself a bit of a wash.

The water was running calm enough, but it was too shallow near the bank for him to bathe. Leaving Storm to drink, he walked upstream to find a deeper pool so he would not have to wade out too far and risk fighting the current. He stripped and splashed into the water, shivering with the shock of the cold, and then rejoiced in the numbing and tingling. He was crouched up to his shoulders when he heard Storm's warning cry. He cursed that he had not kept better watch. So that was what the dream was about! He leapt from the water in an instant, and it cascaded off his body as he splashed his way to his clothes where he had his knife. He grabbed it intending to go as he was to see what distressed her.

At that instant, though, the hair on the back of his neck stood on end and he sensed imminent danger from behind. He turned to see the club flash through the air. He got his arm up in time to take some of the blow, but not enough to keep him from being stretched out on the bank, lost to all light.

Chapter Four

Captured

*T*he knight awoke to a painful pounding in his head. He next became aware of the movement. It was the gentle rocking of a horse. But something was wrong: He was not riding. His eyes flickered open and he found himself staring at the brown flank of a horse. Beneath his head, he saw the ground passing by and watched the horse's legs flicking back and forth. He was slung on his belly over the back of a horse, his head hanging down on one side, his legs on the other. As if that was not enough, he was still naked from washing in the stream.

Ah, the indignity of it all, he thought to himself, and in spite of the pain in his head, he chuckled bitterly at his predicament.

He squirmed, trying to heave himself up, and discovered that his ankles were tied together, as were his wrists, which hung down beyond his head. He was vastly uncomfortable. He squirmed some more.

"He's rousing," he heard a voice call out. Another horse came trotting up, and he was startled by the sting of a whiplash across his bare back.

"Lie still," a harsh voice ordered, "or there'll be more of the same."

Michael took a breath. This will take some figuring out how to escape. First he had to know how many of them there were. Also, he needed to know if Storm was near, and whether she still carried his gear where he could get his hands on his sword.

"Hey," he called out before the horse next to him could gallop off. "What's the harm in letting me ride? I'm not likely to get away. You've got me tied up like a hog."

He listened for some response, but all he caught was a gruff comment and others laughing. Just the same, the horses stopped; several snorted and stamped. He heard someone dismount and walk over to his horse. Strong hands took hold of his ankles and give a great shove, pushing him head-foremost right off the other side of the horse. He was able to turn and take the force of the fall on his arms and shoulders. His skin smarted where it took the impact against the gravelly ground.

They had been traveling along a road. He assumed it was the very road he had planned to ride that morning. As he lay there a moment, there was more laughter. A shadow fell across him, as someone cut the ropes holding his ankles together. He started to sit up. Once again, the whip lashed out and stung him on the shoulders. He winced at the unexpected pain.

"Don't have any bright ideas," spoke a voice at his back. In spite of his hands being bound, Michael sprang nimbly to his feet. Hardly was he standing, his legs were tripped out from under him as a blow hit him along the back of his head. He fell to the ground with a grunt.

"I warned you, no funny business," spoke the voice again. "Now you want to get up, you do it slow and easy."

Michael raised himself to his hands and knees. He shook his head to clear it. He saw between his arms the speaker's foot next to his left elbow. He knew they did not mean to kill him, at least not just yet. He was angry at being so roughly man-handled. Besides, he wanted to know if they meant to knock the fight out of him or were they just mean-spirited? Even with his hands tied, it was a simple move to grab that foot next to his elbow, lean into it and twist. Down to the ground the fellow fell with a deep grunt and a satisfying thud. Michael then swiveled to jam his knee into the man's abdomen and wrest from his hand the whip that had three times struck him.

He looked into the eyes of a bearded face that was painfully gasping for breath. He held the whip up under the man's nose and pressed it against his face. "Just so we understand each other, if you use this on me again, I'll jam it down your throat."

By this time, the two of them were crowded in by other men who had sprung from their horses and now stood behind him threatening with their short swords drawn. Michael stood up slowly with the whip in his bound hands. He gazed around at the circle of faces with a look of mock surprise. "What?" he said innocently, shrugging his shoulders. "Someone had to teach him some manners."

There was a hearty laugh and Michael looked up to see a man on horseback considering him. He had a red beard and blue eyes that gazed sharply at Michael. "He'll do well in the pits," he said to no one in particular, and laughed again. "Looks like we got ourselves a fighter."

Michael took the chance to look around him. Lots of horses, at least fifteen. Most of them with riders, except for the few who had come to surround him. They were dressed as soldiers, wearing tunics with an emblem of a dark castle. They were all armed, many with bows. There would be no quick escape from them. He would just have to bide his time. He caught a glimpse of Storm, but there were too many horses with riders between them.

"What king do you serve?" he asked loudly of Red Beard, who sat on his horse with a grimace on his face, taking the knight's measure.

Red Beard ignored the question. Instead he said, "Give him back his toy," gesturing towards the man on the ground. Michael looked at the handle. It was wrapped in leather and studded with metal. No wonder it had hurt. He glanced down at the man on the ground who stared up at him with a mixture of hatred and fear.

"Remember what I said," and dropped it onto his face. The knight turned back to the rider and walked towards him. The men who had ringed him gave way, but two followed closely behind.

"You wear the tunic of soldiers. Do you serve the king of Gladur Nock?" He asked.

"You'll find out soon enough," Red Beard replied.

"I came here to serve the king of the dragon-held lands," Michael stated.

Red Beard laughed, and then added, "Serve him you will."

Michael realized he was not going to get much more out of him at present, so he changed his tactics. "How about some clothes?" he asked, holding his bound hands up in supplication. "You've already humiliated me. No need to ridicule me as well."

Red Beard gazed at him a moment, as if trying to guess what could cause a man to speak so boldly to his captors. Then he said gruffly, to no one in particular, "Get 'em." The rider nearest him directed his horse over to Storm and returned with the clothes the knight had shed on the shore of the stream. He threw them at Michael's feet.

Michael had little trouble getting his trousers and shoes on, but with his hands bound, he could go no further. He held up his hands again. "If you'd be so good as to untie me, I can finish."

Two soldiers walked up to him, both with drawn short swords. "No funny business," one of them said as a warning.

"I'm not amused by any of this," the knight said gravely. The soldier just stared at him for a moment, but did nothing. Michael held out his wrists impatiently, "Cut 'em already."

As soon as his hands were free, the knight rubbed his wrists to get the circulation going. He was pleased to get out of his bonds so easily. He knew he would have to submit to them again, but he would make sure they did not tie them so tightly. He finished dressing slowly, letting the circulation return to his hands. The soldier watching over him grew impatient and told him to hurry. At last he held out his hands again, but as they were tied, he flexed his muscles. As a result, the bond was not as tight as before. That could come in handy, he thought. Then again, it might only mean a bit more comfort.

They gave him some water to drink out of a skin and a hard piece of bread. He was grateful for even meager refreshment. Red Beard, who appeared to be the captain, rode over to where they stood and spoke to the soldiers guarding him. "Tie him with the others."

They grabbed the knight roughly by the arms and walked him to the outskirts of the troop. There he saw about a dozen men with their hands tied together like his. From each of them a rope ran to a rider. He quickly understood that, as the troop rode, the prisoners walked behind.

He scanned the faces of the others, and was startled to recognize one of them. It was one of the men who had been ready to attack him in the camp, the one with several teeth missing. He spat upon seeing Michael.

"Well, d'ya believe us now?"

"How did they get you?" Michael asked.

"Out huntin'," he mumbled, and then quieter so the others could not hear. "I was trailing you, to see where you might go, when they trapped me. My guard was down."

So that was who he had sensed following him. So much for thoughts of Sounder. A long rope was then tied to the one binding his wrists and handed to one of the riders. They were set up to walk, two per rider, one on either side trailing behind the horse. He was paired with the man he knew from the forest village. The rider holding their rope was the whip man. This setup pleased Michael very much.

Whip Man sat on his horse and gave the rope a vicious tug, jerking Michael from where he stood. He said over his shoulder, "You move when I tell you to, and you stay put when I tell you to. Understand?"

"I see what's needed," the knight responded. "But be gentle with that rope. It's mighty annoying to get tugged along."

"I'll bet it is," the rider said with satisfaction, and gave the rope another pull, once again causing Michael to stumble forward.

The whole troop began moving again, with the prisoners walking along behind. His rider was none too kind about it. Sometimes he let his horse lag behind the others and suddenly spurred it forward to force his two prisoners to run after him. It became a game that pleased him immensely. Michael noticed that he kept the two ropes wrapped around his arms, one on each side. After an hour or so of being dragged along in this manner, Michael decided that Whip Man needed another lesson in manners.

The path had just entered a forested area where tall pine trees grew all around. The riders fanned out. Whip Man began lagging behind again, and the knight knew what was coming. He turned to the man walking beside him. "Are you willing to follow my lead?" he asked in a low voice.

"Sure, if it'll break up the monotony," he answered with a gruff laugh.

"When I give you the word, step briskly to the right of the tree in front of you, circle round it and hold tight to that rope."

"As if I've got any other choice," he commented dryly.

They had fallen back twenty yards or so when Whip Man glanced over his shoulder. He smiled maliciously and spurred his horse. They were just passing between two pine trees that grew not more than ten feet apart. Michael had been waiting for this moment. Couldn't be more perfect, he thought to himself. He looked at his companion and gave him a nod. Then, loudly, he cried out, "Now!"

The two of them stepped to the outside of the trees as the horse passed between them. Grabbing the rope, they both circled around their tree and dug in their heels. Whip Man was pulled off his horse and hit the ground hard with a loud grunt. He lay where he fell, stunned.

The knight was standing over him as several of the soldiers rode up quickly, swords drawn. "This fellow has absolutely no manners," Michael said shaking his head regretfully. Some of the soldiers laughed roughly; a few looked at him with wide-eyed wonder.

By this time, Whip Man had recovered and had gotten to his feet. He was spitting mad. "I'll kill you with my bare hands!" he yelled.

Michael took a few agile steps out of his way. "I'll tell you what," he said. "Untie my hands and let's have a fair fight. You can even have a sword."

"You're a dead man!" he yelled at Michael. "I'll rip out your guts!" He took several steps towards the knight.

"No you won't!" commanded a voice. Red Beard had ridden up and looked at them sternly. "I'm tired of you causing delays," he said to Michael. Then he turned to the guard. "You may not maim him. I want him fit for the pits. You may take an ear or his nose, but nothing more. Be quick about it, too. I want to keep going."

Saying this, he turned his horse and rode away to the front of the pack. Michael realized that he was to find no protection from the captain, but he had not expected any.

With a wicked smile, the guard drew his knife and, taking long steps, made a grab for Michael. It was a mistake. Michael used his tied hands to his own advantage. He swiveled on the ball of his foot and, before the guard realized it, Michael was behind him with his tied hands slipped over the guard's head at his throat. He jammed his knee into the small of the guard's back pulling him off balance. The knife fell to the ground as he groped to free himself and get a breath.

"Help," he squawked to the other riders who were standing around watching. Michael heard him gasping and tightened his hold.

"You got yourself into this," one of them said.

Michael could tell that this fellow was not overly popular. He looked up at the man who had just spoken. "I guess I shouldn't kill him."

"You'd be doing us all a favor. But we'd be compelled to string you up to a tree, and that would be a shame."

"I want someone else to take my rope," the knight demanded.

"I'll do it myself," the same man spoke again.

"Now that that's settled, what do I do with you?" He pulled back even tighter as the guard struggled. Michael put his mouth to the man's ear and spoke so that only he could hear. The guard stopped struggling and listened. "I have killed men larger, stronger, faster and braver than you. I am meaner than a bear in a bad mood and faster than an eagle hunting to feed her nestlings. If you mess with me again, I will snuff you out. You do not have enough friends here to save you. They would be glad to see you go. Do you understand me clearly?"

The guard hesitated, but then nicked his head.

"Nice and easy, then," Michael said loosening his grip. "No fast moves, now. You don't want me to get the wrong idea." He carefully lifted his hands above the guard's head, ready for some treachery.

The guard, though, was thoroughly spooked by now. He staggered away, gasping and holding his neck. Michael backed away from him. When the guard regained his breath, he took his horse by the reins and left without glancing back. The man who had offered to take his rope was looking down at him.

"I want no tricks from you," he said.

"Then treat us decently," Michael returned. "Don't use your horse to torment us. It's bad enough to travel all tied up."

"I take no pleasure in tormenting others," the man said gruffly.

"Then let's be on our way," Michael replied cheerfully.

Part II

The Kingdom of Gladur Nock

Chapter Five

Sparring in the Dungeon

*T*owards the end of day, they were back on the road. Michael's rider was true to his word. He kept up a consistent pace and there were no more incidents. Michael noticed that the road now followed a river. He could not tell if it was the same as the one he had crossed the day before. The water here was much broader, and it was slow moving. They passed by fields where crops were growing. Obviously, he thought, the dragon left these fields in peace. Maybe the people living in the forest had exaggerated their plight.

He looked around at the others. They looked tired, yet all but one was able to keep up the pace. This one was lean and looked flushed. He stumbled frequently and staggered more than he walked. Occasionally, he feebly begged for water.

"Hey," Michael called out to the riders. "That fellow over there looks like he's got a fever."

One of the riders glanced over at him and his face grew grim. "What do you want us to do? Leave him behind?" Some of the guards laughed roughly at this.

"Well, that is an option," Michael pointed out, but they ignored him. The road led mercilessly onward.

The knight was impressed by his first look at Gladur Nock. He admired the strength of its high walls and massive gates. It was built a short distance from the river. The road, however, had not yet turned towards the main gate. He was wondering why when he saw his answer. The road, which had been dirt until now, suddenly became paved with flat stones. Wide enough for a carriage to pass over, it was an impressive piece of work.

The first structure they came to surprised the knight. It was a gallows. Three bodies were dangling at the end of ropes. Michael had seen a lot in his life, and had been exposed to his share of the ugly side. He had never gotten used to hangings, which he considered a waste of life. He walked slower as they passed by and without realizing it, his lead-line grew taut. His rider pulled up his horse to see what was delaying his prisoner. "Make sure it doesn't happen to you," he said.

This jolted the knight out of his reverie. "What did they do to deserve this?"

"They tried to escape," the rider explained somberly. "We find them all, eventually."

"Thanks for the warning," the knight replied dryly.

At that moment, Whip Man came riding by. He pulled up his horse and indicated the hanging bodies with his whip. "That's what's waiting for you," he jeered, and then rode on. Michael winced at the thought and kept walking.

Boats now appeared on the river. There was a line of large vessels, one after another, tied up along the shore. He reckoned that the river must have a very sheer bank here. Each boat sported a colorful canopy. Underneath the awning sat groupings of men and women enjoying the evening. There were servants pouring drinks and, between the revelers, tables filled with food. No sign here of a people living under the shadow of a marauding dragon. As they passed the first boats, the people in them held up their goblets and cheered.

"Welcome back!"

"You've made a good catch!"

"Blessings on our expeditionary forces!"

"Say, take a look at that one," Michael heard someone say. He looked and saw they were pointing at him.

"He'll make fine sport," someone else commented loudly.

Some of the revelers sent servants out with drinks for the riders. The guards returned the greetings. It became obvious that they were being hailed as victors. Michael and the others were their booty.

"Hey, what about a drink for us?" Michael called out as he waited for his rider to empty the goblet a servant had brought. He was curious what sort of response he would get.

"Absolutely," called a jolly, fat bald man from the boat they had stopped in front of. "We must give generously to our surrogates as well. We are grateful for your sacrifice." A servant appeared with a goblet and a cluster of red grapes. The goblet indeed had wine in it.

Michael drained the drink and raised his bound hands to the man in the boat. "My thanks to you, my friend," he called out.

"Oh, our thanks to you," the bald man called back and laughed. All the people in his boat laughed with him.

Michael turned to his companion from the forest. He was greedily eating a peach he had been given. "All right, explain," demanded Michael. "Why did he call us surrogates? What sacrifice are we making?"

The man wiped his mouth on his sleeve before answering. "Each one of us means one less son the townspeople feed the dragon. When all this started, even the rich and noble class had to give up their sons."

They continued their walk down the promenade as night drew on. Lamps were kindled on the boats and along the walkway. It was a festive sight. Small groups of people were strolling the quay, visiting others in their boats. Some boats were empty, but had the remnants of a party left on the table. So this is the other side they did not tell me about, Michael thought. A thriving, comfortable noble class with a great deal of wealth. The dragon had left them intact.

At one point the road turned away from the riverfront and towards the city gates. The whole length of the road was lit with lamps. The parties on the boats along the quay behind them were full of loud chatter, laughter and snatches of songs. People on the road were out taking in the pleasant evening, walking to and from the river. They also greeted the guards like returning heroes. Michael was surrounded by the sounds of merriment. Minstrels carrying their instruments passed them as the night drew on. Michael guessed they were on their way to serenade the feasting nobility and earn themselves some coins in the bargain. All of this was in such contrast to his bound hands and the others imprisoned around him. Again he wondered: Is this the picture of a city oppressed by a dragon?

They were marched up the long approach to the city gates. Michael was suddenly mindful of his conversation in the forest. The immense doors of the gate stood open, allowing passage in and out. Several guards were standing on duty. As they were passing through, Michael leaned over to his companion from the forest village.

"Is this the southern gate?" He received a quick nod. Then he asked quickly, "Which one is Hands?" The man gave him a quick puzzled look, wondering how he might know the name. Then with his grizzled chin he pointed out a guard on the left who stood there studying the faces of the prisoners. When his eyes fell on the man from the forest, his face lit for a brief moment with recognition before returning to an expressionless gaze. Michael memorized this man's features.

He got only a brief look at the broad plaza into which the horsemen rode. The prisoners were herded down stone stairs into a holding area below the streets. The light from torches on sconces along the stone walls shed a dim light. The prisoners were turned over to a set of guards, all with whips in their hands and short swords in their belts. The guards spoke to them roughly and cracked the whips at their legs to keep them moving. They wanted no trouble. The guards had nothing to worry about. The prisoners were tired, hungry and thirsty from their march to Gladur Nock.

About fifteen of them in all, they were led into a large cage. Some called out for food and drink, while others complained about their hands still being bound. Their new keepers instructed them to line up at two points in the cell where the bars were slightly further apart. One at a time, they thrust their hands through and had their ropes cut. Then they were each given a plate of food and directed to a bucket of water in the corner from which they could drink.

Michael ate and drank. He was too tired to start up a conversation with anyone else. The others were equally exhausted. He sat with his back to the stone wall of the prison, another man sitting on either side of him. A few of the men were moaning, others were mumbling complaints, whether to themselves or to others he could not tell. He looked for the fellow who had been struggling to keep up, but he did not see him. He nodded off wondering what they were doing with Storm and whether she was being treated decently.

He held up his shield at the last moment and ducked. The blow from the dragon's foot wrenched the shield out of his hand and sent it flying. All he had left was his sword, which offered little protection from his immense opponent. The dragon's next blow was aimed right at his head. He dove underneath it, tucked his chin and rolled head over heels. His momentum brought him to his feet again in an instant. The dragon's snout was bearing down on him. With a two-handed swing, he smacked the dragon with the flat of his sword squarely on his nose. He immediately dove a second time, tucked and rolled in the opposite direction, once again landing on his feet. He turned to meet the dragon's attack, but there was none. The blow to his nose had sent Star off on a sneezing fit. The boy relaxed and waited for it to pass.

"You're a scamp," Star said when the sneezing had passed.

"Did I hurt you?" the boy asked.

"Only my pride," the dragon said drolly. "Getting your opponent to sneeze himself to pieces is not the most elegant or honorable way of ending a battle."

"Come on, Star," Straw objected. "You told me any win is a good win."

"Well, that was an ugly win, if you ask me," Star responded with a smile.

"A lot better than ending up underneath you again," the boy pointed out.

"Agreed. Although I won't go so far as saying that you beat me, you did succeed in stopping me."

"Say, Star, I was wondering something."

"You usually are," the dragon teased. "What is it this time?"

"All of my practice is with you. And I'm not complaining. But once I'm a knight, I will have to fight with men. Shouldn't I get some practice fighting with men?"

"Once you're finished sparring with me, fighting with men will be easy," Star assured him. "You won't have any trouble with men."

"I guess I'll just have to trust you're right," Straw said.

"Indeed you will!" and Star began to laugh, but his usual chime-like voice was replaced by harsh cracks and snaps. The boy looked at him with incomprehension.

Guards were walking among the prisoners, rousing them with shouting and cracking short whips. A faint morning light filled the dungeon. Michael pulled himself onto his feet and wiped the sleep from his eyes. He looked around with his dreams still clinging to his consciousness. Hadn't there been a dragon here a moment before? The sting of a whip on his arm woke him up completely. He moved with the other men as they were driven from the cage and down a narrow corridor. As the cell emptied out, Michael noticed one man who did not get up from where he lay. It was the man who had struggled to keep up the day before. Whether he was dead or alive Michael could not say.

They were brought into a larger holding cell. Daylight streamed in from barred windows at the top of the wall. Once again they were given food. There was a bucket in one corner to drink from. In the opposite corner were two buckets to relieve themselves in. Once they had eaten, the men began quietly complaining about their accommodations.

"Could be worse," one man muttered.

"In truth? What part could be worse?" another countered.

"I'm not sure," he responded. "But I'm convinced it could be worse." Others laughed bitterly at this.

"At least they fed us," another man observed.

"And it's not half bad," someone said.

"Which means only half of it was worth eating," someone said loudly. Once again there was laughter, this time with more acceptance of their situation.

"What do you think they have in mind for us," a man asked.

"I know what they want with us, and you won't like it." This was spoken by the man from the forest village who had been tied together with Michael. The men grew silent and they waited to hear what he had to say.

"They want to turn us into fighters," he said. "The king wants to fill the ranks of his army."

"Fine with me," one fellow with broad shoulders said. "I'm itching for a weapon in my hands."

"You'll have to learn how to use it first," a voice spoke out loudly. All the men in the cell whirled around. The speaker was standing outside the cell and had been listening to their conversation. He had a scruffy beard and thick hands. He stood of middle stature with a broad build, solid like a wall. He looked like he was made for rough work and enjoyed it. He had a grim smile on his face as he spoke.

"Welcome to the dungeons of Gladur Nock. My name is Mardak and I'm the sword master. I will train you while you are here. I will make sure that you all leave the dungeon knowing how to use a weapon.

When you're good, you will be allowed to join the king's army. And the very best among you will be allowed to earn great honor."

"What if we don't want to join the king's army?" a man spoke up. It was a fellow with broad shoulders and powerful arms, but Michael judged him to be more a farmer than a soldier.

"Let that man out of the cage," Mardak ordered. Guards opened up the door and the man strode bravely out into the space before the cell. "Give him a sword," Mardak said. A guard came forward and handed the man a wooden practice sword. Mardak took one as well. "You can leave when you can fight your way past me," he said.

Then, without any warning, Mardak attacked the man. It took no longer than a few breaths before the prisoner's sword went clattering to the stone floor, soon followed by the man himself as his feet were tripped out from under him. Mardak had struck him in the head and the man lay on the floor with his arms thrown up to protect himself from any further blows. Mardak stepped back from him with a smile. "Did anyone else want to leave?" he asked.

Michael was tempted to come forward, but he knew that Mardak had no intention of letting anyone go. He was making a point, and Michael could see that it had made an impression on the others.

"Welcome to your new life," Mardak announced. "We will feed you and train you. If you work hard, you have nothing to fear. If you are foolish enough to try to escape, you will not get far. I am telling you now so you have no illusions. Those we capture quickly will be beaten. Those who manage to wander further away will find themselves with a unique view of the river. I am certain you saw the accommodations we have prepared on your way into the city. Have I made myself clear?" He was referring to the gallows they had passed.

The prisoners were silent and looked grave. Mardak had made himself very clear.

"You will begin your training this morning," Mardak continued. "When you have satisfied me that you know how to handle a weapon, you will move to the next tier. For now, we will keep you safe down here. Let's move out." At his words, guards filed into the cell and herded the prisoners out into the hallway.

The men were led through a succession of corridors until they came to an open room. The dirt floor had straw strewn over it. Light came from barred windows high above their heads. Michael guessed that the windows were at ground level. There was a pile of wooden practice swords against one wall.

The practice swords were passed out among the men. Guards with metal swords were stationed along the walls. Mardak arranged the prisoners in lines and led them through some basic exercises in swordsmanship. His orders were crisp and clear. He worked the men repeatedly through the same movements until they had broken out in a sweat. Requests for water or rest were ignored as Mardak pushed them relentlessly on to practice. Guards with whips circulated among the men making sure that everyone kept moving.

When they were finally given a rest, a bucket of water was brought in. The pause, however, was brief. Mardak had them soon back on their feet and continuing to practice. Breaks were few and far between. Michael was amused by the elementary forms and the practicing did not tax him. The other men, however, unused to this type of exercise, tired quickly and were stumbling.

When the light coming from the windows above their heads began to fade, Mardak had them stop. Many of the men, exhausted and spent, threw their swords down into the straw and sat where they were.

"Not so quick," Mardak warned. "One more exercise, and then I'll let you go. I want you to pair off and face each other. Come on, let's get this over with."

Grumbling and complaining, the men did as they were ordered. Michael was paired with a large fellow who stood at least a head taller. He suspected what was coming next.

"All right, men. Here's your chance to put into practice what you've learned. I want you to spar. Those men who have been disarmed, go and stand against the wall. Those left in the middle, find a new sparring partner. Do this until one man is left."

This new challenge perked up a number of the men. The thocking of sword against sword filled the dungeon. It took only a moment for Michael to disarm his first opponent, who stood there dumbly staring at him wondering how he had done it so quickly. "I've done this before," the knight said with a shrug of his shoulders. He turned to find a new partner.

After he had disarmed his second opponent, something in the back of his head warned him that he did not want to be the last man standing. In his next match he was up against a scrappy younger man who had more strength than skill. At one sword blow, Michael simply let his sword drop. "I guess that takes me out," he commented dryly and walked to join the others along the wall.

Before long the remaining men had weeded one another out until only one was left in the middle. It was the man whom Michael had let defeat him. The man stood there looking satisfied with himself. Mardak came forward also holding a wooden sword.

"You the last one?" he asked. When the man nodded, Mardak offered that they spar together. Eager to show what he could do, the prisoner charged at Mardak, swinging his sword wildly. Mardak toyed with him briefly, soundly beating him about the arms and shoulders. He finally laid him low with a powerful stroke to the man's shoulder. The prisoner lay in the straw dazed and holding his arm. Mardak had not only disarmed the man, he had made it clear how little skill at handling a sword the man had. Once again, he had made the point that he was the one in charge.

The men were then herded out of this dungeon, down a corridor, and into another room. By this time daylight was gone and torches along the walls were lit. This room had rough tables and benches. This was their commissary. Exhausted, the men ate in silence. After this they were led to another large room that held bunks. The men were instructed to find themselves a berth and go to sleep. It was not long before the room was filled with the sound of snoring.

The next morning they were roused with first light, and the day unfolded as before with instruction and sparring. It also ended the same with Mardak challenging the last man standing. Michael was careful not to be in that position. Their new life unfolded before them, every day a repeat of the day before. If for nothing else, Michael was grateful that he had the opportunity to keep himself limber and active.

Chapter Six

The Pit

*T*heir routine had not varied for the first weeks after being imprisoned in the king's dungeons. They rose at first light and, aside from short breaks to eat, practiced their swordsmanship until the torches were lit in the evening. Some of the men took to it enthusiastically, while others, although resigned to their imprisonment, practiced reluctantly. A few days after their arrival, ten more men joined their group, brought in by another troop of trackers.

Every day, their sparring ended with the last man standing fighting Mardak. The sword master always won, often bruising his opponent. Michael remained cautious and in the background, and had not yet had to fight him. But among themselves, the men had come to recognize Michael's skill with a sword, and many sought him out to spar with one-on-one, sometimes to test their own progress, at other times just to learn more of his technique.

One day, Mardak changed their routine. Following a short noon break, he led them to a caged-in space in which the hard floor was covered with a layer of sand. Daylight streamed down from a barred opening in the ceiling. "This is the practice pit," he told them.

At first he asked for volunteers. Two at a time, the men entered the pit and sparred with their wooden swords. Mardak let them fight until one defeated the other. The reward for the winner was a shower and more rations, which motivated the combatants to fight so vigorously that they often drew blood in spite of the wooden swords. When volunteers were scarce, he chose for them. It was not long before other guards began showing up to watch. They cheered on one or the other of the pair fighting. When Michael saw money changing hands at the end of a fight, he realized that the duels were staged for their entertainment.

Although Michael never shied from a fight, he never used one as a means of entertaining others. He did not like watching the men getting banged up. So far, he had managed to stay out of the cage.

One day he broke his silence. "You don't make skilled fighters out of these men in just a few weeks," he said when Mardak asked for volunteers. The sword master stared hard at him. No one talked to Mardak without being invited to speak.

"You might as well put dogs in the pit," Michael continued. "You're not doing this to train them. You just want something to bet on."

"I've been watching you," Mardak said, staring hard at Michael. "You always hold back, keep yourself in the crowd. But I know your kind. You know how to fight, but you're just too much of a coward to stand forward and be a man."

Michael did not take the bait and remained silent.

"I want a volunteer for the pit," Mardak called out. He looked Michael up and down. "You'll do. Let's see what you're made of. Get into the pit." Michael shrugged his shoulders and walked to the open door. He was roughly shoved from behind. Mardak volunteered another of his group. When Michael glanced over his shoulder, he was not surprised to see who it was. It was Melchi. He stood over a head taller than Michael. His legs were like tree trunks. Michael knew that he would not overcome him with strength.

There was one sword lying in the middle of the sand floor. This was new. Usually they were given swords as they entered the pit. Michael saw that it was one of their wooden practice swords, so at least they did not intend for them to maim one another. It was obvious that they wanted to see who would get the sword first and how he would use it. He was glad, because he had no intention of drawing blood.

They squared off on either side of the sword, each of them bent low to the ground, ready to snatch it up before the other did. What Melchi did not notice was the handful of sand Michael had scooped up. When Melchi dove for the sword first, he got a face full of sand. Michael snatched the sword and tripped up the momentarily blinded Melchi onto his face. It was over in a moment. Michael had not even broken a sweat. He had a knee in Melchi's back and the wooden sword at his neck.

"Can we call this over?" he said loudly. He got only a gruff response that he took for agreement. It obviously had not gone the way the sword master had intended.

Michael helped Melchi to his feet. Melchi looked a bit dazed that it was over so quickly and wiped the sand out of his eyes. As they came to the door to the pit, Mardak held up his hand when Michael tried to pass through. "Not so fast," he said. "The winner gets round two."

Michael wondered if this new rule was in his honor. Mardak now placed two swords on the sand in the center of the pit. So, Michael thought, he wants to see us spar. When Michael entered the space again, he heard the sword master call out not one, but two others. Ah, Michael thought, he does not want to see some sparring. He wants to see a drubbing. Well, the knight thought grimly, I do not intend to take a beating for his entertainment.

The two who came in next looked apprehensive. They had seen what Michael had done to Melchi, whom everyone had considered unbeatable because of his size. They stuck close together, and Michael took note of this.

They squared off over the swords. Michael saw the one to his left give the other a quick tap with the flick of his wrist. He guessed this was a sign between them to dive for the swords at the same time. Michael did not hesitate, and he was not disappointed. As both of them dove for the swords, Michael reached out, but not for a weapon. Placing his hands on the outside of their heads, he shoved them sharply together to knock with a hollow sound. Then he pushed down on their necks, leaving them sprawled in the sand. Michael collected their swords and walked back to the door. "I've told you that it's unfair what you're trying to do. These men are not trained fighters," Michael said, looking directly at the sword master.

The gate opened and Mardak stepped inside. Michael handed him the swords. He turned to leave, but the sword master stopped him again. Michael stood there and watched the two men he had just disarmed stagger out holding their heads.

"We're not done with you," the sword master sneered. He had a harsh smile on his face. He called for a third sword and placed all three into the middle of the sand pit. Then he picked out three new opponents. Michael saw the fear in the face of one, while the other two looked grimly prepared.

Michael stood beside the door and waited until they had entered and passed him by. With these odds, he was not going to wait for them to get settled. He attacked them before they ever reached the center of the pit. It was over in a moment. With well-placed blows to the backs of their legs, he temporarily lamed the two who looked ready to fight. That left only the frightened man who never even tried to pick up a sword. When he turned and saw the other two down, he ran to the farthest corner of the pit as if there was a door on the other side. There was sporadic laughter from outside the cage.

Michael picked up the three swords and walked back with them to the gate. One of the men on the ground dove at him as he passed. As Michael scooted out of the way, he smacked him over the back of his head with the flat side of one of the swords. The man collapsed in the sand with a grunt. Michael leaned over him and said in a low voice, "Sometimes it's better, when you're down, just to stay down."

Mardak opened the gate. He was frowning.

"I told you," Michael said to him. "You don't make warriors with a couple of weeks of training." He tried to walk through the gate, but once again the sword master stopped him. They stood there as the three other men left the pit.

"Get me another sword," the sword master growled.

Michael's patience with this man had come to an end. "Maybe you'd like to show them how it's done," the knight baited him. Mardak stared at him, but before he could respond, Michael continued. "Oh, wait, my mistake. I forgot you know how to lead only from behind your men."

Mardak's eyes bugged out and his nostrils flared. He shoved Michael roughly back into the pit and stepped in after him. He pulled the gate closed with a clang. Then he drew his own sword. Michael was still holding the three wooden swords. He knew they were useless against an iron sword with an edge. He let them drop to the ground. Mardak walked to the center of the pit and looked at Michael.

"Not so quick now, are you?" Mardak taunted.

Michael kept to the periphery. "Is this a lesson or an execution?" he asked.

"Come and find out," Mardak beckoned with an ugly smile.

Michael did not like the odds. Mardak obviously knew how to handle a sword and knew a few tricks of his own. He was also immensely strong. He was going to make it clear to the others never to challenge his rule. This had nothing to do with learning how to fight. It was all about who was in charge.

Something hard hit the straw behind Michael. Was someone trying to trip him up from outside the cage? If Mardak had support from the other side of the bars, it was going to be a difficult fight. He moved to the side and glanced down. Shining in the straw was a sword, and this one was not made from wood. One of the guards had decided to even up the odds. He looked at Mardak and saw surprise and anger in his eyes.

Michael bent to swoop up the sword. Mardak chose that moment to attack. After what he had seen, it was obvious that he did not want to face his challenger on equal footing. Instead of trying to dodge or parry the oncoming blow, and without taking the sword, Michael threw himself forward. His shoulder caught Mardak in the belly. He heard Mardak grunt and his sword clang against the bars of the cage behind him.

Michael wrapped his arms around Mardak's waist and, still bent over, used his momentum to carry them both. The pit was a small enough space that he was able to force Mardak backwards right across to the other side. Michael rammed him against the bars of the pit. Mardak grunted a second time.

Letting go his hold, Michael swiveled and wrapped himself around Mardak's sword arm. With his shoulder still pressed into Mardak's chest to keep him off balance, he cracked his arm repeatedly against the bars of the cage until the sword fell loosely to the floor of the pit. Then Michael drove his elbow into Mardak's midriff. Mardak grunted a third time as he doubled over.

At that moment, a commanding voice stopped him. The gate to the pit flew open, and several guards with drawn swords streamed inside.

"That's enough!" Someone yelled. It was a woman's voice, and it was coming from the barred opening in the ceiling above the pit. The guards pushed Michael away from Mardak and stood between them. Mardak lunged to get at Michael, but they held him back.

"That's enough, I said," commanded the voice from above.

Mardak obeyed and stood there panting with malice in his eyes. "I'll get you," he growled in a low voice, staring hard at Michael.

"How many chances do you need?" Michael asked.

Mardak tried a second time to lunge at him and was thrown back against the bars of the cage by two of the guards. They stood waiting to see what they would be ordered to do next. They did not have long to wait. A door in the shadows of the dungeon opened and a woman walked in flanked by guards. She was dressed all in black leather. Her long black hair hung in two braids that gave her a girlish look. Her appearance startled the knight. He had traveled far and wide in his life, but this was the first time he had ever seen a woman wearing pants. It looked bizarre and unnatural. The braids made her look young, but her manner was brusque and determined. Michael felt an immediate mistrust of her.

"I've seen enough," she barked as she entered.

"But, Your Highness," Mardak began, stepping forward. The guards were no longer holding him. So this must be the princess, Michael thought.

She cut Mardak off before he could speak any further. "It's useless to seek his match in here." She gazed at Mardak and looked like she had eaten something bitter. Mardak scowled and looked away. "I want to see what he can do against a more experienced fighter," she continued. "How about Cole?" She turned to one of the guards. "Bring Cole here."

"But, Your Highness," Mardak protested, "Cole is soon to be sent out."

"So, are you worried for him?" asked the princess. Michael wondered if she meant him or Cole.

"Against him?" the sword master exploded. "I'm more worried Cole will hurt him."

"Really?" the princess said. "I was unaware that you cared that much for anyone." Mardak was visibly stung.

Michael sighed. They were not done testing him. After seeing what he had done to Mardak, she obviously wanted to pull in someone who could forcibly put him down.

At that moment a door opened and the guard reappeared with a man of medium height, and muscular. He had short-cropped hair and his face betrayed no expression. He had a scar that ran from above his right eyebrow across a crooked nose. It looked like a sword slash. "I hate this stinking place," he scowled, looking around. "Why do I have to come back here?"

"To fight," the princess answered sternly. "Do you do something else?"

He ignored her question. He glanced at Michael. "Him?" he asked. And then he scoffed, "I'll break his head open."

"That's why you're here. Give them each a sword," the princess said. "You will fight until one is disarmed. These are wooden swords, so understand this: I want you both to be able to walk out of there. Understood?" She stared at them sternly until they nodded in agreement.

Michael was surprised by her warning. This was not what he had expected. As he walked back into the pit, he had to pass by the sword master. "Now we'll see what a big man you are," Mardak hissed at him.

Michael did not bother to answer. He had to size up this fellow Cole quickly. The slash across his opponent's right eye made him wonder. Instead of squaring off with him, Michael stood to Cole's right. Cole overcompensated when he moved his head to look at him. It was as Michael had hoped: Cole's vision was impeded in his right eye from the old wound.

Michael began his attack, always staying to Cole's right. Cole kept turning to keep him squarely in front of him, and Michael always returned to his weaker side. Cole was a competent swordsman. He had not gotten that scar in an accident, but in a fight. Michael changed his tactics since he was dealing with someone who knew how to fight. Cole's tight, muscular arms told him that he was not going to wear him down. He had to do something decisive and quick, before Cole had a chance to find his weaknesses. And his plan had nothing to do with sword fighting.

Without stopping to think about whether or not it was such a good idea, Michael tossed his sword up into the space between them. He directed it to pass by Cole's good eye. Cole was taken by surprise at this action, and for a brief moment, his eyes followed the sword. This was long enough for Michael. With Cole's guard distracted, the knight lunged at him and drove his shoulder into the man's belly. He heard Cole grunt as they hit the sand, with Michael on top.

Michael next jammed his knee into Cole's solar plexus and at the same moment hit him in the jaw with his right fist. This stunned Cole long enough for Michael to twist the sword out of his hand.

"Enough!" the princess commanded from outside the pit. Michael picked up the second sword from the sand. He stood over Cole who was trying to get his breath back. Michael held out his hand to help him up. Cole looked up at him suspiciously.

"I fought with you because we were forced to, not because I chose this," Michael said in a low voice. He wanted to see what sort of man Cole was. Cole sat up and stared at him a moment. Then he spit at his feet. He had his answer.

"Have it your way," Michael said, backing away from him. Well, he reasoned, did I expect to make a friend by beating him in front of the others?

"I want this one moved," the princess commanded. "Take him out of this bunch and move him in with the first tier."

"The first tier?" Mardak protested. "He's green. We've only just begun our training."

"You heard what I said. Didn't you just see what he did? Do I have to put him back in with you to prove my point? Sword master, I don't care if you don't like him. I want him moved in with the first tier."

When they opened the door to the pit, Michael handed the two swords to Mardak who grabbed them from him. "I'll come back any time you want," Michael said quietly. "Just let me know when you're ready for some further training."

Mardak threw the wooden swords down and grabbed Michael's tunic in both of his fists, pulling him towards him. Michael brought his knee up into the sword master's crotch. Down he went to the floor doubled up and groaning. This got everyone's attention. The princess was staring at him with interest, sizing him up.

"I hope you have a better sword master for the first tier," the knight said to her.

"Be careful it doesn't end up being you," she responded with a smile. Her face relaxed and he saw the spark in her eye. Maybe he had judged her too quickly.

"I wouldn't mind," he said smiling back and giving her a short bow. The guards moved in to escort him away. Michael stepped over the sword master and let them lead him.

They took Michael up a flight of stairs and out of the dungeon. As glad as he was to get back into the light of day, he swore at the stabbing pain in his eyes from the brightness of the sunlight. He was led to what looked like barracks. A group of men were in the area in front of it practicing. Some were exercising alone, others sparred with one another using an array of weapons.

The guards took him inside the building, and they walked him down an aisle with a row of mats on both sides. Michael was reminded of his boyhood in the Dragon Compound. It had not looked much different. For a moment he chuckled to himself, hoping that the food would be as good. Then he grew somber again. The dragon he would find here was not a well-kept Luck Dragon. It would not be Star.

They stopped before a mat that had no blanket. "This'll be yours," one of the guards said flatly. Then they both turned and walked out of the barracks.

"That was simple enough," Michael muttered. "I wonder where I'll get a blanket."

He walked back towards the door. After life in the cells of the dungeon, he had the illusion that he had been given his freedom. He wondered if he could just walk out and never look back. Before he got to the door, a figure entered and blocked his way.

"I just spoke with the guard," he said. "You've been reassigned to me." He was as short and stocky as Michael. His face was clean shaven and browned by the sun. His hands were large and bore multiple scars.

He had a smile in his eyes which his mouth did not betray. "My name is Pommer. If you do what I say, we'll get along."

Michael studied the man a moment before responding. "That all depends on what you ask me to do."

"A fair enough response," Pommer said with a nod. "How long ago were you brought in?"

"About three weeks ago."

"Three weeks ago?" Pommer looked at him skeptically. "So you're the one we've heard about." When he saw the surprise in Michael's face he added, "Word gets around quickly. Although I didn't think I'd see you here so soon. Normally I get to watch a man spar before he's assigned to me."

"It happened sort of suddenly," Michael said. "I think the princess had something to do with it."

"Well, she rarely chooses poorly," Pommer said. "You've seen where the men sleep," he said with a curt gesture. "Come on out and meet the rest of your tier." They stepped outside together. Michael could not see any gates or fences.

"Tell me," he asked. "Are we free to roam around? I mean, what's to keep us from leaving?"

Pommer turned to face him. "Now I can tell that you're newly arrived. I'll explain it as plainly as I can. The men who reach first tier are not only good at fighting, but they like doing it. Each one of these men is eager for a chance to have a go at Scorch. Each one of them is certain he'll be the one to defeat him. They want to be here. They're glad to be out of the dungeons. They're honored by the people until the day comes they can go and try their hand. Understand?"

"Sounds good to me," Michael said.

Pommer continued, "Yes, you do have more freedom. But I do a head count every morning and every evening. You want to be there when I count heads. Otherwise we come looking for you.

"Every now and then, we get someone in here who changes his mind and decides to run. But I'll tell you, there is no place you can run to that we won't find you. No one in Gladur is going to give you a safe hideaway. Your presence means their children don't have to march down Scorch's jaws. And even if you're good enough to make it outside the city walls, the trackers will find you. And I'd rather be in a snake pit than in your shoes when they do. Because I'd die a lot quicker and in a lot less pain in a snake pit. Understand?"

"I think I got the gist of it," Michael said with a nod.

"Good, then let's go meet your tier-mates." Pommer turned on his heel and walked away. Michael liked his manner. Pommer was straightforward and would let him know if he crossed the line.

When the others saw Michael walking behind Pommer, they stopped what they were doing and came over to find out why he was there. There were about ten of them. He noticed Cole in the background with a swollen lip.

"This fellow's joining you," Pommer announced. "He's new here, but he's been moved up by Aina herself, so he must have shown some promise."

"He knows some good tricks," Cole said from behind. Everyone turned to look at him. Cole was fingering his swollen lip. "Either that, or he's just damned lucky," he added. Then he laughed. Michael now knew that the friendship he had offered him in the pit had not gone unheeded.

"Where'd they catch you?" a fellow with a long, golden beard asked. His hair was equally long and braided.

"By the river," Michael stated.

"Where were you headed when they got you?" another asked.

"I was headed here. I had heard about the dragon," he began, but got no further.

"Yeah, the same with me," said one tall fellow with wild dark hair.

"Same with me," another said.

"And me."

"Yeah, me, too."

"Fact is," Pommer said, "most of these men were already on the way here with the idea of challenging the dragon."

This did not make any sense to Michael. "Then, if we were coming here willingly, why humiliate us by making us prisoners?"

"It's for our own good," the man with the braids said.

"It was Aina's idea," Cole added.

"It's like this," Pommer said. "The princess couldn't stand seeing men come here and throw their lives away. She wanted to start a training to make us as skilled as possible before taking on Scorch." Michael saw he had to reassess his judgment of the princess.

"Not that it's helped much," Cole said and the others laughed.

"Why's that?" Michael asked.

"No one's returned from his battle with Scorch to brag about it."

There was silence in the group as this sunk in. Then the one with the wild hair called out, "Hey, catch this," and he tossed a sword towards Michael. He caught it by its pommel. This was not a wooden practice sword.

"If you know some new tricks like Cole said, teach us something," the fellow exclaimed and squared off with a sword in his hand.

"It's a bit dull," Michael said, feeling his sword's edge.

"Supposed to be," the other fellow said. "We agree not to draw blood or break bones. Everything else goes."

"Or gouge out eyes," another added.

"Yeah, that, too," the fellow with the wild hair admitted. "You know, spare the soft parts."

"Fine with me," Michael said.

"Then here's at you," the fellow said, lunging towards Michael and taking a wide swing that Michael neatly parried. Once again, he was reminded of his life in the Dragon Compound. He had grown up sparring with Star. He liked the idea of training with these men. He sensed that they were solidly faithful to one another. And besides, maybe the food would be as good.

Chapter Seven

Bring Me the Dragon's Heart

*E*very once in a while the king has a big banquet and wants us to entertain him," Cole said. They were sitting in the shade eating. Michael was delighted that the food had turned out to be quite good, considering that they were virtual prisoners.

"I assume you don't mean he likes to see us juggling," Michael said.

"If we weren't so valuable, I'd reckon he'd want to see some real bloodshed," Morik said. He shook his long braids to keep the flies from landing on his face.

"I can imagine the princess would welcome an all-out fight," Michael said. He had not seen her again since the day she moved him to the first tier. Every day had been a routine of exercising and sparring. The others had accepted him quickly when they saw his skills and his willingness to share with them what he knew.

"No, you're wrong there," Morik insisted.

"The princess is not like that," Cole agreed.

"I'm amazed," Michael said. "Every time her name comes up, you defend her."

"The king is wicked," Morik said. "Every one of us would agree to that. Even Pommer, and he's local. But Princess Aina is different."

"How different can she be?" Michael asked. "She keeps us here like cattle."

"Well-fed cattle," Cole said holding up his bowl of stew.

"Agreed," said Michael. "Well-fed. But she's also holding us against our will to eventually march off to our death so that her own people are saved."

"Well, makes no difference to me," Morik said. "I came here to fight the dragon. And Aina provides us with companionship, good food and a place to practice our skills. She wants to see us get better at what we do. When the day comes for one of us to go off, she personally sees him off. I'd say she cares a lot."

"Princess Aina looks after us," Cole said. "I'd say she's the one who makes sure no one is hurt when we show off for the king's banquets. If it were up to him, I don't think he'd cry over losing a few of us for his own entertainment."

"Aina's different," Morik said almost with reverence. "You'll see."

"She wasn't so different when she made me fight you," Michael said to Cole.

"Don't you remember that she stopped you the moment you got my sword away from me? Mardak wouldn't have done that. He would have let you continue to bloody me and said afterwards it was to help me remember next time not to let my guard down."

"Well, considering how important we are to her, she doesn't show up very often. I've been here three weeks and I haven't seen her again."

"You wait," said Morik. "She'll come."

They went back to their exercises. Later that afternoon, they did have a visit, but it was not from Aina.

"Weapons down," Pommer called out. "Line up behind the bar." All of the men put down the weapons they were using and walked over towards the barracks.

"What's up," Michael asked Coop, one of the men he had been sparring with.

"When Pommer asks us like that, it means we have a visitor."

"Where are we going?"

"We all stand behind the bar over there."

"That bar?" Michael asked. "I thought that was there to tie horses to."

"It is," Coop said. "But it's also where we stand when we have a special visitor."

Michael went to stand with the others in the space between a waist-high long wooden bar and the wall of the barracks. He wondered if Aina was finally paying them a visit.

A guard of five soldiers approached. They marched in a semicircle around two men. One was obviously King Worrah. He was dressed in thickly woven robes of red and green. His hair and beard showed streaks of gray. He was deep in conversation with another man. When Michael saw him, he felt a jolt of recognition. The last time he had seen him was the day he had been exiled from the Dragon Compound. Although fifteen years had passed and he was dressed quite royally compared to the work tunics they had all worn in the compound, there was no doubt who he was.

"Well," he said to himself. "I'd wondered what had become of him. I guess I shouldn't be surprised." He took half a step behind Cole who was a head taller, just in case he was also as easy to recognize after all these years. He was not ready for Flek to know he was there.

The king stepped forward and addressed the men. "You are my best warriors. I feed you better than I do my own army. Better than my own personal guard. And do you know why? I'll tell you the reason why. Because one of you will bring to me something very precious. And do you know what that is?"

King Worrah paused as if waiting for an answer. Morik leaned over to whisper in Michael's ear. "We all know the answer. But we've learned not to say anything. He likes to do all the talking himself."

"No? You don't know? Then I will tell you. It's time you learned this. One of you will be the hero who brings back to me the dragon's heart. When you go and fight Scorch, one of you will be so skilled in your arts that you will overcome that hated worm and bring me its heart. It must be and it will be."

King Worrah watched their reaction before continuing. "Some people believe that the dragon came here by mistake, that it is a curse on our land. That it sucks our people dry. Nonsense, I say! The land has never been more prosperous. We have never been more powerful against our enemies. The people have never celebrated more. There are nightly parties.

"No, I tell you that the dragon came here by design. Scorch came here because I attracted him, because I wanted him here. And why did I want a beast that would burn up our forests, devastate our fields and consume our crops? A monster that would demand every month a human sacrifice? Because I want his heart. And I will not rest until I get it."

Michael listened to all of this and wondered if the king actually believed what he was saying. "What's the heart good for?" he called out, careful to remain hidden behind the others.

King Worrah scanned their faces, trying to detect who had asked that question. "Let that be my concern," he said harshly. "You bring the heart, that's your concern. That's why you're here.

"And today I have come to you to make sure that you are happy and well fed. And I have an invitation. I am seeking two of you who will be willing to come and provide some light entertainment for my guests. Have no concern. It is merely for display. Princess Aina suffers too much when I let you follow your true disposition. You shall eat and drink from my own table after your brief exhibition."

Michael noticed that the men around him grew restless when King Worrah spoke about the "light entertainment."

"I leave it to Pommer to decide who will come. Any questions? Are you happy? Well fed?" The king asked this in a voice that said he neither expected nor desired an answer.

"Very good," he said curtly. "Return to your activities." Worrah and his attendant turned and walked away, followed by the king's personal guard.

As soon as he was out of earshot, the men began talking among themselves.

"Well, that cinches it."

"I knew it wasn't far off."

"Poor fellows who get chosen."

"Yeah, well, I wouldn't mind going. I'm not afraid."

"Aw, you wouldn't get as far as the forest without soiling yourself."

"Says you!"

"That's right, says me."

Michael got Morik's attention to find out why there was so much stir.

"Yeah, I forgot that you haven't seen one of these yet. This is like the selection of Scorch's next meal. You go give the king a show, then you get a good meal. And after that, you become a good meal."

"Wait a minute," Michael said. "I'm not following you."

"One of the men who goes to the king's banquet is chosen to go to Scorch. It's a going-away feast. The king always makes this same speech, so we know what's coming. Cole has gone twice already. But both times he was bested in the duel and the other was chosen. First it was a fellow named Leften. Last time it was Bodie. I was sorry to see Bodie go, although others didn't feel the same. He had a rather high opinion of himself. Anyway, by now, Cole is probably our top fighter."

Michael had already bested Cole in the pit, but he did not say this out loud. "Who was that with the king?" he asked.

"The king's counselor," Morik responded. "He's got a black heart, that one. The two of them are a good match for one another."

Several others, realizing that Michael had never before heard one of the king's speeches, came over to hear what he might say. "Do any of you know why the king wants the dragon's heart so badly?" Michael asked the men around him.

"No one knows," a tall fellow by the name of Orin said. "Only that it holds great power."

Michael wondered if there was any true loyalty for the king among these men. He looked around to make sure that Pommer was not near enough to hear. He knew that what he was about to suggest would not go over well with him. "Have any of you ever thought about breaking out of here?"

All of their side conversations stopped. This had obviously struck a chord. After a moment of silence, Orin asked, "What are you thinking?"

"It occurs to me that, if we break out and fight united, we can defeat the king's guard. They may number more, but they are no match for us. We're far better trained." There were some mumblings from the others, but Michael was not hearing any objections.

"Yeah, and then we can go get the dragon's heart for ourselves," Coop said suddenly, with a fire in his eyes.

Michael stared at him severely and then a smile flickered across his lips. "You we'll leave behind." The others laughed.

"Look, I want to know, from all of you top tier warriors, which one of you has had any experience with a dragon before." There was silence among the group and a lot of shuffling of feet and clearing of throats. "So I suspected," he said.

"I was married once," Orin said. "She was a real fire-breather." There was more laughter.

"Yeah," Coop said. "I once knew a woman like that, too."

"Well, it only comes close if she was as big a hill," Michael said.

"She was big, all right," Coop said, cupping his hands in front of his chest in a crude gesture. Cole reached his long arm over and cuffed him in the head.

"Look, why can't we all attack it as a group and overpower it?" Morik asked.

"Don't you think the king has already thought of that?" Cole said. "Dragons don't care a twit for armies. They eat 'em up like we might pop a handful of raisins in our mouths."

"A dragon can fly, my friends," Michael explained. "And it will land on top of you. It is covered in scales that are as sturdy as interlocking shields and resist every sword thrust. Its tail has a mind of its own and protects it from behind by sweeping everything, man and horse, out of its way. Its teeth are sharper than a farmer's scythe and far more numerous than the king's personal guard. And its breath is like a fiery furnace. Add to all that, a dragon is far more clever than all of our bright minds together."

"So you're telling us it can't be defeated."

"What I want to impress on you is that you will not defeat a dragon by force."

"Then what will defeat a dragon?"

"Something other than force," he said with a shrug of his shoulders.

"What makes you think you know so much about dragons?" Cole challenged. "It sounds to me like you're just trying to talk us out of what we've all come here to do."

Michael considered a moment before answering. It was not something he liked telling others. This time, though, it would be worthwhile, as long as word did not get out, which was unlikely, since they were prisoners. "Have any of you ever heard of Nogardia?"

There was excited chatter among the men. Then Orin exclaimed, "Every man who dreams of fighting a dragon has heard of Nogardia." Then he recited, "Nogardia needs no guarding. 'Backwards or forwards, 'tis always the same, a singular home for a dragon that's tame.' Every kid knows that rhyme. Why? You ever been there?"

"I grew up there," Michael said softly. The men stared at him while this sunk in.

"Wait a minute," Cole said. "Did you ever know him?"

"The dragon?" Michael asked.

"Sure, him too, I guess. But no, did you ever know him that left? The one they say could make the dragon do handstands. The one they called the Dragon Boy. They say that he left and wandered the land as a knight. Carried a shield with the emblem of a dragon on it."

"A red dragon rampant on a white field," Michael said. "But I never asked him to do a handstand. There would have been no point in that."

There was a lot of shouting among the men at this.

"Not possible!"

"You? I always imagined him taller."

"Makes sense, seeing how well he fights."

"Wait a minute, rumor is you never lost a fight. How did they catch you, then?"

"It wasn't in a fight," Michael said. "I was taken in an ambush."

"Is it true that the dragon did whatever you wanted?"

"I wouldn't go that far," Michael said. "We had an understanding. Star was always very cooperative."

"That's my point," said Cole. He was not yet impressed. "Even if you are that knight, you looked after a tame dragon. Even the verse says it: 'a singular home for a dragon that's tame.'"

"Just like with the handstands, not everything you hear is accurate," Michael said. "There was nothing tame about Star. At least, not in the way a dog is tame. He chose to live the way he did. Do any of you know what became of the dragon there?"

"Sure," Morik said. "They say that one day he just up and left."

"Tame animals don't suddenly get up and leave," Michael pointed out. "Star was there by choice, and when his time was over, he left."

"Where'd he go?" Coop asked.

"That, I wish I knew," Michael said with a shrug. "I have never heard of him since."

"Rumor is that to the south is a kingdom with a Luck Dragon," Morik said.

"In truth, I've heard the same," Michael said.

"That's most likely where your dragon went," Coop said. "He's certainly not anywhere around here."

Cole was not yet finished pushing home his point. "So because you looked after a dragon that was there by choice, you think you know something about a wild dragon?"

"I know about dragon," Michael said. "This one also seems to be here by choice. The only difference is that this one is not cooperative."

"I'll say," Coop said. "He likes regular meals. Say, what did your dragon eat?"

"Not knights," Michael said with a chuckle. "He had a very different diet."

"I know where you're going with this," Morik said.

"Go ahead," Michael urged.

"You want to be chosen to go next to the dragon."

"That is what I was thinking," Michael admitted. "How do you normally choose?"

"We duel among ourselves until two are left," Cole answered. "But I don't see any sense in doing that this time."

"Why's that?" Michael asked.

"It's pretty obvious," Coop answered.

"You've managed to disarm every one of us here in our practices," Orin said. "We all know how good you are. There's not a man here who can stand up to you."

Michael glanced at Cole to see if he would object.

"Don't expect me to stand in your way," Cole said. "If you want to be the next fool to march down Scorch's throat, be my guest."

"But the king will want his entertainment. Don't two of you fight it out to have the honor of going next?"

"It'll be you and me again," Cole said severely. "I'll fight to win. The king will see through anything else. I just have one request."

"What's that?"

"Leave me in one piece."

Chapter Eight

The King's Feast

*P*ommer merely nodded his head when Michael and Cole presented themselves to him as the two candidates for the king's feast. "Sorry to see you go so soon," he muttered as he turned away.

"He usually likes to see us eliminate each other in sparring," Cole commented to Michael afterwards. "He knows me well enough, and I guess he's seen enough of you in action."

Guards arrived and escorted the two into the castle proper.

"I kind of like this part of it," Cole said.

They were brought into a private bath house where they were told to scrub themselves clean.

Michael sat in the hot water and sniffed at the soap before rubbing it into his hair. "Nice stuff."

"Wait 'til you see the food," Cole said, happily splashing away.

Richly embroidered clothing was laid out for them. Plates of fruit and cheese covered the table. Cole stood there still dripping from his bath as he stuffed his mouth. "Eat up," he mumbled through a mouthful of grapes. "It's all we get before we fight. But it's the best."

Michael had to agree. The quality and variety of the cheeses were a delight he had not before experienced.

Once they had eaten and dressed, they were told to wait. While they sat, maidens entered their room and placed flower garlands in their hair.

"Quite an honor," Michael commented.

"Sure, they honor us," Cole said. "We are being sent in place of one of them."

"What happens next?"

"When the hall is full, we're led in and presented. It takes only a moment. They all applaud and then the feast begins. We sit apart, one on either side of the king's table. We don't eat, but they will offer us drinks. We sit and wait until it's time to fight. That's about it. I never got any further than the fight. But this much I know will happen."

It was as Cole said. At one point guards came and led them through a maze of passages, and they finally entered a very large hall. It was well-lit with torches, and colorful banners were hung on the walls. Tables were set up throughout the room, and richly dressed lords and ladies sat at them on long benches. On a balcony behind the king's table, minstrels played, but their music was mostly drowned out by the many conversations of the revelers. Servants rushed to and fro with pitchers and platters. There was a great deal of merriment and chatter. There was a large open space in front of the king's table. He sat on a slightly raised dais with several lords and ladies, and beside him was Flek.

When they entered, they were led before the king's table where they bowed and then turned and bowed to the assembly. Everyone applauded politely. Then they were each led to opposite ends of the table. There was a chair waiting for Michael at the foot of dais and on the floor stood a filled goblet. The hall filled with the sounds of clinking dishes and many conversations.

Cautiously, Michael leaned forward to look at the king's table. Flek had still not taken a good look at him. He wanted to keep it this way as long as possible. He was puzzled that Princess Aina was not sitting next to the king. He quickly scanned the room, but nowhere could he locate her. She had to be there, and he figured she was sitting with her back to him. It was odd she would not be sitting at the royal table.

Michael watched the servants walking briskly about bringing food and carrying away empty platters. Everyone was drinking heavily. He tested what was in his goblet, and found it to be only fresh water. He was pleased by this, since he did not want his senses clouded by wine.

When the diners were showing signs of slowing down, the first of the revelers arrived at his chair. They looked him up and down and made comments to one another about his physical condition. They laughed and joked. A few of them dared to prod him. Michael tolerated all of this in silence. He realized quickly what they were doing when he overheard them comparing him to Cole. They were making bets.

"This one looks quite strong," an older man assessed.

"They're both strong, you fool," his companion said. He was wearing a gold chain across his breast. "How do you think they got this far. It's not strength, but height. This one doesn't have a chance. He'll be crushed."

"I don't agree, Bikko," a man in red velvet said. "Speed and agility will take the day. What good is height when your opponent is faster?"

"We've seen the other one fight now twice," Bikko said. "He wouldn't come to lose a third time. My bet goes with him."

"You have a point," the older man agreed. "Just the same, to make it sporting ..." and they wandered away.

And so they came one after the other to lay their bets. Michael glanced up at the king's table. Flek was in conversation with Worrah. They appeared to be in no hurry to make their choices. Maybe they did not even care, as long as it was not one of them.

One man came who looked like he enjoyed being in a fight as much as watching one. He went back and forth several times between the two contenders. He poked at Michael more forcefully than any of the others, as if wanting to see how he would react. Michael finally stared at him severely to warn him not to do it again. This brought a grim smile to his lips. He looked up to the king's table.

"Hey, Flek," he called out loudly until he had the counselor's attention. "You haven't placed your bet yet. What's your pleasure? You're rarely wrong."

"All right," Flek said standing up. "Time to take a good look."

He left the table and walked over first to Cole.

"Well, we know this one well by now," he commented. The whole hall had grown quiet, curious what the king's counselor would say. "He's a furious fighter who twice could have won, but didn't. Maybe the extra training has taught him some more skills. Is luck with him tonight?"

Then he walked over to Michael. "Stand up," he commanded. Michael rose slowly. Flek ignored his face, focusing on his physical build.

"Well-knit, muscular, good balance," he commented. "But he's short. I never trust much the worth of short fighters."

"More stamina," a man standing nearby offered.

"Perhaps," he said dismissively. Flek's eyes scanned the knight's face for a moment and moved on. Then, as recognition struck, his gaze shot back. His eyes widened and his mouth fell open as if he were looking at a ghost. Then he caught himself, threw back his head, and laughed loud and long.

"What is it that amuses you so, counselor?" Worrah asked from his seat.

"I'll wager this one's full of tricks," Flek answered.

"You act like you know him, counselor," a man wearing a green velvet cap said.

"Know him I do," Flek admitted, walking back to his seat. "The last I saw him, he was sent disgraced into exile, back to the muck of the streets from where he came. I'm surprised you got him so clean. When

I knew him, he was usually smeared in filth. We used to call him Dung Boy."

"So do you place your bets on him?" another asked.

"All my bets go on Dung Boy," Flek said derisively. "I'd like nothing better than to see him sent off to Scorch."

There was a lot of commotion among the revelers as this was said. More bets were shouted out, and many others now rose from their places to get a closer look at Flek's favorite. Michael sat silently, biding his time. He continued to look through the throng, waiting for sight of Aina, but she remained hidden from his eyes.

As the wagers were settled and it quieted down, Worrah stood up with raised arm and announced, "Let the pageant begin!"

The musicians up in the balcony had traded their stringed instruments for large, round cymbals. These they struck against one another, filling the great hall with their reverberating vibrations. All conversation was silenced. The room was filled with the sound.

Michael listened to the ringing of the bronze cymbals and a powerful memory welled up. When he lived in the Dragon Compound, every afternoon after Star returned from the river, cymbals as tall as a grown man were struck until the air was alive with its sound. On some days, Star would unfurl his immense wings and lift himself into the sky. Circling above the compound, he mixed his own song with that of the cymbals.

"Well, they got that right," the knight thought grimly to himself. He wondered if this was something Flek had designed.

The beating of drums was added to the ringing of the cymbals, creating a bass tone to anchor the higher vibrations. The raised energy in the room was palpable. Suddenly through side doors a train of dancers entered the hall. It was a single-file row of women whose heads emerged from a long rippling costume that connected them. In the front was an immense head beautifully crafted to resemble a dragon's face, yet light enough to be carried by just one dancer underneath it.

The dragon wove into the hall between the tables, circling around the room until it ended up in the open space before the king's dais. The long tail whipped back and forth, the head rose up and down, its immense jaws able to open and shut. Michael was mesmerized by the beauty and grace of the dancers' movements. For a moment, he wondered if Aina was among them, but their faces were all thickly painted with intricate designs and he could not recognize any features.

Then with a shout, a single figure emerged from a side door. Another dancer, dressed as a knight now entered the room. She carried a shield and sword. She also made a ceremonial tour of the room, weaving between the tables of revelers.

When she reached the center of the room, together with the dancers that made up the dragon, they bowed before the king. Then the battle began. The reverberations from the cymbals and the steady deep cadence of the drums continued to fill the hall. The fight between the dragon and the knight was obviously staged and intricately prepared, yet it was a vigorous dance with many twists and turns and slashing of the air.

Although they never made any physical contact, they made it appear as if dragon and the knight engaged in a furious battle. Three times the knight fell to the ground and rolled out of the way just escaping the dragon's great jaws. Three times, the knight sunk her sword into the dragon's side, causing it to falter and sink down before rising up again to the attack.

Finally, the moment arrived when the dragon's jaws were about to swallow up the knight. The clashing of the cymbals and the drum beat had risen to a fever pitch. The warrior raised her sword and buried it into the roof of the dragon's mouth. This appeared to be the death blow. The dragon staggered, tossed its head back and forth several times as if to shake off death, and finally lay down on its side. The drums and cymbals became a murmur in the background.

The knight drew her sword out of the dragon's mouth and drove it into the dragon's flank one dancer behind the head. She thrust in her arm and pulled out a felted shape. It was a deep red color and larger than both her fists together. Michael realized with a jolt that it was meant to represent the dragon's heart. The knight walked over to the dais and offered it to the king. Worrah stood up and received it from her. In exchange, he gave her a finely decorated bag that was tied closed. She took the bag and skipped a victory round circling the dead dragon. Then, to the continued applause of the revelers, she wove through the tables holding the bag up high. The sound of the cymbals again filled the hall. By the time she had left the room, the dancers making up the dragon had also left the space before the king's table.

Then there was silence. Michael had to admit to himself that the pageant had stirred up his heart. He was ready to engage Cole in battle.

Worrah clapped his hands and a servant rushed in carrying two swords. They looked to be wooden, such as the ones he was used to in their sparring. Michael was content that no one intended them to seriously harm one another. The swords were placed crossed on the floor in the middle of the open space. Michael realized that this was the signal for them to fight. He glanced up at the dais and saw that they were all staring at him. He looked back to the open floor and there stood Cole with a sword in his hand, the second one on the floor behind him. He had known what was coming next and was not going to wait for Michael to figure it out. He was now armed and had the advantage.

Michael rose slowly from his seat, deciding the best way to proceed. The last thing he wanted was to hurt Cole. He chuckled to himself at the thought that he did not want to get hurt trying to protect Cole from harm. He believed what Cole had told him: He would be fighting his hardest.

Michael considered how he could win as quickly as possible. He had been training the others, Cole included, in many of his techniques. Cole had studied him well and by now could outguess many of his moves. That called for him to do something he had never done before. Michael picked up the chair he had been sitting on and began walking slowly towards Cole. If he had no sword, at least he could have a makeshift shield. When Cole saw what he was doing, he looked uncertain. That was the effect Michael had hoped to create. That had always been one of Star's most central teachings: Do the unexpected.

Michael raised the chair so that the legs were pointed at his adversary. Cole stood his ground, but he looked like he did not quite know what to do next. When Michael came within range, he took a swing at the legs, but the wooden sword clattered against them and did them no damage.

Michael circled around Cole until he had him with his back to the low dais. He thrust the chair towards him twice, almost to announce what his next move would be. He wanted Cole prepared, and the warnings did not go unnoticed. Michael took a short step backwards, and then charged him. Cole was not able to sidestep the legs and backpedaled as quickly as he could. A moment later, he crashed into a leg of the king's table from behind, knocking it back. Michael noticed with grim satisfaction that Flek had been thrown off his chair onto the ground, cursing and scrambling to get out of the way.

Michael now had Cole pinned against the table with the chair legs. He put his shoulder into the seat to hold him in place and quickly bent over and under. He grabbed hold of one of Cole's legs and, yanking at an angle, pulled it out from under him.

On his way down, Cole first hit the low platform on which the table was raised and then the floor. The sword fell beside him. Jamming his knee into Cole's chest, Michael snatched up the fallen sword and pressed the edge into Cole's neck. Nearly strangled by the sword, Cole stopped struggling.

Michael wondered what would end the fight. He had forgotten to ask Cole ahead of time what determined the winner. He glanced around the room, looking for some clue how to continue. Most of the revelers had risen to their feet, and he became aware for the first time that they were shouting encouragement.

Suddenly Flek was standing over them. "They wish to see blood," he said coldly. "An extra bag of gold to your credit if you finish him. He's lost three times now. They don't want to see him a fourth. I suggest you break his neck."

Michael knew it would be a long and ugly death if he only had the wooden sword to use. Besides, he had no reason to harm Cole. They had become comrades in arms.

"Nothing's changed," he said to Flek, glancing up. "I'm still sickened by your motives." So saying, he carefully released his hold on Cole and stood up. If he had to continue to fight, he would.

Cole slowly sat up. The revelers were chanting something and it took a moment for Michael to catch the words.

"Dra-gon slay-er! Dra-gon slay-er! Dra-gon slay-er!" they chanted. The room rocked with the sound. Two guards appeared and stood one on either side of Cole. They led him out, his head bowed in defeat. Michael threw down his sword and wondered what would happen next.

Two servants quickly reset the table on the dais and took away the swords and the chair. Another servant appeared, carrying two more swords. These, however, Michael immediately saw were made of polished steel. For a moment he wondered why Cole had not told him about this, when he realized that he had never gotten this far before.

Flek was still standing there watching the servant cross the swords on the floor. Then he turned to Michael.

"Now we'll see how really clever you are." He turned on his heel and returned to his seat. From the musician's balcony, the drum began to beat again.

With a terrifying scream, a warrior rushed into the hall. He was dressed in scarlet robes with a yellow sash. He wore a carved mask over his face. The mask was a grotesque and exaggerated image of a face with large white pointed teeth and tusks. Along the brow of the mask were carved human skulls.

Without a moment's hesitation, the warrior snatched up one of the swords and screaming, rushed at Michael with the sword raised high. Michael threw himself out of the way as it came crashing down onto the king's table, smashing a pitcher and wedging itself into the wood. Now the tables were turned, and Michael was the one having to deal with the unexpected. He was now in a fight for his life.

With a quick upward movement, his attacker freed the sword from the table. Michael, however, had by this time fetched the second sword. He was not going to try and deal with this one unarmed.

The warrior charged him a second time. Their swords clashed and the battle was joined in earnest.

As they traded blows, Michael was impressed by the vigor and agility of his opponent. In a protected chamber of his mind, he wondered who he could be fighting. And why? Was this the final test before being sent off to Scorch? Who was this champion?

The dinner guests remained on their feet yelling and cheering them on. Michael had no doubt that the betting continued all the while they fought. The drums beat a rapid cadence in the background.

Never letting his guard down, Michael remained aware of the space around their battle. He was wary of some treachery from Flek. Were a second and a third opponent about to appear from the wings and join in the fight?

Michael wanted to disarm this opponent rather than harm him. He already respected his skills at swordsmanship. He remarked that this warrior, like himself, was short in stature. In fact, he appeared to be slightly shorter than he was. Would he be able to wear him down and in a moment of fatigue take away his sword? He was uncertain what else to do to avoid bloodshed.

It became clear that this swordsman was doing everything he could to kill him. Although his opponent's sword play was exceptional, Michael already knew that he was stronger, and that the force of the blows against his sword was growing steadily weaker.

He hoped to use the mask to his advantage. His opponent was looking through the oversized, gaping mouth. He could clearly see his eyes in the shadow of the disguise. He hoped that the mask would limit his opponent's peripheral vision and create a blind spot he could use.

His challenger, however, was quick, and every time Michael tried to swerve to the side, his foe turned quickly with him, keeping him in front. Michael, though, was patient and worked methodically. He set a rhythm of swerving to one side and then the other, creating an expectation of which side he would swerve to next. Once he was satisfied that his opponent was predicting his moves, he changed the rhythm.

When his challenger expected him to zig to the right, Michael zagged to the left. It was the split second he needed. He slipped under his opponent's guard and drove his shoulder into his chest.

He heard a yelp of pain escape through the mask and wondered if he was fighting someone with a healing wound. He looked into the mouth of the mask and saw two large eyes staring at him. The eyes reflected both intensity and pain. They were now grappling hand to hand, trying to disarm one another. Then a mocking voice spoke to him. "How do you want to fight a dragon if you cannot even defeat me?"

Michael was jolted by this question. This was almost word for word the challenge he once gave to a warrior king named Malvise who had come to the Dragon Compound looking to provoke a fight with

Star. Although at that time he had never before fought a grown man, he had beaten the warrior king and forced him to leave.

He was even more startled, however, when he realized the voice was a woman's.

Michael was trained to turn his surprise into action. Without thinking, he extended his leg and, with a swift forward movement, tripped her up. She fell hard with Michael landing on top of her. When he jammed his shoulder into her breast, he understood her shriek of pain.

He was determined to end this as quickly as possible. He wanted to avoid hurting her any more. He deftly pinned her arms down with his knees. Although she struggled and squirmed, he out-muscled and outweighed her and she could not escape. He applied only enough pressure to keep her in place. He did not want to bruise her any more than he might already have done.

She did not appreciate his consideration. "If you are this gentle with Scorch," she spat at him through the mask, "he will swallow you like an appetizer before a meal. He won't even stop to taste you going down."

She spoke with such fervor that Michael was taken aback. What did she want him to do? He had already subdued her. She answered his silent question. "Don't you understand?" she hissed. "Scorch will show you no mercy. You cannot afford to show him any. Otherwise you've failed before you've begun."

Michael was astonished by her words. Who was this warrior maiden who fought with such unparalleled excellence and fiery spirit? He did not have to wonder long.

Michael became aware that the yelling in the hall had subsided and the drumming had stopped. Guards appeared beside him and took hold of his arms to prevent him from doing his opponent any more harm. By the care they were taking in pulling him off her and helping her up, it was suddenly crystal clear who she was.

Princess Aina now stood before him, the gruesome mask hanging from her hand. As a servant unfastened a red cloth wrapped around her hair, she stared at Michael with utter contempt.

The king was standing at his place, holding his hands up for silence. "Well, Aina," he asked from the dais, "what do you think of this champion?"

"Worse than the rest," she spit out. "He doesn't have a chance."

"You are much too severe," Worrah said conciliatorily. "We have never before seen a champion defeat his opponent so creatively. Nor so quickly. And he did conquer you as well. That, too, is a first. Wouldn't you agree?"

"He never laid a sword on me," she responded. "He only disarmed me. Is he going to try and disarm the dragon? If he cannot beat me, how will he fight Scorch?" So saying, she turned on her heel and quickly left the room.

"Tut-tut," Worrah said with a sour look on his face. "She is never content. Regardless, before us is our champion. Do you not all agree?" He was now addressing the assembly.

"Dragon slayer! Dragon slayer! Dragon slayer!" the chanting of the revelers echoed off the walls in the great hall.

Worrah descended from the dais and walked up to Michael. "Come, sit at my table and eat with us. Refresh yourself from your exertions. You have won for yourself quarters inside the castle and the freedom to wander our fine town at will. Until the day you set off to fight the dragon, you are an honored guest in Gladur Nock. Come, rejoice with us."

A place was set at the table, and Michael sat looking out over the great assembly gathered there. Platters of fruit were now being carried to all the tables. Michael, however, was brought all manner of food. His goblet, he noted, was now filled with a fragrant wine. He was hungry from his exertions, and ate to still his fatigue. He was not happy, though, and was barely aware of what he was eating. Aina's words kept echoing through his mind. He knew that she was right. He had no hope of defeating a dragon. Star had painfully brought that lesson home to him time and time again. And Star had been a gentle Luck Dragon.

Chapter Nine

The Portrait

The next morning Michael awoke and was for a moment disoriented. His bed was soft, he was alone, and there were curtains drawn over the windows. Then in a flash it all came flooding back to him. After the feast, guards had escorted him down several corridors, up a flight of stairs and down a hall. They told him that this room would be his new quarters until he set out to challenge the dragon.

He stretched and fully appreciated the softness of his mattress and the warmth of the blankets. He yawned and wondered what new surprises were in store for him. He did not have long to wait.

The sound of several pairs of boots on the wooden floorboards echoed down the hallway outside his door. Were they just passing by or was he about to have visitors?

As the pounding of the boots reached his door, there was not even a knock. The door flew open and two colorfully dressed guards walked briskly into the room carrying long staffs with spiked ax blades attached at the top. They took a position, one on either side of the door and rapped the butts of their staffs on the floor.

"Rise for the king's counselor!" one of them announced in a voice loud enough to carry across a banquet hall.

Michael sat up in the bed and stared at them with a bemused expression. Flek, a dark brown cloak hanging from his shoulders, sauntered into the room.

"I suggest you do as they order," he said with a small smile. "Otherwise they will force you."

The guards rapped their spears against the floorboards a second time and again one of them ordered in his massive voice, "Rise for the king's counselor!"

When Michael made no show of getting up, they briskly stepped over to the bedside. "Tell me, Flek," Michael asked. "Were these men present at last night's entertainment?"

"They are the king's own personal guard. Of course they were present. What difference does that make? Get up."

The two guards were waiting for a sign from Flek, ready to grab Michael and force him to his feet.

The knight calmly looked up at them without moving.

"You saw what I did last night, unarmed, against the other champion. I am going to challenge a dragon to battle, by my own choice. Do you really want to tangle with me?" He waited until he saw this question etched in their faces. "Now, step back away from my bed." It was more a warning than a request.

The guards gave one another sidelong glances. They hesitated and looked back at the king's counselor.

"Get out!" Flek shouted with a dismissive gesture. "Out! Wait for me in the hall."

The two guards retreated and left the room. Flek was seething. "You've not changed in the least," he spit at Michael. "Arrogant and cocky." His right eye twitched. "And you still stink, Dung Boy."

Michael sighed. He threw back the covers and stood up. Flek took half a step backwards, as if frightened that Michael might attack him. "Flek, this place suits you well. A downtrodden people and a king with a taste for gambling money and spilling blood, as long as it's not his own."

"Blab on, Dung Boy. Another few days and you'll be only a bad memory. This dragon won't eat out of your hand so quickly. Scorch will swallow you down like all the rest of them."

"Why did you come here, Flek? Certainly not to wish me luck. If you're done gloating, you can go now."

"As a matter of fact, I am here to congratulate you and wish you good luck in your upcoming battle. The king's counselor always visits the king's champion once he is chosen." Here Flek smiled. "To make sure that all of his needs are met."

Michael considered this a moment.

"In that case," he said. "I would like my sword back. And my armor. And my horse. They were all taken from me when I was ambushed."

"That's not going to happen," Flek said with a delighted smile. "What was taken from you was distributed among the trackers that captured you. Not only does the king recompense them well for their services, they may keep whatever they have plundered. What they took from you has long since been sold, melted down, and the horse, unless it showed promise, was most likely slaughtered and its meat given away. You will be issued standard equipment and as good a horse that will not be missed. After all, you will not be returning, so why throw away good armor or horseflesh?"

"You know, Flek, when I'm done with rescuing your worthless king from the scourge of this dragon, I'm coming back." As he spoke, the knight slowly walked straight at Flek, causing him to back up, step by step.

"And I am going to settle with you. I'm going to settle for all the undeserved teasing, baiting and outright meanness that I tolerated from you while we were growing up together. It cost you nothing to leave me alone, but my very existence was a thorn in your side. And you never stopped trying to pluck me out until you finally succeeded in getting me thrown out of the Dragon Compound. If it had been left up to you, you'd have had me stoned. Don't think I've forgotten." By this time Michael had backed Flek up to the wall, and although Flek was half a head taller, if he could have passed through that wall to escape, he would have.

"And when I come back, I am going to finally even the tally between us." With a gesture of finality, Michael suddenly raised his right fist underneath Flek's nose with his pointer extended.

The movement was so sudden, Flek flinched. "Keep your hands off me," he bellowed. "I am the king's counselor. Guards! Guards!" he cried. He pushed Michael's raised arm to the side and fled from the room. "Nothing but a lame horse you'll get," Flek shouted from the hallway. "A lame horse and a blunt sword!"

Michael heard hurried steps moving away from his door. He turned and leaned against the wall, chuckling to himself. He figured that Flek had enough power to make good his threat. He would have to look out how to get a good charger to go after the dragon. He winced at the thought that someone would have made a meal out of his faithful and beloved companion Storm.

"Well, anyone who can both annoy and frighten Counselor Flek can't be altogether hopeless," spoke a soft voice behind him. Michael was taken by surprise, something that did not often happen to him. He turned around to see Aina standing in the doorway.

"May I come in?" she asked. She wore a simple, beige dress, with an apron colorfully embroidered with flowers, her hair tucked under a bright blue scarf.

Michael stepped back to give her room to enter. "Your Highness, I am honored," he said with a bow.

"The honor is mine," she responded with a curtsy. Michael noticed that she was smiling.

"Have you come to continue to remind me that I am no match for a dragon?" he asked, carefully watching her expression.

"Oh, no," she protested, holding up her hands. "I've made my point and I am finished. I have a different role now."

"And what may that be?"

"Until you leave, I shall be your guide and companion," she said pleasantly. The sincerity in her voice caused Michael to pause.

"And why the change?" Michael asked.

"This is the service I provide every champion before he marches off to the dragon. It's the least I can do," her expression had now turned somber.

"My thanks, my Lady," Michael said making a bow.

"A fitting title," Aina said mysteriously. Her expression remained thoughtful and sad. She returned his bow with a curtsy. "I am here to see that your needs are met. Tell me what you'd like, and if it is within my powers, it is yours."

"Well, that is a welcome offer," the knight said warmly. "First of all, I'm going to need a worthy mount to ride and a solid shield and well-fitting armor. A long spear and a sharp sword will fill that out. Preferably the horse and armor I came with, but Flek assured me that I have no hope of getting them back."

Aina's laugh was a delightful warble. "And you want all of that right now?"

"No," he responded. "First I'd like a good wash and then a hearty breakfast."

"Now, that will be easier to come by," she said with a broad smile. "Follow me, and I will lead you to the bath house. Then we can break the night's fast together." So speaking she walked out of the room and down the hall, beckoning Michael to follow her.

After a pleasant wash, Michael dressed in clean clothing that smelt of rosemary. He walked back down the hall to join Aina in a well-lit chamber overlooking the marketplace. They sat at a table that was well provided. They dined on bread, cheese, fruit and cold meat. Their goblets were filled with a very delicate, light wine with a trace of fruit in its aroma.

After he had eaten his fill and was nibbling on some grapes, a thought occurred to Michael. "Are you chosen to accompany me to make sure that I don't try and escape? You've already proven yourself to be a worthy opponent. I wouldn't want to clash arms with you again."

"Thank you for the compliment," Aina said with a smile and a nod of her head. "No, I am not here to guard you. But I do want to warn you that, although you have the freedom of our town, you will be followed everywhere you go. And even if you were to manage to escape, I assure you that the trackers will find you. And once captured, there is only one fate left: They will deliver you to the dragon. But this time you would go without mount, without armor, without even a sword. I don't recommend that you try and escape."

"I have no intention of leaving," Michael assured her. "I am only trying to understand why you are with me. And why you are so friendly towards me. Until now, I have only gotten to know, well, let's say, your more brusque side. You are far more attractive in a dress than in pants."

Aina raised her cup to him in acknowledgment of the compliment and took a sip of wine before responding. "These are desperate times," she said somberly. "I have no leisure to be a lady, let alone a princess. My land is beset by two evils. They devour all that is good and wholesome and beautiful. I have no choice but to be harsh and relentless. I owe it to my people." Her eyes flashed as she spoke.

"Yet what is different now?" the knight asked.

Aina took a deep breath and the light left her eyes. "For the moment, all has been decided and I can no longer influence the course of things. Even though it's fruitless, my only hope is to await a champion who will deliver us from both evils. This time, you have been chosen. I honor you and I respect the sacrifice you are making. You are, after all, going to your death." This last she spoke in a low voice.

"I have not chosen to go die," Michael said with a penetrating stare.

"It makes little difference," she said averting her eyes. "The dragon will choose for you."

Michael was uncomfortable being reminded of this. He distracted himself by trying to puzzle out something Aina had said.

"You say the land is troubled by two evils. The dragon is easy to see. What is the second evil?"

Aina looked up sharply at the knight. "Are you blind as well as foolish?" she asked bitterly.

When Michael looked at her questioningly, she spoke again, but it left the riddle unanswered. "Or perhaps that is where your own sympathies lie. Whatever the reason, I'll leave you to live what little life you have left in ignorance." She abruptly got up from the table and left the room. Michael was puzzled what he had said to upset her. This warrior-maiden presented him with many riddles to be unraveled.

Not wishing to be left alone, he also left the table and followed the princess. She passed through a short hallway, and two connected receiving rooms that were set with fine furniture. Then they passed through a sitting room that was hung with several portraits richly framed. Glancing at them, Michael thought these must be portraits of the royal family. One in particular caught his eye. It portrayed a young woman in stately dress and wearing a diadem set with gems. Yet she carried in her arms a basket filled with onions, leeks and garlic. The knight was puzzled why a lady of the royal house would let herself be so portrayed. Was this an indication of her connection to the common folk?

He studied her face. It looked oddly familiar. Her eyes in particular awoke strange memories in his heart. He felt both longing and sadness rising up, yet could not understand why.

"Your Highness!" he called out. She was near enough to hear and returned to where he stood.

Her expression was pleasant again. "What is it?"

"This portrait. Do you have any idea who she is?" He asked in a choked whisper. He was having difficulty speaking. Why would someone he had never known take his breath away. What did she remind him of? He had little hope Aina would know. Castles sported portraits of ancestors dead for a century or longer.

"She was my grandmother. Why do you ask?"

Aina's grandmother. Indeed, he now saw that they shared a similar look about the eyes.

"Is that what I'm seeing?" Michael asked himself. Still, there was something more. Something unknown was nagging at him, prodding him, mocking him.

"Did you know her well?" he asked.

"I did not know her at all," Aina answered. "Funny you should ask about her. Why do you want to know?"

Michael continued to stare at the figure's eyes and suddenly he knew for a certainty who she was. He noticed the distinctive pattern in the scarf that was lying across her shoulders. How could he have missed it until now? He grunted as if the wind had been knocked out of him.

"What do you know about her?" he demanded.

"Well, some say that she was a commoner. Others insist that she was a queen in her own right. I like to think that this portrait was made to say that both were true. The older people, those who knew her, still talk about 'My Lady,' with great reverence. They say she was as kind as she was wise. She brought radical reforms in favor of the common folk. She supported the poor and instituted courts that did not favor only the wealthy. My old nurse who served her when she was queen used to tell me that I resemble her."

"Indeed, you do," Michael commented. "What else do you know about her?"

"Nothing much. She left when my father was a babe. When her husband, the king, died, she wandered off, never to be seen again."

"Do you know where she went?"

"No. She just disappeared. She was never spoken well of for having abandoned her crown and her young son. But when I look at her portrait, I can't believe that. There must have been some other reason." They both stood in silence a moment, staring at the portrait of a young woman watching them from the canvas with a knowing smile.

"There were other stories about why she left," Aina continued in a low voice. She glanced around, as if to make sure that no one else was around to hear. "Some say she was tricked into leaving," she spoke, almost in a whisper, "that influential members of noble houses wanted to get rid of her and, while she was in mourning for her husband and distracted, they feigned the death of the young prince. It's whispered that she left in grief over her loss. The nobility were glad to see her go. They reversed most of her reforms within a few years. They did raise my father to be king, not daring to harm the head of the rightful heir to the crown. My nurse maintained that he had known his mother long enough to be touched by her mercy and kindness. As soon as he took his place on the throne, he brought back many of her reforms." She paused and studied Michael a moment. "It's strange, but you act like you know her. Do you recognize her?"

Michael did not answer. "What else do you know about her?" Aina hesitated before speaking.

"Well, there are rumors about her, of course. That's to be expected."

"Rumors?" He decided to risk a guess. "Were they rumors about her connection to a dragon?"

Aina looked at him astonished. She continued to speak in a low voice, stepping closer to him. "Odd that you should ask. Indeed, there are those who say that the dragon plagues us because of her. That she was really a witch and put a curse upon the land. That she could speak with dragons and she summoned this one to destroy us, in revenge for how the barons tricked her. None of it really makes much sense. I believe it was invented by those who wished to defile even the good memory of her that she left behind. I can't believe that she wished anyone evil."

"Nor can I," Michael spoke softly. "Nor can I."

Chapter Ten

The Dragon Maker

*T*he next morning, Aina appeared at Michael's door to take him for breakfast. She was polite and pleasant, yet avoided any serious conversation. She appeared preoccupied with other thoughts. When he asked how long before he was going to be sent to fight Scorch, her only answer was that it would come soon enough. After eating, she disappeared, saying that she would come visit him again at supper time. She told him he was free to explore the town at his leisure.

Michael lingered at his window overlooking the marketplace. He enjoyed watching the hustle and bustle of the shoppers. One young woman caught his eye. She was leading a donkey that was laden with sacks. Something about how she moved and what little he could see of her face were familiar. Although she was dressed in the commoner fashion of homespun cloth, she bore a striking resemblance to the princess! He watched her disappear down a side alley, leading the donkey.

He spent the day walking around the town. He made a point of going down to one of the main gates and talking to the guard on duty. It did not escape him that he was indeed being followed, though discreetly, as Aina had warned him. That evening he sat at the king's feast, and made a point of speaking only when addressed. He was still much discussed by the nobles, and he could tell elaborate bets were being wagered. Flek, he was pleased, only glowered at him, but left him in peace.

The next morning Aina again arrived to have breakfast with him.

"My lady," Michael began. He saw her cheeks redden at his words. "I would much appreciate it if you would give me a tour of your fine town today."

Aina hesitated a moment before speaking. "I cannot do that. I am needed elsewhere. But I will ask one of the servants to take you around."

"That won't be necessary," he replied. "If you cannot take me, then I will wander on my own. Tell me, have you found me a horse yet? Or a sword?"

He had not expected her to have taken his request seriously, so he was surprised when she answered, "I have not yet been successful. I hope to have an answer soon."

When they had finished eating, Aina excused herself. As soon as she disappeared down the hallway, Michael got up and found the quickest way out to the marketplace.

The young woman from the day before emerged from a stall leading again a heavily-laden donkey. She walked along the edge of the market and headed down a narrow alleyway. Michael was not far behind her. By the time she had turned down two other alleys she had left the commotion of the market behind. Michael quickened his pace to catch up with her. The young woman heard his footsteps and turned to see who was hastening past her.

Brief shock fluttered across her face. Then she looked stern. "I told you that I am busy today."

"Your Highness, this must be an important mission if you have to go disguised." He noticed that she looked quite attractive with a shawl across her shoulders and a scarf tied over her long braids. He was struck again how young she appeared, hardly more than a girl.

"And a mission I prefer to do alone," she said, still not ready to welcome him.

"The back streets of any town can be treacherous for a beautiful young woman. Just think of me as your chaperone."

"As if I needed any protection," she huffed.

Michael laughed, remembering the excellence of her swordplay. "You have a point," he acceded. "Still, I hope you will let me accompany you. If nothing else, so I may stretch my legs in good company."

"If you come with me, you must be ready to serve me without question," she said firmly. "Are you ready to do that?" she asked with a challenging look.

Michael bowed to her. "I follow my Lady's orders," he said. Once again, he noticed her cheeks flush, and wondered why.

"Good enough," she said turning away, continuing to lead the donkey. "We have work to do."

They walked in silence through a maze of streets and alleys. The further away from the palace they walked, the more run-down the houses appeared. The alleys grew narrower, and the streets were no longer cobbled, but packed dirt and covered with filth. The people they passed had dark looks and watched them suspiciously. The children were dressed in rags and, although some ran about playing, others sat on the side of the streets looking listless. It did not take long before Michael knew they had come to the part of town that did not bother to go to market. They had nothing to trade and no money to buy much with. Finally, Aina spoke.

"These people are in need. My grandmother used to help them. I do what I can as well."

They came to a small plaza. Aina stopped and called out loudly, "Bring your pots!" Then she said to Michael. "Untie one of the bags."

Hardly had Michael taken a heavy bag from the donkey's back and untied it than a crowd of people arrived. There was a lot of jostling and friendly bantering as they tried to get close to him.

"Fill their pots," Aina commanded.

The bag the donkey carried was filled with barley. Michael took each pot in turn and filled it with the grain from the bag. The people thanked him with shy smiles and went their way. Aina was surrounded by several older women who were weeping into their aprons, telling her some tale of woe. Aina nodded and comforted them.

As the bag was emptied out, Michael began to see some had returned with another pot for seconds. They smiled and winked and spoke their thanks. When the bag was empty, the people dispersed.

"What do we do with the rest?" Michael asked, gesturing to the still-laden donkey.

"We move on to the next little plaza. They'll be waiting for us. Word will spread that we're coming."

"Does the king know you do this?" Michael asked as Aina led the donkey away by the reins.

"Yes, he tolerates it," she said bitterly. "But he could do more, if he were only willing. He complains that I spoil the people, making them think they can have something for no work. I tell him he is starving his own people, but he doesn't care. Well, my grandmother cared, and my mother did what she could, and now so do I."

They walked from plaza to plaza until the last bag had been emptied. They had traveled to the furthest edge of the town.

"We will have to hasten to get back in time for supper," Aina commented. "Thank you for your help. I didn't expect you to be willing to do this."

"And why not?" the knight asked.

She studied him a moment before answering. "We were born into a privileged class. We are willing to share, but only on our own terms. And our terms always work to our own advantage, even when it looks like we are helping others."

"As for myself, I wouldn't know," Michael said. "I grew up on the streets. I know the pain of hunger from my childhood. I admire you for doing this. It is plain to me that you are drawing no advantage from this."

"You're not from a noble house?" she asked astonished.

"I was an orphan," he confessed. "I don't know who my parents were."

She stared at him hard. "I judged you based upon your advanced skills at arms. I thought you were born and bred to be a knight," she murmured. "You keep surprising me."

"I was just thinking the same thing about you," Michael laughed.

For the next two days after breakfast they went again to pass out food to the poor. They were full days in different parts of town.

"Do you ever run out of neighborhoods to visit?" Michael asked as they walked beside the donkey, now free of its burden.

"There's no shortage of hungry in our fair town," she replied. "Although some areas have grown more deserted. Before the Warrior's Compound was founded, Scorch's sacrificial meal came from among the poor. As a result, many townspeople have left. Where they have gone, I cannot tell."

Michael recalled his visit to the village in the forest. He pondered whether he should tell her about them. He thought it might comfort her to know they were looking after themselves. At the same time, he realized it would distress her to hear that they lived in constant fear of being found and attacked by the king's trackers.

He decided that if she knew about them, she could have some influence with her father to leave them in peace. He was about to speak, when he noticed that two guards had walked up to within a few paces behind them in the narrow alleyway. Aina also noticed.

"That's odd," she said in a low voice to him. "They don't ever follow this closely."

"That's because they're closing the door behind us to make sure we don't escape," Michael said flatly. Aina looked up and saw two more figures appear at the other end of the alleyway walking straight towards them. Michael recognized with grim amusement that one of the men was none other than the king's counselor.

"And so you pay me another visit," Michael said addressing the approaching figures. "You've chosen an interesting place for it."

Flek did not bother to respond. He blocked their way and spoke loudly, as if issuing a proclamation. "The king's champion is found guilty of threatening the safety of the princess Aina."

"He has not!" Aina protested.

"The king's champion will be punished according to the laws of our kingdom."

"Punished? For what?" demanded the princess. Fleck ignored her.

"Furthermore, the king's champion has striven to elude and otherwise escape his captivity. He has wandered into questionable quarters of our town and exposed himself to risks that would endanger the successful execution of his duties. The king's champion is valuable property—"

"You make me sound like livestock," the knight interjected.

"—yet he may not violate the king's orders. He will be punished in accordance with his rank."

Windows above them in the narrow alley opened and heads were stuck out to see what the commotion was about. When they saw what was going on, they quickly closed themselves in again.

"Flek, is that the best you can do?" Michael asked, glaring at the king's counselor. "Do you have to disguise it with a royal proclamation? If you want me beaten, have the courage to challenge me personally."

Flek only smiled and continued in a voice too loud for that narrow space. "Furthermore, the king's champion has dared to leave the palace under disguise and lead the princess Aina into danger. He has contrived to compel her to dress as a commoner, below her true station."

"He's done nothing of the sort," Aina said firmly.

Flek continued relentlessly on. "The king's champion stands under scrutiny for witchcraft. His punishment shall be justly meted out." Flek looked at Michael and, lowering his voice, said with a wicked smile, "Dung Boy, this is just to make sure you don't have any clever ideas about harming the dragon. Scorch is much too valuable an asset to lose. Not that I worry about it, but there are others who do not share my confidence." Then he commanded in a loud voice, "Guards, proceed to carry out the punishment."

The guards pulled short clubs from their belts.

"I protest!" Aina said. "I command you to stand down."

"It's all in order," Flek finally addressed her. "We know what we're doing. Just step aside and in a few moments we will lead you back to safety. I know this scoundrel. He's full of tricks. We will deal with him. Just stay out of the way and you won't get hurt."

"I'll do nothing of the sort," Aina warned.

Flek gestured with his hand and one of the guards behind them made to grab hold of the princess. This was the moment Michael had been waiting for.

The knight grabbed Flek by his tunic and, with a great shove, thrust him into the guard beside him, throwing them both off balance. He pushed the donkey between them and swiveled on his heel. He hit one of the guards behind him in the throat with the heel of his hand. This caused him to drop his club. Michael swooped it up and with a quick, hard jab to the stomach, left that man lying on the ground struggling to breathe.

He turned back again to the guard beside Flek. He had by now regained his footing and gotten the donkey out of the way. He attacked Michael with his club raised. Stepping forward, the knight raised his left arm to block the blow and threw his elbow into the man's face, breaking his nose with a dull popping sound. His own club then came down onto the side of the man's head above his ear. The guard went down like a stone, hitting the ground hard. Michael was not fighting merely to defend himself. He was fighting a battle, and he wanted to minimize the chances that his opponents would get up again very soon. His blows were fierce and ruthless.

In the meantime, the guard who had tried to restrain the princess was also lying face-down on the ground. Aina was standing over him, his club in her hand.

"That wasn't necessary, Your Highness," Michael said with a smile. "I could have handled him."

"Oh, believe me," she said with passion in her voice. "This was my pleasure."

The only one left standing was Flek. He stood there baffled and shocked, looking down at his fallen guards.

"Don't worry, king's counselor," the knight said. "They won't be getting up again for awhile."

Although Flek's face was ashen white, he had not lost the use of his tongue. He looked at Aina. "If you choose to throw your lot in with him, Princess, that's your doing, not mine. I tried to save you from this filth. If you want to go down with him, I won't mourn your loss."

Michael swiftly reached out and took hold of Flek's cape where it was held together by an ornamental brooch underneath his chin. He lifted him up and shoved him hard against the wall of the narrow alleyway. "You're a coward and a bully, king's counselor," Michael said to him. "You still rely on the strength of others to do your dirty work. Now listen carefully to what I'm going to say. If anyone tries this again, or dares to lay a hand on the princess, whether you're with them or not, I will personally come after you. Make no mistake. The princess Aina is under my protection, since it is obvious that she is not under yours."

The knight dropped Flek after saying this. The king's counselor lost his footing and fell to the ground on top of one of the guards. He quickly scurried out of the way.

"Let's go home, Aina," Michael said to the princess. Taking the reins of the donkey, the two of them walked down the narrow alley and away. They hastened down three more lanes, Aina frequently looking behind them.

"I'd wager there's no one following us any more today," Michael said. "We'll be halfway home before any of those guards are back on their feet. And I don't think Flek has enough courage to follow us alone."

"I agree with you," Aina said. She looked like she was struggling with a hard decision. Finally, she said, "There's someone I want you to meet. Let's go this way." At the next crossing she turned away from the direction to the palace. Michael was intrigued where she was leading him.

They walked until they came to a street that had more foot traffic. They were passing a line of shops. There was a cobbler who had set up his work in front of his door in the afternoon sunlight, pounding leather into shape on his small anvil. Michael could tell the baker's shop from the strong pleasant smell coming through the open windows. Then there was a shop selling all manner of tools which were hung in the window. A large whetstone for sharpening knives and plough-shares stood next to the front door.

At the next shop, the knight stopped in his tracks. Through the window, he could see dragons. Not life-size dragons, but small models of them, carved out of wood and painted with bright colors.

"This is where I wanted to take you," Aina said.

"What sort of shop is this?" he asked amazed.

"It's the toymaker's," she replied. "Some call him the dragon maker. He's a friend of mine. Come on. I want you to meet him." She tied up the donkey to a post and they entered the front door.

The shop was lit only from the light coming from the street. It was dim inside, but Michael could see that the walls were filled with shelves. And on every shelf were displayed dragons in every possible posture and gesture.

"Dragons," he gasped. He was amazed and delighted.

"I know," Aina sighed. "They're beautiful in some strange way, aren't they? I think that's what troubles me the most."

Aina's comment was odd, but he was too distracted by what he saw to question her. Beside each dragon were miniature horses and knights in gestures of engagement, as if before him were a massive battle between an army of knights and a gathering of dragons frozen in time. He stood studying one after another. The dragons were so carefully and accurately done that the knight was quickly convinced they could have been made only by someone who knew dragons very well.

Then he came to one dragon on the shelf that caused him to gasp. This one stood alone, no horses or knights nearby. He carefully picked it up in his hands and walked to the window to let more light shine on it.

"Perfect," he murmured. "Just perfect." He turned the wooden figure over and over in his hands, a broad grin covering his face. It was an exact replica of Star.

"Aina, who has done all of these?" he asked, his voice full of excitement and wonder. But she did not respond. Aina was not standing next to him any longer.

Michael looked around, but could not see her. He saw a curtain that looked like it covered a door leading to a back room. He heard her voice coming from there. That's when he paid attention to the other voice that spoke with her.

"Princess, you've hesitated bringing this one to me." It was a man's voice. "I've spent a lot of time wondering why."

"I've been uncertain and confused about him," he heard Aina reply in a low voice. "At first, I thought he was like all the others. Gallant, brave, but a fool. I'm not as certain any longer. He's different. He really is. He goes with me to bring food to the poor. And for some reason Flek hates him. I've never so much not wanted—"

"Hush, Your Highness, some things you don't want to voice," the other interrupted. "Let me take a look at this different one."

The curtain was pushed aside and an old man appeared. He wore a funny round cap over his long white hair. His long beard was equally white. He wore a tunic of dark purple that hung to the ground. Michael was surprised seeing him, because judging by his voice, he expected a much younger man.

"I see you have a good eye for dragons," the old man said coming nearer, indicating the carved figure in the knight's hand. "There are many kinds of dragons, you know. There are the wild ones, like Scorch. But there are Luck Dragons as well. Like the one you're holding there. They do exist, you know, in spite of what people say. By the way, welcome to my shop." He smiled at the knight and made a welcoming gesture with his arm.

Michael was astonished and intrigued by what the old man had just revealed. "You know about Luck Dragons?" He held up the figure in his hand. "What do you know about this dragon?"

"It's important that children grow up learning about all kinds of dragons, don't you think?" the old man replied. "Of course, some say," he rambled on, "that in the end, there is only one kind of dragon and it is the company the dragon keeps that determines whether the dragon is wild and destructive or will bring blessings and good fortune."

He now had Michael's full attention. "Where did you learn that?" he demanded.

The old man ignored his question, as if he had not heard. He turned his back on the knight and wandered away behind a counter. "I wonder if the same is true of Scorch?" he mused. "Probably not. Most say this one is thoroughly evil. But you never can tell. I think you'll find that there is more to this dragon than what meets the eye. And considering how big a dragon is, that's saying a lot!" The old man laughed at his own joke.

"Who are you, old man?" Michael was peering directly into his face, trying to locate a memory that was tickling him. He was certain he had seen this man before. He just did not know where or when.

"Who am I? Well, you might call me the finder of what has been lost," the dragon maker said with a chuckle, avoiding looking the knight in the eyes.

"Sometimes a child gets lost, sometimes a memory," he continued. "Lost children are usually relatively easy to find. Memories, on the other hand, are difficult when they get misplaced. I've found my share of lost children." He glanced up quickly and met Michael's eye. The knight was jolted by that look.

"I've also found a number of lost memories," he continued. "I've done a lot of digging to find the one about dragons. And once a memory's been found, it's such a puzzle to whom it belongs. You don't want to give it to someone who won't take care of it. It will just get lost again. The same goes for lost children, of course. If you can't return them to where they belong, then you have to go to the trouble of finding them a new home. One has to be careful placing an orphan. Not just any place will do, you know."

The old man's eyes suddenly rose again to meet the knight's. Recognition shot through Michael. "It's you," he gasped.

"Orphans are troublesome, you know," the old man continued. "It's tricky to find them the right place and put them in touch with the right people. Usually, they are orphans because they had no chance of meeting who they had to meet where they started. Some orphans are accidental, and then there are others who are intentional, for that very reason. It can be quite a bother to set it all up, but we do what we can. Yes, the intentional orphans are the ones we have to keep an eye on." The old man turned his back on Michael and began pushing some curtains aside that hung on the wall. There were open storage cabinets behind them. They were packed with random objects, baskets, clothing, tools, pots of paint, unfinished carvings. The old man was looking for something.

"Now *things* are a different matter, although they can be as troublesome as an orphan. Some things, when found, you have to hang on to until you can return them. Just because you find an item, doesn't mean that you've found the owner. A most taxing process. Then the owner appears, and you have to remember where you stored the item in question. Now let's see. I thought I left it here."

He rummaged a little more. Michael was so astonished to realize the old man's identity that he stood there speechless. He was fascinated by his rambling monologue.

"People misplace the strangest things. Boots, stockings, gloves. And then I usually find only one, which isn't much help, you know, if you've got two hands and two feet. Hats are a lot easier, of course. You need only one of those, unless you've gone and lost your head." He paused to chuckle. "Had a friend with that problem. Couldn't decide for the longest time what to do with his hat. Finally, I kept it for myself," he said gesturing to the round, felt cap on his own head.

"Some things aren't so valuable, you can imagine, and are best left lost," he said, his back now turned to the knight. "Things like embarrassment, cruelty, guilt or shame. And gossip. Dreadful thing, gossip is. I'd prefer it was never found, but it is often kept while something worthwhile is discarded. Then there are other things that are priceless and worth all the trouble they put you to. Such as love, or forgiveness, or a sense of devotion. Ah, here it is. "

The old man turned around holding in his hands a long bundle wrapped in a rug. At one end, a metal handle appeared. It only took a moment for Michael to recognize it.

"I heard you'd been missing this," the old man said with a smile.

"My sword!" He reached out to take it from the wizard.

"I went to a lot of effort to get this back. Don't lose it a second time."

Michael held it in his hand and let the rug fall away. A thrill went through him as he felt its familiar weight. The handle fit his hand perfectly. He swung it in the close confines of the room.

"Careful, careful!" the old man warned. "It's been newly sharpened, and I don't want you damaging my dragons. Save it for the one you've come to fight."

"Aga, how can I thank you?"

"By doing what you came here to do."

"I have so many questions to ask you."

"And we haven't time for any of them. I've done what I came here to do and I am urgently needed elsewhere."

"But Aga, now that you're here, couldn't you go out and deal with Scorch?"

"I might, but it would do no good. Even if I were successful, and that is highly questionable, he'd just appear elsewhere. You've been trained for this moment and your destiny awaits you."

"Aga, I just don't know how to go about this. You know I was trained that there is no way—"

The old man interrupted him, "There is but one thing standing between you and success. And it has nothing to do with Scorch."

"I don't understand."

"Nor do I expect you to. That day outside the walls of the Dragon Compound I gave you what Star was not able to in order to complete your training. Everything you've done from that day to this has been in preparation for the battle that awaits you. This much, I think, you can understand."

The knight took a deep breath, pressed his lips together and nodded his head in silence.

"Good," continued the wizard. "I'm glad you agree. It's time for all of us to go. But don't leave by the front door. You know you're followed everywhere. I have a back door; use that. I also have something else that I've wanted to return to you. You'll find it behind my shop."

"But Aga, there's so much I want to know."

"Everything you want to know you've already learned. It's up to you to remember what you've forgotten. Now go."

The wizard pulled back another curtain that covered a dark passage leading to a back door. Reluctantly Michael walked through it. Behind the shop was a small courtyard. A horse was tethered to a post. When it saw him emerge from the shop, it whinnied loudly and shook its great head. The silver bells on her bridle tinkled merrily.

"Storm!" Michael ran over to her. "Storm, how did you get here?" He ran his hands over her strong neck and she nuzzled him in the chest. He stood there gazing lovingly at her, his hands busy stroking her. To his further delight, the knight saw that his armor and shield were tied to her saddle.

"I'll never understand the ways of wizards," he muttered to himself.

"And it's a good thing you don't," Aga spoke behind him. Michael turned to see him striding away from the shop door. He had put on a hooded cloak and carried a long staff in his hand. He had a bag slung over one shoulder.

Before he could disappear, Aina emerged from the shop and ran over to him. She took hold of his cloak and held him back.

"Are you still so certain?" she pleaded.

Aga smiled down at her. "Maiden, I have no doubt whatsoever. He is the one we've been waiting for. If he cannot manage Scorch—well, that is too dreadful a thought to entertain. He will have to do what he can. Yes, I am quite glad he has finally come, because it now frees me up. There are pressing matters that cry for my attention elsewhere."

"You're leaving?" she asked astonished.

"Yes, my dear. It's time for me to go. But have no fear. I am leaving you in the best hands possible." He saw the shock in her face and cupped her cheek gently in his hand. "Despair not, maiden. I doubt that you have seen the last of me. For the moment, however, you have no further need of my services. When the day comes again that you do, I shall not let you down. That much, at least, I owe to your grandmother. For now, it is enough that the two of you have found one another."

With these words, Aga turned and walked away. He never looked back as he disappeared around a corner.

Michael stood holding Storm's forehead to his own. Tears were running down his face. "I thought I'd lost you," he whispered to the horse, caressing the side of her head. "How did you know to bring me to him?" he asked Aina when he felt his voice would not crack.

"He has had me bring every champion to him," she responded. "You are the only one to whom he ever returned horse, armor and sword. He seems to think highly of you. Where do you know him from?"

"He knighted me." He acknowledged Aina's look of surprise. "He did more than that. He gave me my sword, shield, armor. Even my horse. This horse. My beautiful Storm. I owe it all to Aga."

Aina gazed at him fully in his face. "You are the king's champion," she said in a whisper. "Yet I have not even asked your name. I've never cared about the names of the champions. They come, they go and never return. You are so different. Please, tell me now. I would like to know. What is your name?"

"Michael." He pronounced it Mi-kah-el.

She looked startled when he said it. "That is the very name," she muttered. "When Aga first arrived, he told me, 'I am waiting for one named Michael.' He pronounced it the very same way. 'When he comes,' he told me, 'bring him to me immediately.' But over time, I forgot. I even gave up asking the champions for their names."

"It seems like you have known him for quite awhile."

"He appeared soon after the king began sending off human offerings to the dragon."

"How did he win your confidence?"

"He told me he had known my grandmother," she said, shaking her head. "He told me stories about her, about her life. Some of it was what I knew from my nurse, and so I chose to believe him, although I never knew for certain. There was something about him I trusted."

Michael almost spoke at this, but decided the time was not yet right.

Chapter Eleven

The Ruined Lands

The knight made an inventory of his armor and went through his saddlebags. "It's all here," he murmured in wonder. Even an old tattered piece of embroidered cloth that he had carried around with him since the day his grandmother had died, tucked away at the bottom of one of his bags. "Nothing's missing. How did he manage that?" He looked around at Aina. She had her back turned to him, staring in the direction Aga had disappeared around a corner.

"What are you thinking, Your Highness?" he asked.

She lifted her hands to her face before turning. Her eyes were glistening, and he saw she had been crying.

"I asked you for my horse and armor," the knight said softly. "I thank you for their return."

"It was all his magic," she responded. She bit her lip and looked searchingly into his face. Michael wondered what she was thinking, but did not ask a second time.

"We'll need some more magic to keep this safe," he said instead.

"That won't be quite as hard," Aina said with a smile. "I have many servants who are still faithful to me. Among them is a groom. He will keep both horse and armor safe. Even if the guard sees us return with them, once under my protection at the palace, no one will dare touch them."

Michael took the reins and Aina led him quickly away. She bade him wait at a corner and she left him, to return a few minutes later leading the donkey that they had left tied at the front of the toy-maker's shop. She led them through many turns and windings of the circuitous back streets. She knew them as well as the maze of hallways inside the palace.

At one point, Michael stopped her. "How close are we to the south gate?" he asked.

"We pass close by," she answered.

"Take me there," he said.

"Surely, not," she responded. "It is out of our way."

"Surely, yes," he said with a smile. "I wish to see it."

"It will endanger our safe return to the palace," she warned.

"It will endanger us more if I do not go there now."

She shrugged her shoulders as if to give up any responsibility for what the outcome of this detour would bring. She turned down the next lane and led them through a series of alleys between the houses, one built shoulder to shoulder with the next. They emerged into an open space with more foot traffic and ahead of them loomed the large towers of the city gates. This was the way down to the river. It was here that Michael had entered Gladur Nock as a prisoner.

"Take the reins until I return," Michael said, handing her the lead-lines from his horse.

"Where are you going?" she asked astonished.

"Just paying a visit. Wait for me. I'll be right back." The knight strode into the covered opening to the gate, leaving Aina staring after him with surprise.

Out of the shadows a sentry strode forward to challenge him. "Who goes there?" he said in a strong voice.

Michael stopped to face him. "The king's champion," he replied.

"The king's champion?" the sentry said, obviously impressed. Then he composed himself. "If king's champion you are, you'll not be passing through this gate. Go back the way you came."

Michael sized up the sentry. He was an average-sized man with average-sized features. He glanced behind him, peering into the gloom of the keep. He could see the portcullis on the other side and the open fields behind. In the distance, he caught sight of the sun glancing off of the river.

"Do you challenge all who pass through this gate?" he asked.

"Man, woman and child I challenge, coming and going. No one passes through without my leave. And you do not have my leave."

"Nor am I asking for it," Michael assured him. He wondered if he had come on a fool's mission, but continued in spite of the sinking feeling he had.

"I go soon to the dragon," he said.

"So we've heard," the sentry replied. "We all wish you good luck. I've got five coppers bet on you myself," he added with a big grin. "I've heard you're mighty handy with a sword. I've given you an hour."

Michael must have made a sour face.

"Don't think I don't have faith in you," the sentry hastened to add. "Rumor is that most champions don't even get their swords drawn before Scorch takes them down. Why, if you go the full hour, you'll win me a month's wages. I'm on your side, you know."

"I only wish you were," Michael mumbled under his breath. Then he spoke loud enough for the sentry to hear. "Look here, I intend to last longer than an hour. I intend to return."

"From Scorch? Now that would be a feat."

"So put your money down on that," Michael said. "And you will be a made man." The sentry laughed at the absurdity of his statement.

"And when I return," Michael continued, "that is when I will be looking to see who is on my side. That's when every man—in town, in field or in forest—will count, once the dragon has been dealt with. That's when I'll be looking to see who stands by me."

"Strangely you talk for a champion," the sentry said scratching his scraggly beard. "In town, in field and in forest, you say?"

At that moment a large man stepped out of the shadows of the keep and came to stand beside the sentry. "What's the problem here?" he asked.

"No problem," commented the sentry. "This here claims to be the king's champion."

"King's champion," he said, looking Michael up and down. "Then he shall find no passage here. Go on your way, king's champion, back to the palace. You've gone astray and your keepers will be looking for you. You will not pass through here."

Michael turned and walked away. Over his shoulder he could hear the sentry's excited chatter. "Captain, did you hear what he said? He said he's coming back from Scorch."

"I heard him, sentry," the Captain of the postern replied. "I heard every word of it."

Michael thought to himself, That will have to suffice. He returned to where he left Aina.

"What was that all about?" she asked.

"Me? Oh, I'm just getting to know your lovely town," he said. "The longer I stay here, the more it intrigues me."

"You are a most uncommon king's champion," she said peering at him.

"Of this, I hope you are right," Michael said with a laugh.

They entered again into the maze of streets and byways. They finally emerged from a narrow alleyway right into the large market plaza before the palace walls. They crossed to the doorway from where Aina had received the donkey that morning. She took the reins for Storm. "Wait for me here." She entered with both animals and returned quickly.

"All is well. Your horse is safe," Aina said. She took him by the arm and wanted to lead him into the palace. He held her back. "What is it?" she asked.

"Your Highness, can you steal me out of here?"

She stared hard at him before answering, thinking she had misjudged him. Her manner was suddenly cold. "Is that why you went to the gate? Look, I told you, there is no escape. You will not manage a full day before the trackers find you again."

"I'm not looking to escape," the knight said. He saw the relief in her face. Then he added, "I want to go and see the dragon. I want to see Scorch." Aina was shocked.

"Are you out of your mind? You can't just ride out for a visit, you know."

"I have to know what I'm up against," he said somberly. "Can you take me there? And then bring me back again."

Aina stood silently considering his request. Twice she started to speak and stopped herself. She was obviously struggling with something. "There is a door in the palace wall we could leave by," she finally explained. "It opens into a wood bordering the city. If we left before first light, then we would have a chance that no one would try and stop us. The trackers are watching all of the roads that lead away from Gladur. But I am certain they do not watch the roads that lead to the dragon. No one rides to the dragon on purpose."

"So, you'll take me?"

"It's foolish and foolhardy," she objected.

"Well, that about sums it up for me," he laughed. "The very sort of thing I'd want to do."

"Let's get a bite of supper and retire," she said in a low voice. Her face was a mask showing no expression. "I will come and get you an hour before first light." He was curious how he had been able to talk her into it so easily.

The silver bells on Storm's reins jangled merrily in the darkness of the predawn day. The air was cool and crisp, although the bright stars overhead promised that the morning would turn warm. Michael was leading Storm as he walked on foot beside Aina, leading her own horse.

"This is not quite the silent escape I had been thinking of," Aina said in a low voice to him. He chuckled.

"Well, the groom closing the gate behind us does not make our leaving very secret."

"He won't tell anyone," she said. "In fact, he will keep watch to open the door again when we return. I suggest we don't come back until after nightfall to reduce the chances of being seen."

"That suits me. I'm glad to stretch my legs and get out of the town, if even for a day. Don't you think we'll be missed?"

"If we're lucky, no. Even though we're followed wherever we go, they'll think that we rose early and gave them the slip. Most likely they'll spend the day scouring the town looking for us. When we show up in the evening, they will just conclude we stayed out of sight. We are going to be back by evening, aren't we? You haven't told me yet how much of a look you want to take."

"That's hard to say. It depends on how hard he is to find."

"We won't have to worry about that. Once we're there, he'll find us." They had entered the protective cover of some trees and she said, "We can ride from here."

"You know the way? In the dark?"

"Yes. I know the way."

Suddenly the knight realized why. "You've done this before, haven't you? This isn't the first time you've snuck away to take a look at the dragon."

Aina stopped walking and Michael wished he could see her expression in the dark. "I've gone before," she admitted in a low voice.

"How often?" he asked. Her lack of response was already her answer. "You go regularly, don't you?"

"I can't keep away," she admitted, sounding defeated. "I'm drawn to him. If I don't go, he haunts me in my dreams. I have no peace from that cursed beast."

"Has he ever seen you?"

"No—yes—I don't know. Several times I thought that he was looking right at me. But I had to assume that he wasn't, because I came away alive. If he had seen me, he would have eaten me, don't you think?"

"Dragon's have an excellent sense of smell," Michael mused. "So this is why you know that the trackers won't see us. Tell me, what goes on inside of you when you see him?"

Aina did not answer at once, as if struggling with what to say. "It's strange that you ask me that. He's terrifying," she finally answered. "But he's also thrilling. And there's something majestic and beautiful and noble about him. And when I say that, I feel like I am betraying my own people, because I hate Scorch for what he's done. Every time I go, I'm so confused about my feelings. They're all mixed up. And the worst is that I can't keep away."

Michael reached out in the dark and found her hand. "Now you know a little bit how I feel and why I have to go and see him. If you know the way, then lead on before the light overtakes us while we are still within sight of the city walls."

They mounted and walked their horses until there was enough light to see their way clearly. After that, they rode at a gentle gallop into the morning. They passed through forests spotted with open meadows and streams running through them. Twice they passed a small herd of deer grazing in the cover of the trees. Michael was thinking what a peaceful land this was. Then he smelled it and pulled Storm up suddenly. Aina stopped with him.

"There's been a fire," he said.

"There's been a dragon," Aina responded sourly. "Once we can smell it, we're close to the ruined lands."

They rode a little longer among the trees before Aina said, "Let's dismount and walk our horses from here. It happens rather suddenly."

They led their horses by the reins. "What do you mean, it happens rather suddenly? What happens?" Michael asked.

Aina had come to a stop and gestured towards the thick wall of foliage before them. There had been no road or trail to follow for some time. They had been finding the best way between bushes and around trees. "Look through there. It's rather like a curtain."

Michael walked up and parted the branches that cut off his view from what lay ahead. He was astonished at the scene before him. The land that had been green and alive with forest and shrub was gone. Nothing but a black wasteland extended as far as the eye could see across a landscape of rolling hills.

"Didn't you notice that we haven't seen any deer for awhile?" Aina asked. "There are no birds hunting or nesting this close to the destruction. Squirrels and chipmunks are missing. Nothing will live this close to Scorch. Even the insects avoid it."

Then Michael realized that what she said was true. He had not seen any animals since he first smelled the burn. Nor could he hear a single bird chattering in the branches. It dawned on him how unnaturally quiet it was. The knight grimaced as he peered over the blackened and bare land. Nothing stirred. "Well, how do we find him?" he asked.

"It's odd," Aina admitted looking around in all directions. "I don't understand it. Every time I've come, no matter where I end up, seeing there's no trail to follow, when I look out, he's always somewhere in sight. This doesn't make sense, that we can't see him."

"It makes sense to me," Michael muttered. "I know what I'll have to do." He turned and mounted onto Storm.

"Hold on," Aina said with big eyes. She grabbed hold of Storm's reins. "What are you doing? Where are you going?"

"I'll be back," he said looking down at her. "Wait for me. But no matter what you see or hear, stay here." He did not wait for her reply. As an afterthought, he added, "If he eats me, run for your life." He gave Storm a sharp kick and she sprang through the trees, carrying him into the black, ruined land.

Chapter Twelve

Scorch the Terrible

One moment there was deep forest and uncanny silence. Then suddenly, as Storm rode forward, it was like passing through a gateway, and a wall of forest stretched to his right and left. He blinked at the bright sunlight unfiltered by trees. Before him lay the great wasteland of Scorch the Terrible. Scorch had done his work well. The desolation was complete. Not a tree remained standing that was not a blackened skeleton of its former glory, mocking the dreary sky with its angular arms beseeching uncaring gods for help. Bushes fared even worse, having been burnt to stubble along the scorched ground. There was no sign of green anywhere. The knight's throat grew tight and parched. Scorch had been careful not to let a single blade of grass return after he had spent his fury on what had once been rich rolling hills tickled by wooded streams and crowned by thick forests. It was Scorch's way of intimidating all comers who dared to think that a dragon was nothing more than a fat, overgrown lizard and a quick road to glory and a hero's reputation.

The knight took all of this in as he dragged his eyes along the scene before him. It was painful to look at. Scorch had made his message clear: He would deal with anyone who dared oppose him as mercilessly as he had the land he claimed as his desolation. The knight snorted, and then sneezed, the intense smell of the burnt land, at places still smoldering, invading his nose with irritating acidity. He had to calm Storm, fearless companion of his campaigns, who was growing uneasy at this unnatural, widespread destruction.

"The smell has got stuck in your nose now, too," he said, leaning over to stroke her neck and whisper into her ear. "Get used to it. It's the smell of evil. Never forget it, and beware. We've come to meet it head-on, my sweet." He paused a moment, and added soberly, "But then, we've never fought together any other way. This will likely be our last battle together. Let's take it on bravely." Then both man and horse sneezed at once. "Ach, Stench they could have called you as well, you loathsome beast," he mused bitterly, speaking loudly at the ruined hills through which they rode.

"Where are you, you evil thing?" he bellowed out suddenly, making his horse shy and sidestep on the loose, rocky soil beneath them. "Show your wicked, ugly scales," he called out. "You're not a cat, nor am I a mouse, so stop your slinking." His voice fell flat on naked hills around him. He spurred his horse to come to the top of a rise of land to give him a better look around. "Let's just get it over with," he mumbled to himself under his breath.

"You!" he bellowed out again, twisting in his saddle to look in all directions. "Scorch! Show yourself! I bring you challenge, you wretched, cowardly worm of a beast!"

There was silence from the ruined landscape around him. Only the unhindered wind whistled coolly, ruffling Storm's mane. The quiet was unnerving; no song of bird, chatter of squirrels, burble of running water. Not even the rustle of wind in the leaves. Nothing. Nothing except Scorch's desolation. It was a picture of hopelessness.

He rode on, further into the depths of the black hills, leaving the green edge where the ruination met the forested land behind him. He spurred his horse up another rise and repeated his challenge loudly in all directions. Again, he was answered only by the silence carried in the wind. His words fell dead in the empty landscape. He rode even further into Scorch's ruined landscape, coming to another rise and once more bellowing out his challenge. He wondered how many more times he would have to repeat this.

After his fifth try, standing at the top of a naked hill, as he gazed out over the ugly, blackened hills around him, the hair on the back of his neck stood up. There was nothing concrete, more a feeling than a sound of an unfathomable heaviness from behind. An unfathomably nimble heaviness. Beneath him, Storm felt it as well. She nervously side-stepped and pulled at her reins as if she wanted to bolt from that spot.

He did not even bother to turn and look. Some old reaction, pulled out of the sleepy depths of his unconscious told him urgently that he did not have time to look around. With a cry, he gave Storm the free rein she was demanding and dug his spurs into her sides. Suddenly released from his firm hold and urged on by his heels, she sprang forward with a spray of gravel, leapt off the crest of the hill and flew down into the ravine below them.

He felt the forceful gust of the dragon's immense body as it landed heavily, though relatively silently on the spot where he and his mount had stood a moment before. Storm kicked and leapt, with sudden fright in her eyes as she twisted her head about trying to glance at the danger from behind as she galloped ahead. A lesser rider would have been thrown from the saddle.

"Nice evasion," murmured Scorch calmly. "And I don't give compliments easily. How you knew I was there is beyond me." Scorch, of course, was speaking more to himself than to the knight. He was so used to keeping his own company, not being inclined to keeping anyone else's for very long. But Scorch's comment was not lost on the knight, who realized that his escape was a gift of life that had come from his childhood drills. He sent up silent thanks to Star. He also marveled at Storm's reaction. She had also sensed the dragon's presence and, though the knight may have hesitated, she had not.

Michael had now confirmed one of the things he had come to find out: Scorch had the ability to speak. And of equal importance, Michael had the capacity to understand the dragon's speech. However, Scorch's voice had a quality that was all its own. Star's voice had clear bell-tones, quite like chimes blowing in the wind. Scorch's voice, on the other hand, lacked any pleasant music. It was dull and flat, full of clicking sounds, like the striking of a tin cup with a spoon.

The knight galloped off to a safe distance before he reined Storm in and turned to face the dragon. Once Storm saw the dragon before her, her tail flew into the air and her mane stood on end. She pawed the ground like a bull preparing to charge. Michael had wondered how she might respond faced with the dragon, and here was his answer. Rather than turn tail and run, she was eager to carry him fearlessly into battle. The knight held the reins tightly, holding her in check. He had not come prepared to fight. He wanted only to size this dragon up.

Scorch lay flat on his stomach on the crest of the hill. His sudden appearance was part of his dragon cunning. For all their size and bulk and weight, dragons are uncommonly swift and silent. If Michael had not played this game a dozen times a month with Star, and come to know from behind the feeling of a pouncing dragon, he and Storm would have already been crushed beneath the dragon's heavy clawed feet and finished off by the rows of razor-sharp teeth lining its ponderous jaws.

The dragon lay there, outwardly showing little concern, while he sized up this new opponent. The knight took this opportunity to do the same. Scorch was an immense dragon with very mature lines. He was finely scaled and carried himself proudly, as if he knew that among dragons he was particularly well formed. The knight could not resist the thought that cleaned up, he would be quite handsome. Even though the scales showed only a very dirty, muted brownish-green, his practiced eye could see the potential beauty beneath.

A week in the stream underneath my scrubbers, he thought to himself, and he would make a beautiful Luck Dragon. Michael wondered idly how he had fallen. He wondered if there was any chance that Scorch would tell him.

"Hail, Scorch the Terrible," he finally called out flatly.

"Hail, nimble mouse," Scorch returned, not thinking for a moment that the knight before him could understand his words. "You will help me work up an appetite before I eat you."

"I did not come to be eaten by you. I did not even come to give you battle," the knight calmly responded.

The dragon had been carefully practicing indifference, so as not to betray his admiration of the knight's recent escape from certain death. However, when the knight responded to his words, he could not hide his wide-eyed wonderment.

"You, little worm of a man, you understand the ancient tongue."

"You, monstrous worm of a wretched beast, I am surprised you know any civil tongue at all."

This comment stung, for Scorch actually had a high opinion of himself. After all, for a wicked, wild dragon, he felt that he fulfilled the description very well. He drew his shaggy brows together.

"I thought we had eaten the last of the ancient race."

"Not quite," commented the knight dryly. "I am left still."

"Then I will have the pleasure of ending with you all ability to pry into dragon secrets."

"That, of course," said the knight, "still remains to be seen." He had, after all, deftly avoided the dragon's first attempt at ambushing him.

The dragon laughed openly. "There is no way for a mortal man to defeat a dragon," retorted Scorch. As if to emphasize his point, he thrashed his long, snaking tail and opened his immense jaws, exposing row upon row of razor sharp teeth, and then shut them with a threatening snap. Storm pranced sideways and reared up as Michael pulled on the reins and spoke softly to control and calm her. He sensed that she felt no fear, only eagerness to engage.

The knight could not help flinching at Scorch's comment. It had always been Star's first and final observation to him whenever they sparred. "There is no way to defeat a dragon. Never forget this." It was one thing to hear this statement from a Luck Dragon whom he knew loved and protected him from harm. It was something quite different to hear this from a wicked, evil beast of a dragon who unapologetically planned to eat him. Something inside the knight grew cold and for the first time he was afraid. Yet what was fear? Fear was the closed door to keep you from going further. Open the door and enter new adventure. After all, what had Star trained him for, except to fight dragons? It was his destiny that all battles in his life had led to this encounter. There was no question of turning aside. He had come to find this dragon, and now they were finally engaged, even if for the moment nothing further than sparring with words.

"That may be so," he said at last. "That may be so. We shall probably put it to a test. Yet, perhaps it is not necessary."

Scorch raised his head and peered at him curiously. "What do you mean, little worm?"

"What I mean is this. It is true that I know your tongue because I am of the ancient race. I am a dragon master. It is my destiny to tame dragons. If you come with me peacefully, we can avoid a great deal of trouble." He tried to sound convincing, but Scorch only laughed.

"I am a dragon. It is my destiny to destroy all who oppose me. I know no master. I eat dragon slayers. I eat dragon masters. That is why there are none left."

"Except for me," interrupted the knight.

"Except for you," repeated Scorch. "But not for long," he added staring directly at Michael. The knight quickly avoided the dragon's gaze. "I wonder how you have escaped 'til now," mused the dragon. "If you are truly what you claim you are."

Michael decided to avoid this issue. The last thing he wanted Scorch to know was that this was his first encounter with a wild dragon. "What makes you so certain that you are right?" He hoped to distract Scorch and give himself some time to think of a better plan than getting eaten.

At this the dragon laughed scornfully. "Right about what? That it is my destiny to eat you? Or that you cannot have any hope to defeat me? Both are easy to answer. I know I am right because I am stronger."

"If you are really so much stronger, you can help others and share what you have with those who are weaker."

"Share?" Scorch belched short, orange flames out of his mouth with this word. Storm took several steps backwards in the face of the unexpected heat.

"Why should I share? I have worked hard for what I have. Look about you and see how I have labored. Let others work as hard and get their own."

"Yet, if you came with me in peace and offered your blessings to the people of this kingdom, the dwellers of the town would shower you with gifts."

"The foolish, dirt-eating townspeople already shower me with gifts, and I shower them with my curses in return. It is a good enough trade for me and they are content with it. Look, they have now sent you for my next meal. It's been awhile since I had some horseflesh."

"I've not come to fight you, Scorch," the knight quickly responded. "I have not been sent by the townspeople. Not yet, at least. I came of my own free will to speak with you."

"Did you come to mock me, then?" the dragon demanded. "If I let you go, you will boast far and wide that you escaped me. Who knows what lies you will spread!"

"You can plainly see that I come unarmed," the knight protested. "What honor does Scorch win by eating an unarmed knight? I've come to let you know that I will be the next to come and challenge you. As a courtesy between us."

"I need no warning and I seek no courtesy," Scorch said acidly. "These are human frailties. Fool, what is to keep me from eating you now?"

"You like the sport of battle," Michael said. He had no idea if it was true, and was appalled at the thought that Scorch might pounce on him at any moment. He had not gotten this far along in his plans when he had decided to come meet the dragon. "Besides, you also enjoy the conversation. Why end it now when you can have both your sport and more conversation when I return?"

Scorch snorted, and for the moment he accepted the knight's reasoning. "I will be waiting for you when you return. I am ready for any challenge you can bring. I am always ready. I fear nothing and no one. Go make your boasts and enjoy the moment of glory it gives you. It will be your last." Scorch stared at the knight, his eyes narrowing. Then he added with a hiss, "Nor do I have any need for your sport or foolish conversation. Go before I change my mind."

It was the dragon who now turned and began to stalk away. Michael knew that their meeting had ended. He did not want to wait in case Scorch reconsidered things. He was just turning Storm when he faintly heard from the direction of the forest Aina's voice yelling some warning which he could not clearly understand. He glanced back and saw why the dragon had turned away so suddenly. Scorch's tail was swiftly bearing down on him and Storm. If he did not move from there quickly, it would mow them both down.

Michael gave Storm a hard kick in the sides, but she did not need it. She had also caught sight of the immense tail flying through the air and sprang away at a hard gallop. The dragon's spiked and horny tail missed them by less than the length of an arm. Scorch, glancing back to see the horse and rider escape, roared in defiance as he quickly disappeared over the next hill and beyond.

Storm rode at full speed towards the line of trees. She did not stop when she came to them, but went crashing through the wall of foliage at the edge of Scorch's devastation. Only when they had put the trees and bushes between themselves and the dragon could the knight quiet his mount.

Aina came running up to them and grabbed hold of Storm's bridle to help settle her down. "I saw it all," she gasped. She looked white with fear. "He tried to kill you, twice. And you were talking with him. How do you do that? Can you understand what he is saying?"

Michael dismounted and first gave his attentions to Storm. He reached up and caressed her muzzle. "Calm down, Stormy girl. That was your first dragon, and you were great. The next time we'll know what we're in for." Then he looked at Aina. He became aware that he was shaking and took a deep breath. He hung onto Storm's bridle to steady himself before answering. "Yes, I could speak with him. Now I have an idea what to expect when I come to challenge him. But at least I've put some doubt in his mind. Let's hope that he's convinced that I am more to reckon with than anyone else he has ever fought before. It may be my best advantage." Then he laughed at himself. "Let's hope it won't be my only advantage."

"Tell me what happened out there," Aina said.

"Not here," the knight responded. "I want to put some distance between us and the burn. This is too close for comfort."

They mounted and rode slowly away from there. Michael did not relax until they had traveled far enough that they could once again hear birds singing and see squirrels scampering in the trees. Aina noticed that Michael was looking drained and unsteady in the saddle. When they came to a glade in the forest she pulled up her horse.

"Let's stop here," she said, dismounting. "I want to hear what you found out."

The knight was grateful for the rest. Once off Storm, he found his legs still weak. He sat down in the shade of a tree and gratefully drank from the flask Aina offered him. He then told her about his conversation with Scorch. She was fascinated by his report.

"I don't understand why he didn't just eat you on the spot," she wondered.

"Probably for the same reason he doesn't eat you every time you come to visit. He's intrigued. Or maybe he just likes the company. Perhaps we'll never know. But I think when I come to meet him in battle, he'll be more cautious in dealing with me, and that in itself will be worthwhile."

"If you can speak with him, can you not somehow reason with him? Maybe convince him to go away?"

"It's not that simple. But now I see a way maybe to avoid a fight. At least I have his attention and he is looking forward to my return. I will just need a little time to come up with a good plan. And some time to rest. I hate to admit it, but I am drained from this meeting with Scorch. Can we rest a bit?" And before Aina could even agree, he lay on the ground and closed his eyes. He was asleep within moments.

The knight awoke with a start. He had wanted to shut his eyes for only a moment, but he saw the sun slanting low through the trees on its pilgrimage to the horizon. He looked around and saw Aina sitting close by. She was embroidering stars onto a piece of blue cloth.

"I'm sorry," he said when she saw he was awake. "I didn't mean to sleep."

"Don't be hard on yourself," she said softly. "You faced a wild dragon today and walked away to tell of it. I don't know anyone else who could claim that."

He sat up and looked around. "Should we get going?"

"Rather not," Aina answered. "Darkness will overtake us before long, and since there will be no moon tonight, I won't be able to find the way."

"Will this cause a problem back in Gladur?"

"Most likely, but I don't care any longer." Aina gazed at the knight searchingly, as if she were trying to answer some question about him. She looked immensely sad. He wanted to ask her what she was thinking, but she spoke first. "We'll leave tomorrow at first light. I brought some food we can cook and we both have blankets."

"We should have brought you a pavilion," he commented with a weak smile.

"As befitting a lady," she said bitterly. Then seeing the pained expression on Michael's face, she added, "The blanket will do," indicating the one she had been sitting on. "I like sleeping out in the open. The stars in the night sky are so comforting. I would never get to see them cooped up in a pavilion."

"Let's have something to eat before it grows dark," Michael said. "I guess we'll have to eat it cold. We don't want Scorch to know we're still so close."

Aina looked at him in disbelief. "Do you really think he doesn't know we're still here? Haven't you noticed how quiet it's grown? All the animals have gone into hiding since we arrived. It's not because of us. I am sure that he is hovering on the edge of his destruction and smells the horses. Perhaps he can hear us as well. I tell you, a dragon's senses are extremely keen." After saying this, she began walking around gathering dry wood.

"You're going to make a fire?" he asked surprised.

"Why not? Scorch is very patient," she lectured him. "He knows we haven't gone away, and he'll wait for us to make the first move. I'm certain that we could have a raging fire burning all night, and he wouldn't bother us. He'll sit quietly and wait for us to walk into a trap of his own making."

The knight watched her quietly as she brought the wood to an open spot and cleared it of vegetation.

"You seem to know the habits of this dragon very well," he finally commented.

"And you seem awfully naïve of dragons for a dragon-fighter," she returned sharply.

"I half suspect that, given a sword, you'd go fight him yourself," he said watching her carefully.

"Give me a suit of armor, a lance and a horse and, yes, I'd rather do battle with that beast than wait passively for it to come and eat me." She said this savagely and with great passion. "I hate this dragon," she added fiercely. "I despise him. He has destroyed everything I love, everything I care for, any hope I ever had. Scorch has taken away everything noble in my life and left behind nothing but ugliness." She was nearly crying now. "And I'm stuck in this woman's body and can't even go and give battle. I can't even have the satisfaction to die fighting him. I feel so powerless against him."

Michael was taken aback at this onslaught. He was used to meeting fierce opponents, but he still had not learned how to deal with the fierce words of a woman. "I imagine you've lost many fine knights," he finally said.

"All of them!" she nearly screamed in reply. There was desperation in her voice.

Something in the bitterness of her words prompted him to ask, "Including one you loved?"

It was the wrong thing to say. At these words, her eyes grew big, and she picked up one of the branches she had collected and threw it at him with all her might. He ducked to avoid getting hit. Then another branch flew at him, and then the next. She had excellent aim, and the only way to protect himself was to deflect them with his arms. She kept the branches coming so quickly, he could not even catch his breath long enough to call out to her to stop.

As suddenly as it had begun, the attack ended. Aina crumpled onto the ground, her face in her hands, sobbing. Michael walked over to her and sat down beside her. He placed his arm around her shoulders and she turned to let him hold her. She cried inconsolably against his neck.

"I am so sorry for your loss," he said quietly. He truly felt sorry for her pain. At the same time, he noticed that he also felt sorry for himself. He envied that knight who had been so fiercely loved by this passionate maiden-warrior.

She continued weeping for some time, although the spasms that wracked her body slowed down and finally grew quiet. With her face buried in his shoulder, she seemed to have gone to sleep. The sun had disappeared behind the trees and it was growing dark. The evening chill was settling in. They happened to be sitting next to Aina's blanket, and Michael reached out and grabbed it. He was going to cover her and go make a fire, but she held firmly onto him. He accepted this, and as he stretched out his legs to be more comfortable, she stretched out beside him. With a free hand, he covered them both with the blanket as well as he could, and they lay there holding one another.

Michael drifted in and out of a pleasant doze. He was so delighted with her warm presence that he had to consciously overcome feeling guilty about enjoying it. After all, he was merely there to comfort her. Although it had grown too dark to see her face, at one point he awakened and knew that she was awake as well and that her eyes were open. He could feel her warm, comforting breath against his cheek.

"I'm sorry," she sighed. "I lost control of myself. I get so desperate sometimes. When it hurts so badly, I don't know what else to do."

"There's no need to be sorry," he spoke softly, holding her a little tighter. "You have suffered great loss."

"Scorch has taken everything away from us, everything that I have loved," she continued.

"You must have loved him very much, this knight of yours, that the dragon took away," he said into the darkness.

"I still do love him," she breathed into his ear. "And I am so desperate because Scorch will take him away from me before the next moon and I don't know how to stop it."

Chapter Thirteen

The Wager

*T*he next morning they rose as soon as it was light enough to find their way. They rode back in silence. The whole way Michael mulled over what Aina had said to him in the night. Had she really meant him? His roaming life had never given him long enough in one place to develop relationships, let alone to have a chance to fall in love. This was new for him, and he did not know how to react. He was about to face a wild dragon in a fight to the death. How could he freely express the feelings of his heart? When Aina did not mention it again, he decided to accept that her comments were a passion of the moment and had passed. She must have realized by now the impossibility of any relationship between them. Aside from the extremity of their situation, their stations prohibited it: She was a princess and he an orphan raised on the streets. He was relieved when she did not refer to their conversation from the previous evening.

They arrived back in town mid-morning. Aina led them directly to the door in the wall they had exited from the day before. As Aina had predicted, the groom was waiting for them and took their horses.

"Your Highness, I am so relieved that you are safe," he said. "I expected you yesterday evening."

"We were delayed. Were we missed?" she asked.

"Yes, Your Highness," he responded. "How could it be otherwise? Guards were out all day in town searching for you. The palace was turned upside down when you did not show up in the evening."

"Were you questioned?" she asked.

The groom had been standing with his head slightly averted. At Aina's question, his hand went instinctively to his face. "Yes, Your Highness, I was. But not for long."

Aina put her hand gently on his chin and raised his face so she could see him clearly. His left eye was bruised and swollen and there was an open wound above his eyebrow.

"The dogs," she cursed. "I shall have you avenged."

"Your Highness, your return is enough revenge for me. As I said, they did not question me long. It will heal. I will take the horses now." The groom walked off, leading their mounts.

"He's a good man," Aina said. "There are many in the palace like him. They risk their lives in order to watch my back. Without them, Flek would have gotten rid of me a long time ago."

"Then let's see what we can do to change that," the knight said. "What's our next step?"

She thought a moment and then smiled broadly. "Have something to eat. I'm famished."

"Now that's a plan I can stand behind," the knight said laughing. "I could also use a good meal."

They had barely entered the first hallway when a guard approached them. He bowed to the princess and then to the knight before speaking.

"The king sends greetings to the king's champion," he began. "And hopes that his stay has been comfortable."

"It has been quite comfortable," Michael replied cautiously. "Please relay my thanks for his hospitality."

"That won't be necessary," the guard said. "You will have the opportunity to speak with him yourself. The king requests his champion's presence at this evening's farewell banquet."

"Farewell banquet?" Aina said. "To whom are we bidding farewell?"

"Why, to the king's champion," the guard said. "The king wished me to tell you that clothing befitting the occasion has been selected and prepared for you. The feasting will begin this afternoon. You will be awaited." Having delivered his message, the guard turned and walked away.

"He was waiting for us," Aina said, gravely. "That guard. He knew we were coming and was waiting for us."

"Well, it had to come," Michael said.

"But not so soon," she said vehemently. "Never so soon. There is always at least two weeks between choosing and sending. I'm certain this is Flek's doing. They will not question that we were missing, but this is clearly their response."

"I would have preferred more time to pass before I went to meet him again," the knight sighed. He was not hesitant to go fight Scorch. He was reluctant to leave Aina. "At least I have my horse and armor back. And now that I've met with Scorch I can go any time. But I'm concerned for your safety, after what Flek said to us in town. And now we see what they thought they could get away with doing to your groom."

Aina's expression was grim. "You don't have to worry for me. I will take care of that." Before he could ask what she planned to do, she said, "We will go to our chambers and rest. Dress early for the feast. The king will not suffer you to come late. Not after our disappearance yesterday. Besides, this is his last chance to show you off."

"If this banquet is coming ahead of the usual time, how will he gather enough of a crowd?"

"Oh, don't worry about that. The nobility are always available for a banquet. Particularly one that involves the king's champion. They will clear their schedules of whatever other leisure they had planned. You will see."

Michael returned to his chamber and found festive garments already laid out for him. A servant came to his door with a tray of food and a message from the princess to eat and rest well. In the afternoon he rose and washed. Then he dressed and admired himself in the mirror. He had never worn anything so fine before.

He turned left and right, enjoying his own image. "I wonder if he'll let me keep it," he murmured to himself. There was a cap to go with the rest, which he now placed on his head at a jaunty angle. The cap had a colorful feather. He smiled at himself. "This is what I would look like if I had grown up among the nobility," he commented to his image. And then he laughed. "I did grow up among the nobility. And we weren't dressed anything like this."

His thoughts ran away from him then, and he wondered what had become of his good friend Colin and twin sister Alis. And there were Frog and Stomper as well. They were all children of the nobility. In the Dragon Compound, though, where they grew up, there were no fine clothes or fancy feasts. It was all hard work and good companionship. At least when Flek and his friends were not around.

Michael left his chamber and walked down the corridors that led to the great feasting hall. He had not been there since he had won the right to be the king's champion. He entered and was amazed to find all of the tables already filled with revelers. The moment he walked into the room he was spotted. A man sitting near the door rose from his seat, raised his goblet and bellowed over the buzz of voices, "Good health to the king's champion!"

At this, everyone's attention was drawn to him. All around the room feasters rose from their seats with their goblets raised. "Good health to the king's champion!" roared from all sides. He raised his arm in greeting and bowed to them all.

At the raised dais, the king rose from his seat and gestured to an empty place at the end of his table. Flek was sitting at the table as well, and glared at Michael as he approached. He was grateful that his place was on the other side of the king from Flek. When he walked to it, he saw that two places were empty. He was directed by a server to sit at the end. He wondered briefly who was to have the place beside him. He only hoped it would be someone he could tolerate.

He took a moment to look out over the assembly. His eyes scanned the room, looking at their faces. He realized what he was looking for. He hoped to find Aina. She was the one bright light for him in this place. Then he remembered that she had not attended the last feast. At least, not as a diner. He sighed and reached for his goblet. The fragrance of a light, fruity wine rose to his nose. One would never know that they were beset by a dragon, he thought. Something inside of him rankled. He was suddenly not so willing to go offer his life so that the nobility could go on feasting while a large portion of the people suffered and went hungry. The more he thought about it, the more he was disgusted at the idea of being their sacrifice.

At that moment another figure entered the hall from the same door he had. He was attracted by the brightness of the gown she was wearing. It was Aina. She wore her long black hair flowing over her shoulders and a golden diadem sparkled from the crown of her head. Her blue gown was studded with golden stars. His jaw dropped looking at her. She was beautiful.

The princess walked in front of the dais and curtsied to the king who acknowledged her obeisance. Then she walked over to stand in front of Michael. She beamed up at him and laughed when she saw that he was gaping at her.

"Well, aren't you going to invite me to sit with you?" she asked.

He then realized that the empty place was set for her. He quickly stood and went over to take her hand.

"Your Highness," he stammered. "I am honored."

She openly admired him in his festive clothing. "You clean up nicely for a street orphan," she teased, and he blushed. "Lead me to my place and sit beside me," she spoke softly into his ear. "I must coach you through this evening."

The food was plentiful and the dishes sumptuous. Servers walked around to make sure that plates stayed full and the wine flowed generously. Once again from behind the dais musicians played softly as a backdrop to the buzz of voices.

"When they've had their fill of wine, the bidding will begin," Aina said to him.

"What do they have to bet on now?" he asked astonished.

"You, of course," she said. "What else?"

"But it's already been decided that I go to fight Scorch."

"Wait," she only said.

Michael did not have much appetite. He had to repeatedly put down the rising anger that these people were not worthy to go fight for. Because of them, he had to leave Aina. He turned his attention to her. She ate lightly, and he noticed that she did not touch her wine, as if she wanted to keep her head cool and clear. He was fascinated by her dress. The golden stars that were embroidered over the whole dress evoked some memory, but he could not call it forth. The crowd, the noise and the spiced wine drove it out of him.

When the feasting had slowed down and the drinking was their sole activity, Michael saw what Aina had been waiting to happen.

A man in the first row of tables stood up and raised his cup. The feasters grew silent to hear what he had to say.

"My compliments to the king and the king's champion," he announced. "I'll open up the wagering, seeing that someone has to. I like the looks of this champion. I think he has a good chance. I'll wager five gold against half an hour. Who will take my wager?"

The man remained standing while a servant with a tablet walked around the room calling forth, "Five gold against half an hour."

It did not take long before another man several tables back stood and declared, "I'll take your five gold if you add five silver to it, to make it sporting."

The first man bellowed, "Done!" and both sat back down as polite applause rippled across the room.

Another man stood, raising his goblet. "That was a meager gamble," he said frowning. "And an insult to the champion's worth. I'll double it. I wager ten gold against an hour. Who will take me up?"

Again the servant walked up and down the tables calling out, "Ten gold against an hour."

It didn't take long before another man stood. "If you're giving your money away, I'll help you out. I accept ten gold against an hour!" The servant kept the record on his tablet.

"What are they betting?" Michael asked Aina softly.

"How long you'll last," she said turning to him. She gave him a penetrating look. He was astonished at her words.

"You mean, they're betting how long I'll live until the dragon eats me?"

"That's quite correct," she said. He felt the blood rush to his head and he clenched his fists. It was the same thing the guard from the south gate had told him. He grew resolute.

"I'll put a stop to this," he said firmly. He was about to stand up, although he was not sure what he was going to do. Aina quickly placed her hand on his arm and held him tightly.

"Don't," she cautioned. "Trust me. Just listen. Your time for action will come. It's not now." The authority in her voice made him pause and trust her.

The betting went on for quite a while longer. The opening wagers were modest compared to what came later. When revelers were offering up to three hundred gold coins, a small fortune, the applause that had been polite at the beginning had grown strong and prolonged. The length of time he would survive also grew. The longest anyone gave him, though, was until noon. The betting also became more detailed. Some wagered when he would break his lance. Another when his horse would buckle under him. And another when his sword would shatter. Michael grimly wondered if their experience of past champions informed their betting.

The gambling was slacking off and coming to a gradual end. Aina turned to Michael and looked him in the eye.

"How long do you give yourself, Michael, king's champion, before the dreaded Scorch makes a meal of you?" She was not mocking him. Her eyes, sad and large, said that she was asking in all seriousness.

"He will not make a meal of me," Michael answered steadfastly. "I'm coming back to you." Their eyes locked, and there was nothing in the room for the knight but Aina.

"That's good enough for me," she said and took a deep breath. Then she surprised Michael by suddenly standing up. She raised her goblet and spoke. All eyes were upon her.

"I greet the king and the king's champion," she said steadily in the way many others had begun. "I, too, wish to make a wager."

The king looked at her with open astonishment on his face. "Aina, never before have you placed a bet. This is quite unexpected."

"With this champion, I make an exception," she said with a smile.

"What will you bet, Princess?" Flek asked from his seat leaning forward to see her. "A bag of barley?"

If there had been any conversations in the hall, they stopped at this comment. There was absolute silence as if everyone held their breath to hear what the princess would answer.

"Even better than a bag of barley will I wager, king's counselor. Better than a wagon-load of barley. I offer my golden diadem." With these words, suddenly a hundred voices began to speak at once in hushed whispers into the silence.

"Aina, what is this rashness?" the king asked. "Or are you making a jest?"

"No jest, o king," she said. "And I stand by my wager. The only question is if there is someone who will take it."

There were so many voices speaking that the room hummed. Aina stood waiting. Then one voice spoke above all of the others.

"Well, we've heard what you will offer, Princess," Flek said loudly. "But you have not yet told us the terms. How long will this champion last? Half an hour? Half a day?"

Aina looked around the room, her goblet still raised, waiting until she could hear nothing but her own breathing. "My wager is that this champion shall return."

The moment she said it the room exploded again in excited discussion. Michael was stunned and deeply pleased at the same time. What was she up to? Did she believe that much in him?

As excited talk raged through the hall, the servant walked along the aisles between the tables calling out loudly above their chatter, "Princess Aina wagers her crown that the champion returns."

Suddenly what the server was saying struck the knight. Aina was not offering a piece of jewelry. She was offering her right as next in line to rule the land. He looked up at her standing beside him. She was watching the crowd, waiting for someone to accept her offer.

"Aina," Michael spoke to her. "You can't do that. You can't stake—" but he got no further. Flek had stood up with his cup raised.

"Princess, with joy I accept your wager."

The hall grew silent. Aina stared at him.

"You're not worth that much," she said and smiled. There was mocking laughter from the crowd. "You will need a backer."

"My victory is assured," Flek answered with self-confidence.

"Just the same," Aina responded. "You cannot wager without having something of equal value to cover it."

Flek turned to the king. Worrah was not looking at either of them.

"Your Majesty?" Flek said. There was a moment's pause, and then the king nicked his head and quickly looked away. There was loud murmuring from the crowd.

"As you can see, Princess," Flek said with an insincere smile. "I have sufficient backing. I accept your wager."

A man jumped up from his seat with his goblet raised.

"Huzzah for the princess!" he bellowed. Around the room people likewise jumped up from their seats and holding their goblets high called out, "Huzzah for the princess! Huzzah for the king's champion!" Applause filled the hall.

Aina did not sit down, although she did place her cup back on the table. After acknowledging the crowd's approval, she held up both hands. The revelers grew quiet to hear what she still had to say.

"I thank the lords and ladies of the court for their approval. I wish to announce that tomorrow when the king's champion goes off to face Scorch, he will not be guided and accompanied by the trackers as is our custom. Since so much is at stake, I will see for myself what his fate will be against the dragon. I will personally escort him."

"Princess, certainly we cannot allow that," Flek protested. "Your safety cannot be put to such a risk."

"I am touched by your show of concern," Aina responded coldly. "But you need not be worried for my safety. I will, after all, be with the king's own champion. And considering the real risk I am taking, I will not be satisfied with any reports from your lackeys. I will go myself to see the outcome of this challenge. Enough said. Bring out more wine!"

Aina sat down and applause approving her announcement thundered in the hall. Michael looked first at her and then at the king and Flek beside him. Although Aina was beaming at the revelers, Michael could feel her whole body trembling. Worrah and Flek had scowls on their faces.

More servants emerged from the side with full pitchers and the wine began to pour again. While some drank deeply, others began to leave the hall. One servant veered away from the others and, carrying her pitcher, came directly towards Michael and stood before him. He realized how parched he was and drained his cup. Irritated, he clapped it back onto the table harder than he had intended. He watched the servant fill his cup, and without thinking snatched it up and drained half of it before turning to Aina.

"Why did you do that?" he hissed. Sitting now beside him, she looked exhausted. She took a deep breath before turning to answer him.

"You would not be the first champion that the trackers quietly disposed of. You heard Flek the other day. The king doesn't really want any harm done to the dragon. If I escort you, no one can do any mischief to you ahead of time."

"That's not what I meant," he said quickly, "although I'm grateful for your protection. Why did you wager your crown?"

She gazed deeply into his eyes and smiled weakly. She looked spent after what she had done. "Well, it is mine, after all. But I am somewhat depending on you to help me keep it." She held his gaze a moment longer before looking away. Her face was ashen. "Come, drink up. What happens next is for you."

She picked up his cup and handed it to him. He looked at her questioningly and she motioned with a nick of her head towards the side doors. The room had grown hushed again and in the flickering lanterns the knight saw white-clad maidens entering the hall, each carrying in her hands a small earthen vessel with a flame within. An ornately carved and decorated chair had been place in the middle of the open space before the dais.

The princess had risen and was gently tugging on the knight's arm, urging him to stand up. His head was already swimming, from his irritation with her wager he thought, and he accepted her guidance. She led him to the chair and left him sitting there. He realized that he had his goblet in his hand, not knowing how it got there and full once again. Absently, he swallowed, felt the dryness in his throat, and drank again deeply.

The maidens, their white gowns swirling, circled around him, dancing, moving without pause. Their movements were coordinated, rising and dipping as they danced, the clay vessels in their hands raised and lowered in sequence with one another. Their white dresses swirled away from their twirling bodies, giving them the impression of being airborne. His eyes followed them, turning to watch as they circled around and behind him. They reminded him of the undulating gait of a dragon, and he laughed gruffly at the thought.

His head was giddy. Was it their movement? Was it the wine? He looked down at his cup and felt like he might pass out soon. He did not want to spill the wine, so he drained his cup before letting it fall from his hand to the ground. He leaned his head back in his chair and for the first time his hands felt the texture of the carvings on the armrests. He looked down at them and saw that they had been carved like scales. Dragon scales.

He could barely keep his eyes open. The movement of the lights in the hands of the maidens constantly in motion circling around him was overpowering. He closed his eyes a moment to relieve his dizzy brain. When he felt himself slipping away, with a great effort, he forced his eyes open again. The dance was still going on, and for the first time he noticed the hypnotic rhythmical beating of a single drum and the eerie playing of a flute. More like the wind than music, his fogging mind reflected. More like an animal cry than the wind. The flickers of flame blurred together in flashes of white dresses. He closed his eyes once more and did not open them again.

Part III

Michael and the Dragon

Chapter Fourteen

In the Forest

He was standing on the dragon's broad back scrubbing the scales. Beside him was a bucket of water. He was at peace with himself and his life. He looked up to admire the white billowing clouds above and the darker ones on the horizon. There was a breeze in the air and a storm approaching. That did not bother him, since it was the season for storms. Star shifted his weight and the boy had to use his scrubber to maintain his balance. He looked up to see what had caused the usually immobile dragon to stir and was surprised to see Flek approaching, followed by a crowd of his cronies. They all bore weapons of some sort, and Flek, in their lead, wielded a long spear with a wickedly barbed point. They marched up to Star, and without a word, Flek drove his spear right into Star's heart. The boy looked on helplessly from where he stood as the dragon shrieked in pain.

The knight's eyes shot open. He was panting, in a sweat, and his heart was beating furiously. Michael blinked his eyes, trying to make sense of the world he had escaped to from his nightmare. He was looking at trees in the forest. But he was certain he had not gone to sleep in the forest. Where had he been? Then the memory came crashing down on him: the banquet, the princess and her wager, the dancing maidens with their dazzling lights. And the wine.

Yet how did he get here? And where was here? The sound of bells as a horse shook in its traces caused him to sit up. There was Storm looking at him, expectant and waiting. She shook her head again. All of his gear was secured on her saddle, even his shield and lance.

They had released him! He was free to go. A sudden rush of relief flooded his chest. He could ride from this cursed place and never have to return. His ordeal was over. Whether this was the doing of the princess he would probably never find out. He was simply grateful to escape what he had known all along would be certain death. What a fool he had been to believe that he had wanted to go and fight Scorch. He would end up as dead as all those who had gone before him and all those who would follow. No one can defeat a dragon in battle. Living was far better than dying just to prove—what? That he had taken care of a Luck Dragon when he was a boy? What foolishness. The idea of fighting the dragon had possessed him like a spell. Aga was wrong. He was not destined to face a dragon just because he was dragon-trained. What nonsense! And by some stroke of good fortune, he had escaped this madness.

A horse nickered nearby, but it was not Storm. Reacting to the sudden noise, the knight whirled around. He was startled to see a second horse grazing in this small clearing. And then he was shocked to see Aina sitting close by. She had been sewing and the needle was still in her poised hand. He felt his heart leap into his throat.

"Welcome back," she said in a gentle voice.

"Wha'? Where?" He could not find the words.

"They swear to me that it leaves the head clear," she smiled pleasantly. "Perhaps you need a bit more time."

"The wine," he said with an accusing tone. "You gave it to me to drink. You told me to drink it."

"I did not know how to avoid it. Every king's champion is drugged in this manner. It is to prevent his getting cold feet the night before and trying to escape. I knew you didn't need it, but I could not give my reasons for why I believed so. There was too much to have to explain. Besides, there was no reason to make public that you know about dragons and have no reason to run away."

Michael's face reddened, but the princess could not guess why and she let it pass without question. "The drug also insures that the chosen warrior has a restful night's sleep before going off to battle," she added. "I hope that you slept well."

"How did I get here?" His voice was hoarse and his words were slightly slurred.

"They carried you out. The trackers have many functions."

The knight glanced around. "Are they nearby?"

"The trackers would have stayed with you until you went to the dragon. Although in your case I feared that they might not have let you awaken at all. Flek considers you much too dangerous, and after watching you with the dragon, I can understand why. How Flek knows, I don't yet understand. Anyway, that was why I made the wager. To insure that you get to Scorch."

The knight was silent. In spite of himself, he was weighing what his chances would have been against a handful of trackers. But then, if they had intended to kill him, they would have kept him firmly bound, or worse yet, killed him in his drugged sleep. Still, he could not stop himself from wondering, and it embarrassed him. He was feeling like a coward.

"I have food and drink, if you wish to refresh yourself," Aina said, breaking his reverie. She picked up a bag that lay near her and opened it up. She pulled out bread, cheeses and fruit, which she placed upon an outstretched blanket. "Come, eat this for now. Or if you want to make a fire, I can cook you some porridge."

Michael sat with the food between them. He stared at it without reaching out, a frown on his face.

"Is this the effect of the drug, do you think?" she asked.

"What?" he snapped. He was startled by her question. He was afraid she would see how he truly felt.

"I was wondering whether it is the effects of the sleeping draught that you are so sullen. Or is it in anticipation of the dragon? Or perhaps both?"

"Too many questions," the knight grumbled. He picked up a bunch of grapes, hoping to quench his parched throat and distract his racing mind. Aina sighed and went back to her sewing. They sat in silence as he chewed on the fruit.

His mind was bursting. A moment earlier he had been relieved to have escaped from this misadventure. Now, when it looked inevitable, his thoughts were jumbled and confused. There was that part of him that *did* want to fight Scorch. That was why he had come to Gladur Nock, and here was finally his chance.

"Are you frightened?" she asked breaking into his thoughts. Her question took him unprepared. Did it show? "I could understand if you were."

"You don't understand," he said, but did not know how to continue, and fell silent.

"You *are* going to defeat him, aren't you?" Aina probed. "You said that you could defeat the dragon. I wagered my crown that you will be a match for the dragon. Was this a mistake?"

"Are you, too, having second thoughts?" he asked.

"Oh, dear," she said, looking suddenly pale. "Is there no hope?"

Hearing her despair forced him to rally his courage. "Aina, I will go and meet this dragon. I know about dragons, and I have been trained for this battle. You saw me speaking with him." He sounded convincing, even to himself. But he said nothing about defeating the dragon, and he hoped that Aina would not notice.

"Then I am content," she said quietly and lowered her eyes.

· ✳ ✳ · ✳ · ✳ ✳ · ✳ · ✳ · ✳ ✳ · ✳ · ✳ ✳ ·

The knight gave Storm free rein to pick her way through the trees and around bushes. Aina's horse carried her lightly, keeping step with Storm. There was not any particular trail to follow, not even a path well tread by forest animals. As before, he let Aina lead them. This time, however, they did not hurry their horses, but rode in a leisurely manner.

The forest leaves shone bright green with reflected sunlight, and sporadic birdsong filled the air. As they rode, the knight pondered deeply upon Aina. This girl-woman pleased him greatly and he forced himself to stop thinking about where they were headed. They had not spoken since they had broken their first camp. What more could there be to say? He wished for nothing more than to ride another path and take her with him.

"We'll camp near the devastation for the night," she said suddenly. "That way you can engage Scorch in the early morning." She took his silence for agreement.

Around midday, they came upon blackberries growing in the shade of the great trees. Whether they had passed berry hedges the day before, the knight could not say. Their pace had not allowed them to tarry.

"Come," the knight said pointing out the berries. "We owe ourselves a bit of a rest."

They dismounted to refresh themselves with the sweet fruit. Michael watched Aina eat the ripe berries. It was not long before her hands and face were stained purple from the sweet juice. She giggled and pointed at his face. He guessed he must also look like her.

Aina relaxed as they ate and seemed to push her own dark thoughts away. Looking at her, Michael reflected that she was little more than a tender child who had had far too much pain and responsibility thrust upon her at an early age. He wanted to protect her from more.

"I'm not as young as you think I am," she said, as if reading his thoughts. "I braid my hair to keep it out of the way." She held him with an intense gaze. "I left childhood behind a long time ago."

He recalled their sword battle and knew that she was a warrior in her own right. There was so much about her that confused him. He looked away. "Odd," he commented.

"What? That blackberries grow in the forest? 'Tis not odd, 'tis normal. They are always ripest just when the leaves begin turning."

"No, not the berries. I find it odd that your father let you risk your crown," he said.

"My father would have *never* let me risk my crown," she responded, her eyes narrowing.

"But that he did," Michael objected. "He even backed up Flek's wager, which I find even more astonishing. How can he favor Flek over you?"

"My father never knew Flek," she said with finality.

Michael was stunned by her statement. He could not make sense of her words. Then suddenly, with the force of a thunderbolt, the truth dawned on him.

"What a blind fool I've been!" he erupted. "Of course, it all makes sense now."

"You didn't know, did you?" she said smiling at him. "Well, I forgive you your ignorance."

"How was I to know? He the king, you the princess."

"By the simple fact that he and I are nothing alike. Do you not remember that I told you that my father had been touched by the same kindness and gentleness as my grandmother?" He did remember, yet he had not paid any attention to it.

"But if Worrah is not your father," he asked, "who is he and what is he doing on the throne?"

"My father died when I was yet a child. My memories of him are sketchy. My mother took over ruling the land following his death. She was a strong woman, and I loved her very much. And the people loved her. She was not as giving to the common folk as my grandmother had been, but I think the demands of the crown were great and she did what she could.

"But the fact remains that she was a woman, and over time the barons began muttering. It wasn't long before the muttering became loud protests that it was not enough for a woman to sit on the throne alone. They demanded that she marry, in order to properly guard our fair city and provide a proper heir. I was her only child, and the barons wanted a male heir. Of course, they expected that she would choose a husband from among them. That was about the time Worrah showed up. He was gallant and brave, claimed a noble lineage, and pretended to truly care for my mother.

"She married him. Over time, his true nature came out. Not long after Worrah came, Flek appeared, and the two of them became inseparable. Worrah isolated my mother from the affairs of the land. It didn't take long before he had isolated her from everything. He even began replacing her servants, until there were few in the household that remained faithful to her. In a castle, fealty follows power, and Worrah wanted all of it. After several years, she died of a broken heart."

"And what about you?" Michael asked gently.

"I saw what was coming, and I had my mother's support. The nobility wanted a male child so he could fight and defend the crown. But my mother fled early from Worrah's bedchamber and never gave him a child. So I studied the way of the sword. I had the best teachers in the realm. They were amused to be teaching a girl, the princess herself. They never expected how seriously I would take it up. By the time my mother died, no one dared stand up against me. I can defeat most men."

"To this I can attest," Michael said with a laugh.

"I think that Worrah wanted to get rid of me quietly, but I was anything but quiet, and this tickled the barons. My disappearance would have undermined his power, so he let me be. I made myself useful by creating the warrior training."

"Why that?"

"It was the dragon maker's suggestion, actually. Aga was a blessing, once I had found him. I would go to him for any advice I needed, and it was always sound. When Worrah's guards followed me, they only thought that I had a liking for the dragons he made. I did end up giving a lot of them away."

"What did the warrior training give you?"

"The dragon is a scourge to our land and people. But for Worrah, it's a blessing. Flek admitted it when he thought he was going to get away with having you beaten. Worrah is so repressive of the people. I think they would have long since risen against him, but the constant threat of a dragon at our gates drains us and distracts us from how bad a ruler he is. You see how he lives, how lavish and wasteful. He serves only himself and a hall filled with nobility, and lets the people starve. Once the dragon is gone, we will have a chance to change things."

"Men like Worrah don't need a dragon," the knight said sadly. "I have wandered the world enough to have seen that. Kings like Worrah are plentiful. They find some enemy real or imagined and lead their people into endless, drawn-out wars. They find a threat from outside, and if it's not big enough, they do everything they can to increase it. It is the people's fear of the enemies the king has created that keeps kings like Worrah in power."

"So that is why I am so confused by how I feel about Scorch," Aina continued. "Scorch fascinates me. I even find myself looking forward to the days I go to watch him. Yet I hate him because he keeps Worrah in power. He's destroyed so much land and killed so many of my people. He is an evil plague. I created the Warrior Compound to get rid of Scorch, so one day I can get rid of Worrah."

"Aina," the knight began, "there is another option." He had hesitated saying this before, but after hearing Aina's story, he felt emboldened.

"Another option for what?" she asked, looking interested.

Michael took a deep breath before continuing. "We could leave Worrah to Scorch. They deserve one another. Over time, one day, the dragon will be his end. It's just a matter of being patient."

Aina was shocked by his words. "Are you suggesting that we just ride away from this?" When he nicked his head in agreement, she stood up abruptly. "You would abandon my people to the viciousness, greed and cruelty of both Worrah and Scorch?"

Michael saw how she was taking his suggestion, and realized he had made a grave mistake. "I didn't mean it like that." The moment he said this, he knew he was backpedaling.

"How else could you mean it? If I leave, then there is no longer any buffer between the people and an insatiable nobility. They will continue to drain the common folk of their goods and feed their sons to the dragon. Scorch will destroy Worrah only after they have both destroyed my people." She stared at him in disbelief. Tears were brimming in her eyes. "If you're not willing to go fight Scorch, then just say so. I should have known. How could I have believed in you? Why would you be any different than all the rest?"

"Aina, let me explain," the knight said.

"There's nothing left to explain," she exploded. "Aga was wrong, that's all. It's my fault for trusting a foolish old man. Go, if you can't face him. You're not the first to run. You won't be the last. You really fooled me. How clever of you; you already fulfilled your promise. You met the dragon and walked away alive. Just nothing is changed. Scorch is still here, keeping Worrah in power. Go on, the trackers are waiting for you. Have you seen the gallows at the edge of town? I didn't know you were in such a hurry to be the next one hanging there." Tears were streaming down her face and her eyes flashed with anger. She went over to her horse and jumped in the saddle. Without looking back or saying another word, she rode off.

"Aina!" Michael called after her. "Aina, come back! You don't understand." He stood there with his head in his hands, berating himself for making such a mess of things. He finally admitted what he had kept unspoken until now. "Ach, if only I hadn't fallen in love with you. Then staying alive wouldn't be so precious."

He knew he would make things worse chasing after her. There was nothing he could say that could make up for his words. Only his actions could do that. Although he could not be certain in this trackless forest which way led to the dragon's devastation, he figured that if he kept going in the general direction she had been leading him, he would find it. Her reaction taught him that he had already determined his choices. He had committed himself to fighting Scorch, and he now felt an unwavering resolve to go through with it. His only hesitation came from having fallen in love with Aina. He just wished he had not alienated her on his way to finding this out.

The knight mounted Storm and continued with a heavy heart. Grim determination focused his mind and will as he bent his thoughts on one thing alone: his battle with the dragon.

· ✶ · ✶ ✶ ✶ ✶ ✶ ✶✶·   · ✶ · ✶ ✶ ✶ ✶ ✶ ✶✶·

It was first the penetrating smell, and then the uncanny silence of the forest that let him know he was coming once again to the edge of Scorch's wasted lands. The faint scent of burnt earth quite suddenly grew so intense that the knight pulled in Storm as a reflex. They were standing in a forest glade, Storm's ears perked, her nose already registering that something was gravely wrong.

"We're near," he commented out loud, if for no other reason than to break the silence.

The forest that had been so peaceful and welcoming all this time suddenly became sinister and threatening. Michael looked around and shrugged his shoulders. It looked like any of the other glades they had already passed through. Only the burnt smell and the silence made it different.

"I guess this is as good a place as any," he said to himself. He dismounted and began to make his camp for the night. He did not make a fire. The smell of burnt wood was already so strong in the air, he could not stand adding to it. He looked through the food that hung in a bag on his saddle and separated it into two portions. One was for his evening meal. The second portion was for the next morning before he sought out the dragon. He did not make a third.

The knight lay on his bedroll looking up at the stars sparkling between the trees. I can't see them all, he thought. I can see only a part. The rest is hidden from me. With this he fell into an exhausted sleep.

"Star," he said, looking up at the dragon. Just gazing at him filled his young heart with what he understood as love. The dragon's scales were freshly washed, and they shone with brilliant rainbows in the sunlight at the edge of the river. "I still have a question."

The dragon looked down his long snout at the boy. "I imagine you have a lot of questions. You're still quite young."

"Do you mean, that as you get older, you have fewer questions?" Straw asked.

"Is that the question you had?"

"No, but what you said made this one come first."

The dragon chuckled with the sound of chimes blowing in the wind. "From my experience, as you get older, you know more and begin to realize that you understand less. For some, that leads to asking fewer questions, because the answers do not necessarily increase your understanding."

The boy thought about this for a while. "So, are you saying that I should ask fewer questions?"

Star laughed again. "I can see that I've confused you and sidetracked you from what you wanted to know. Ask the question you began with."

Straw pursed his lips, looking for the right words. "Why are we doing this?"

"Do you mean, why do we sit here and talk? Or why do we come every day so that you can scrub me down when once a week would do just as well?"

"No," the boy smiled brightly. "I know why we do that. It's so we can spend time together. Sometimes I think that was the reason I knew I had to find a way into the compound. I had no choice but to get closer to you. I knew, somehow, that we were supposed to spend time together."

"It sounds like you have answered your own question," Star said.

"All of that part makes sense. But the sparring. Why that?" He gestured at the wooden sword and shield that lay in the grass.

"Would you rather we stopped?" the dragon asked.

"Not for the world!" Straw exclaimed. "It just feels like a part I didn't know about. I knew I would one day scrub your scales. I knew I loved you. I knew I would spend all the time I wanted with you. But this, the sparring, somehow I didn't know."

"There are times we have to open one door to find out what is in the room behind. We know only that there is a door and we must go through it. All of your attention has been on the door: getting into the compound, getting close to me, having time together. You have now entered the space beyond, and usually, that is when the mystery unfolds. It is just a question whether you have the courage to go through the door."

"I know now that I want to be a knight," Straw said with determination.

"And now, becoming a knight is your next door. There is a room behind that door, too," Star said, gazing fondly at the boy.

"When will I discover what is in that next room?" he asked.

"Only when you have opened the door and decided to walk within."

Chapter Fifteen

A Spiny Meal

*T*he knight awoke and caught his breath. "Star!" he called out, but there was no response. The stars still shining overhead sparkled mutely down at him. He gazed at the sky and let his eyes blur. He imagined himself lying beneath his beloved dragon, staring at his starry coat.

"Is this my next door?" he whispered to them. "Was I trained for this moment? I don't suppose I will ever find out. Nor does it even matter. What's important is that I open the door. That is all that ever mattered."

He took a deep breath, and though the air was oddly thicker than normal, his nose could no longer smell the burn. He had been there long enough to no longer sense it.

He watched the stars fade and the sky turn a predawn grey. As soon as there was enough light, he rose and began his preparations. He ate his meal and stripped off his leathern traveling clothes. He folded them neatly and placed them in a pile on top of his bedroll. He went through his saddlebags and took out everything that would not serve him in the upcoming battle with the dragon. He left all these things neatly at the base of a tree.

There was one piece of cloth that he did not put aside with the rest. It looked like it had once served as a woman's scarf, although now it was faded and ragged along the edges. Now pale with age, it had once been dark blue with golden stars embroidered all over it in a random pattern. He held it in both hands and stared at it. This piece of cloth held some of his earliest memories. He now recognized it as the same pattern in Aina's dress the night of his farewell banquet. He knew that he would take it with him when he went to meet Scorch.

After saddling Storm, he carefully put on his armor. It had been specially designed so that he did not require a page to help him. When he had donned everything except his gauntlets and helmet, he picked up the embroidered scarf. Using his teeth and one hand, he tied it on the outside of his armor, just above his left elbow. When it was securely in place, he was satisfied.

"I go to battle in the name of the Lady," he announced to the surrounding trees. "In the name of the Lady who taught my heart love, and in the name of the Lady whose heart taught me to remember my path."

Michael secured his sword at his side, put on his helmet, then his gloves. He walked over to Storm and heaved himself into the saddle. He slipped his arm through the straps of his shield and shifted it to his back. He had brought two lances, both now leaning against a nearby tree. He chose the stouter one, leaving the other behind.

At that moment, he was startled by the sound of a strangled roar that sent chills up and down his back. Storm whinnied and side-stepped nervously.

"Impatient?" he asked out loud. "We'll be there soon enough." Taking hold of the reins, he turned Storm towards the sound, and she carried him to the edge of the devastation.

When they came to the dragon's ruin, Michael paused a moment and glanced around. Scorch was not in sight. This meant little, though, since he had managed to sneak up on them last time. There were enough gullies in these rolling hills to hide him. The knight took a deep breath and urged Storm onward.

They rode out and across the barren landscape, Storm's hooves kicking up clods of blackened earth. They rode to the third hillock before Michael reined Storm in and stood up in the stirrups.

"Scorch!" he called out. "Where are you, vile worm! I've returned as promised. Show yourself!" There was no response and nothing stirred. They rode deeper into the dragon's desolation.

Each time they reached a hillock, Michael repeated his challenge. "Scorch! Come out from hiding, you creature from hell!"

He was walking Storm down into a ravine when suddenly, the hair on the back of his neck stood on end. He whirled Storm around. There on the neighboring hill, which he could have sworn a moment before had been empty, lay the dragon. "So, my breakfast has arrived," Scorch commented with an ugly chuckle of his clicking, tinny voice.

"You will find that I am a spiny meal," Michael returned, lifting his lance into the air. "Careful I don't choke you on the way down."

"Every tiny mouse has tiny teeth," Scorch sneered. "But that does not stop the fox from eating him. You are but a morsel, yet you will do, you will do."

"I'm going to have to disappoint you," the knight said.

"I think not," Scorch responded and said no more.

At that moment, Storm surprised the knight. She started walking of her own volition, straight up the ravine directly towards the dragon. At first Michael was puzzled why Storm would do this without his lead, but quickly realized what was happening. Scorch had caught the horse's eye, and their gazes had locked. Scorch was using his dragon power to draw the horse right to him, without having to use any force at all. Michael knew well this attractive force of a dragon. Star had often used it with him, and trained him how to resist it. Storm did not have a clue how to break the power of a dragon, and was merrily marching right towards Scorch's cavernous mouth, ears perked and tail swishing.

In one swift movement, Michael dug his spurs into Storm's sides and yanked strongly on the reins to the left. Storm whinnied at the pain and gave a sudden jump following the direction of the reins. This turned her flank to the dragon and broke the eye contact. With that, the dragon's spell was broken, and Michael casually led Storm out of the ravine at an angle away from the dragon, acting as if nothing had happened. Without intending to, Scorch had helped the knight end up on higher and flatter ground. The knight glanced at the dragon and saw the look of wonderment in his face. For the third time now Michael had foiled the dragon's plan and gotten away. He did not want to give Scorch any more time to think about it.

"Look around at the destruction you have caused," the knight said waving his hand at the surrounding devastation. "You are so large and powerful, what is the need for such violence? What do you have to fear? Do you really like living in this wasteland?"

The dragon glanced up for a moment to take in the complete desolation of his surroundings and sighed. "It is safer this way. I can overlook everything much easier. No need to worry about anyone sneaking around." The dragon now pinned the knight with his gaze. "You yourself know that there are many forces that want to destroy me. You are one of them."

Michael could feel the dragon's pull himself as he looked deeply into Scorch's eyes. It was so inviting to simply direct Storm towards him. He allowed his gaze to lock with the great dragon. He felt the numbness beginning to cloud his thinking like snake venom running through the blood to the whole body from the point of the bite. His limbs began to grow heavier and it was becoming difficult to move by his own will. A bubble of warmth and peace wove itself around him. It would be so easy to surrender.

Just as he was on the edge of losing the will to resist, the knight broke the eye contact by looking away. It was really that simple, although a dragon's gaze is so fascinating that few ever realize, before it is too late, that all one need do is look in another direction. He took a deep breath, and sighed. He knew that he could have stopped it earlier. He was testing himself to see how much he could resist. He was satisfied to know that he could come to the edge of giving up and still look away.

He heard a dull, metallic sound, as if the dragon had clicked his tongue in disappointment. Then, as if nothing had happened, Scorch said quietly, "If you find me cruel and ruthless, it is in defense of what is mine, rightfully mine by conquest. I will not let anyone get in my way. Not even a self-styled dragon tamer." Scorch said this last in a very low voice. "This territory is mine. If you enter it, prepare to die, for I will defend it." Scorch stated this calmly, as if there were nothing to discuss.

Michael knew that Scorch was biding his time, waiting for the moment when he could catch both knight and horse off guard. Twice now the knight had deflected the dragon's tricks. The battle had already begun, and in their first sparring, Michael had come away with the upper hand. The dragon's usual tricks and natural enchantments would not serve him here.

"It's been long," continued Scorch, "since I have had anyone to talk with. I find it nearly pleasant. It will be a shame to have to kill you." His voice sounded almost wistful. Michael continued to slowly shift his position. He wondered how long he could keep the dragon talking. He wanted to be at least on equal footing with Scorch, if not a bit higher. After all, when the dragon raised himself to his full height, he would tower over the knight mounted on his horse.

"Tell me, little worm," continued Scorch in an almost light, sing-song voice, "what makes you so tired of life that you want to march down my throat? I am surprised at myself, but I almost feel sorry for you."

"What makes you think I'm tired of life?" Michael asked, desperately keeping his voice from shaking.

"If you are a dragon master, as you pretend, you know full well that there is no hope for you once we fight."

I spent my youth battling dragons, the knight thought. Or more correctly, one particular dragon. It had been an integral part of his experience to fight with Star, lose, and get up again to do it the next day. He did not like to be reminded that there would be no next day for him following this battle.

His silence made the dragon curious. "Do you pretend to me that you have fought with a dragon already?"

Michael was not sure how to answer. Should he tell Scorch about his days with Star? He wanted to prove to this arrogant degeneration of a worm that he knew dragons very well, that he had been trained by a dragon, a true dragon, not such a shameless, filthy, cruel and greedy beast as crouched before him on the hill, waiting for his moment to pounce. He wanted to boldly announce that he had already survived this long in their encounter because he knew dragon so well.

Scorch sensed the knight's hesitation and continued to probe. "Well? What can your experience with dragons be, after all? If you had fought one, you would be dead. This is the reason I consider you an impostor, even if you can speak the ancient tongue. You are an impostor—or completely naïve."

Scorch was definitely puzzled. The knight obviously knew more about dragons than was comfortable. How much did this little stinging fly know? He wanted to find out how great a threat he really was. Well, not really a threat, but how annoying would he prove to be?

"The only dragon you are likely ever to have seen was in your grandmother's imagination as you sat on her knee listening to her stories," Scorch continued. "Unless, of course, you had the misfortune to encounter that aberration of my breed, which can hardly be honored with the name dragon. They are misfits, malformations, a mockery to our whole race. Too weak to live as true dragons, they rely on handouts from self-styled tamers such as you and are kept penned up as pets and a curiosity for sightseers." He spit this out with obvious disgust.

Michael nearly spoke, and then abruptly stopped himself. He was seething that Scorch would call Luck Dragons misfits and malformations. He himself had lived with Star's beauty, grace and strength, which far surpassed anything this mountain of hate, greed and destruction could ever come close to achieving.

"It is a goodness that they have all but died out," Scorch continued, watching the knight carefully. "Now, it wouldn't be one of the fallen members of my proud race who has given you the mistaken idea that you know something about dragons, would it?"

Hot in the face, agitated by Scorch's harangue, the knight was about to blurt out all sorts of proof that a Luck Dragon is the noblest creature on the earth. What stopped him was the look on Scorch's face. If Michael had not lived with a dragon day in and day out, he would have missed it, most likely. After all, who can claim to know dragons well enough to read the subtleties of their expressions?

What Michael had noticed was a look of intense curiosity. Scorch was baiting him, watching to see his reaction. Perhaps it was already too late, and he need not say another word for Scorch to already know everything about him. The dragon had been craftily leading him to divulge anything that would give him the advantage in their inevitable clash. Scorch had already guessed that Michael's experience came from associating with a Luck Dragon. Was he probing for a final confirmation? Michael was not ready to give it to him so easily. Realizing what was at stake, he suddenly grew very calm and changed his whole attitude. The dragon had won the first round, but the knight was not ready to concede the game.

"I will let you decide what I know and from where I have it," he said. "I have no need to prove anything to you, wasted worm that you are. I will give you one last offer: Come with me in peace and I will assure your safety."

"My safety?" roared the dragon, rising up suddenly high onto his haunches. Higher and higher, he used his great tail to counter-weight his body to gain even greater height. With the full length of his upper body, he towered over Michael and Storm, his back legs and tail anchored on the ground. He looked like a thundercloud about to break. "My safety is your end!" Scorch bellowed and, amazingly, continued to rise into the air even higher, mushrooming straight out of the ground.

This was an abrupt end to their conversation, and Michael knew that this was his chance. If this had been the first time he had ever watched a dragon rear up, he would have undoubtedly stood there dumbfounded until Scorch picked him flailing from his horse's back. As awesome as the sight was, though, Michael had seen it too often before and knew that he had to act. He hoped that the years of campaigning with Storm had prepared her to trust what her rider was about to ask her to do. His only hope was boldness. If Storm faltered, all resistance would end right here. But if any horse was bold, it was his trusted and faithful Storm.

The dragon was rearing himself for one lightning-like pounce. He rightfully expected that if rider and horse ever regained their senses and took in his immense size, they would turn tail and run. With one well-timed leap, using his wings to give him the needed loft, he would be on top of them in a moment. It had worked every other time. He was certainly not prepared for what happened this time.

Chapter Sixteen

The Commonality of Dragons and Knights

Before Scorch could pounce, Michael dug his spurs into Storm's sides and cried out loudly and clearly, "For the Lady!"

He leveled his lance and charged straight for Scorch's belly, diving right underneath those powerful forelegs and sharp talons. Scorch was not expecting this and delayed a moment, which was exactly what Michael was depending on. Well-armored everywhere, with no weaknesses in his scales, Scorch was not worried that the knight's paltry lance would do any real harm to his underside. Let the human worm try and sting him. It would be both the first and last blow dealt in their battle.

Scorch now doubled over to catch knight and rider beneath his heavy feet. But now the rider did something else unexpected. He did not attack the dragon's belly as Scorch had anticipated and where the dragon had hoped to crush him. At the last moment he swerved off to the right, making no contact at all. Scorch's taloned feet hit the ground hard right where he thought the rider would strike, only to slam against empty rocky soil, jarring the dragon for a fraction of a moment. But it was long enough. He looked down and saw nothing. Where had that rider gone?

Michael had guided Storm to swerve around the dragon's exposed belly, around his back legs, to ride pell-mell alongside the dragon's tail, the latter half of which had been sticking straight up into the air. Scorch rallied quickly and turned to catch the little mouse that was scurrying behind him. But when he twisted his body around to the left and looked where the rider had been a moment before, Michael was gone.

At almost that same moment, he heard the knight's battle cry, "For the Lady!" and he felt an annoying jab of pain in his right leg. With an enraged roar, he swung around to catch the rider there, only to find him gone again.

After Michael had cleared the dragon's back leg, he cut left to pass directly behind the dragon's raised tail. He had ridden quickly, and when Scorch was looking for him on the left side, the knight had jabbed him with the lance in his right leg. He did not wait for the dragon's reaction, but wheeled Storm around and rode again towards the back of the dragon, once again, slipping behind the raised tail.

While Scorch was searching, annoyed and bewildered on the right side, Michael's war-cry sounded once more, "For the Lady!"

He stabbed him with the lance on the left side. Once again, as the dragon twisted to find the new source of this stinging beast, off rode Michael around the back. This time, though, Scorch regained his bearings enough to turn his whole body around to keep the rider from passing behind him. He wanted this annoying fly in front of him where he could make an end of him.

Michael sensed the dragon turning, and gave himself more space to maneuver, but still rode hard to keep himself behind the beast, circling as the dragon turned. Once again, Scorch found no one to fight. "Stand still, you pesky, stinging fly!" he bellowed out.

"Why? So you can swat me?" But Michael only thought this, not speaking a word. With their conversation ended, he was well aware now that he was fighting for his life. He had already divulged too much to the clever Scorch. From this point on, he was focused and silent. He jabbed Scorch again with the lance, this time in the tender side-wall of the dragon's long tail. The tail was still well covered with overlapping scales, but less thickly than in front, leaving the beast slightly more vulnerable from behind. Michael figured that slightly was far better than not at all. A quick jab, and off he dashed.

Reacting to the pain, the dragon turned and once again found no opponent. Michael was not sure how long he could keep this up. At some point the dragon would stop reacting to the immediate pain and turn to catch him as he came careening around the tail to the other side. He knew he had taken the advantage for the time being, and did not want to press his luck any further. It was time to change tactics.

This decision came not a moment too soon. After the last jab, Scorch feinted to the side where he was hurt, but turned quickly to the other side to catch Michael coming around from behind. But no rider showed up.

During his conversation with Scorch, Michael had scanned the surrounding land. He had seen what he was hoping to find, not far away from the place where they were now sparring. He turned tail and galloped off towards a stand of boulders. He was very pleased when he arrived at them. All of them had relatively flat tops, broad enough for him to stand securely. Not only were they differing sizes, but they lay so well placed to one another that he could use them as stepping stones. In addition, there were spaces in between where he could quickly and comfortably fit his whole body. This would come in handy.

By the time the knight reached the boulders and had wheeled Storm about, Scorch had located him and was staring at him with intense malevolence. Michael hoped that his next move would work. Although Storm gave him the advantage of speed, he knew that he was still, in some ways, more vulnerable on horseback. Besides, all of his sparring with Star had been done on foot. That was how he was accustomed to fighting with a dragon.

Among the boulders, he felt he had a good chance of holding out for awhile. He avoided completing the thought of what he was holding out for. For time? For victory? Till the end? Yes, that would do; until the end. At any rate, he needed to give Storm a rest. He dismounted onto one of the boulders and gave her a sharp slap on the backside.

"Off you run, my beauty!" and he stood a brief moment to follow her direction as she galloped off without him. He hoped for two things now. First that she would not spook and ride completely away. Secondly, that Scorch would come after him and leave her in peace. If she stayed within earshot, he would be able to whistle her to him again later and continue the battle from horseback. He realized with a sigh that he had no way to keep her from totally leaving the battleground. But he could influence whether Scorch would take out his anger on his horse.

"Hey, you bloated night-crawler! Have you ever gotten slow! Hey, do you think you can catch up with me if I stay in one place on the ground? Come on over and let's find out."

Scorch saw only red. His eyes flashed and he clenched and unclenched his claws. His long spiked tail thrashed from side to side, throwing up clouds of blackened sand, and he tossed his head with a roar. The rows of horns on the crown of his head were standing straight up. His own questions had been now clearly answered. This knight knew about dragons. He knew their soft spots and he knew their habits. He knew how dragons moved and how they fought. Yes, he had had a good teacher. But now on the ground, there would be no more dashing away. No more running around behind him to sting him in the side. Scorch gloated. Now he had this foolish knight cornered. It was only a matter of time to end this cat and mouse game. And how can the cat possibly lose? This foolish and arrogant knight had offended his pride and would suffer for it.

"Scurry, little mouse," Scorch called out in a voice hoarse with anger. "Scurry and squeak. I will eat you yet. You help me build up a good appetite. You are already a dead mouse." With these words, he came bounding over to the boulders.

"You've got to catch me first," Michael taunted back. "And I'm not dead yet," the knight added, muttering this mostly to himself, partly because it was true, partly because he needed to give himself courage. "Nor am I a mouse," he said defiantly, pulling his great sword from its scabbard and flashing it in the air. This he said loud enough for Scorch to appreciate.

The dragon hesitated, stopping abruptly in his forward leap towards the boulders. He had never liked swords. Nasty, sharp things, swords are, and this stinging fly looked as if he knew how to use it. He had proven that he knew a trick or two.

It was true, that Scorch was well-armored with overlapping scales. Just the same, a sharp sword in the wrong hands in a prolonged battle could do even an armored dragon some serious damage. This knight had already shown that he could dance circles around him. But that was while he fought with horse's legs. Now he had only his own, slow feeble ones by comparison.

Just the same, Scorch decided to be cautious until he knew whether the stinging fly was as dangerous with a sword as he appeared to be. He covered the last yards to the boulders slowly and stopped out of range, yet close enough for a sudden, quick leap. The knight stood ready to receive him.

The two stood sizing one another up. The knight chuckled to himself that even after all of his experience, a dragon was still a lot to size up. Finally, he spoke. "Have you answered your questions about me yet?"

"Not all of them," Scorch responded. "One thing I'll say. You had a good teacher. I will be sorry to finish you off."

"Thanks for the compliment."

"You're welcome. Dragons don't give them easily."

"Yes, I know."

Scorch sat back on his haunches and considered this knight. If there is anything a wild dragon can appreciate, it is courage. Scorch had seen so little of it lately. After all, what mortal man had the mettle to charge straight into the belly of a rearing dragon? Yes, this knight had plenty of courage, that had been made quite clear. Scorch also appreciated his fine fighting technique. He did not recall ever facing such a worthy opponent. It takes unshakable courage to challenge a dragon and sharpened skill to be able to survive even the first onslaught. Scorch was impressed by the knight's qualities. He also knew that it took one thing more in order to fight a dragon—a love of battle and blood. It demanded a clever deceitful mind and a readiness to use any trick, no matter how unfair, in order to succeed.

"It's not too late, you know," Scorch said, watching for the knight's reaction. He was not disappointed.

"Too late for what?" Michael asked, puzzled by the dragon's comment.

"To go. Leave. Move on."

This was a new tact. Where was Scorch taking this?

"I can't believe that you're afraid to continue to fight me," the knight said.

"That's just it," Scorch responded. "I see that you are not afraid to continue to fight me."

"So what is there to stop us?" the knight responded, raising his sword.

"Only my great respect for you," Scorch said. "Look at it from my side. I do not remember the last time I faced an opponent who could match you for courage and skill. You are, after all, quite unique. Why waste such a specimen as you are? Take your chance. You've faced a dragon and survived. You stay here and no one will ever know of your feat. I enjoy eating the slow and the amateurish. But a knight with your skills, it seems a pity."

The knight had not expected anything like this, in spite of the number of times Star had warned him: When it comes to dragons, expect the unexpected. "What makes you suddenly so interested in my survival?" he asked.

"I can identify with you," Scorch said. "We have a lot in common, you know."

"Oh, really? I hadn't yet noticed. Certainly not our looks."

"More than you realize," Scorch continued, enjoying the knight's moment of doubt.

What new trick does he have hidden behind his scaly elbow? Michael wondered.

"Yes, we have a commonality in many ways. Yes, even our looks."

The knight began to protest, but Scorch stopped him. "I am armored, am I not? I come this way out of the heavens."

"From hell," Michael murmured, but loud enough to be heard.

But Scorch chose to ignore the comment. "You are armored, too, in case you hadn't noticed."

"But I can lay my armor down," the knight quickly pointed out.

"Then do so," dared the dragon.

"I am no fool. I need it for my defense and protection from you."

"As do I need mine, to protect me from you," Scorch answered. Michael only scowled. "Remember, it was you who came here to challenge and attack me."

"All right, you hateful worm, tell me where else we are similar."

"Well, little man-worm, you have proven yourself to be very brave. Bravery is a dragon's noblest qualities."

"As if there were anything noble about you," Michael scoffed.

"And we are both very skilled in battle," Scorch continued. "I by nature and you by some fortunate accident of training. We are both very clever and enjoy a good battle. We are both obsessed with power. We do not trust anything but our own strength. You are cruel where cruelty is called for. You overpower others when you are strong enough. You say you are doing good, but you rejoice in exercising your power and putting others down. You even like to be feared. That in itself is a protection that you welcome." He made these last points very slowly and deliberately, and watched to see the effect on the knight before adding lightly, "I would say that makes a good many points of similarity."

Michael was uncomfortable with Scorch's line of reasoning. Star used to do the same thing to him. There was just no way around a dragon's logic. He would be happier with a frontal attack.

"And there are two more things that occur to me," Scorch added, pleased with himself for quieting the knight's quick tongue. "We hate one another intensely, and want to see the other dead. I count those together as one." And then he stopped talking.

Curiosity got the better of the knight. "And what is the other thing? You said there were two." He was hooked; he wanted to know.

Scorch was satisfied that he had the knight's full attention. It would help for what he was about to offer. "Although neither of us wants to admit it, we both admire one another tremendously."

This stung deeply. Michael did not want to say it, yet he had to agree that Scorch was right. Even though he wanted to remove this dragon from the face of the earth, he could not but admire and even love him for all of the dragon qualities which he carried naturally within him. Michael fully shared the confusion of feelings that Aina struggled with. Fallen dragon or not, there was still so much beauty in Scorch to admire, even if it was raw and uncontained. Many of the qualities that he had loved so deeply in Star shone through all of this beast's ugliness and wickedness.

Scorch saw the effect of his words on Michael's soul. He was every bit as good at reading human thoughts as Michael suspected. "You are, after all, very like a dragon," Scorch said.

The knight began to splutter and protest. He barely got out a few incoherent words. Then he stopped and took a deep breath. There was truth in this that he could not honestly deny. "All right," he spit back. "Perhaps you have a point. It takes a dragon to fight a dragon. I accept the compliment that you find me as ugly as yourself."

"Only your soul," Scorch said softly.

Michael screamed and brandished his sword. "Come!" he yelled. "Enough childish banter. Let's fight, then, like the beasts we are." The dragon's words had stung him deeply. It was true that he loved to fight, he loved to show how powerful he was, maintain the upper hand and have people admire or fear him. He had never offered any other choice. He never let anyone lord it over him, which is why he wandered his whole life, never accepting the yoke of anyone whom he would have to call master. It always sounded noble to claim that he traveled to bring good into the world. The honest truth was that he trusted only himself.

"Not so quick," said Scorch, smiling to see the turmoil in the knight. "There is time enough for battle. I want to make you a small offer."

"Offer? What can you have to offer me?"

"We have an opportunity here that we should not pass up. After all, it is not every day that I meet up with a human who speaks my tongue and is as much dragon as I am. Except perhaps in size, you understand."

This brought a flicker of a smile to the knight's face.

"Good," he continued. "I am glad to see that you are amused and listening. This is a unique chance to get more of what we both love."

"The only thing you love is yourself," the knight spat out.

"Precisely," the dragon answered calmly. "And what is a dragon, after all? Power. Pure, incarnated power. And with power comes freedom."

Michael had to admit to himself that his attraction to dragon stemmed from his unabashed admiration of its immense and uncontainable power. A dragon does have great power, but there is more than that. It rubbed him the wrong way that Scorch's views were so limited. Michael had known the other side of dragon. He started to say so, but Scorch interrupted his thoughts.

"I am almost willing to bet my scales that you have spent your life wandering about the world because you will call no man your master. Am I right?"

Michael was taken aback by this insight, yet he did not want to agree, so he merely said, "Go on."

"Well, we have this also in common. I have spent many centuries wandering about the face of the earth. I, too, will call no man my master. But I am not against a partnership."

What was this dragon after? "What kind of partnership are you talking about?"

"One of like minds, like desires, like souls. One that you and I could easily agree upon."

"What can you possibly gain from our working together? You already hold the whole kingdom here under fear and dread. They will do anything you wish, as you pointed out yesterday."

"I really don't need more, if that's what you mean. Talking with you, though, I realize that I miss conversation. For all we know, none of the ancient race is left, but you. There aren't any other dragons for me to spend time with. The fact is, we don't tolerate one another very well. I am willing to strike a partnership with you, in return for your companionship. We understand one another. That is not something to hastily throw away." Scorch paused after saying this, and then added, as if as an afterthought, "And if it doesn't work out, after all, I can always eat you later."

Michael snorted audibly. He was intrigued by the turn of the dragon's thoughts. He leaned on his sword and commented, "I can't see you offering this out of fear."

"Not at all, I assure you," Scorch answered quickly. "I offer this out of greed. I want it all, of course. I want the power, the freedom, and the companionship."

Michael was furious at the dragon's arrogance, and at the same time curious. Scorch was right about one thing, there was time enough still for fighting. "What would this proposed partnership look like? What do I get out of it?"

"Well, I suppose you've had a chance to meet that excuse for a king that rules over this land that I have conquered."

"Yes, I've met him. I am not impressed."

"So, you know what I mean. Have you seen how he treats his people? He does not consider himself one of them. He acts like a stranger in their midst, which I believe he is. He behaves as if he has every right in the world to lord it over them. He doesn't have a dragon's breath to scorch the land, but he has done a good job of robbing from them and hoarding for his own advantage."

"I'd expect you to have a higher opinion of human dragons."

"Very little dragon-like about him other than greed!" Scorch exclaimed. "He lacks the sort of courage that dragons admire. He has the courage only to steal from others who are weaker."

"Well, what about him?"

"I propose to place you in his stead. It's the perfect plan. You can rule as ruthlessly as he, and replace his timidity with your courage. And there is more, if you're interested."

Michael merely grunted, "Go on."

"Well, perhaps you also noted that this king has a beautiful daughter, a princess."

Michael raised his eyebrows. How did this dragon come by so much information? "I know her," he admitted.

"Normally I eat princesses for breakfast, but this one I have let live, and it has been a mystery to me why. She has certainly offered herself to me on a regular basis. I began to almost look forward to her visits. Now I understand why I never harmed her. I was waiting for you. If you remove this fattened calf of a king, you can take his daughter and rule the kingdom. An opportunity like this doesn't come very often. Don't make the mistake of believing you will ever be made such a fine offer again." His eyes glistened conspiratorially. Scorch looked absolutely proud of himself, certain that his arguments would win the knight over.

"So, tell me what you think," the dragon prompted.

Michael's thoughts rushed furiously. Was this the escape he had been looking for? Instead of facing certain death in battle with Scorch, he could leave this desolation to inherit a kingdom and gain a wife. He could peaceably put an end to the dragon's devastation and return a hero. Aina would be his, Worrah defeated and the people saved! The kingdom would welcome him joyfully if he released them from not only Scorch's destruction but the king's tyranny as well. He would be heralded as the man who tamed the dragon and freed the country from its shackles. This was how he would tame the dragon. It was a faultless plan!

Scorch interpreted his thoughts. "Just think, everyone would believe that you'd turned me into a Luck Dragon. That's what you want after all, isn't it? Your fame would spread to all lands. Just imagine how you would be feared. Your authority will never be challenged."

Yes, it was perfect. The trouble was that it was too perfect. Scorch's last words had jogged him out of his illusion. Was he so naïve to think that Scorch was reformed, let alone transformed?

"Is it really that simple?" the knight asked. "I don't think so."

"Why does it have to be complicated? After all, isn't that the way of the world? What do you really know about Luck Dragons, anyway? Every Luck Dragon has made his peace with someone. Who wouldn't mind thirty years of easy living? I can always go back to marauding afterwards when I get the itch."

Michael's stomach turned at this. Everything that Star had meant to him was at stake here. He was not ready to believe that Star had been nothing more than a wild dragon who had struck a bargain with someone. He had known Star too well, too intimately. He would have seen through any façade. Besides, there was no one else who could talk with Star. Before he had come along, Star had resigned himself to keeping his thoughts to himself. And added to this, Star was by nature kind, gentle and giving. Quite the opposite of Scorch.

Michael felt a grim determination. He had to call the dragon's bluff. "You know, Scorch, I am touched by your offer."

"I knew you'd like it. All we have to work out are the details. And we have plenty of time for that. First things first: Get the king out of the way."

"You'll have to act with kindness and generosity, you know."

"Sure, sure. I can put on a show. We don't have to worry about that now."

"It also means that you will have to bless the land, the livestock, and the crops, and even the little babies that are born."

Scorch lost some of his enthusiasm at these words. He eyed Michael with a menacing look, and then commented caustically, "These are details that we can work out later." Seeing the determination in Michael's face, he added, "You seem to know a lot about this."

"So you can draw your conclusions about my past from what I'm telling you."

"Indeed I can. So as long as you're stuck on this, tell me what else is expected from me?"

"This desolation will become a garden."

"I wouldn't mind the extra offerings," Scorch commented sarcastically.

"Any offerings you receive will be blessed and returned. You will pretty much give up eating."

"I don't eat now," Scorch growled dangerously. "I gorge. What do you expect me to live on if I don't eat? Air?"

"Precisely," said the knight dryly. "Air and light. It is the only nourishment a Luck Dragon needs. Are you still ready to strike this partnership?"

Scorch saw that the knight had an agenda of his own. He should have known. He had already guessed that Michael had had his training from a Luck Dragon. That he was stubborn as well as foolish he had also long since figured out. He pawed the ground angrily, throwing up great clods of hardened dirt. "What sort of fool do you take me for?" he bellowed. "No one knows these things except you! We can establish whatever rules we want and tell everyone that it's normal."

"Anything different and you wouldn't be a Luck Dragon. And I wouldn't be keeper for anything less than a Luck Dragon."

"I'm not looking for a keeper!" bellowed Scorch, his eyes flashing.

"Well, then less a keeper and more of a guardian, let's say. To look after you, you know."

"I do not need keeping, I do not need a guardian, and I definitely do not need looking after! I look after myself! I was proposing a partnership. Partners in power to maintain power. You want to turn me into a hand-licking lap-dragon."

Michael smiled at the image of Scorch fitting in someone's lap. "Then our partnership doesn't seem to your liking."

"To my absolute disliking," growled Scorch, thrashing his tail. "You can't trifle with me like this and think I'll settle for it. I don't need you. I've lived this long without your company and lacked for nothing. As for your conversation, well, I'd rather have silence."

"Then have at you, worm," Michael said calmly. He was content. He held his sword before him, ready for Scorch's attack.

There were no more words between them. The dragon struck, Michael parried, then counter-strike and counter-parry. Their battle swayed back and forth, one attacking, the other parrying the attack. Michael fell into a very familiar rhythm. Inside his head he could hear Star coaching him, warning him, goading him, stretching his strength, his endurance, his knowledge of the wily ways of dragon. Michael felt confident that he could keep up his side of the battle all day long. His limbs felt light. His heart rejoiced to be sparring with a dragon once again.

Only this was not simple sparring, but a battle to the death. And although he kept pushing it away, at the back of his thoughts he could hear Star's confident warning, "When you fight a dragon, no matter how long it lasts or how well you have fought, the dragon will always end up on top. You cannot defeat a dragon by force."

His mind became a battleground to mirror his activity. He fervently wished to vanquish those words: "You cannot defeat a dragon by force." Every time he pushed them away, every time he managed to banish them from his consciousness, they came raging back to taunt him, snap at him, claw him. Attack and defend, lunge and parry, the battle with Scorch raged on, fighting for his life with his body and with his mind.

In some calm place within him he became aware that the day was waning. What would nightfall bring? Would they call a truce until morning? Or would they continue the battle in the starlight? He knew that dragons had keen sight even in the dark. Scorch would not be willing to let him rest.

Michael did not want to think about this. He had to stay present in the moment. It was just one more thought to push out of his awareness. One less thought gave his body the freedom to lunge and parry, attack and defend.

Chapter Seventeen

The Dragon's Heart

*I*t did not take long for news of Scorch's victory over the king's champion to reach the royal chambers. Even though Worrah had assured the princess that he would let her accompany the knight alone, he was not satisfied to leave the outcome up to fate. He gave his trackers orders to keep their distance and stay out of the way, but to report back to him without fail. And if necessary, if the dragon for some reason did not act according to its most ferocious reputation, they had orders to intervene. Soon after night had fallen, the first tracker returned with an account of the battle and what they had seen of how it ended. Once again the king's champion would not be returning. Worrah was fascinated to hear that the knight had had discourse with Scorch before the battle.

"I warned you that he has a way with dragons," Flek said dryly.

"Not *has*, my dear counselor, *had* a way with dragons," Worrah said. "He has gone the way of all the others. But I had no idea that the worm could talk. This opens up whole new possibilities. I see a negotiation partner." Flek was not as hopeful.

The following afternoon, the remaining trackers returned to report upon the fate of the princess. Their orders had been to insure that she also not return to the palace. They assured the king that they had seen her ride off and were certain that Scorch had acted with his accustomed finality. After they were generously paid for their services, some remained in the town, while others returned to patrolling the highways and byways leading into and out of Gladur.

As for the knight Michael, they had indeed seen him fall in battle. They had watched Scorch worry and torture the warrior's beaten body. They had watched as the dragon carried his broken corpse off to a secret place they had never dared to follow and find. They had seen this before, and clearly knew the signs. This was the end.

On the other hand, those who knew the ways of dragons knew this had been only the beginning of a prolonged torturous end for the defeated knight who was indeed broken, but not yet dead.

Michael found himself moving through a funnel of darkness, drawn forward towards a point of light. It was the way out, and the warmth of the light beckoned him on. He was not aware of moving his legs to approach that light. He was caught in a current, as if he were in a river, and the flow moved him forwards. He wanted to yield, to let the current do its work and carry his exhausted body. Yet he had a nagging feeling that he had left something behind.

He glanced back the way he had come. The darkness was nearly impenetrable. But way in the distance, he perceived a faint, flickering ember of a light, a single pale star flimmering in that darkness. He saw it and at once desired to return to it. It would be so easy to let go and be carried towards the beckoning light before him. But the flickering light in the other direction was so compelling that, without knowing why, he forced himself to turn around and, using every ounce of strength left, he laboriously fought against the current and retraced his path back into the darkness and away from the growing light.

He fixed his eyes upon the one anchor in that blackness and strove with all his might to regain it. It glowed faintly, and as he struggled, its light strengthened minutely. He strove towards that dim star shining in that vast and permanent darkness. And then he was overcome by nothingness, and gratefully dissolved into it.

At some point, it glimmered in Michael's dulled consciousness that night had fallen. Not even sure who he was any longer, let alone where he was, all he sensed around him was the steady, rhythmic, calm beating of a drum which seemed to come from outside of him, but was so overpowering that it penetrated right through him. He was too benumbed and bewildered to even wonder who might be beating a drum and for what reason.

And there was the darkness, a darkness greater than the absence of any source of light, a penetrated, inky night. It was so thick that it was like being immersed or wrapped in some opaque substance. Was this the great night of death he had so long been able to avoid? Was he now dead?

As he floated in this sea of darkness, vague images drifted through his soul of a great battle with a powerful dragon. Slowly the memory surfaced as if arising from dark waters; he was a dragon fighter. He had died fighting a dragon. Sudden, bursting flashes of color intruded upon him, although revealing nothing of his surroundings. He was not even sure that his eyes were open. The flashes of light only left him more desolately alone in the sea of darkness in which he floundered.

The first real hint that he might not be dead came when he realized he was breathing. Short and shallow, it pushed itself into his consciousness that breath means life. It made him curious, in a detached sort of way, whether there was still a body connected to that breathing.

The moment he made his first attempt to move, he regretted it. He had been at peace floating in what he had taken for the inky sea of death. The slightest attempt to move sent lightning streaks of pain through his body and up and down his spine, jolting his senses. He had enjoyed feeling detached, and the rude throbbing was unwelcome. Even attempts to breathe more deeply brought stabbing pain to his sides. Although this confirmed that he was still alive, it was no consolation. With his body feeling so raw, he wished to be relieved of it. Still, the spirit to fight against all odds had lived in him for many years. More out of habit than desire, he was willing to battle through this pain one more time.

Something wise in him cautioned to proceed with small movements. He tried wiggling his feet. He found that his right foot could swivel slightly, but the left one felt buried under a great weight, numbed, heavy and dead. Perhaps there was no foot there at all. In fact, his whole left leg was immobile, perhaps missing altogether. Not that it mattered much. Next he tried his fingers. As with his feet, he could not detect his left hand or the arm that went with it. Was one whole side of his body missing? Had he been ripped in half? He *was* able to locate his right hand, his fighting hand. All of the fingers hurt to move. He discovered vaguely that this hand was grasping something, although he was not yet interested in finding out what it might be. It was enough to feel its firmness pressed between fingers and palm. It had a settling, reassuring effect.

Taking stock, he pieced together that one side of his body would not respond to him at all. In fact, over most of his body, there was a great, crushing weight lying upon him. The image passed through his mind that he was buried and the weight he felt was that of the earth piled on top of him. A sudden thrill of terror raged through him at the picture of being buried alive under the ground. And then it passed as quickly. Would that be so bad, after all? He already felt detached from his body. Perhaps he had been found and taken for dead and some good folk had done the decent thing and buried him. In that case, it would soon be over. He owed them a debt of gratitude for the favor.

Then something remarkable happened. The heavy weight that he had taken for earth piled over his body, shifted. He could definitely feel it grow lighter over some parts of his body and more oppressive over other parts. Suddenly he could no longer stir his right foot. It was as if something alive was holding him down, rather than the inert weight of mounded dirt.

Something alive. A fleeting, terrifying picture began to glimmer in him that he was indeed buried, buried under a mountain of primeval life. Was it possible, that he was lying underneath the dragon?

The very thought caused his heart to race and his lungs sought deeper breaths. His mind tried desperately to remember what he once knew about dragons, had been told, taught, trained to know. He was certain that he had not killed the dragon he had been fighting. And with a sudden flush, he knew the name of this dragon: Scorch the Terrible. Scorch had played with him as a cat does a mouse. Certainly, he had dealt annoying, even injurious blows, but a mortal his size can offer nothing lethal to a dragon. He had been taught that long ago, over and over again. Had not Scorch even taunted him with this knowledge? When Scorch had tired of the game and the knight had grown weary of parrying and outmaneuvering, the dragon, with one deft movement, had simply mashed him. He had no direct memory of the final blow. Chances were that he had been too exhausted to even see it coming.

So the dragon was alive, he was certain of that. He ruled out the possibility that he had killed the dragon and that, in its death throes, it had collapsed upon him. So how did it happen that the dragon was now on top of him, shifting its weight again to lie even more oppressively?

He started to drift off to sleep. It was comforting to disconnect again from the pain in his body and the pain of his memories. A voice warned him that he was leaving his body and truly dying now. Rally, the voice insisted. It's not time for that yet. This brought him to his senses again. He moved slightly and purposefully, enough to awaken the pain again. He was not ready to die, not quite yet. Not as long as there was a mystery to unfold. Another door, Star had said. Behind which lay another room. Mysteries were always his undoing, but in this case, it kept him alive.

He had it now. He remembered what he had been taught about the habits of wild dragons. And there was no question that Scorch was completely wild. He had been taught that once a dragon had defeated its mortal enemy, it dragged him to its lair and added his body to its already highly-piled bed of booty. Preferably, the dragon brought the knight alive, to let the death be as slow and painful as possible. And then the dragon would lie upon his victim, slowly pressing what little life was left right out of him. It was a special cruelty particular to dragons, and Star had always been careful to point out that this was how it always ended. Always.

Now he was really awake, or at least as awake as his battered condition allowed. He was alive, broken, defeated, yet breathing, lying in the dragon's lair underneath Scorch himself. It was a miserable picture. He took in a ragged, shattered breath, as deeply as he dared. He let out a muffled whimper. If he had had more strength, he would have wept out of misery for his wretched condition.

He had no one to blame but himself. Had not Star warned him and nagged him and lectured him endlessly and forever that a mortal man cannot defeat a dragon? That it was just ridiculous and full of misguided pride to think that he could? He had hoped, somehow, that he would be the exception. After all, he was an exception. He could understand a dragon's speech. He had been trained by a dragon. Hadn't Aga told him he had been trained for this moment? Somehow, he had believed that he could outwit Scorch, if he could not overpower him. Instead he had ended up exactly where he had been told he would. Exactly where he had ended up after every sparring bout with Star. Underneath and defeated.

He tried licking his parched lips. It did little good, since his mouth was dry as well. There was grit around his tongue, and he tried to scrape the dirt off of it using his lips, since he did not even have the strength to spit. The wish for a drink of water rose to the surface of his consciousness and floated away. He resigned himself to swallowing in a half-choked manner. He moved the muscles of his face, making a grotesque grimace. Then, to his surprise, he rotated his head and discovered that somehow his head was free of pressure. He also realized that his eyes had been closed all of this time. He needed to open them. He was not sure that he wanted to confirm with his eyes what he suspected. Still, he had to look.

His eyes felt like there was sand in them, and his left eye was swollen shut. He did not particularly remember the exact slap to the face that had done it, since he had received so many. His right eye, however, was able to open, and he tried to take a look. At first he could only tell that it was indeed night and completely dark. He blinked repeatedly, trying to clear his vision, and tears rose up and washed his good eye of the grit that stung it. He shook his head slightly and blinked several times in a row to clear his vision. Dark, inky, thick night. The last he remembered of the battle was the sun sinking below the horizon. Enough time had passed to let it grow dark, very dark. A few more blinks, and then, in a blurred, one-sided manner, he saw them.

Stars! His head must surely be quite free from beneath the dragon to have such a complete view of the starry heavens. Even through his blurred vision, they appeared so clear and spectacular. And near! So near that if his hands were free, he would be able to reach out and touch them. This feeling brought on giddiness and once again a certainty that he had in fact died and that this was a vision to his spiritual eyes. He closed his good eye a moment to ponder this. How could the stars appear so close unless he had left his body behind and his soul was upon its final journey through the heavens?

He heaved on his arm, and once again the stabbing pain brought him back to accept that he was trapped beneath the victorious Scorch. And yet the stars! What could it mean? It did not make sense that the stars could appear so near. He tried again to reason it out. He had battled with Scorch and lost. Scorch had dragged him to his lair and added him to his pile. He was still alive, and Scorch was going to press the life out of him, slowly and painfully. It was a dragon's right by deed of victory. His body was held firmly in place by the dragon's weight. His head was free and able see the sky. Yet the stars in the sky seemed close enough to touch. Some far away memory was jostled and tickled. Stars close enough to touch—why was that so familiar?

He watched them, asking himself what was the missing piece of this riddle. Then, to his amazement, the stars moved. They not only twinkled, but actually moved in space. It happened so suddenly that, were he not already lying on his back, he would have fallen down. He was certain that it was not dizziness from his wounds, nor the blurriness from his one-sided seeing, but that the stars themselves had shifted. And then in that moment everything fell into place, and with a rush of emotion that caused his throat to swell, he remembered and knew.

He was looking at the dragon's coat.

But how was that possible? This was Scorch the Terrible, not Star the Beautiful. It had never occurred to him, in all the years he was together with Star, to ask him whether his coat was unique. He had merely assumed it. Maybe all dragons have such a similar coat that shows the pattern of the starry heavens in the night. Was it out of ignorance that they had called him Star?

This thought nagged at him. He resented that this dreadful, damned beast of a fallen dragon should have the same beautiful coat as his beloved Star. It was just not right to mix the fairest with the foulest. He wished even more fervently that he could have defeated this beast. His deep love for Star made him burn to destroy this misrepresentation of dragon. His misery grew greater than he could endure. He began to weep silently.

That was when he heard the beating again. The beating. It had been the first thing that he had become aware of when he had emerged from the nothingness. Regular and rhythmical, it had been easy to ignore. However, it was not the beating of a drum, but was much richer, deeper, more silent, more felt than heard. He realized how it had been in the background of his awareness since regaining consciousness. Was it the pounding of his own blood in his ears? No, although it affected his body, he was certain that this sound was outside of him. And then with a shock he recognized it for what it was: the beating of a heart. It was the dragon's heart.

He was lying underneath Scorch, pressed to the ground by the dragon's weight, but not enough to completely crush him. His head was free and he was directly beneath the dragon's great, beating heart. It felt as if it were knocking at the door of his soul, asking the same question over and over again.

If the great and terrible Scorch had a coat so similar to his beloved Star, would this dragon also carry that same secret chink in his armor as well? Were all dragons as vulnerable as Star? Was this part of dragon lore, or simply Star's own peculiarity?

If it were true, he thought, if it *were* true, then not all was lost. He had one last great, noble chance to overcome this dragon. The battle was not over and the thrill of this idea caused him to clench his unpinned fist. This led him to two remarkable discoveries.

First, he realized that the firmness he had felt all this time in his right palm was the pommel of his sword. Somehow, although he had lost consciousness and been dragged to this spot by the dragon, he had never let go of his weapon. His faithful sword was still there beside him, awaiting the moment when he could resume battle.

Secondly, although both his legs and his left arm remained pinned under the dragon, his right arm was free. He moved it slowly and quietly. Although it was immensely sore, it was not broken.

He tucked the sword next to his body, careful to be able to find it again. He marveled how much more secure and confident he felt, knowing the firm length of it was along his side. Then, with his arm free to move, he began to slowly and gently feel around the dragon's coat. He burned with a determination and a certainty. This battle was not over. He was not destined to walk away from it, but he wanted to make sure that the dragon was not going to either.

He touched gently as far as he could reach to the right, but he found no sign of what he was searching for. Now he moved his hand in a great arc above his shoulder along the side of the creature. He did not have far to reach before his hand stumbled upon it. A slit in the skin, so cleverly grown that it would be missed in battle since it folded over upon itself, like a lapel over a pocket. Yet his hand found it easily and slipped inside. And there within, just an arm's length away, was the dragon's heart!

Although a thick membrane separated him from the heart itself, it beat forcefully against his hand and he felt the immensity of its strength. It was hot beneath the dragon's coat and he quickly removed his arm, fearful that Scorch would sense his movements and in one protective gesture crush him. A thrill passed through his body and he knew what he must do next. There was no question or hesitation. In fact, hesitation meant risking getting his arm pinned beneath the dragon and missing this one chance the dragon in its pride had given him.

He groped around for his sword and found it. He grasped it again by the stout pommel, rejoicing in its firmness. He moved the sword around so the point could lay at the opening, the chink in the dragon's armor that gave him access to the great, vulnerable heart. If he were able to position it straight, with one strong thrust he should be able to drive it into the beast's heart. Although it would mean his own death, he prayed for nothing better than to take the dragon with him. It was for this moment that Star had so painstakingly trained him. Star had always insisted he could never stand up to a dragon in battle, that he could never win. But here was the way to be victorious. He could destroy the dragon through his own defeat.

As he slowly maneuvered the sword into position, he heard the pommel drag along the loose stones and gravel next to his head. He froze, knowing that a dragon's sense of hearing is keen. He realized that although he needed to move quickly, it would have to be inch by inch so that no suspicious movement might arouse Scorch's attention.

It was then that he heard another sound, one that had been present all this time, but only now finally penetrated its way into his consciousness. It was the far away sound of chimes gently knocking against one another in the wind. Yet these were no ordinary chimes. It was the sound of the dragon's contented purr when sleeping.

At that sound, memories showered down upon him, fond, warm, happy memories of his years with Star. How often had he heard this sound and been comforted by it! The countless times he had nestled in a crevice of Star's immense back and drifted off to sleep to the sound of those chimes. Oh, how he loved the very majesty and gentle strength of a dragon. It was what gave his own life meaning. Memories of his bond with Star flooded his heart and he thought it would burst. Instead of driving his sword into the dragon's heart, he felt one was being thrust into his own.

Scorch's words before their battle came back to him. It was all true, all of it. He was so very like a dragon, from the armor he wore to ward off the world to the desire in his heart for power. He had always told himself that, just like a dragon, he could match his own energy and moods to fit his surroundings. He had done a fine job of it here. He had met the violence of Scorch with his own violence. What if he had met him with love, or at least acceptance? How might this have proven a worthier defense against a wild dragon? What right did he have to feel in the slightest bit nobler or more worthy than this great beast of heaven that now loomed above him in the darkness? He loved all dragons, yes, even this wild, destructive one. How could he ever think to kill it? How could he even want to?

Michael let the pommel of the sword drop as tears streamed down his face and sobs racked his body. He wished to be a boy again and return to Star's firm guidance and intense devotion. But he was a man, a man who had received the gift of a dragon's training. What was it worth? What was the essence of that training? What was the lesson that Star had been so insistent on teaching him? For all of the times Star had repeated it to him in so many different ways and forms, here, when it counted the most, he had failed.

What is the true nature of a dragon? It was not power, as Scorch had insisted. A dragon has power, great power, given to him to serve others, and misdirected when the dragon serves himself.

And now Michael realized that his calling was to serve something greater than himself. He had been fooling himself all these years. Scorch had been right—he was only looking out for himself. That was why Aina had left him in the forest. It had taken a wild dragon to finally teach him this and make him face the truth.

A dragon's true being is the same as in every man and woman. It is the being that is able to bless a land and bring countless gifts to its people and to the countryside through unhindered generosity. That being is love and a desire to help and to give.

Michael knew that he had no business lying beneath a dragon with a sword. As the tears streamed out of his eyes, all of the lessons of his youth poured out of his heart. He was grateful to Scorch for this teaching. He was grateful to have finally faced himself and, for the first time in his life as a knight, to find defeat. For out of that defeat came self-knowledge and humility.

Michael's hand sought out the opening, the vulnerable chink in the dragon's coat. He slipped his hand between the scales and reached upwards, stretching his arm to its full length until he could feel the regular, firm pulsations of the dragon's heart against his hand on the other side of a thick, yet penetrable membrane. He could feel the intense, animal heat of the dragon's body, but most of all, he could feel its love, the love that was hidden in every sentient being's heart, the love that can be misdirected and easily turned to violence through fear and greed. It was the love he had denied himself since leaving Star and hidden away behind his own coat of armor. It was the love that had been revealed briefly before parting from Aina. He held his hand firmly in place.

"We be of one heart!" he cried out in a strong, hoarse voice to the night, to the dragon, to the stars. "We be of one heart, thou and I. We be of one heart." And with these words, a force flared forth from the dragon with an immense surge as powerful and irresistible as any river in spate, coursing up his arm, through his shoulder and exploding in his breast as a blinding-white lightning flash of illumination.

Chapter Eighteen

Flowering Fields

*T*he knight was uncertain what happened next. He was so overcome that he lost track of time. There was a strange stirring above him, and through his one good eye he could tell that the stars were shifting again. The great weight lying on him was lifted. He thought this must be an illusion, and that it was more likely that he was losing the feeling over much of his body. He had stopped sobbing, and he now filled his lungs as deeply as the pain would let him, emitting a long groan.

Suddenly, a warm and comforting breeze blew over him. There was no mistaking this. He tried to penetrate the darkness and see what was going on, but all that he could tell was that the stars above him had shifted dramatically. He could no longer tell where the dragon had gone. Again he wondered whether he had died. Then he recognized the source of the warm breeze. It was the unmistakable smell of flowering trees. The dragon was leaning over him sniffing at him, breathing on him. The warm breeze was the dragon's breath. Yet how this dragon could have a breath that smelled so sublime was a mystery that his burdened and swimming mind could not begin to penetrate.

Then he heard a voice that, although somewhat gruff, had a deep gentleness, warmth and caring to it, and most shockingly, he knew the voice as well as his own. "And we be of one mind, thou and I," a voice like chimes spoke from just above him. "One heart and one mind, we be one together. We are one."

The sky swirled above the knight and the stars twinkled against one another as if the heavens were filled with chimes. "Is that you, boy?" asked the strangely familiar voice with immense gentleness and caring. Without waiting for an answer, it continued, "Bless my scales, boy, what a powerful strange dream I've been having."

"Star," the knight gasped, tears blurring his vision completely. He had to struggle to catch his breath. "Star? How is this possible? Oh, let it be true. My Star, my beloved Star!"

· ✶ ·* ✶ * * ✶ ✶ * ✶ *   · ✶ ·* ✶ * ✶ ✶ * ✶ ·

The last of the brightest lights in the bowl of heaven were still glittering in the deep velvety blue sky. The inky darkness of night was reluctantly giving way to the promise of a radiant day. The dim pre-dawn flush revealed a desolate landscape, burnt, hopeless, devoid of life, not fit for human or beast. The prevailing color was black; all plant life had been reduced to charcoal and ash. Any animal life that had once graced this land had long since fled or been destroyed. All water had been mercilessly and systematically dried up.

The dawning light, however, revealed a curiosity on the crest of a hill: a man and a beast. The man sat on a stone, slightly leaning to one side and somewhat hunched over. Beside him lay a pile of armor, which he had, with great effort, recently removed. The clothing beneath was dyed dark with blood in places and the cloth was stiff. At several points, it stuck to the dried wounds which had previously bled so freely. The man was filthy and smelled strong and sour from his recent great exertions. He had taken a frayed linen scarf that was embroidered with golden stars and awkwardly tied it around his chest, as if to hold himself together with it.

Before the man was a beast. A great mountain of a beast. A dragon and, as dragons go, not a very pretty one. Its great scaled coat was streaked with filth. The trained eye would even notice that at places his scales had been marred and even dented in the battle of the day before. In the dim light, the dragon was moving around slowly, with its great snout just a few inches above the ground.

In that dim light, the man watched the dragon dumbly, numbed by exhaustion and the surprising turns of the past day and night. Then something awakened in him, he blinked a couple of times, and curiosity brought him to speak.

"Star, whatever are you doing?" he asked quietly. "You've been at it for the past however long," by which he meant, for as long as he had been watching him.

The great dragon paused and looked up at him. "I am awakening the earth."

"You're doing what?" He was much too exhausted to try and understand this.

The dragon chuckled. "I'll make it simple. I am breathing on the earth."

The knight tried to think about that, but he encountered a blank wall between his thoughts and his understanding. "What's that going to do?" he finally asked.

"Awaken the earth," the dragon replied patiently, continuing what he was doing.

"Do what?" he asked again, too numb to know how to ask more.

"You'll see. By this afternoon, it will make sense to you. For now, perhaps it would be best to sleep."

"Ah, sleep," said the man, as if remembering something long forgotten. And he whispered to himself again, "Sleep," as if the word alone were a lullaby. He slowly leaned to one side and slid to the ground. His movements were those of a man in great pain, and cautious of doing anything that would cause more pain. Beside him lay the padding he had worn between his armor and his body. He nestled his head upon it and closed his eyes. A deep concern flickered through his mind, and he forced his eyes open again. "Star," he called out weakly.

"Yes, boy?" came the familiar response from somewhere he could not see.

"You'll still be here? When I wake?"

"I'll be here, boy," the dragon responded. "I've work to do before I can leave this place. Sleep deeply, I'll be here."

"You're not just a dream?"

"Boy, I am a dream. I am something the stars dreamed up. But still, I'll be here when you awaken. Sleep now. Sleep deeply."

The knight sighed with relief and his body shuddered involuntarily. He could let go of his troubling thoughts now and fall asleep. He closed his eyes again and felt himself being swept away by a strong current of darkness, carrying him to a dreamless, untroubled land where healing takes place.

The dragon continued his slow progress across the barren, burnt land. As he had told the knight, he was breathing on the earth. There was something else, though, something he had withheld and, which in the dim light, the knight could not see enough to question. Great tears were brimming out of the dragon's large eyes, rolling down his long, scaly snout, and dropping onto the scorched earth like rain.

Star stopped moving across the earth for a moment and looked over to the man lying on the cold ground. He moved nimbly there and hovered above him. He placed his snout barely a few inches over the crumpled body. He breathed on him, as he had been doing on the earth, and the tears rolled from his eyes, dampening the man's thin, soiled clothing. Deep in sleep, the man groaned once and sighed, and his body grew more relaxed and less crumpled. When the dragon was satisfied, he left the man lying there and returned to the place on the earth where he had left off.

The knight Michael perceived the light through his closed eyelids before he was fully awake. He registered in his sleep-drugged mind that it was bright daylight and that he had overslept. Day is for action, and he had to get moving. His eyes flickered open, but the light was so strong that he had to quickly close them again. Something in him did not want to wake up. Foolishness, spoke a voice from deep within. The day is slipping by, and there are deeds that need doing. He forced his eyes open again, compelling himself to wake up.

The day was so bright that he went through this game of opening and closing his eyes several times, often even slipping a few moments into sleep again before some stronger voice within him commanded him to stay awake and get on with the day. He was rather enjoying the game and relished secretly slipping back into the darkness for quick little dips. Finally, though, he put an end to it by stretching.

The pain jolted him awake. And with the pain came flooding back the memory of where he was and how he had gotten there. He sat up cautiously and looked around. Beside him lay his pillow of padded clothes. Beside that were the untidy heap of ruined armor and his battle-worn sword waiting patiently for its master's guidance.

He looked around to orient himself. The sun was halfway in its path to the horizon, but the day felt old. It must be mid-afternoon, he concluded. Had he slept all day? Considering what he had been through, it was possible. He scanned the landscape, but what he was looking for was nowhere to be seen. The dragon was gone.

"Star!" his voice croaked, empty and small in that broad wasteland. He sighed and sat upright to take stock of himself.

"Well, I haven't died, it seems," he mumbled to himself, moving first his arms, then slowly his legs to assess the extent of his injuries. "Hurts too much to be dead," he laughed bitterly. That morning, or whenever it had been, he had been too numb with exhaustion to acknowledge much more than general pain. Just about any movement hurt, and he suspected several cracked ribs and a left leg that he could not stand on. He had wrapped Galifalia's scarf around his chest to give his ribs some support so breathing would not hurt so much. He remembered one eye being totally swollen and closed. And then there were the fingers of his left hand that had refused to do his bidding. He realized that he was more aware than he knew about the status of some of his injuries.

Strange, though, that he could see again out of both eyes. He blinked several times and then reached up with his hand. He found that his face, although still tender and slightly swollen, felt almost normal, and he was able to see out of the eye that had been swollen shut. He located a nasty cut on his forehead that was sore and scabby but no longer bleeding. To his added surprise, he realized that he had just been using his left hand to explore his face, and the fingers that had been numb and broken after the battle now obeyed his command, though stiff and tender.

He took a deep breath and discovered that the pain in his ribs had subsided. This was all so odd that he could only shake his head with wonder. It was then that he looked around for the first time, and what he saw made his wonder increase immensely.

Small, white flowers, tinged with crimson covered the burnt ground. From where he sat, a field of flowers extended in all directions. Each flower was no larger than his thumbnail and hugged the ground on a short green stem with radiating leaves larger than the blossom. He was so astonished, he stood up and hobbled around to inspect the flowers growing on all sides. In his excitement, he did not even notice that he was able to walk.

"Where in the world did these come from?" he wondered out loud.

"They're from me," spoke a voice behind him that was filled with warm light and music. He turned quickly at the words.

"Star," the knight said and smiled broadly.

There stood the dragon, quietly, patiently, as if he had always been there. But Michael knew that just a moment before that place had been occupied only by flowers.

"Star, the flowers, where'd they come from?"

"Do you recognize them?"

The knight had a good working knowledge of medicinal herbs, since it came in very handy in his profession. He looked carefully at the delicate petals, so bright white, rimmed with a hint of red. Many flowers were still budding and the sepal was a striking crimson. Red buds, white flowers, there could be no other like that.

"Unless I'm mistaken, these are dragon-tears," he finally said.

"What do you know about them?" the dragon asked.

"Well, they are said to be the first growth after a fire," he answered. "They do for the earth what myrrh does for a man. They heal it."

"You've learned well," Star replied with satisfaction.

Michael shook his head in disbelief. The day before this land had been completely barren. What had happened to make it bloom with such sudden ferocity? He knew Star held the answer to this riddle.

The knight stared at the dragon. Star's emerald green scales shone in the sun like countless rainbows. This did not make the least bit of sense. "Star," he stammered. "I don't understand. Your scales are filled with rainbows. But yesterday, you were a dirty brown."

"Oh, that," sighed the dragon. "I sloughed it off just before dawn. It's still over there," he said with a toss of his great head. "Who knows, it might somehow come in handy. In the past, some have used my sloughed skin in place of chain mail. I am told it will turn a blade far better than links of iron."

The knight looked in the direction the dragon had indicated. Lying in a heap was a dark mound of the dragon's skin. Michael shook his head. It was all more than he could comprehend.

"Star," he said, "my mind is so muddled. There is so much that I don't understand. And my body! Do you realize I can move my fingers again? I can actually walk, although my joints ache, and I can see again out of both eyes!" He would have continued to list for Star all of the discoveries he had made about his healing wounds, but the dragon interrupted him.

"Here comes one. I think it best if you would handle this."

"What? Here comes one what?"

Star did not need to answer, because then Michael heard the challenge himself. The words floated lightly on the wind. "—to honorably do battle with me, thou most hateful, vile and deceitful worm!"

He turned looking for the source of the words. On the crest of a neighboring hill stood a horse and rider. The rider was dressed as a knight, though he wore a knight's leather jerkin and leggings rather than a suit of armor. In his muddled condition, they looked to him strangely familiar. Who was this knight? Where had he come from?

"—to meet with me in battle," the knight's shrill voice continued, "until death finds one or both of us!"

The challenger held a lance, but did not carry a shield. Michael blinked twice, but could see no sword at his side. The voice was strangely familiar but was so out of place that he could not identify it. The knight lowered his lance and prepared to charge. Michael could only dumbly watch as the rider gave spur to his horse. When he focused his attention on the horse, recognition shot through the muddiness of his thinking. It was none other than his own Storm.

Then everything fell into place and just as suddenly he knew who the rider was. He had to stop this madness before it went any further. He stood up and waved his hands over his head. "Stop!" he yelled, his voice still too hoarse to carry far. "Stop, no, stop. All is well."

As soon as Michael stood up, the rider quickly reined Storm in.

"You're alive!" the knight called out in astonishment. "Thank the gods, you're alive!" And then with great urgency, "Michael, watch out! He's behind you, the dragon's right behind you! Run! I'm coming! Quickly, run. Save yourself!" So speaking, the rider gave Storm the spur again, lowered the lance and with a tremendous yell charged forward to the rescue.

Chapter Nineteen

The House of Michael and Aina

*T*he knight Michael did not know what else to do. If he did not act quickly, horse and rider would charge headlong into Star, who sat there passively, showing very little involvement in what was going on and absolutely no intention of defending himself. Michael curled his tongue and blew a shrill whistle. It was the battle command for Storm to stand still and hold her ground. He had trained Storm to respond to his words, to the pressure of his knees, and to his whistle. Storm heard her master's signal, and came from a gathering gallop to a sudden standstill, throwing up clods of dirt. Unprepared for this, the rider toppled over Storm's head and landed with a dull thud on the ground in front of her.

Michael hobbled as quickly as he could over to the fallen knight. He was concerned for the rider's safety, but he saw immediately that it was not necessary. The rider quickly rose and ran, lance still in hand, to meet him. They fell into one another's arms.

The rider was, of course, Aina, and she was nearly hysterical between joy and terror. "You're alive, you're alive!" she shrieked, holding his face between her hands. Then she looked past the man at the great dragon that loomed tall behind him. She pulled him frantically towards the horse. "Come! Come! Escape on Storm." Placing herself between the man and the dragon, brandishing her lance, she screeched, "Ride off, I'll hold the beast. I'll do it! Save yourself!" The fierceness in her voice told him that she meant to take on the dragon without a moment's hesitation.

Michael knew that he had found the warrior-maiden he had dreamt of his life long. How had he been blind to it before, seeing only a tender girl-woman? But then, she was all that as well; he still had this to learn.

"Aina, dear heart," he said, wrapping his arms around her from behind, holding her back from advancing on the dragon. "Put down your lance. Put it down. There is no more fighting. The battle is over."

She thrashed and resisted him a moment. Then she heard what he had said and, struggling with his words, tried to make sense out of them.

He took advantage of her stillness. "Aina, I tamed the dragon." He repeated these words slowly. Then he added, "The battle is finished. The dragon is tame. There is no more danger." From behind, he took hold of the lance and pulled it gently from her hand.

This startled her and she grabbed it back from him. "You're crazy! You can't tame a dragon. You're under his spell!"

He held firmly onto the lance. "Yet it's true. The dragon is my friend." As she turned slowly to face him, he gazed into her face, betraying with his eyes how happy he was to see her. "You came back. Thank you for coming back."

Struggling hard to make sense of what was happening, she did not seem to have heard him. Her hands went to touch his face, search his wounds, stroke his hair. Trying desperately to find words she repeated in a choked whisper, "Battle is finished?"

Michael smiled and nodded his head. "No more fighting."

Aina sank into his arms, and he let her down gently to the ground, where she began to sob. He sat with her, holding her, letting her pour forth her grief at having lost him and her relief that he was still alive.

"I watched yesterday," she said, when she was able to speak. "From the trees, I watched you fight. I hated you when you said you wanted to run away. I came to fight the dragon myself. I wanted to let him eat me. I had given up. And there you were. I watched you talk with the dragon. I watched you fight, and then you talked again. And then you fought. You were magnificent."

"Just not magnificent enough," he said caressing her long hair that he had freed from his leathern helmet.

"You fought long. You were beautiful, how you commanded the battle. I was certain that you would prevail. But you grew weary, and the dragon was full of tricks and never grew tired. Finally, I saw the dragon...kill you." This last she could barely speak in a choked voice.

"It must have looked like that. But he took me alive to die on his treasure-heap."

"I thought you were dead," she sobbed. "I saw him carry your body away, and I knew that I wanted to die, too. All hope was lost. I found the clothing you had left behind, and all morning I mourned your death, and then I mourned my own. When I finished, I was resolved to come to seek my end."

Michael then related to Aina all of what had happened from the time she saw him defeated by the dragon until now. She listened carefully and with apparent disbelief. When Michael finished his tale, she was silent. Aina looked up at Star who had until now kept a respectable distance from them. He had been coming closer by degrees, so as not to frighten her. He had remained quiet all this time, but now finally spoke. "This must be the lady," he said quietly. "I remember you called upon her frequently."

Michael laughed grimly at this comment. "Yes, Star, this is the Lady. In her name I did battle with you. In the name of this Lady, you and I fought, and in the name of the love I did not have the courage to express to her. I was brave enough to face a wild dragon, but lacked he courage to tell her of my love."

Aina stared at Michael with wide eyes when she heard him say this. Her lips moved, but she could not fashion words. She took his hand in both of hers and held it firmly. She gazed at him warmly and a smile lit her face.

"She has something of my Lady in her," Star mused. "I can feel her heart, and it is good and pure. How can this be so, boy?"

"It is simple, Star," the knight explained. "Her grandmother was the Lady Galifalia."

"O, wonderment," the dragon said and shook his great head. "That I should live this long and be surprised by the weavings of the threads of fate. That I should be led to this land and that the two of you should meet. I do not doubt that she will feel the intent of my heart as did my Lady. Do not worry. She may not understand my words, but I believe she can read my heart."

Aina shook her head at listening to their interchange. "Why are you speaking with him about my grandmother? What does she have to do with this?"

"Remember what you told me about your grandmother, how there were rumors that she had dealings with dragons?"

"What does that have to do with anything? Just vicious rumors."

"They weren't rumors. They were true."

"You're lying! That's not possible."

"When your grandmother left here, you said she was in mourning. She went to be near an old friend, on whose love she could rely. She went to live near a dragon that she had tamed. This dragon. Star and Galifalia were very close."

Aina's eyes blazed in protest. "How can you say such a thing? How can you know anything at all about my grandmother? This is ridiculous. She would never have had dealings with Scorch."

"Not with Scorch," Michael said soothingly. "But with Star, yes. Star loved Galifalia."

"My Lady," Star chimed. "She could read my heart. Maiden, I sense you have a similar power, though I cannot explain why."

Michael did not have a chance to translate Star's comment.

"You have no proof of this," Aina objected. "You're just trying to confuse me."

"Perhaps this will convince you," Michael said. He untied the frayed piece of cloth that he had secured around his chest the night before. It was the same cloth he had worn on his arm during his battle with Star.

Aina gasped when she saw it. "Where did you get that? It bears the crest of the women of my house."

"It was your grandmother's," Michael replied.

"How did you get it?" Aina demanded.

"I have carried it with me all these years. It is all I have left of the woman who raised me."

"You? My grandmother raised you?"

"I told you that I was an orphan. I was given to your grandmother. Do you remember when I asked about her portrait? I recognized her then."

"Why would you have been given to her?" Aina asked.

"As far as I can tell, to make sure that Star became familiar with me. She was my link to the dragon. Galifalia died when I was still a young boy. By the weavings of fate, Star took over raising me."

"I am amazed by what you're telling me," she said. "If it were not for this piece of cloth..."

"Perhaps that is why I kept it all these years," he said. "I am also amazed that I would meet Galifalia's granddaughter and have the chance to help her. Galifalia was everything good that you've heard about her. I loved her dearly. She was the only family I ever knew. Until Star. If she had not cared for me, Star would have never taken any interest in me. If I had not been trained by Star, I would have never come to challenge Scorch. If I had not come to fight Scorch, I would have never met you and known love. There is more at work here than just coincidence."

"What could that be?" she asked.

"It's always handy to have a Luck Dragon around," chimed in Star, who had been quietly listening to their conversation. Michael laughed and told her what he had said.

"I was raised by a Luck Dragon," he added. "This dragon. And his name is Star."

"This dragon is an evil beast that had terrorized my kingdom," Aina protested.

"It is a dragon's nature to live a generation among the people who care for him," Michael explained. "He blesses the land and brings good fortune. But at the end of that time, the dragon reverts to his wild state until he is tamed again."

Aina turned her back on him, but he continued anyway, hoping that she was listening. "It is true that Star lived here and was wild and destructive, drawn by Worrah's evil character. But now he is tame. You can hear the change even in his voice. You can see it in his coat."

Aina shook her head. Everything she had known as true was being turned upside down. "How can I believe any of this? It is preposterous."

"You have to trust."

"Trust the hateful beast that has destroyed my land?"

"No, not the beast. But can you trust me? I know the great good that Star can bring. I lived with it every day for years," the knight said calmly, sensing her frustration and pain that none of this was making sense. "Look, he's already begun. All these flowers, they're from him. These hills will be covered by thick grass by the time winter comes, of this I am certain. Cattle will be grazing on it in the spring."

"I don't care about flowers," she said with tears streaming down her face. "He tried to kill you."

"And still I love him," the knight said, sounding defeated and sad. "We tried to kill each other because we were both blinded by hate and fear. When I came out to do battle, I was no better and no different than he was. I was armed and armored, full of mistrust and self-righteousness, looking for an enemy to destroy. If you can feel the goodness hidden in my heart, then seek it, too, in his. I'm certain you can find it."

Star had been listening intently to their words. He laid his head on the ground and great tears began rolling from his eyes and down his long snout to the ground. "Boy, tell your lady that I sorrow for the pain she has suffered. For her sake I would dwell in this land and bless it. As I once served her grandmother, the Lady Galifalia, I am willing to follow her as my lady. I will gladly become her servant and rebuild what has been destroyed."

Aina did not give Michael a chance to tell her what Star had said. "Just because his voice is changed you want me to believe that he is different? Because of him my mother is dead. You want me to believe that Scorch is really a Luck Dragon. That he is not by nature cruel and that all this destruction is not what he normally does?"

"It's far more complicated than that, but the simple story is that this dragon's name is Star and he is tame."

"I don't want a simple story!" she shouted. "Look at what he's done! He's destroyed everything," she said gesturing at the ruined land around them. "Because of him Worrah is king."

"What does she mean, that Worrah is king because of me?" Star asked. "He's her father, is he not?"

"No, Star. Worrah is not her father. Her father died some years ago and her mother married Worrah. He is not the true king."

"Well, this is wonderful," the dragon said brightly. "Far more wonderful than I could have imagined."

"There's nothing wonderful about it," the knight objected. "Worrah is what attracted you to this place and he is still in power."

"What is wonderful is that your lady is the rightful ruler of this land. Worrah has no true claim to it. We just have to drive him off. It's really quite simple."

"Tell me. What's he saying?" Aina asked, eyeing the dragon with suspicion. "He sounds happy about something."

"You can feel his heart," Michael said with a broad smile. "Star is not only happy, he is outright brilliant." He turned to the dragon. "Star, when you were Scorch, you made me an offer. I think with a little adjustment, I am ready to take you up on it."

"I am prepared, o Dragon Master, to follow where you lead."

"What's going on?" Aina demanded.

"Aina, if Star were to help you to overthrow Worrah and place you on the throne, would you believe in him then?"

"Is that what he is offering?" she asked. "This is all so confusing." She sat in silence.

"Scorch is gone and will not return," Michael said. "This is Star and you hear him speaking. Listen to what your heart is telling you."

"And you understand those sounds he makes as words?"

"As clearly as I now hear you speaking."

"I must admit, his voice is beautiful," she said reluctantly. "I do hear that. It sounds like chimes in the wind. But can he be trusted?"

"It's really more a question of whether you are willing to trust him. I tell you, by his nature there is no guile in a dragon. He is devious only when faced with devious leadership."

"Such as Worrah and Flek," Aina said.

"We can defeat them," Michael insisted. "All we need is an army."

"Oh, well, that's a relief," Aina said with a lopsided smile. "So, in other words, we have lost before we've begun."

"Not at all," Michael reassured her. "I think I know just the place to find what we need."

Aina peered at Michael and shook her head. "You have surprised me from the beginning. When I first saw you in the pits, I thought you were just another foolish knight, skilled at arms, but with not much more in your head than wanting to prove that you were the best and the strongest. At every step, you have shown me you are far more than what meets the eye. And, in addition to everything else, you *are* the best and the strongest. "

He laughed. "You are not the first to notice that."

"But what do we do now with the dragon?"

"That is mostly up to you. Can you trust now what I am telling you about him?" Michael asked.

Aina was silent and studied the ground. "I'm so confused," she confessed. "I do want to trust him. I have always felt in my heart that there is great goodness in the dragon. And then that frightens me because a voice warns me that this is part of the dragon's deceit, to trick me into trusting him."

"Tell your lady that I have been turned from the evil house of Worrah. I now follow the house of Michael."

When the knight had repeated to her what Star had said, the princess added, "The house of Michael and Aina. In that I will put my full faith. With you beside me, I will trust in what is yet to come." She took his hand and held it firmly, her eyes fixed upon the dragon tears spreading over the land like a carpet of stars before their feet.

Part IV

To Seed the World

Chapter Twenty

Scorch Is on the Move

Watching from a safe distance, the trackers had left when they saw the princess ride out to challenge Scorch. They had seen before what Scorch could do to a horse and rider, and they took no joy in witnessing it again, particularly since this was no seasoned warrior, but a woman. Although none would admit it, too many of them suffered from bad dreams having watched the dragon kill in the past. They had no desire to freshen the memory. As a result, they missed out on all that happened when Michael whistled Storm to halt in her attack on the dragon.

The king quickly spread word of his champion's defeat. He followed this up with an alarming announcement that the princess was missing. He left the people to draw their own conclusions based on rumors that he carefully planted. Although some would remain hopeful, he was confident that the people would eventually conclude that she was lost and dead. He wanted to give them time for mourning before he made his next move. He was very pleased with the turn of events, and therefore puzzled by Flek's hesitation to rejoice.

"They're gone, my good counselor. I realize that you cannot show your true emotions publicly, but we are among ourselves. Why such somber looks?" They were drinking spiced mead together in the royal chambers, and looking out over the rooftops of the town.

"I know this man," Flek said with a frown. "I have seen him turn defeat into victory before and once even rise up from the dead. I won't be convinced he's gone until I see his lifeless body."

"Well, you have little chance of that, good counselor, seeing that our dear Scorch has made a meal out of him. It is so convenient to have a dragon close at hand. This Scorch has earned every bit of the land he claims."

"What do you plan to do next?" Flek wondered.

"With Aina gone, you are now officially the next in line for the crown. How accommodating she was to wager her inheritance and then get herself eaten. I could not have planned it better myself. While we wait out a respectable period of mourning, I suggest you take yourself a wife. Without Aina here to object and stir up trouble, I can also do the same. Not even the conservative barons can fault me now for siring an heir. Let's hope that among our happy children is a matching pair that we can one day guide towards marriage. This way, we will rule without opposition forever."

"And what about the dragon?"

"Scorch? He is far more useful than any border wars we could have stirred up. Sooner or later, we would have to make peace with our neighbors. Scorch remains a permanent enemy and threat to Gladur. There is no reason it should ever end. As long as he is there, the people will accept my rule. It is a never-ending war, only without all of the cost of having to keep an army equipped and in the field. As long as the people fear Scorch, they will turn to me for protection. Our goal is to keep Scorch content and well provided with regular meals."

"There should be no trouble in that," Flek added. "Aina assured this herself by establishing the Warrior Compound."

"Exactly," Worrah agreed. "She had no idea of the great favor she did us. But for now, my good counselor, in your best interests, find yourself a wife. Do you have any prospects?"

"I was thinking of the Baroness Delica. I find her quite beautiful. And she holds a great deal of land."

"Baroness Delica? The last I knew she was still married to Baron Brunam."

"Who is a thorn in your royal backside, if I may say so."

"All too true," Worrah mused.

"Which leads me to conclude, that if Baron Brunam were to suffer a mortal accident while out riding, you would not mourn his loss for very long."

"Look less to how long I would mourn and more to how long Delica might. It is the baron's widow you wish to marry, not me." They both laughed and poured themselves more mead. The king was satisfied; his counselor was cheering up. "Ah, I do enjoy being king," Worrah mused.

· ✶ .* ✶ * ✶ ✦ ✶ *✶·   · ✶ .* ✶ * ✶ ✦ ✶ *✶·

For two days, Aina was simply happy to have Michael back and alive. However, as she began to grow more aware of the situation, questions arose. "We are headed back to Gladur Nock," she said one afternoon, as they made their way carefully through a forest. "We want to overthrow the king. The king has an army, in fact, a sizeable army, and there are just the two of us. And on top of that, your wounds are far from healed. You are in no shape to fight."

Their horses were ambling around bushes whose leaves showed off their gay autumn colors. "I'd like to point out, Your Highness, that we also have the dragon," Michael said with a wan smile.

"Ah, the dragon," she responded. "I'd nearly forgotten." She was only half-joking. The dragon was indeed there, but she found it had the uncanny ability to accompany them silently and unseen. Although the forest here was not particularly dense, Aina rarely caught sight of him. In other places, regardless of how thickly the trees grew together, Star always managed to find a path to fit his bulk and remain relatively hidden from view.

"But you told me that the dragon won't fight," Aina pointed out.

"True," Michael conceded. "Star will not engage in any more battles. If he did, the wildness in him would be aroused once again. That is the nature of a dragon: He reflects whatever powerful emotions are directed towards him. If attacked by the army, he would destroy everyone in his sight. We would be rid of Worrah's army, but we would have little chance of surviving."

"Which leaves me where I began, that there is the king, with a large army, and there are just two of us, and you are weakened from your recent battle."

"Well, I agree that it does look that way at the moment," Michael replied. "But then, my experience has been that when dealing with a Luck Dragon, expect the unexpected."

"That's not a lot to go on," Aina said, pausing to snatch her skirts back from a large brambly bush that had grabbed hold of them. "Maybe your Star is a little out of practice being a Luck Dragon."

"I admit our situation is lacking something," Michael said. "But just the same, I'll put my faith in Star."

They had emerged into a large glade. The late afternoon light shone brightly into it, and its reflection was blinding. As Aina left the cover of the trees, she was so shocked by what she saw there, she quickly reined her horse in. Her hand rose to her face in surprise.

Michael pulled up Storm and looked around, a broad smile on his face. "Now this is the sort of luck that I was talking about."

A throng of armed men filled the glade. The sun shone off their armor, helmets and weapons.

The two dismounted and stood gazing at the armed encampment. Aina's hands cupped her cheeks. "These are not the king's. Where did they come from? Have we been invaded?" she asked in astonishment.

The army had been taking a rest, and many faces turned to look up at the knight and the princess as they came out of the trees. There was a long moment of silence and then a rumor began running through the throng of men. At first it sounded like a meaningless murmuring like the wind in the trees, but as it grew louder the words that were spoken by so many of the men became clearer.

"Aina...the princess...it's her...she's come...she'll lead us...Princess Aina." And then their voices joined together as they clashed spears to shields and cheered, "Princess Aina! Princess Aina! Princess Aina!"

Several of the men detached themselves from the mass of soldiers and came towards her. They drew their swords and knelt at Aina's feet. They placed their swords in the grass of the meadow, hilts towards the princess.

"Your Highness," one of them spoke above the many voices still celebrating around them. "We come as your faithful servants. We have ever been loyal to the crown, your crown, the true crown. Lead us into battle. The time for change has come." These words renewed the cheering among the throng of soldiers and another round of "Princess Aina!"

One of the men who had knelt at Aina's feet rose and stepped over to the knight and the two men clasped arms. "We got your message," Aina heard him say. "But we had no idea that you would be bringing the princess. This is even better than we expected."

"Will, I am grateful that you trusted me enough to answer my summons," Michael said to him.

"It took a bit of convincing," Will admitted. "The fact that you sent it through Hands helped convince the more reluctant. We've traveled long days since then. We are ready to do as you bid. Are we to go against the dragon first? Where are the others?"

"Others?"

"The vanguard," Will said looking past them into the forest. "The rest of your followers. The loyal citizens who have joined you."

The knight blinked several times and was at a loss for words. He had not expected this. "Well, first of all," he stammered, taking a deep breath, "we're alone. And as for the dragon, you see, the dragon, well, the reason I called you is, well, it's not to go against the dragon."

"That's not making a lot of sense," Aina said, smiling at her companion's difficulty.

"I just don't know how to tell them," he said looking helpless. Aina could not keep herself from laughing at his predicament.

"Tell us what?" Will asked. The soldiers stood silently waiting for him to continue.

At that moment a shadow passed over them from above, and a wave of fear swept over the army gathered in the glade. "Scorch!" voices shouted in dread.

"To arms! To arms!" the captains commanded with booming voices, as several horns blew to call the men to form ranks.

"Archers to me!" Will yelled above the gathering noise as he sprinted away from Aina and her knight. "Archers to me! Form your ranks!"

Looking up, Michael saw that Star had taken flight. He was soaring in a sweeping arch that would bring him to pass over the glade where they stood.

"He knows how to make an entrance," he sighed to Aina before he limped off at a gimpy run. He had to stop this before it turned ugly. He knew that all of the fear, dread and aggression that the army could direct at Star would turn his calmed and peaceful heart to violence once again. He had a fleeting thought that perhaps Star had taken flight to put some distance between himself and the hostile soldiers. He hurried to the nearest bugler who was still blowing a call to arms and wrested the horn from his hands.

"Hey, give that to me," the bugler protested trying to grab it back.

"In the name of Princess Aina," Michael said urgently, "you must do as I tell you." He locked the man's eyes with is own. "Will you follow my lead? For Aina's sake and for the true crown?"

The bugler hesitated a moment, but could not resist the knight's penetrating eyes. "Tell me what you want of me," he said.

"Good man!" Michael exclaimed and grabbed him by the sleeve. "Follow me!" he ordered. Half dragging the bugler, he hurried to where Will had gathered the archers. He was surprised how out of breath this made him.

"Will!" he shouted as loudly as he could over the tumult, "let me lead the archers. I know what must be done."

"Gladly," Will shouted. "They stand ready at your orders."

The archers stood in ranks, arrows knocked and bows drawn, heads thrown back towards the sky. They were only waiting for the order to shoot as soon as the menacing dragon came within range.

Michael was still holding onto the bugler's sleeve. "Will you do as I ask, without question?" Michael demanded.

"What do you want me to blow?" the bugler asked.

"Give the call to stand down," Michael ordered. "Give the call to lower their weapons. It is our only chance."

The bugler looked astonished at Michael's command and glanced up at the sky where the dragon was wheeling on long wings, closing the circle to pass directly overhead. "You're mad!" he declared.

Will looked as amazed as the bugler. He glanced up at the dragon and then at Michael's face. He saw fierce determination there. He opened his mouth to speak, but words failed him. Then he seemed to make up his mind, shaking his head forcefully as he looked up again to see the dragon coming into range. He turned to the bugler to speak, but at that moment Aina came running up to them.

"Bugler, do as he orders you, by my command," she shouted. "Now!"

The bugler's eyes widened as he acknowledged the princess with a quick nod and raised the horn to his lips. With loud, clear tones he played the notes ordering the army to lower their weapons.

Around the field, all eyes turned to the knot of archers and the bugler. Confused murmurs broke out everywhere. But when the other buglers saw that the princess herself stood beside the man blowing the order to end all opposition, they accepted this as if they had been commanded personally. One horn after another took up the call for the army to lay down its weapons.

Reluctant and confused, the men lowered their shields, their spears, and their swords. The archers relaxed their bows and pointed the arrows to the ground. When the horns stopped blowing, silence ruled the field, and all heads were turned upwards. Michael could see in their faces the fear that the dragon was about to fall upon them without their being given a chance to raise a hand in their own defense.

And then he saw puzzlement and wonder begin to smooth the hardened lines in their faces. The horns had stopped blowing, the clanging of arms had ceased, alarmed voices were no longer crying out. Only one sound was left, and it was coming from above.

The air was filled with the deep sonorous vibrations of cymbals. It was a soft, yet penetrating sound that seemed to come from nowhere. It filled the whole glade and surrounded them. Men shook their heads in disbelief. "What beautiful music," Will whispered, as if afraid to break the spell.

Star circled above them, in ever widening circles, flying, singing.

"What's he doing?" Will asked in a low voice.

"He's happy at your coming," the knight answered. "And he bids you welcome."

· ✻ ✲ · ✳ ✳ ✲ ✳ ✳ ✶ · · ✻ ✲ · ✳ ✳ ✲ ✳ ✳ ✶ ·

"Scorch is on the move." Flek had run breathless into the king's chamber.

Worrah looked up, annoyed. He was sitting at a table, a cup of wine at hand and several documents before him on which he had been writing. "What is that supposed to mean?" the king asked with a scowl.

"Trackers have just come in to report that Scorch has left the area of devastation." Flek went over to a side-board where he filled a cup with wine from a standing pitcher. He took a long drink.

"Unpredictable things, these dragons," Worrah grumbled. "No gratefulness, whatsoever." He reached out, grasped his cup, and took a careful sip. "Was bound to happen sooner or later. We knew it would. With Aina out of the way, I have no further need of him. Let him go."

"Worrah, you don't seem to understand," Flek said with a look of fear in his eyes. "Scorch has not gone anywhere."

"But you just told me he'd gone," Worrah said raising his eyebrows.

"Left the area of devastation, yes. But he has not left the kingdom. He has moved to a new area to the north, into the pine forests."

"Well, we can't let him settle elsewhere and destroy more good land," Worrah said with a dark look. "That timber is lumber waiting to be felled and sold for profit. Scorch can't go turning it into charcoal."

"And how do you propose to stop him?" Flek asked, plopping himself down in a chair. "Scorch is going to do whatever he pleases."

"You're the one who grew up with dragons," Worrah said. "Take care of it. Either drive him back or drive him out."

"I grew up with one dragon, and it was a tame one," Flek pointed out. "This one is wild. Wild dragons do what they want, and this one is no different."

"This is just not acceptable," Worrah said with a dismissive wave of his hand. "Tell the trackers to drive it back. I certainly pay them enough. It has a perfectly good corner of devastation to live in. Drive the worm back, I say."

"The trackers, my good king, are very quick to protest that they were never hired to engage the dragon. Besides, they report that they have already lost several of their number since the dragon left its devastation. Apparently when it began to move, they did not get out of its way quickly enough and they have gone missing. The trackers are skittish now. They will follow where the dragon leads them, so they can lead us to it, but they are keeping a safe distance."

"Oh, bother!" exclaimed the king, slapping his hand down on the table top. "Finally the princess is out of the way, and now this has to happen. What good is a dragon if it won't obey? Didn't you say that he could talk? Can we bribe him?"

"The only one who was rumored to be able to talk with a dragon we already fed to him. We have nothing left to offer as a bribe at this point."

"Then threaten him! We've dealt with him this long, why should it be so difficult? Why can't he be happy with what we've given him?"

"Perhaps you remember that we haven't given Scorch anything," Flek said impatiently. "Whatever Scorch has, he's taken. If he chooses to take more, I don't know how we're going to stop him."

Worrah sat a few moments deep in thought. "Then let's think like a dragon and turn this to our profit," he finally said. He grabbed some parchment and began to hurriedly write on it. "We will send word to King Melham of Warrensfold to the north and King Ribod to the east. They hold lands comparable to ours. We have kept the dragon contained all this time. No need for them to know that we've had no influence over it. We will tell them that the dragon, which we have protected them from all this time, is on the loose. If they doubt me, they can come and see the truth of that. It's time for them to come and help us control the dragon's ruin. As our allies, they are compelled to send us their armies."

"Have you gone crazy?" Flek protested. "What good will that do? You want to overrun our land with their armies? How is that a sane defense?"

"But an excellent offensive move," Worrah said with a gleam in his eye. "We will give them the position of honor in battle against Scorch. They will lead their own forces. If we play our cards right, we can have them march right down the dragon's throat. Scorch can serve me by destroying the armies of my neighbors."

"Whose thrones you can claim once their defenses are ruined," Flek said. He bowed towards the king. "How much I admire your ingenuity, o king!"

"Thank you," Worrah smiled accepting Flek's acknowledgement. "I am rather proud of the plan myself."

"There is only one large fly in the ointment," Flek continued.

"What could that be?"

"How will you keep Scorch from destroying your forces as well?"

"We will go to engage Scorch while he is still some distance from the capital. We will hold our forces to the rear of our neighbors' armies when we attack, thus cutting off their retreat. Once Scorch has gorged on the armies of my allies, he will be satiated and we can withdraw our troops. We might lose a legion or two, but such are the risks of war.

"Now here's another idea!" he continued excitedly, slapping the table with the flat of his hand. "We will make an elite force out of the men in the Warrior's Compound. They've been trained to fight the dragon. Let them march against him. Let that be the lost legion. No skin off my nose."

"Brilliant," mused Flek. "This way you need not lose a man of your army."

"And as to Scorch," Worrah continued, "what does it matter if we give to him a new sector of land? After the feast we deliver to him, he will be content to stay put for awhile. Then we will expand our boundaries into the lands to the north and the east. My kingdom will double, even triple, in size. That's how I will make a deal with the dragon. Once we have control of the surrounding kingdoms, what does it matter if Scorch increases his devastation? Let him repeat this every five years, for all I care. Eventually, Scorch will get me crowned emperor."

Flek raised his cup. "I salute your brilliance, my king. Once again you have proven your right to rule this land."

"I thought you might like it," Worrah said with a nod, and returned to his writing.

· ✶ ✳ ✶ ✶ ✳ ✶ ✶ ✶ ✶ ✶ · · ✶ ✳ ✶ ✶ ✳ ✶ ✶ ✶ ·

"Master Sound-the-Alarm!" Michael said with obvious pleasure. "I half expected to see you here."

The boy stood before the knight with his chest puffed up, trying to make his small stature look larger. "I've come to fight with the army," he said proudly.

"Have you, indeed?" Michael said with a nod. "And here I thought you'd come to collect that ride on my horse that I promised you."

"That, too," the boy said with a big smile. "I haven't forgotten that you promised."

"I didn't think you would," the knight replied. Then his face grew serious. "Come, walk with me a bit. Let me borrow your strong back for a staff." He placed his hand firmly on the boy's shoulder to steady his walk and favor his aching leg.

Sounder could not help but notice. "Sire, you are injured," the boy said with concern.

"Fighting is not child's play, Master Sounder," the knight said seriously. "For that I'm not happy to see you here."

"No, sire, fighting is not for boys," Sounder agreed with a vigorous nod. "That's why I've come with the army. We've a man's job to do."

Michael stopped and turned to peer at the boy with a penetrating eye. "Does your mother know that you are here with the army?"

Sounder looked uncertain for a moment before responding. "I've come to take my father's place," he said resolutely.

"Now, how does that work?" the knight inquired.

"He fell seriously ill right before the army left, and he couldn't come. My ma is tending to him. I'm taking his place."

"So, that answers my question, and it is as I feared. Now see here, Master Sounder, your place is by your ma, helping her in her need. By running off, you will worry her to death."

"I'm old enough," Sounder said petulantly. "I shan't go back! She doesn't need me, the army does. I've come to fight. Besides, we've got the dragon on our side. It'll do whatever you want. I saw it with my own eyes. It won't be dangerous for us at all. We will win this battle easily."

"Now see here, my young hot-headed and misinformed boy," Michael began, but got no further. Will had hurried up to him.

"Can you come with me? I'm in need of some advice."

"Lead on, Will," he said. But before going, he turned to Sounder. "I'm not finished with you, young man."

"I'm going with the army," Sounder insisted as Michael limped away. And he added for good measure, "And I can ride your horse, too! I stole her once, and I can stay in the saddle." Hardly were the words out, he knew his mistake. He clapped his hands to his mouth, looking quickly around to see if anyone else had heard him.

"We have an awkward situation," Will explained to the knight as they walked.

"More awkward than marching with a dragon, seeking a battle we have little chance of winning?" Michael asked with a bemused smile.

"Well, when you put it that way," Will laughed. "This, I fear, simply complicates matters. We have some prisoners. And we can't decide what to do with them."

"Prisoners? Already?" the knight was puzzled for only a moment before he realized who they had captured. "Of course," he said with pleasure. "If you hadn't, the king would already be marching against us."

"Exactly," Will said. "We knew they were watching the roads, so we sent our own trackers out to ambush them. The last thing we want is for Worrah to get wind of our movements."

"Do you think any got away?"

"We are fairly certain that none escaped us. We were puzzled why we didn't encounter more of them, but Scorch showing up yesterday seemed to answer that riddle. With the dragon on the move, they are keeping a safe distance."

"Which means they won't see our army on the move, as long as we stay close to the dragon," Michael completed the thought. "So, how many did you capture?"

"Six," Will said. "Two separate hunting parties."

"And you haven't put any to the sword yet, I hope," Michael said.

"We're not murderers," Will replied with exasperation. "Although there are voices among us who would like to do just that. The trackers make our lives miserable, forcing us to live in hiding. Anyone they capture is turned over to the king's dungeons."

"As I know well," Michael pondered. "I also have no great love for them. But I agree, putting them to the sword makes us no better than Worrah. I'm wondering, though, do the trackers come from Gladur?"

"No, they're strangers to us."

Michael brightened. "Perhaps we can turn that to our own advantage. Let's take a look at them."

They had come to two guards who stood before a clump of trees. Sitting on the ground, their hands and eyes bound, sat six trackers. Michael immediately recognized one of them from the troop that had captured him. Good fortune, he thought. "That one," he said pointing him out, speaking in a low voice so only Will could hear.

"The one with the red beard?"

"I know this one. He was in charge when I was captured."

"That explains why he gave us quite a fight when we overtook him," Will said. "He's probably one of their captains. But he's been quiet since then."

"Have him brought out to speak with us alone," the knight said.

The guards pulled the tracker roughly to his feet and led him to stand before them.

"Take off his blindfold," Michael ordered. The man blinked in the bright sunlight. His eyes glanced a moment at Will, and when he saw Michael, he face betrayed fear.

"Payback time," he muttered bitterly.

"So you remember me," the knight said.

"That I do," he said steeling himself for what might come next.

"Fear not," Michael said. "I won't harm you any more than you harmed me. You showed me neither favor nor disfavor. You did what you were paid to do."

The tracker gave a quick nod of acknowledgement.

"Tell me," Michael continued. "To whom do you owe fealty?"

The tracker looked puzzled. "I work for the king," he said.

"But do you owe him loyalty? Is he your king?"

"Worrah?" the man grunted. "He's not my king. He's my paymaster."

"That'll do," Michael said to the guard. "Take him back to the others." As the tracker was being led away, Michael turned to Will with a smile. "I think we have a solution to our dilemma. Now, someone find me that boy."

Early the next morning, the knight was sitting at a campfire with Aina and Will and several other leaders of the army, enjoying a breakfast of warm porridge. One of the soldiers walked up to him.

"Well?" Michael asked, looking up at him. "Did you find him? Where is he?"

"Gone, as far as I can tell," the soldier answered. "His sleeping mat was cold and I've searched the camp, but no one has seen him this morning."

"Who are you looking for this early?" Aina asked.

"Oh, just a boy who came with the army. I owe his mother a favor."

"You know a family living in the forest village?"

"Well, when I was a young, untried knight, the boy's mother provided me with my first adventure. And a much needed meal," he added with a smile.

"Well, that's a story waiting to be told," Aina said with interest. She straightened her skirts about her and folded her hands in her lap. "I'm ready to listen."

Before he could speak, one of the grooms who looked after the horses came running up. "Gone!" he shouted, obviously agitated. "Your horse, such a fine mare, she's gone. I don't understand it. I went to water the horses in my care, and your mare is missing! I swear she was there when we set them out to graze yesterday at day's end. She was hobbled with the rest. I swear it."

"I believe you are blameless in this matter," the knight said calmly. He turned to Aina. "Now, how odd is that? A boy missing and a horse missing. What do you think are the chances that they're together?"

The soldier reacted first. "I'll send riders out after him. We can track him and overtake him." He turned to give orders, but Michael stopped him.

"Wait. Let the boy go for now. Besides, you'll not overtake Storm so easily if he is riding her full out. You know, I did once promise him a ride on my horse. Perhaps he's taking me up on my offer. Maybe he just wanted an outing before breakfast. Let's give him a chance to come back on his own."

"Is it wise to let him ride off?" Will asked. "What if the trackers see him?"

"A lone boy on a horse will arouse less suspicion than a troop of armed soldiers riding in pursuit," Michael reasoned. "He's a boy, and a bit headstrong, as boys can be. He has ideas of his own, I've discovered, and doesn't like to be told what to do. He reminds me a bit of myself when I was young. In fact, I'm probably still like that!" the knight said, striking his leg and laughing with obvious delight. "Let him have his ride. He'll come back to us when he's ready."

Chapter Twenty-One

A Trap Well Sprung

I have excellent news, Your Majesty," Flek said, sitting down beside the king in the banquet hall. Worrah had called an evening of feasting and entertainment for the noble families. Musicians played in the background while servants walked among the tables keeping goblets filled with wine. News of Scorch leaving the area of devastation had unsettled many. Their comfortable lives had been interrupted, and fear gripped Gladur Nock that Scorch might attack the city. When Worrah announced his plans to march against the dragon bolstered by the armies of their allies, many were reassured that the situation was under control.

"I have need for good news," Worrah growled at his counselor. "I hope you've come to tell me that our good neighbors have accepted my proposal."

"No, my liege," Flek said. "It is too early to have heard back from them. My spies tell me that the kings are having a difficult time getting their nobles to agree to this undertaking. Some argue that anything that weakens us is a good thing. They are in no hurry to pit themselves against a marauding dragon."

"Then we need to offer them some persuasion," Worrah said, keeping his voice low. "Send some trackers into the forests that border our lands and set a few fires. Make sure to set them on their side of the border. Not so big as to burn down a whole forest, mind you, but enough to get their attention. Then send messengers to their kings to claim that Scorch was responsible. That should be incentive enough."

Flek thought about the king's idea for a moment. "I continue to be impressed by the wiliness of your mind," he said with open admiration.

"Do you think I became king because I am honest and simple-minded? Now, what good news have you brought me? Cheer me up, loyal counselor."

"You know the rumor of a rogue village of your less loyal citizens living in the forest?"

"You've found them? Now that's a forest I wouldn't mind burning to the ground, even if it is my own."

"Better yet," replied Flek. "Trackers have reported that the fools have taken arms and are planning a sneak attack against Gladur. They must have heard that Scorch is on the move and decided they could mount a rebellion while we are distracted."

"They can have but a paltry and ill-equipped army," Worrah said with astonishment.

"Indeed, that is the report," Flek rejoined. "It is a desperate move by a desperate group."

"Then we will go meet them and crush them. Any prisoners we take will reveal to us under persuasion of bribes or torture where the rest are hiding. Then we will have them all. Fools—walking right into my hands. We will lay them a pretty trap."

"This will be an excellent time to try out your new troops, wouldn't you agree?" Flek pursued. "We can place the soldiers from the Warrior Compound at the head of our forces and watch them cut this rebel army to pieces."

"Is there any chance that Scorch will get in the way of these plans? I don't want to run the risk of an encounter with him until we are reinforced by our neighbors."

"The trackers assure me that the rebel army is moving in a different direction than the dragon. They only spied the army by chance and came quickly to report to me."

Worrah paused, thinking about this news. He motioned for a server to fill Flek's goblet. "You are a man after my own heart," he chortled. "Have the trackers been well cared for?"

"They will feast tonight in their own quarters. They will lead us on a campaign against the rebel forces as soon as we can get our troops in the field."

"Excellent. No rest for you tonight, my good counselor, but you will be rewarded for your efforts," Worrah said clapping him on the back. "All of our interests move forward as if by design. But tell me, Flek, how is your own campaign advancing in winning the hand of Lady Delica?"

The two men looked where she sat at the feast. Although dressed in black, she was engaged in a lively conversation with others at her table across the room. Her neighbor nudged her to notice the king and his counselor looking in her direction. She raised her goblet in a toast. Flek and the king lifted their goblets in return, looked at one another and laughed.

Flek left the banquet early, and he did not get much sleep that night. He was busy with the officers of the king's army giving orders, making plans, and preparing for a successful campaign.

· ✶ ✶ · ✶ ✶ ✶ ✶ ✶ ✶ ✶ ✶ ·   · ✶ ✶ · ✶ ✶ ✶ ✶ ✶ ✶ ✶ ✶ ·

"Right through there," the tracker said pointing. "Our path lies through those narrows." The army had been moving through pine woods following a line of high, rocky cliffs. They stood at a jagged cleft in the cliff wall about the width of three men standing shoulder to shoulder. The break was not straight and from where they stood, they could not see where it led.

The army had been traveling for four days. And for four days they had not seen any sign of the rebel army. The trackers assured the king that the rebels were not far behind.

"You want me to take the army through those narrows?" Worrah said, looking where the tracker pointed. That these trackers knew his own land better than he did made him uneasy. It was an instinctive mistrust, but mistrust all the same. "Are you sure it's safe? Your men have checked it out? I mean, it looks like a perfect place for a trap."

The tracker scratched his red beard before responding. "These narrows are not long and get wider as you pass through. They funnel out into a wide plain on the other side. I've had my men check it out. Look up, and you'll see them on watch at the top of the cliffs." The king looked where the tracker pointed and saw several figures silhouetted against the sky.

The tracker continued. "If you position your army on the other side of these narrows in the plain and wait for the rebels to file through, you can trap them against the cliffs on the other side and they'll have nowhere to escape. I told you I'd lead you to a place you can trap them. This is it."

"But I take one look at it and grow suspicious. How do you expect them to be fools enough to walk right into it?"

"When they come by here, we will make them think that going through these narrows is their escape," the tracker pointed out. "I'll station my men so they can open an attack as they are passing by. They will see these narrows as their way out. Once they've filed through, you'll be there with the army to pin them against the cliff walls, and we will seal off this side to prevent them from returning."

Worrah nodded his head and looked pleased. "I can see you've thought this through. Well, if the other side is as promising as you say, it may indeed work." He turned to Flek who was riding beside him. "Send riders off at once to our allied neighbors and have them led here. Encourage them to come and help us rout out these rebel forces, the cancer of every king's rule. Then we can march together against Scorch."

Flek wheeled his horse and rode to the commanders of the army. He gave messages to the couriers who immediately set out at a trot. They had alerted their allies of the coming battle, but waited to summon them until they knew where the battle was to take place.

"How far behind us do you think the rebels are?" Worrah asked the red-bearded tracker.

"They are within half a day's journey, o king. We should expect them by this afternoon. I suggest you get your forces into position in case my men miss intercepting their scouts. We don't want to frighten them into taking another route."

"So be it," Worrah said decisively. He raised his voice so that the commanders could hear, "Give orders to pass through the narrows. We will set up position on the other side once we see the lay of the land."

The king rode at the head of the army as it filed through the narrows between the high cliffs. But Worrah was still troubled. Something nagged at him to be wary. He had achieved his successes by following his deeper instincts, and they warned him now that something was not right. He glanced again up to the high cliffs and saw trackers still standing on the heights. This gave him some comfort, but he was uncertain of the trap he was about to prepare.

Yet it was exactly as the tracker had told him. Worrah pulled his horse aside as the army passed him by. He looked around to get a feeling for the land. Indeed, the narrows opened up into a wide plain of rolling hills, backed by the high cliffs forming a box canyon, along which the army was now riding. At one side was a thick growth of trees that grew right up to the cliffs and extended at an angle far into the plain. Excellent cover, he thought, to hide his men. They could be concealed easily by the growth of trees and underbrush, watching the unsuspecting rebels enter the canyon. In his imagination, he saw his forces waiting for his sign to ride out and corner the rebels with no retreat possible once the narrows were cut off by the trackers. However, the trackers were too few to seal the way completely. He would reinforce them with cavalry from his own regulars.

He gazed at the line of the forest. The leaves on the trees in the fall sunlight gleamed in vibrant reds, golds and yellows. He imagined his own forces lined up amid those gay colors, watching with grim and silent expectation, weapons in hand, waiting for the sign to attack.

He called over one of his captains and outlined for him how he wanted the men to be stationed out of sight. He wanted to do this quickly so that his soldiers had time to grab a bite to eat before the long wait for the rebel army to arrive. He decided to hide a preliminary force in the trees, with the bulk of the infantry out of sight behind. The cavalry would be furthest away, since they could come the quickest.

He was giving orders to one of his commanders, gesturing towards the line of trees, when his eye caught a movement that should not have been there. He saw between the leaves and branches what looked like the head of a horse shaking off the flies. There was a momentary gleam of the sun off of burnished metal. Panic seized his heart. He stood up in his stirrups and shouted as he waved his arms. "Get back! Get out! It's a trap! Back through the pass!"

Hardly had the words left his lips, than there was a great commotion among the foot soldiers entering the canyon. They no longer marched in orderly ranks, but surged with urgency, pushing those before them into disarray. Worrah heard cries of "Attack!" and "Rearguard under attack!" For a moment he thought he heard several panicked voices cry out "Dragon!" but he had no time to follow it up. His attention was riveted by what happened next in the plain.

Only moments before, Michael had been standing with the princess Aina and Will behind the cover of the last clump of trees, watching what was unfolding in the box canyon.

"It's all going as you planned," Will said. His voice was edged with excitement. When the knight did not respond, Will looked at him, wondering if he had missed something. "It is all going as you planned, isn't it?" he asked.

Michael paused before answering, watching the disarray of the king's forces as they realized they were being attacked from behind.

"Yes, so far it is all as we planned," he said. His voice sounded cautious and guarded.

"You know we can't defeat them, don't you?" Aina asked. Her question startled him, but instead of answering, he peered into her face. "We're outnumbered three to one." There was despair in her voice.

He shook his head. "I don't think it's hopeless. Not yet. After all, we have—" But his voice faltered as he was distracted by the action of the king's army.

"Yes," Aina finished his sentence for him. "We have the Luck Dragon." Her voice had a tinge of bitterness.

"He's obviously made a showing on the other side of the pass," Will said excitedly. "He's chasing the rest of the army into the canyon."

"I can't stand this," Aina said desperately. "These are my people. But the soldiers in the army are also my citizens. I just can't stand here and watch them butcher one another."

"You won't have to," Michael said firmly. "I promise you—" But he never finished what he was going to say. At that moment Will cried out that a lone rider was approaching swiftly from behind. Both the knight and the princess looked.

"Who could that be?" Aina asked.

"It's Storm," Michael said with joy in his voice. "He's come, at last."

A moment later Storm reached them at a full gallop and might have kept on riding past them if the knight had not whistled shrilly. Storm came to a sudden halt, throwing up dirt and a cloud of dust. Her sides were heaving heavily and she snorted loudly. An exhausted boy who had been until now desperately clinging to Storm's mane slid off the horse's back into the knight's waiting arms.

"Is all well?" the knight asked, peering into the boy's drawn face.

"Yes," the boy gasped, before his eyes rolled up into his head and he lost consciousness.

The knight laid the boy on the grass and stood up to his full height, his eyes blazing. He drew his sword and commanded at the top of his voice, "Charge! Full engage! Now! We haven't a moment to lose!"

At his order, the air was suddenly rent with the blare of trumpets. The forest exploded, expelling riders and foot soldiers. The rebel army that had been hiding amid the trees and foliage now charged into the open space, blocking the king's army from spreading out and taking position in the plain. From the chaotic cries coming from the pass and the panicked soldiers charging into the backs of their companions, nearly knocking them over, Worrah realized that their retreat was blocked. His whole army had been confined in the box canyon. It was indeed a perfect place to lay a trap. But the trap had been sprung on him! The hunter had become the hunted. It was slowly dawning on his army that they had walked into an ambush, and panic spread among the men.

Worrah spurred his horse, riding among the foot soldiers, flaying with his whip left and right to get the men's attention away from the danger before them, to listen to their commanders. He was not alone. Every commander on horseback was doing the same, riding among the milling men, using his whip to get the soldiers to reform ranks and listen to orders. The trumpeters were the first to regain their wits and blew the call to reform ranks. The soldiers responded quickly to the sound of the trumpet, and in short order were prepared to meet the frontal attack of the rebel army.

Worrah swore under his breath, yet was satisfied. His forces had been well trained and now that the initial shock of walking into a trap was over, they were lining up and resisting in an orderly fashion. Worrah, swore again. These upstart rebels would pay for this, and pay dearly. He spread the orders among his troops: Give no quarter, take no prisoners, show no mercy. Now that he had them, there would be no escape. Because his own forces were so superior in number, he schemed how to counter-spring the trap back on those who set it. Knowing there was no retreat, his army would fight all the more fiercely.

The front line of the battle was in tumult where his soldiers engaged the onslaught of the rebels. Behind the front line, the rest of his army eagerly awaited their turn to give battle. The narrowness of the canyon prevented them from circling around and flanking the rebels. Let the rebels attack as long as they wished. The king's front line was so deep, there was no possibility of its ever breaking. It was like the ocean crashing against the cliffs: The rebels, like the waves, would be continually thrown back, making no headway.

Worrah was delighted with what he saw. He held his horse on the outskirts of the battle line as couriers on horseback moved to and from hotspots in the battle. He was able in this way to direct his forces. He sent word to the warriors from the training compound to take their places in the front lines. He had no doubt that their superior skills would soon rout the rebels.

It did not take long for it to dawn upon the rebel leaders what Worrah had already recognized. Their plan to contain his army in the box canyon could be turned to their advantage only if they had enough forces to overwhelm it. Greatly outnumbered, they now saw what Aina had realized before the battle began, that their own forces would grow weary and their line eventually crumble. It was like a dam holding back flood water. All it would take was a single chink to open up and Worrah would engulf the plain with his army. Already, with the arrival of the king's warriors from the fighting compound, the line was wavering and bulging at places. The poorly equipped rebel forces could not stand up for long against a better trained fighting force. They knew only one thing could bring them relief, and the troop leaders hoped it would come soon.

The din of battle was deafening. Waiting impatiently, Worrah shouted encouragement and orders that no one could hear. Flek appeared at his side. "What took you so long?" Worrah shouted at him over the noise of the fight.

"The press and throng are intense," Flek shouted back at him. "I came as quickly as I could. What do you want?"

"Go to the front line," the king ordered. "Break it! Break through, no matter what the cost. Wedge an opening, force it open! Go now, quickly! Let's make an end of this."

Flek looked out over the battling forces. Immediately he saw what the king wanted. If he could force an opening in the middle, he could split the rebel army in two and then encircle both halves.

As ideal as it might be to wedge an opening in the middle and so divide the rebel forces, that was where the fighting was fiercest and where the line of rebel forces was the deepest. It would be a costly foray on both sides. Flek surveyed the line for a moment until he found the point he was looking for. At the near end, next to the cliff, the rebel line was beginning to thin out, as fighters were moving across to defend against a bulge that threatened to break in among them. He gathered a small troop of soldiers and made his way through the throng, collecting more as he went, right towards the edge.

Progress was slow, but his plan was simple enough that he knew it could not fail. Along the way, he ordered reinforcements to put more pressure onto the bulge. He knew that if there were enough distraction at the point that was threatening to break, he could open up a breach at the cliffs that would get him through.

His plan worked perfectly. By the time he reached the edge against the cliff, the rebel line had grown so thin that his troops easily broke through. They succeeded in opening a gap through which the king's army could then flow unhindered into the plain and circle around the rebels. He made it past the first line of defense with a handful of soldiers.

What happened next, however, was not according to his plan. Instead of the gap allowing more troops to funnel in behind him, suddenly it constricted and was choked off altogether, trapping him with his followers behind enemy lines.

Flek and his men were now surrounded on three sides by fiercely fighting rebels. There was no retreat, and behind them were the walls of the cliff. He saw no choice but to rally his men and, instead of fighting defensively with their backs to the cliff walls, to drive them in a wedge right towards the bulge. It was a reckless plan, and many men fell on both sides.

The effect, though, did not take long to be noticed. In spite of his losses, Flek gained enough ground that those forces holding back the bulge were suddenly attacked from two sides. He was not certain, but he thought he caught a glimpse of the king's own crested helmet with a fiercely flashing blade on the other side of the bulge. As he drove his men on with greater impulse to unite his small unit with the forces striving to break through, Flek could sense the panic beginning to spread among the rebels around him.

Suddenly the rebels in front of Flek melted away. His men were thrown against the shields of the king's soldiers. It was all they could do to keep from getting skewered by their own forces. He was reunited with Worrah's army, but he could not tell if they had made any headway into the rebel lines.

It had indeed been Worrah's crest that Flek had seen over the heads of the fighting men, and he found himself now face to face with his king. Worrah was openly cursing and his eyes were fierce. "Fool!" he cried out. "What have you done but waste good fighting men? Turn and fight or I'll run you through."

Flek was stung by the king's outrage, but this was no place to defend his honor. As he spun around to face the rebel forces, he realized how many of the men who had joined him had fallen. There were only a few left standing, and, bleeding freely from their wounds, they looked exhausted. He himself had a cut on the leg and bleeding gashes on his face and sword arm.

Over the clash of arms and the yells and cries of men in pain, defeat and victory, there was a sudden faint blare of trumpets. Flek glanced over at the king. The surprise on Worrah's face told him that these trumpets had not been sounded by his orders.

Chapter Twenty-Two

The Duel

*T*he intensity of the battle slackened as everyone paused to listen to the call of the trumpets. For a moment Worrah had a look of fiendish joy on his face. "It's our reinforcements. It has to be. They've arrived with good speed." But a moment later he was uncertain. He looked at Flek with menace in his eyes. "Did you order this?" he demanded.

"Not I," he swore.

All along the line the battle was tapering off. Exhausted and injured men were backing away from one another, lowering their shields, letting tired arms drop to their sides. Following well-trained drills, fresh forces immediately replaced the front lines on both sides, while those who had been fighting retreated to the rear of their lines to rest or to have their wounds bound up. The trumpets continued their call to cease the hostilities.

"A truce?" Worrah bellowed. "I didn't order a truce." Yet as ready as he was to reengage, the soldiers on both sides were thankful for a respite to at least find out from where the order came.

At that moment the rebel forces suddenly parted in the middle, leaving a corridor between them through which the trumpeters walked, still sounding the call to cease fighting. Worrah now saw his chance. The rebels were opening for him the very gap he had been trying to drive through them. With a single order he could wedge his army into the opening breach. The fools had decided their own fate! He was already hurriedly giving the order to be passed on to his own trumpeters: Charge full on! What he saw next, however, caused his blood to run cold and he found himself clinging to his messenger, keeping him from carrying out his command.

A lone rider was trotting his horse up the space the army had opened. It was a knight in armor upon a white mare. He bore a battered shield, though its emblem was still clear: a red dragon rampant upon a field of white.

"It's not possible," he gasped. "He's dead, his horse eaten. They swore to me, he's dead." The king turned to Flek for some explanation, but his counselor stood there with his arms hanging, his mouth open in shock.

The ranks around the king opened up, and the rider directed his horse through. One of the trumpeters walked with him. When they stood before the gawking king, the trumpeter served as the knight's herald. "Devious and false king!" he spoke in a loud voice.

The field of battle had grown eerily calm and quiet. Everyone strained to hear the herald speak. Worrah winced at his words and a scowl covered his face. "You are called out in challenge to fight in single combat. Here, in witness before your people, before the army that obeys you only for the wages you pay, and before your people who have deep and enduring grievances against you for your intrigues, misdeeds and false-heartedness. You are hereby called to account for inciting rebellion among loyal citizens through an oppressive, cruel and dishonest rule. You are hereby called to single combat. O, king, do you accept this challenge?"

When the herald finished speaking, silence reigned the field. Everyone awaited the king's response. Worrah looked up at the knight who sat impassively on his horse. His visor was down, and the king could see only two fierce eyes boring into him, filled with hate. He did not hesitate. Throwing his arm into the air, he cried out in a loud voice,

"I accept! And let the opposing army lay down its arms to the victor!" A great cheer rose up from both sides.

Before the sound abated, the king quickly turned his back to the knight and pulled Flek to him. "Here is the chance we've been waiting for, my dear counselor. Don't disappoint me. I'm willing to wager my life that he is weakened from his battle with Scorch. How he escaped, we may never know. Nor is it my intention to give him a chance to tell his tale." Holding Flek by the arm, he walked away from the knight as a space opened up between the two armies, large enough to contain the combat between the king and his challenger. The knight dismounted from the horse and stood with sword drawn and shield raised, ready to engage the king. Worrah continued to whisper instructions into Flek's ear.

The king turned suddenly, clashed his sword against his shield, and with a great bellow charged his opponent. The knight did not wait for Worrah to come crashing into him, but skipped deftly out of the way, tripping the king as he passed. Worrah was on his feet in a moment, enraged by the knight's maneuver. He charged again, this time more cautiously, determined to make contact. Sword clashed against sword and shield against shield. The knight was very light on his feet, twisting and turning to avoid the vicious blows from the king.

Worrah, who was immensely strong, was accustomed to overpowering his enemies. His blows repeatedly missed their mark and instead slashed through empty air, throwing him off balance. Each time, the knight took advantage of the lurching king, striking him hard with the pommel or the flat of his sword.

"Stand still and fight!" the king roared. "Stop dancing around and fight me like a man!" The knight did not respond, but continued his agile moving around an ever-growing frustrated and furious king.

All this time, Flek had been busy following Worrah's last instructions. He walked among the resting soldiers, moving the fighters from the Warrior's Compound to stand as a buffer between the dueling combatants and the rest of the army.

"Here is your chance to show where your loyalties lie," he spread the word down the lines. "The king will reward you greatly for your deeds this day. You will become the leaders of his army once you show what you're made of. You are his personal body guard. Act quickly when I give the sign. At my sign, strike down the enemy in your way."

While he was gathering them and giving instructions, Flek continued to follow the course of the battle. He had little doubt that Worrah would win. He knew him to be ferocious and overpowering in combat. But he was surprised by the knight's tactics. There was something familiar about how agile and nimbly he moved his body. It was strange, but it all reminded him of someone else, not of the knight who had gone off to battle the dragon, not of the knight who had been a thorn in his side all the years he was growing up. This was not the way he fought. Something was wildly wrong.

Then the last thing the king had yelled at the knight sank in, and he knew exactly where he had seen this style of combat before. He had a moment of grim amusement at how ironic and perfect this was all working out. He grabbed a spear from one of the soldiers and stepped out onto the edge of the circle of battle. The knight was moving around the space so quickly and deftly, Flek had only a moment to wait until the two were coming towards him. By now the king had been soundly beaten around the head and the ribs, and had barely succeeded in landing a blow against his opponent.

As the knight passed in front of him, Flek stepped forward and from behind, stuck the long handle of the spear between his legs. The knight went sprawling onto the ground. Before he could scramble to his feet, Flek was standing over him, the point of the spear pressed against his throat.

Everything went deathly still among the armies. Then, just as suddenly, there was vehement protest from the rebel army.

"Remove the helmet," Flek ordered the king who was staring dumbly at this unexpected turn of events. "Quick, before they can act." Worrah did not need to be told twice. He bent over the prone knight and with his knife cut the laces that secured the helmet.

"Oh, false knight!" Flek accused, as the king worked quickly. With the point of the spear at his neck, the knight could only lie still to avoid sudden death. "False knight, you bring shame upon us all. Citizens and soldiers, look upon this false knight!"

Worrah had finished with the helmet and roughly drew it off of the knight's head. Long, black hair cascaded forth, covering the ground around the knight's head. There was a gasp from all who were close enough to see.

"Well met, Princess," Flek sneered so quietly only she could hear. "Did you bring me my crown?" He removed the threatening spear from her throat and stepped back. Princess Aina rose slowly to her feet.

"I marveled how Dung Boy could be so light on his feet," Flek said softly to the king. "Something wasn't right. How the princess cheated death before is a mystery, but it won't happen twice."

"And the knight?" Worrah asked. "If she be here, what about him?"

"Either dead or useless, I reckon," Flek assured him. "Otherwise she would not have come to challenge you herself."

By this time, word had passed from mouth to mouth that the king had been fighting against the princess. Even the rebel army was astonished. Worrah knew he had to make the most of this moment. "Faithless girl!" the king condemned in a stentorian voice. "To raise arms against your lawful king. Would you depose me and place yourself in my stead? Why such an act of traitorous desperation? Have you forgotten so quickly that you forfeited your crown?"

At these words there were astonished murmurings from both armies. The king turned to speak to the men standing around them.

"Yes, good soldiers and good citizens alike. This very princess, who falsely disguised herself as a man and attacked me so wildly, renounced her crown and claim to the throne, not ten days ago, at the farewell ceremony for the king's champion. She had so little regard for her royal inheritance that she recklessly and foolishly gambled away her crown and all her rights as a ruler of this land. No wonder she comes disguised, hoping to wrest back through deceit and brute force what she desperately and thoughtlessly lost. But you will lose more than your crown by challenging your king," he now addressed Aina. "This will cost you your head."

There was rumbling through the crowd as they disputed questions and possibilities in loud whispers. Then they grew quiet and looked to Aina to see how she would respond.

"I've lost nothing, false king," she spit back at him. "True, I wagered my crown to silence the spiteful tongue of your despised counselor. But I did not bet frivolously nor have I lost my wager. Far from it, I have kept my crown most firmly."

"It is easy to make claims, Princess," the king scoffed. "But we see no proof here. You come disguised, dressed in his armor. What further proof do we need that he is dead? Produce your champion. Let him step forward and show himself if he is still among the quick and the living. That was the bet, after all, wasn't it? That your champion would outlast all previous champions. In fact, you wagered that this champion would even survive and return from his battle with the dragon, did you not? What a ridiculous thing to believe, to imagine that anyone could battle a dragon and survive."

"You don't have to imagine it," Aina declared. "You have only to see it with your own eyes and then you will believe." So speaking and with a sweep of her arm, she gestured behind the rebel army towards the plain. All heads turned to look. Immediately the shriek of panic rose up, tired arms groped for swords and shields, and there was a general confused call to form protective ranks. For looming behind the rebel army stood a dragon.

"To arms!" cried King Worrah, his eyes wide with terror. His army was already recoiling from the sight of a dragon so close to them. If they could, they would have clambered up the canyon walls to escape. The rebel army, on the other hand, did not stir or show the slightest unease.

"Peace!" Aina called out. "All of you, peace, I cry. Be still and hear my voice!" At first she was drowned out by the astonished, fearful cries of the soldiers. But as there was nowhere for them to run, they girded themselves for what they feared was an inevitable attack and grew grimly silent.

"Hear me!" Aina called out loudly, gesturing to get their attention. When they saw that the dragon did not stir, they turned to hear her speak. "The dragon will do you no harm as long as you do not raise arms against it. It comes with a message for the king. Be still, I pray, and let that message be delivered."

At these words, all eyes watched as the dragon began to walk through the space provided between the divided rebel army.

"Witch!" Worrah flung at Aina. "Like your grandmother before you."

Up the dragon walked, carefully, intently, towards the king. Worrah cowered there, firmly gripping his sword, fearful of treachery and sudden attack. Flek stood by his side, clutching his spear, eyeing the dragon. Then an astonished look of recognition crossed his face.

The dragon halted when it came to within a stone's throw of the king. Then, to everyone's amazement, the dragon spoke. "Your time has come, o king. This is the end of your miserable rule through fear and force. Lay down your arms and flee with your life—or die."

Flek knew that voice, and it was not coming from the dragon. Overwhelmed by the sudden appearance of the dreaded beast, he had not noticed the man riding on the dragon's neck. "You, again," he growled, recognizing him. "You have more lives than a cat."

Flek stepped over to Worrah and grabbed his arm to get his attention. "That's not the dragon speaking," he hissed into his ear.

"What? Who then?"

"Gaze upon the beast's neck. You'll see him there." Dressed in his leather traveling clothes, Michael sat upon Star's neck.

"Unbelievable!" Worrah gasped. "How is he alive?"

· ✦ .˙✦ * * ✦ ✦ ✦ ✦· · ✦ .˙✦ * * ✦ ✦ ✦·

"This is a desperate plan," Star had warned him earlier in the day before the battle had begun.

"It is the best we can devise," the knight had answered. "I am still too weak from our battle to challenge the king. Our army is too small and untrained to defeat the king's forces."

"Yet why send the maiden? I know she can be fierce. She was willing to attack me single-handed. But she was throwing her life away, and she accepted her fate. There is no need for that here."

"This is Aina's wish," Michael explained. "The king is a usurper. He has brought suffering to her land and her people, and she blames him for the death of her mother. She is well trained in the ways of arms. I have fought against her myself and can attest that she is a formidable opponent. She has every chance of defeating the king, and she demands her revenge."

"And if she fails?" Star asked.

"If she cannot defeat him, you and I will have to make an appearance. It will also be the only way to save her life."

"I agree with all you say," Star nodded. "It is a bold plan, and nothing less than boldness will succeed here. But you are aware that if they attack me, I shall retaliate. I will return kindness with kindness, but also force with force. It is my nature and I cannot overcome my nature. I will once again return to my wild state. I will destroy both armies in the end, and you most likely with them. You will not be alive to tame my heart again. What will be the gain of that?"

"Star, I have no intention of letting them attack you," the knight responded. "You are too dear to me for that. At the first hint of any hostility, I will have you out of there. But I still live by the advice you gave me when you were training me."

"Do the unexpected," Star said solemnly.

"And taking a Luck Dragon into battle is the most unexpected action that occurs to me. Besides, why should you suddenly not bring me luck? You have never failed me before." At this, the sound of chimes, the dragon's laughter, filled the air.

·✱.˙✱ * ✱ ₊ ✱ * ✱·   ·✱.˙✱ * ✱ ₊ ✱ * ✱·

Now, sitting upon the dragon's neck, glaring down at the king, Michael was even more confident. Even though Worrah had spotted him, the effect was what he had hoped for. The king was pale with fright. His army looked ready to bolt. This desperate plan might work after all.

"Lay down your arms, Worrah," he commanded. "Fleeing with your life is more than you deserve. You have ruled your land with a harsh and cruel hand. You have driven good and loyal citizens into exile. You have sent brave men to certain death. And all for what? So that you and the nobles can continue to feast off the fat of the land while the people are kept at the edge of poverty. Shame on you, for your self-serving life. As a king, you have an obligation to lead your people in peace and prosperity and to defend them against the aggression of foreign kings. Instead you rule with fear and hunger. You cultivated a wild dragon to terrorize the people into following your misguided lead. Be gone, I say, before I set the dragon against you."

Many in the king's army were already laying down their arms, ready to believe that their safety from the feared dragon depended upon their turning away from the battle.

Worrah was also wavering. He knew defeat when he faced it. Somehow, this king's champion had not only survived his battle with the dragon, he also had some mysterious command over it. Whether it was witchcraft or not, he did not have the power to combat it. He was already weaving a plan in his mind how he could escape to a neighboring kingdom, raise forces, and return to take back the throne by strength of arms. He knew he had enough support among the nobility to succeed.

Only Flek looked undisturbed. The whole time that Michael had been speaking, he had been studying the dragon. Convinced that he was not mistaken, he now stepped in front of the king. "I don't know how you managed it, Dung Boy. You were always a clever one," he sneered. "Much too clever for your own good. It got you thrown out of the one home you ever had, you wretched orphan. What did you do with Scorch, dung boy? I know you could not have ever defeated him. Is he still prowling around the forests somewhere? And where you found Star and how you got him to come here, I'll never guess. Did he convince Scorch to move on? Never mind, I don't even care for the answer."

He paused and looked around to see what reaction he was causing. The soldiers were listening with rapt attention. The rebel army was fully focused on his words. He cared little for any of them. It was the king he most needed to reach.

"I know dragons!" he declared in a loud voice. "I have always told you that. I know all about dragons. Why? Because I grew up taking care of one. This one, this very one! And I know that this dragon will no more attack you than a grasshopper will. I know because I made his comfy bed up for him every day. This dragon is tamer than a lap dog. At least a lap dog will show its teeth if you threaten it. Why this one even has teeth at all is a mystery I'll never understand. They serve no purpose, neither for eating or defense."

Flek was delighted with what he now saw. Soldiers were picking up their arms again. Michael had a surprised look on his face. And best of all, Worrah no longer looked like he was ready to run. He paused a moment to show the king with a subtle motion of his head what he had noticed in the distant plain behind the rebel army.

"Dust," Worrah muttered. "There's an army on the move."

"What did she promise you, dung boy?" Flek directed his gaze at the knight. "Did she promise to make you a prince? Did she offer you lands? Maybe she said she would make you her king. What a joke! You've spent your life being a pretender, fooling others into thinking you deserve to have what others have earned. But the truth will always stick to you like dirt. You were raised an orphan in the gutter, an orphan because no one wanted you. Here you are, a nobody, making yourself big and important. Well, we've all noticed you! But what we see is the dung of the gutter still sticking to your clothes."

Flek's words shot home and Michael was stung by them. A grimace passed over his face.

"Promises are cheap," Flek yelled up at him. "And so are your threats. Get you gone! And get your imitation of a dragon out of here. I always told you he was a useless pile of scales. Get you gone before I take a stick to you!" And so speaking, he picked up a stone and threw it hard towards the knight and the dragon.

His aim was better than he could have hoped for. Distracted by Flek's words, the knight did not even see it coming until it was too late to dodge out of the way. The stone hit him squarely in the chest and the force of the blow nearly unseated him. The leathern clothing gave him some protection, but he was stunned and had the breath knocked out of him. He grabbed at Star's horns to keep from falling.

Aina was ready. She had also noticed the dust of the approaching army and knew that she did not have a moment to lose. She raised her sword high, her black hair flying about her head. "Citizens, arise and attack! Follow me!" And with these words, she charged at the king, intending to renew her battle with him, determined not to let him escape or issue further orders.

With a cry as if from one voice, the rebel army was on its feet and charging forward to follow their princess. They would not let her rush into battle without them. The cries of, "Aina! To Aina!" filled the air.

Flek had also not hesitated. A moment after throwing his stone at the dragon, he snatched up his spear with both hands and swiveling on his foot, stepped in front of Aina as she charged the king. Her momentum and the point of the spear did the rest. Flek had only to hold on to the shaft firmly. Aina crumpled to the ground clutching at the wooden haft of the spear. It happened as quickly as a breath is released.

Seeing Aina fall, a great cry of despair rang out from the throats of the rebel army. They were incensed and enraged to see their princess impaled by Flek's hands. Instead of giving up the battle, as Flek had hoped, they were maddened to even greater passion and anger. The army charged as one man towards the front line of the king's forces. Flek immediately disappeared behind a wall of armed men. The warriors from the fighter's compound which Flek had so carefully placed around Aina's battle with the king now closed around him, sealing him off from any attack from the rebel army.

Seeing Aina fall, the king raised his sword high. "Victory is ours today! See," he cried pointing out over the plain. "Our allies have arrived. Double wages for every man with blood on his sword! Charge!" Worrah led his soldiers with a crashing ring of swords, shields and splatter of blood against the front line of the enemy. Once again, the air was filled with the cries of fury and pain.

All this time, Michael had been desperately guiding Star away from the armies. It had been a stroke of luck that the stone Flek had thrown had not struck the dragon. Had it struck Star, there would have been little chance for him to calm the dragon once he mirrored Flek's scorn and hatred. With what little breath he had left, Michael was whispering his enduring love into Star's ear and begging him to take them both to safety. He glanced back for just a moment, and what he saw turned his blood to ice, choking the little breath he had out of his throat. He saw the moment Aina crumpled to the ground clutching the haft of the spear. Every ounce of his being cried to go to her, but he knew that doing so would bring utter disaster upon them all. He had no choice but to guide Star away from the battle. Tears of frustration, fear and pain sprang forth from his eyes. "Star," he wept, "o my beloved, take us away from here. Quickly."

With a great heave, Star was suddenly airborne. Through the blur of his tears, Michael saw the army grow smaller below him. He saw the empty plain behind the warring forces. He saw galloping horses carrying riders with swords drawn, rushing to join the battle. The flowing white hair of one figure in their lead caught his attention for just a moment. But his mind was growing numb with the pain in his chest and the pain of his loss. He heard Star bellow an ear-splitting roar, and he knew that he had been too slow in getting him out of there. Star was once again wild. Then all went dark.

Chapter Twenty-Three

The Commander from Nogardia

*A*h! I think he has decided to come back to us. Go and tell the others." It was a deep sonorous voice that he knew well. In fact, it was a voice he had known his whole life, though he had not heard it often. It was a voice connected to everything good that had ever happened to him. It was a voice worth returning to, after the troubled dreams that he had been having. "Well, my knight, are you ready to face the consequences of your decisions?"

Michael's eyes shot open at this question. He was not prepared for the strong light around him, although he lay in a shaded place. He blinked his eyes and the tears running down his cheeks brought back his last painful memories: Aina falling at Flek's hands, a hostile force overtaking the rebel army from behind, and the greatest disaster—Star going wild once again. He wiped his eyes on a sleeve to clear them.

"Aga!" he exclaimed. Beside him sat the old wizard, a look of concern on his face.

"You have left us waiting quite awhile for your return," the wizard said gently. The knight began to raise himself, but half way up the pain in his chest caught him with a gasp. Aga tenderly pushed him back down.

"You're not quite ready to spring back to action," he said with a smile. "But it's all right to rest. Your services won't be needed for awhile."

"Aga," Michael gazed upon him with astonishment. "Where did you come from? What are you doing here?"

"Well, my fearless knight," the old man said with a chuckle, "that is the art of a wizard, is it not? To be in the right place at the right time. And once I have arrived, I must help things happen. I'm happy to say that I didn't botch anything up this time. I will be the first to admit that I've made some pretty messes in my day." Again the old man chuckled. These words brought Michael away from his astonishment at seeing the wizard and back to the memory of the battle.

"Oh, Aga, I've ruined everything," he moaned, and began to count off his pain. "I led the rebel forces into an indefensible position. We trapped the king's army but we had no way to contain it. And Aina, I failed her completely. And now I've lost her! I should never have agreed to let her fight against the king. But I was too weak after my battle with Scorch. And Aga, Scorch wasn't Scorch, but Star, my own beloved Star, and I took him in among the armies and I promised him I would get him out in time, but when he saw the third army bearing down on the battle the wildness overcame him. I heard him. I don't know why I'm even alive. I have to go and find him and tame him again. I can't leave him wild again."

Aga had let the knight rattle on until, out of breath, he ended with a choked-off sob. When Michael tried to get up again, the wizard gently, yet firmly, pushed him back down. Michael was in such distress, he buried his face in his hands.

"I guess you just have to let it all come out, first," Aga said. "And then maybe you'll be still enough to give me your attention. Take a look at this." He held something up in his hands. It looked like a dirty-brown piece of cloth, though it had a stiffness to it unlike normal fabric.

"What's that?" Michael asked.

"Take it and you tell me," the wizard said, offering it to him. "I believe you are far more familiar with it than I am."

Michael took the material and stared at it. It was not cloth at all. It was a large piece of skin, skin covered with scales. It had a slit in the middle of it.

"Scorch's skin," he gasped, now recognizing it. He felt the edges of the slit. "This was the piece..." and his voice trailed off, frightened of stirring hopes that would be dashed.

"That's right," Aga continued for him. "This was the piece of skin that Scorch sloughed off. You had Star use his talons to cut it to size, didn't you? Nothing else could penetrate it. You had him cut a slit in the middle so it could fit over someone's head. Do you remember who you gave it to?"

"I made Aina wear it underneath my armor," he said excitedly. "I insisted that she use it as an extra layer of protection. Does this mean...? But I saw her fall."

"Without this to protect her, no doubt, the spear would have passed through her body. It certainly broke through your armor. But the point could not penetrate the dragon's skin. She fell to the ground because the wind had been thoroughly knocked out of her."

"Then, she's alive?" the knight asked, once again trying to rise from where he lay. "I must see her."

"All in good time," Aga said, keeping a firm hand on his shoulder. "She was badly bruised by the blow. Star has been tending to her, much as he probably did to you after your battle with Scorch. I am confident that she is in the best of care. You will be able to question him thoroughly, once you are up."

"Star? Star is here? How is that possible? When he saw the approaching army, I heard him roar. You mean he's not gone wild?"

"Not in the least, my friend. What you heard was not the roar of an enraged dragon. You heard the joyful call of greeting to old friends. You disappoint me, gallant knight. I thought you knew the language of dragons. Have you been fooling me all these years?" Aga had a big smile and Michael knew that he was being teased.

"Then the army—they weren't the allies of the king? You mean, they came in time?"

"Indeed we did."

"Then that was you at their lead," he said, remembering the figure with the flowing white hair.

"That was me," the wizard confirmed, "although I usually try to avoid battles. They are nasty, unnecessary things and I find them completely distasteful. This one, however, I did not think I should miss. The rout was rather spectacular, if I do say so myself. I'm sorry you missed it. I'm sure you would have appreciated all the finer points."

At that moment, a boy approached carrying a tray with a pitcher and two goblets. He hesitated at the edge of the shade the tree provided.

"Ah," the wizard said seeing him. "Approach young squire. I see you bring refreshments."

"Sounder!" Michael exclaimed.

"Here you are, sire," the boy said, placing the tray on the ground beside the wizard. Aga patted a spot on the bed, and Sounder sat down. Aga poured a drink for the knight and handed it to him. Then he poured one for himself. Michael was grateful to wash away the dryness in his throat.

"Master Sounder has spent every moment by your side since Star brought you back," Aga explained. "He is very devoted to you."

Michael looked at the boy and a weak smile crossed his face. "I am glad to see that you've recovered from your ride."

"I think I have taxed you enough for the moment," Aga said. "I leave you in Master Sounder's good care to make sure that you stay put until I return." So speaking he lifted himself lightly to his feet and strode away.

Sounder was staring at the knight with unabashed adoration. Michael recognized the look and could barely keep himself from laughing out loud.

"Well, say it already. You are obviously bursting with something."

"You have a dragon," the boy sighed.

"Are you not afraid of him?" the knight asked in a threatening voice. "He's big, boy, as big as a mountain on the move."

"He's beautiful," the boy sighed. "And he does whatever you want."

Michael had to laugh. He was reminded of when he was a boy no bigger than this one and his first meeting with Garth, the Dragon Master at the compound in Nogardia. He had spoken to Garth as incoherently and love-struck as this boy.

"So you don't like my horse any more?" Michael teased.

"Oh, sire," the boy said perking up, "don't get me wrong. Storm is the most wonderful horse any man or boy could ever wish to ride. She never tires, she's smart, she's fast and I don't think I stayed in the saddle as much as she kept me in the saddle. No, sire, Storm is the finest of horses. The longer I rode her, the more amazed I was at how much horse she is. But Star, well, Star is, I mean, do you think you could let me ride him?"

Michael's chuckle was cut short by the pain in his chest. "Who knows? Perhaps we can work something out. But first tell me how your ride on Storm went. You found Nogardia? That's amazing in itself. How did you get them to listen to you?"

"No, sire, I never did make it to Nogardia. And it was a good thing, too. For if I had made it, and had to convince them to come, they would never have made it here in time. And they came in the very nick of time, they did. It was a wonder to see."

"Hold on a second," Michael stopped him. "If you never made it to Nogardia, who came to our aid?"

"The very ones, sire," Sounder said with wide eyes. "But I never had anything to do with it."

"Now you're confusing me, boy. Go slowly and tell me things by degree."

"It was like this," Sounder explained. "I stole away on Storm like you told me to. And no one ever followed after me. Or if they did, then Storm outran them. And I never saw no one along the whole way, except maybe some people working their fields. I followed the way you told me, sire. I let the evening star guide me. It was bright in the late-day sky and at night, after it set, I used the belt of the Great Hunter to show me the way, just as you told me to. But mostly I just let Storm find her way. I slept on her back, and when I did she trotted easy so I wouldn't fall off, and I could only hope she knew better than me which way to go.

"Then on the third day, we were following a road and we came to a crossing. I didn't know which way, and Storm seemed undecided, too. Or maybe she was distracted. An old man was sitting there on his horse, not going anywhere, just sitting there, like waiting for someone. Storm went up and nuzzled his horse. I asked him if he knew the way to Nogardia. And then he did something amazing. He greeted Storm by name, he did, I don't know how he knew her and she acted like she knew him, and he asked me more questions than I was able to ask him. Then he muttered something like, 'Now I understand why I've been standing around waiting at these crossroads like an old fool.' He told me he'd take care of the rest and that I had to return posthaste to you and tell you that they were coming. He even spoke of you by name and said you probably had the dragon with you and that he would hurry."

The boy was out of breath after giving this history. Michael offered him a drink from his goblet, and the boy gratefully took several gulps. "He knew everything so well, I had to believe him," he concluded.

"And it was a good thing you did," Michael said.

Suddenly Sounder jumped to his feet. "Oh, sire, forgive me. I've been chattering away so much I've forgotten to do my duty."

"What have you left undone? You have performed a deed at your young age that bards will sing about as long as there is memory. They will call it 'The Ride of Sound-the-Alarm.' It will be part of every campfire entertainment from here to the mountains."

At these words Sounder blushed a deep red. "Nay, sire, I mean not that. I promised to tell the commander of the forces as soon as you were awake. He wishes most urgently to speak with you."

"Do you mean Will?"

"Nay, sire, not our forces. But the forces we summoned. The ones you sent me to go and seek. The ones the old man brought."

Michael drew a deep breath. Sounder meant the commander of the troops from Nogardia. It was one thing to try and summon them. It was a rash act, but the only gamble he had. Now that they had come, and the battle was over, he had to face them and thank them for riding to his aid. He had left Nogardia years before as a young man distressed and in disgrace. He had violated the strictest rule of the Dragon Compound, and he had been banished for his transgression. Did they know who it was they had come to save? What would they think? Would he know any of their captains? After all, he had grown up among the children of the nobility. By right of birth and training, they would be the very ones who would have taken on the leading roles in the army and the realm. Were any of his friends still there, or had they, like Flek, moved on to find their own fortunes?

He had no choice but to face them. "I had much preferred to seek out Aina," Michael muttered.

"He said he would take you to her," the boy said cheerily.

"Who?" Michael asked, startled at the boy's answer to his comment.

"Why, their commander, of course," the boy said. "But he wants to greet you first."

"Well, in that case, we shouldn't keep him waiting," Michael said, resigned. "Boy, help me to my feet. It is only fitting that I receive him standing."

With some effort Sounder helped Michael to stand up. The knight held onto the boy's shoulder until his light-headedness passed. He took a deep breath and felt the soreness in his chest where the stone had hit him. "All right, Sounder, I'm ready. Go and fetch him."

Sounder looked to make sure that Michael was not about to keel over, and then he ran off. The knight took this moment to get his bearings. He had been lying in the shade of a clump of trees. Looking around, he saw many horses grazing not far way. The smoke from numerous campfires rose off to his right beyond other trees. He saw many figures walking, but too far distant to tell who they were. Star was nowhere to be seen.

Sounder came running back. "He's coming, sire," he said, breathless. Michael placed his hand onto Sounder's shoulder again to steady himself. The boy craned his head to look up at him. "Are you troubled, sire?"

Michael laughed bitterly. "Does it show?"

"You're shaking, sire. Perhaps it is your wound? Should I tell him not to come? He was so looking forward to speaking with you."

"No," the knight said with a shake of his head. "Let's get this over with. And there is no reason for you to hold me up to do this. Sounder, I want you to take the pitcher and return with it full and bring a goblet for the commander of the army."

"Yes, sire," Sounder said. He snatched up the empty pitcher and bounded away. He passed the commander of the army as he was coming around the trees. Sounder saw that he had a big smile on his face. Then from behind him he heard a cry of surprise. He did not stop to find out what had happened. He hurried off so he could return all the sooner.

Sounder had to walk slowly coming back with the pitcher. He did not want to spill anything or drop the second goblet. When he came around the trees into the small grove where Michael had been cared for, he saw the two men sitting on the ground knee to knee. When he came closer, he was astonished to see that both men had been weeping. He stood before them holding the pitcher.

"Sire, is all well?" he asked concerned. "Should I call for help?"

"Drink is all we need," Michael exclaimed, wiping the tears that continued to fall freely from his eyes. "See and learn, young squire," Michael said to him. "See men cry. Although we may hold back tears when we are in pain, in joy we can let them flow freely. Come, squire, fill our cups to match the fullness in our hearts."

As Sounder poured from the pitcher he glanced from face to face. Both men looked as pleased as if something treasured had been returned to them that had been long lost.

"Let me introduce my friend to you," the knight said. "Master Sound-the-Alarm, this is Colin, the commander of the king's army. And a finer, more faithful friend I could not find anywhere."

"You know each other, sire?" Sounder asked amazed.

"We grew up together," Colin now spoke.

"And when all things went against me, I still had at least one friend," Michael added.

"Two," Colin corrected. "Alis always believed in you. She loved you as dearly as she loved me. After you left she spoke up in your defense even to our parents."

"Dear Alis," the knight said nodding his head. "Oh, how I sometimes ache for the carefree days we spent together. And here we are so many years later and so many adventures behind us."

"From all I've heard, my life has been boring compared to yours. But are you not at least a little surprised to find me here in this position?"

"A little is an understatement," Michael laughed. "I must admit that I never thought of you as joining the army, let alone leading it. I always thought you would follow in your father's footsteps and become an ambassador for the king."

"So did my father also believe," Colin pointed out. "It was not easy to disappoint him. To make things worse, Alis used to tease me, saying I'd never make a knight. Maybe that spurred me on even more to try harder. You were an inspiration to me. After you left, I devoted myself to working with arms. I didn't have a dragon to train me, but there were plenty of other good teachers around."

"You knew about that?" Michael asked astonished.

"Rumors got around, and the rest we guessed. You know, once Star left, we had to find some means of defending ourselves against warlords like Malvise. He never returned, but there have been others. Without a dragon, Nogardia was suddenly in need of guarding. More than once there were bitter grumblings from those who knew you that it was a big mistake to drive you away. You were the very thing we needed after Star left. So some of us decided to take your place. Before I knew it, I was assigned to keep the soldiers in defensive shape. After that, I took over as commander of the army. When Aga brought your call for help, I was so happy to hear from you, we set out immediately.

"Here," he said, pulling a piece of clothing out of a bag he had slung over his shoulder. "I have something from Alis. She sends this to you." It was a tunic bearing the sign of the dragon. "It was one of yours when you lived in the compound," Colin explained. "She kept it for you all these years. Typical thing a girl would do, sentimental and all. She held out the hope that someday she'd be able to return it to you. She would have loved to come as well."

"Is she well and happy?"

"She is very busy, you know." Then Colin slapped his forehead. "Of course, there's no way for you to know this. Alis married King Pell's son. Alis is the Queen. Don't tell anyone I said so, but having the queen for a twin sister did make it a bit easier to get assigned as commander of the army."

"King Pell's son is now king?" Michael was astonished. "Did he ever spend time in the compound? Did you know him?"

"He was there together with us," Colin said smiling. "You knew him, too. Didn't you know? Well, of course, when you came we all had known each other since we were born. And he wasn't the type to introduce himself to you like, 'Hello, I'm going to be king one day.' "

Both men laughed. Sounder sat there, his mouth hanging open in astonishment, listening to the conversation between the two friends.

"He didn't like anyone making a big deal out of it," Colin continued. "We were all just kids anyway, and the kings of Nogardia have a tradition of making sure their children are treated the same as the others. He was never the type to brag about anything. I think that's one of his best qualities as king. Anyway, that's another reason why Flek stayed away from us and never gave you a hard time when he was around. Flek knew who his rivals for the crown were, and every day there was the boy first in line right in front of his nose."

"Well, are you going to tell me who it is?"

"Why, Frog, of course."

"Frog?"

"Well, we don't call him that any more, you know. At least, not in public. Anyway, when Aga came with your message, Frog didn't hesitate a moment. Good thing for you he liked you. He would have come himself, if Alis would have agreed. But she said it was too dangerous. But now I'm baffled. If you didn't know he is king or that I'm in command of the army, how did you know anyone would come at all?"

"It was Star's suggestion," Michael explained. "He was convinced I might have some friends left in Nogardia."

"One or two, as you can imagine. We've never forgotten you. Parents use you as a bedtime story for their children. Particularly for the ones feeling down on their luck. By now there are more legends than truth about what you could do with Star. And it all started before you had been gone even a week. I guess that's what got Mixer going."

"Mixer?" the knight flinched as if he had been slapped.

"Yeah. Mixer was convinced from the beginning that you had been sent off to be a wandering knight. I don't know where he got the idea. But he made plans to join you, and one day he just disappeared and never came back. To this day we don't know what happened to him."

"Mixer did find me," the knight said with obvious pain in his voice. Colin studied his friend's face before responding.

"I can tell there's a story there to be told, and from your bearing, it does not promise to be a happy one. Perhaps by wine tonight you will tell me about our friend. We have long wondered, and his family has a right to know."

"Yes," the knight admitted. "It is best that I tell you. But as you say, let it wait for later."

"Anyway, after Mixer disappeared and not long after that the dragon left, Garth told several of us who had been close to you what really had happened between you and Star. We knew in our hearts that you never endangered the dragon. From that time on, Frog and I made a point of following your exploits."

"How could you?"

"People love to talk and tell tall tales. Whenever visitors came and told stories of a mysterious knight whose shield bore the figure of a dragon, we knew it had to be you. Garth told us what your crest looked like."

"Is Garth still alive?"

"He's as old as the hills and one of the king's most trusted counselors," Colin said with a broad smile. "No one dares go against his advice when he stands his ground. They say he consorts with wizards and knows things before they happen."

"Well, one wizard for certain," Michael commented, looking around as if he expected him to appear at any moment. Then something occurred to him. "Say, I'd nearly forgotten. Young Sounder here told me that you were going to take me to the princess."

"That I am," Colin said, getting to his feet and helping Michael to his. "If you need to, you can lean on me."

As they walked along, Colin pointed out the different camps that had been set up since the end of the battle. "Over there is where we are holding the king's army. Most of them swear they will be loyal to the queen."

"What queen?" Michael interrupted him. "Do you mean Alis?"

"Not at all. I guess I should still call her the princess. But she'll be queen now with Worrah out of the way. It only makes sense, you know. She will be the supreme ruler of her people."

"Of course. I hadn't thought of that, but you're right." For the first time, the full consequences of Worrah's defeat began to dawn on Michael. He heard again in his mind Flek's last words to him: *What did she promise you, Dung Boy? Did she promise to make you her king? What a joke! Raise an orphan out of the gutter, he's still got dung sticking to his clothes. Promises are cheap.*

An intense sadness filled his heart.

Chapter Twenty-Four

Something More and Something Less

*A*h, there he is," Colin pointed, breaking Michael out of his reverie. It was Star standing among some trees. "I had forgotten how beautiful he is. Of course, he still completely ignores me, same as always. But what did I expect?"

Star stood looking down at a man. It appeared to be one of the officers in the army. He looked to be an older man, judging by his grey hair. Michael thought he must be one of the commanders. It struck him as odd that Star was showing him so much attention. Particularly after Colin's reminding him that Star had the habit of ignoring almost everyone who cared for him. And unless he was mistaken, there was a marked tenderness in their encounter. As they came closer, Michael could hardly believe his eyes. Although he had aged, there was no mistaking him. "Mali!"

"Straw!"

The two men embraced and once again Michael's tears flowed. Sounder, who had trailed silently behind, was baffled to see men whom he considered hardened warriors weeping freely. He could only shake his head in disbelief.

"I never thought I'd see him again," Mali was saying, gesturing towards Star. "Or you either, for that matter. I was telling him how much I've missed him. He seems to understand every word I say. Is it true that he can speak?"

Michael was so astonished to see him that he missed his question. "Mali, what are you doing with the army? I hope Colin does not make you swing a sword and face others in battle."

"Mali is my trusted quartermaster," the commander of the army said. "He keeps the troops fed, well-equipped and cared for. Just as he always did for Star. The men love him more than they do me."

"Well, that's understandable," said Mali. "I make sure that their bellies are full three times a day. What do you give them? An opportunity to get themselves killed."

"They are soldiers, after all," Colin said shrugging his shoulders. "I mean, that's their job, isn't it?"

"You have come to see Aina," the dragon broke in, speaking to Michael.

"Ah, the dragon speaks," murmured Colin. "So back to Mali's question. Tell the truth. Do you really understand all that tinkling of bells? That's what Garth told us."

"It's true," the knight explained. "Although I cannot tell you how. It's just something I can do." He paused a moment and looked his friend full in the face. "Oh, Colin, please forgive me that I never told you. I didn't understand it myself at the time. I understand it even less today. I just didn't know where to begin, and everything Star and I did we had to keep anyone from knowing."

"Don't worry about it," Colin said, laying his hand on Michael's shoulder. "I'd have probably thought you had gone crazy. As it was, I already did think you were nuts to willingly take a dragon, all alone, down to the river to scrub every day, for years. It wasn't until later that we found out you were doing something more interesting than splashing in the water. Now, let's go find this princess of yours."

This uncommon party, three men, a boy and a dragon, walked slowly, enjoying one another's company. Michael looked up at the dragon. "Aga told me you have been caring for Aina. Is she seriously hurt?"

"I have done what I can for her, as I did for you following our battle, and I believe she will heal, though it will take time. The spear would have run her through had it not been for the protection of my skin."

"Is there anything else we can do for her?"

"What more there is to do is being done," Star said cryptically.

"Explain," requested the knight.

"There is a woman, well, something other than a woman, something more and something less than a woman, who is also tending to her. My help is general in healing wounds. I believe she has arts that are more specific to a woman."

"Now you are speaking in riddles," Michael protested. "Something other than a woman. Something more and something less than a woman. Whatever are you trying to tell me."

"What an odd conversation," Colin interrupted. "You realize that we are only getting one half of this exchange. If it is a riddle for you, imagine how befuddled we are!" They all laughed.

"Star just told me that there is some woman tending to the princess, but there is some mystery about her he won't reveal."

"Well, we'll soon find out," Mali said. "We have come to where she is resting."

They had been walking across the open field and now came to another grove of trees at the foot of some high cliffs. A line of men was standing guard. As the unusual companions approached, the men stood and raised their weapons. The knight could tell that they were agitated at the approach of the dragon. They eyed him cautiously, watching his every move.

"They are not comfortable around me," Star said. "I will go out of the way so that we don't aggrevate one another." The dragon slipped quietly around the edge of the trees and out of sight. The men on guard relaxed visibly.

When Michael looked at them, he realized with a shock that he knew them all. "Morik! Coop! Pommer! Cole! What are you doing here? The last I saw in battle you were fighting for Worrah." The men from the Warrior's Compound crowded around the knight touching him, slapping him on the back, even bumping him about in their joy to see him again.

"We are warriors, and that was the side we happened to find ourselves on. We make no excuses." Morik explained with shrug of his shoulders. "We're glad to see the queen's champion is back on his feet again. Is it true that you fought that blasted dragon and won?"

"Wait a minute," Michael said. "Don't you mean king's champion?"

"Ah, that's just what we've been calling you," Coop interjected. "She'll be queen now and you're the one that gave her back her rightful crown."

"And we're the queen's guard," Cole said. "And we'll fight any man that gainsays us."

"So be it," several voices cried out.

"We claim our right to stand by the queen and defend her from harm," Morik said, looking ready to single-handedly fight anyone who disagreed with him.

"And the queen has yet to send us away," Pommer added.

Michael looked to Colin for some explanation.

"It's true, what they say," Colin said. "Aina has given permission that they remain on guard around her. And no one has wanted to fight them over that. And they did, after all, prove their faithfulness in battle. If not for them, Aina would have been trampled after she fell. And then there is what happened to the king's counselor."

"Flek!" Michael exclaimed. "I'd completely forgotten him. Where is Flek? And where is the king, for that matter?"

"Well, Flek we can tell you about," Morik answered. "When that great coward ran her through with his spear, we were as one man agreed. We were not going to abandon the princess. She has always been good to us. She hand-picked each one of us out of the training pits, same as she did with you. She treated us with respect and care like a ruler should."

"Not like Worrah did, like a pack of dogs that you can kick and mistreat and send off to die," Cole added.

"And besides," Coop said, "we're fighters and we have sharp eyes for what happens in battle. When Flek speared her, none of us saw the spear come out on the other side. That would have been her death. So although she went down, we weren't convinced that we had lost her."

"We surrounded her to protect her body," Morik continued, "in case there was some chance she could be healed after the battle."

"That's when we realized we had also surrounded Flek," Cole said.

"We could have let him go," Morik said. "But no one was taking a vote. He treated us worse than the king, being the king's tongue and teeth, so to speak. He always treated us as if we were his slaves. If you had been around longer, as some of us have been, you would have seen some of the whippings he handed out. He did it just to instill fear, not because anyone had crossed a line." Michael was reminded of the day Flek cornered him and Aina in an alley of the town with the same intention.

"Anyway," Pommer concluded, "once we saw we also had him in our center, and he had just tried to kill the princess, we knew what we wanted to do with him."

"We made sure our swords came out the other side," Morik said grimly.

"Flek's dead?" Michael said, aghast. He looked to Colin.

"Flek left Nogardia to find his fortune," Colin said. "He threw in his lot with a king so cruel and manipulative that he attracted a wild dragon. He always complained that his native land was too tame and too small for him. I will report to his family that he found the fortune he was seeking, and died in battle fighting for it."

Michael could only shake his head in disbelief. "It is not the end I would have wished him."

"Yet the one he earned," Mali said, placing his hand on the knight's shoulder. "Let it be."

After a moment, Michael seemed to accept the fate his old nemesis had brought down upon himself. "Men," he said looking up, "I am happy to see you. It is fitting that you should serve as the queen's guard. So I ask the guard, may I be permitted to enter into her presence?"

"The way is always open for the queen's champion," Cole said. Banners had been hung on the branches of the trees to form a wall and a door. Members of the queen's guard held them aside to let Michael and the others enter into the grove of trees.

The craftsmen in the army had worked quickly. Aina lay upon a raised bed made from tree branches that had been firmly lashed together. They had sewn two banners together for bedding and filled the space between with soft, fragrant grasses. They had done the same to make pillows. She was asleep, and looked as comfortable as if she were lying in her royal chambers back at court.

Around her bed hovered four ladies-in-waiting. Aga was also among them, gazing down at her. When he saw Michael and the others, he held a finger to his lips to indicate that they should be silent and not wake her.

Colin held onto Michael's sleeve and spoke quietly into his ear. "We will wait outside until you rejoin us." He then herded the others back out the way they had come in. Michael walked over to the bed and stared down at Aina. She looked worn, but there was color in her cheeks, and this gave him hope that she was going to be all right. Aga motioned for Michael to follow him. They walked far enough away among the trees that they could talk without disturbing the sleeper.

"There is someone here who has been waiting to speak with you," Aga said. Michael glanced around, but saw no one else in the grove. "I must prepare you for this," Aga said. "So it will make sense to you."

"Aga, what are you talking about?"

"You know that this world is full of mysteries," Aga began. "After all, you have been trained by a Luck Dragon. What could be more mysterious than that?"

"I don't think there could be much left to surprise me," admitted the knight.

"And yet, let me caution you," warned the wizard. "You have shared in one of the more obvious of the many mysteries of life. After all, how can you overlook a dragon? Once you've seen one, you have no choice but to believe in its existence."

"Aga, what are you getting at?"

"There are much more subtle mysteries that you have no idea about. And they are no less real and no less true." A cold shiver ran up Michael's spine and the hair on his head stood on end.

"There is no end to what we can learn, if we are willing and keep our senses open," Aga continued. "So I want you to be very open to what I am going to show you."

"Is this the something more and something less than a woman that Star was talking about?"

"Her name is Mellifor," Aga said. "She is an elf."

"An elf!" the knight exclaimed. "Elves don't exist."

"Nor do dragons, if you've never seen one before," Aga said with a slight smile. "So call her a nature spirit if you prefer. She is an elemental being with a far more subtle body than any woman. Yet her life forces are far greater. So, indeed, one might say, she is less than a woman and more than a woman."

"So that is what Star was talking about," the knight mused. "What does she want with me? Why is she here?"

"Well, the strange thing is that she and her people are always here, living and supporting what we generally call nature. They just prefer to keep themselves hidden from our sight. They don't care much for human company, and, truth to tell, they don't feel particularly safe in our presence. They spend their time tending the trees, bushes and flowers. Even the simple grasses give them more pleasure than dealing with us. From an elfin point of view, they find us a harsh and uncivilized nation. Not as bad as dwarfs, perhaps, but we seem to have few redeemable qualities."

"Dwarfs?" the knight exclaimed.

"Don't let me distract you. It is an elf that has come to see you."

Michael shook his head in disbelief. "All right, why is she here? What did you call her, Melli-something?"

"Mellifor is her name. And she has come by free will to help Aina for the sake of her grandmother."

"Galifalia?" the knight asked astonished.

"So, I am pleased to hear that the two of you have figured out this unusual connection you have to one another. I feared that if I had told you, neither of you would have believed me."

"Her portrait hangs in the palace," Michael said. "Although she was young when it was painted, the resemblance is still striking. You know, Aga, something happened between Galifalia and Star and everyone always talks about it, but no one has ever told me what their connection was. How did she begin in Gladur Nock and end up in Nogardia?"

"Galifalia actually spent her youth and old age in Nogardia. And where she began her life is another story altogether. As far as her connection to Star, Mellifor could tell you more than I can. I know only bits and pieces of what happened, although I will admit I was the one to introduce Galifalia to the elves. I have heard there is a journal of sorts telling the whole story, written in Galifalia's own hand, that lies locked away and forgotten in the archives of Nogardia. Typical of the Lady that she never told me about it. I was on my way to Nogardia with the intention of finding it when your message came. When I leave here, I will resume my search. Once I find it, I will share with you what it contains. As far as Mellifor is concerned, I know only that she insists on speaking with you before she goes her way again. Are you willing?"

"Of course I'll speak with her. Why wouldn't I? Where is she?"

"I am here," whispered a voice. It had the sound of the wind playing with the leaves in the trees. He could not even tell from which direction it came. Suddenly the scent of flowers filled his nose, as if carried on the breeze from a nearby field. But there was no breeze blowing through the glade. At first Michael thought that Star might be near, since his breath always smelled of flowering trees. But this was a different fragrance, a more earthy smell. The knight looked to the left and right but saw no one. Then he thought he saw something out of the corner of his eye in the deeper shadow of the trees just a few paces away. As he looked more closely, one moment there was nothing, and the next moment there stood a woman.

Her figure was so faint that he could almost see through her. She was dressed in a gown of green, yet at its edges it faded to brighter yellows and oranges, as if she was mirroring the change of foliage in the trees. He approached her slowly, as he might step towards a wild animal, fearful of frightening her away.

"Did you come to help Aina?" he asked.

"I have treated her with herbs that bring healing and health," she said. Michael marveled at her voice, neither human nor animal, with a lilt that transcended music.

"Thank you," he said sincerely. "Will she be all right?"

"She will heal," Mellifor said. "But you must care for her still. The blow was a great shock to her body. Star's healing works best on a man's robust physical nature. My herbs are meant for a woman's more complex and subtle life forces. Aina's body is made to bear children into the world, not bear arms and wounds from battle. Help her to do more of the former and less of the latter."

Michael blushed and laughed in spite of himself. "I'm afraid that won't be up to me." The elf gave him a puzzled look, but he ignored it. "Aga tells me that you knew Galifalia."

"I knew the Lady," she answered.

"I marvel at that, I must say," Michael said. "By your looks, you are younger than Aina." He could not help but admire the smooth lines in her face, her full, flowing hair and the fairy delicacy of her figure.

"We do not age in the way humans do," she said. "This form is but an illusion I provide so you can see me. I knew Galifalia. I was with her on the great adventure."

"The great adventure? I have not heard mention of that before. What great adventure?"

"I have not come to speak with you about what we did together," Mellifor said. "I have stayed to speak with you about something else."

"So Aga told me. What is it you want? I will help you in any way I can."

"They say that you can speak with the dragon," Mellifor said.

"I can."

"Then I wish to ask the dragon a question and that you tell me his response. Will you do that?"

"If Star will answer your question, I will tell you what he says," Michael replied.

"Then let us go to him. This way," she said when he turned to go out past the queen's guard. "Follow me through the trees. He is waiting for us where we can be alone." She walked between the trunks through the glade, but to Michael it was as if her feet never touched the ground. The knight followed and behind him walked Aga.

They came through a tangled mass of bushes, and when the underbrush opened, there stood Star, watching them as they approached. Amazed, Michael looked around and wondered how the dragon had managed to come through the trees that grew close together in all directions.

"You've brought the elfin woman," Star said with the sound of chimes that was his voice. "Is she the one who was with Galifalia when she made her journey?"

"Yes," Michael confirmed. "She says they were together."

"What are her questions?"

Michael turned to Mellifor. She was staring at Star with the same wonderment he had seen before in others facing the dragon for the first time.

"He is so majestic," she sighed. "To think that there are dwarfs, humans and sadly, even elves, who would be willing to rip the heart out of his breast. As if the heart holds some greater magic or nobler truth that the dragon in his wholeness lacks. I will never understand that part of our journey, that any of the nations could believe or seek that."

She stopped speaking and stood gazing at Star. The dragon returned her look as they stood in silence among the trees. After awhile, Star began to purr, and the grove was filled with the music of his chimes. "I wish I could read him as I can a tree," Mellifor said.

"That is why we have speech," Star responded. "Ask what you have come to find out." Michael told the elf what Star had said.

"I want to know about the berries," she replied.

"Were they not returned to you?" Star asked. "And did your people not plant the seeds and did not new trees arise from them?"

When Michael translated for her, she nodded her head. "All that has happened. I have been asked in the name of the elfin nation to thank you."

"If you come but to thank me, why have you not come sooner? Did it take until now to find someone who would approach me? Rarely does the elfin nation appear to humans. Even more rarely do they appear to me."

Mellifor laughed with a sound that running water makes. "We are a people who keep to ourselves. The fact that nature is renewed and you have forests to live in is the sign of our thanks. But today we seek you out because we also had a question, and there is none among us to understand your speech. We had to wait until this one had come," and here she indicated Michael, "who can speak with you.

"What is your question?"

"We are concerned. For now, the balance in nature has been renewed through the gift of the berries. However, even among elves there is greed, stupidity and fear. What if we squander the gift we have and the world once again begins to fade and die? Can we depend that you will be there as before to guard the last seeds until we come to seek them?"

"This was not the first time that the elves succumbed to their weaknesses," Star responded. "And they are the most constant among the three nations. Yes, in some ways, even more steady than the dwarfs who turn tradition into lawfulness. Yet the elfin folk must still learn that it is not always about succeeding. It is also about striving. If we do not strive, there will never be any success. And even our failures bear the seeds of new life. As every tree must one day die, so will every nation one day fade from the earth. Yours will be no exception. What you leave behind will be the fruits of your striving and the promise for the future." When Michael translated, Mellifor looked downcast.

"You do not like my answer," Star said. "Perhaps there is a reason why you cannot speak with me. Perhaps you must strive without any guarantee that your efforts will succeed, or as last time, be rescued from a slow obliteration."

When Mellifor heard what the dragon had to say, she bowed to him. "I will pass on the wisdom of what you have told me, although your words bring no comfort. Before I go, I wish to offer you this intention, that as long as my words are remembered, the elfin nation will not join in a dragon hunt again."

"Even if it save the world?" Star asked.

Michael did not have time to share Star's last words. Mellifor faded before his eyes. A moment later, it was as if she had never been there.

"All right," the knight said, looking from Star to Aga. "What was that all about?"

"I've never quite understood the elves," Star said with a laugh. "All that appearing and disappearing. Maybe that's why I prefer humans. They stay in one spot until they move and they can't even run all that fast."

Michael looked up at Star and put his hands on his hips. "You're not going to tell me, are you?"

"Wouldn't do you any good anyway," Star responded.

Michael now turned on Aga, who had been a silent witness to the whole conversation. "And you?"

"Me?" he said with a shrug of his shoulders. "I'm just an old man, you know."

"You two will drive me to distraction," Michael said and walked back to see if Aina had woken up yet.

Chapter Twenty-Five

The Emissaries

*A*re you certain?" Aina asked.

The tracker glanced at the others sitting in council. They were grim-faced men, not to be trifled with. He hesitated a moment before answering. "Your Highness, this is the best information we have. I believe there is no guile in the report. With a handful of his personal guard, Worrah has made it safely to Warrensfold in the north."

"The king of Warrensfold has long coveted our northern frontier," Aina sighed.

"Then Worrah chose well to retreat to him," Will said. "He hopes to find an ally in the king."

"Thank you, you may go," Aga said with a wave of his hand to the tracker. "You've ridden hard to deliver this news. Go and refresh yourself with food and drink at the fires." The tracker bowed and left the grove where Aina had kept her sick-bed. This space had now become their council room. Will was about to say something, but Aga raised a hand in warning for him to remain silent. The wizard waited until the tracker had left the enclosure before speaking.

"I pray you, all of you, be cautious of speaking either your insights or plans in front of others. Princess, your crown is not yet securely set on your head, and all those who are not devoted to you are, by my reckoning, hedging their bets. They will throw their lot in where they see the most determination and chance of success. It is imperative that we let no plans get into the hands of someone who might be willing to sell them to the highest bidder."

"Aga is right," Will said. "Your Highness, we must return to Gladur Nock as soon as possible to prevent an uprising of the nobility. Those who supported Worrah and profited from him will not be happy with your sitting in his stead."

"And yet I am certain there were many who only endured his rule because their other options were to leave or be disowned by the king," Aina said. "I think we can also count on others who will be swayed by the prevailing winds, as long as their own wealth and position are not severely impacted."

"A coronation!" Colin said brightly. "That will rally the people and the nobility behind you, Your Majesty. It will reassert your position and establish your authority. My forces will escort you home, and I guarantee that at the sight of them, any thought of rebelling against you will be quelled. I will send word back to Nogardia at once. Even if the king can't attend, I know that my sister, Queen Alis, would not miss this for the world."

"My thanks to you, commander. I will never be able to repay the good you have done."

"You already have," Colin responded. "It has been enough to be reunited with old friends and to make new ones."

"Then we are agreed," Aina said. "We will return home in the company of our allies from Nogardia. I will send orders today that preparations are made first for a royal wedding and then a coronation."

"Do you think you are well enough to travel, Your Majesty?" Will asked.

"I feel stronger every day," Aina said. "I can ride a horse again, as long as we travel slowly. Based on everything we have heard, it is important that we put our intentions into action."

"Excellent plan," said Aga clapping his hands together. "Don't you agree, Michael?" He peered at the knight. "You've been strangely quiet. What do you have to say?"

The knight looked uncomfortable, as if some great burden pressed upon him. "Your Majesty," he began, glancing up at Aina, but not making eye-contact. "I have a request to make."

"Speak," she said with a puzzled look on her face. "Are you not excited to move forward with our plans?"

"I am, Your Majesty, but I have someone to care for, and to him I owe my first loyalty." Aina and Will looked confused, but both Aga and Colin knew what Michael was talking about.

"This is about Star," he continued, speaking softly. "It is my responsibility to look after him."

"I see," Aina said. She considered this for a moment before speaking. "Can he not return to Nogardia? Don't you think they would be happy to have him back?"

"Not possible, Your Majesty," Colin responded. "We would indeed welcome Star, but we have already kept this Luck Dragon for a generation. He will never return to our kingdom again. He must live elsewhere. That much we've learned about the habits of dragons."

"Your Majesty," Michael began again, "I said I have a request. I have spoken with Star. He would like to settle here, in your land."

"He already did, once," Aina pointed out, an eyebrow arched.

"That wasn't Star," Michael said quietly.

"We are not dealing with two dragons," Aina remarked.

"Yet, in a way, we are," Michael insisted. "If we can accept that there are two dragons living within one. And both dragons have very different characters. When Star sloughed the skin that saved you from Flek's spear thrust, he also sloughed off Scorch. Have you forgotten that Star offered to deliver you from Worrah and return the crown to your head?"

"Yet he refused to fight. I think that the dragon had very little to do with it all," Aina observed.

"Aina, it depends on how you look at it," Colin interjected. "Let me tell you about the good fortune a Luck Dragon brings. I knew a boy when I was young. He was an orphan living on the streets. Yet he managed to gain entrance into a compound reserved for children of the nobility. He lived there for years keeping a secret that eventually got him sent into exile. Bad luck, wouldn't you say? Not at all! The same hour he left, he was named a knight and wandered the world helping people wherever he went. Then one day, he was captured and thrown into a dungeon. More bad luck, right? Landing in the dungeon, however, led to his being named king's champion. But he was sent off to fight a dragon. What a disaster! Yet instead of suffering a miserable death, he tamed the dragon."

By this time, Aina was laughing, and the men at the table wore big smiles.

"Aina, you are alive and you won your battle against Worrah, but it was not because you had a superior army. Although we arrived in time, it was not because we had a wizard leading the way. It was because you had a Luck Dragon on your side. His workings are subtle, but there is no denying the good fortune he brings. You will never regret having him living in your land. In fact, you will count it as the greatest of your blessings."

"You yourself have said that you can feel the goodness in him," Michael continued.

"I am less worried for myself than for my people," Aina responded with a frown. "In spite of any lingering hesitation I have, I bow to your arguments. You tell me that he even helped heal me from my wound. But he has terrorized my people for years and brought countless sorrows upon them."

"How do the people who lived in exile feel about Star?" Michael asked, turning to Will. "They left their homes because of Scorch. Do they now live in fear and dread that there is a dragon here in the camp?"

"The people left their homes because of the insatiable dragon living in the heart of the king," Will replied somberly. "Since our first encounter with Star, the army has shown a growing awe and trust in him. Your Majesty, I don't think there will be a problem, once your subjects get to know Star."

"Well, then, assuming that's the case, what is the nature of your request?" Aina said turning to Michael.

"I wish to have a Dragon Compound built," he said looking to Colin who smiled and nodded. "I know our friends from Nogardia will help us in the design. And I ask that we keep Star as our honored guest for as long as he wishes to stay. I will recruit a staff to care for him from both the common folk and the nobility. I will make access to Star broader than it was when I grew up. I suspect I already have one devoted scrub boy here in the camp. Helping to look after a dragon will keep him from stealing my horse again." They all laughed, knowing he was talking about Sounder.

"And I propose that I myself act as Dragon Master," Michael continued. "I will insure that he is cared for properly. So that is my request: Build for Star a compound and appoint me as the Dragon Master." After speaking he stared at his hands, unable to meet her eyes.

Aina looked at him, concern creasing her fine features. "Is that all you request? Is there nothing more that you wish from me?"

Michael took a deep breath and looked up. "I will stand beside you as your knight, if you allow me. Your personal guard already calls me the queen's champion. I will live up to that title. In addition, I will train others so that you may never fear for your crown."

Michael was stunned by Aina's furious response. "I don't want you as my knight!" She sprang up and stormed around the glade waving her arms.

The others reacted quickly. "We'll leave you now, Your Majesty," Colin said bowing. He pulled Will by the arm, and the two of them quickly left the enclosure. Michael was also on his feet, following behind Aina. Only Aga sat calmly and watched them both.

"Have you forgotten everything we said to one another after your battle with Scorch?" she yelled at him, tears brimming in her eyes. "The promises we made? The vows we took? Do they have no meaning to you?"

"Aina, we had both just survived what we thought would be certain death," Michael replied. "I am offering to release you from hastily made vows. I want to do the honorable thing."

"I don't want the honorable thing!" Aina cried at him. He was reminded of the day in the forest when she had left him. How had he managed again to say the wrong thing? Aina continued, "I don't want to be released from anything! I meant every word I said to you. I am talking about love, not honor. I want a husband, not a knight!"

Now Michael felt his own heart burst. "Aina. Your Majesty—"

"Don't majesty me!" she cried out. "Marry me!" She ran over to him and pounded him on the chest with her fists. Then she openly wept and he enfolded her with his arms.

"Oh, my beloved Aina," he said softly, his face pressed into her hair. "You are a princess by right of birth. You will soon be queen. I am an orphan. Flek was right when he said that the dirt of the street will always cling to my cloak."

"Flek is dead," she groaned. "Let his twisted words die with him."

"You and I could forget his words. But there will always be others who won't. If you want to hold the crown, you must marry a man of noble birth."

"You are far nobler than any of them," she countered fiercely. "Who of those worthless nobles would have a dragon following his every order?"

"I never give him orders. Star acts of his own free will."

"Why are you arguing with me?" she cried. "You can be king."

"Aina, the nobles will bow now, but sooner or later, they will begin to grumble that I am a pretender. And worse, they will reject any child that I might father. As your knight, I can strengthen your crown. As your king, I will weaken it."

At that moment, a guard slipped through the makeshift door and stood sheepishly at the entrance, staring at the ground, waiting to be acknowledged. "Your Highness," he said in a cautious voice.

"Not now!" Aina barked at him.

"Your Highness," he repeated, determined to deliver his message. "Emissaries, Your Highness. They wish you see you immediately."

"Emissaries?" she roared. "From the king of Warrensfold? Already?"

"No, Your Highness," the guard said. "I'm not sure where they've come from. They spoke of a King Radabinth."

"Excellent," Aga said springing to his feet. "I thought they'd never get here. Or find us, for that matter. Thank Star for that. Send them in at once and have refreshments brought as well." The guard bowed and left. "Never underestimate the attractive forces of a Luck Dragon," Aga said with a broad smile. Aina and Michael stared at him bewildered and confused.

"Come, come, wipe your faces," he said, handing Aina a handkerchief that he pulled out of a bag by his side. "It is not fitting for the royal pair to be caught weeping," he added with a gesture to the handkerchief. Aina stared at it. It was a piece of dark blue cloth, ornately embroidered all over with golden stars.

"This is the royal crest of the women of my house," she said with astonishment. "How did you—?"

"Not just of the women," Aga pointed out. "I thought you had figured that out already. Have you not seen the piece that Michael carries with him? You haven't lost it, I hope," he said to Michael, raising an accusing eyebrow.

"But it wasn't mine," the knight said. "I have carried it all my life because it was all I had from Galifalia. To remember her. She used it for a headscarf."

"Yes," Aga agreed. "She had her own. But what you could not know, and she obviously never told you, is that when I brought you to her, one of the blankets you were wrapped in was also so adorned."

"You brought me to her? *You*?"

"You were never an orphan, not really," Aga said with sadness in his eyes. "I was entrusted with delivering you to the only relative you had living in Nogardia. That was Galifalia. Don't look so astonished. Of course, it was me. How do you think I knew your name? Have you forgotten the day I gave it back to you?"

"Aga, what are you telling me?"

"I am rather unsuccessfully trying to unravel events that have long been concealed from you," he said laughing. Then he grew serious. "Michael, you are born of a royal house. And not just any house. As Star must have told you when you were still a boy, you are descended from the ancient race of the Dragon Keepers. You are born from that royal house."

"But I was an orphan!" Michael protested.

"By design," Aga countered.

"They purposely set me out?"

"We purposely sent you away," a voice spoke. The three of them turned to see the speaker. Two men dressed in long scarlet robes stood at the entrance to the grove. Their heads were covered by felt hats. Their brown, bearded faces were creased with lines as if they had spent their lives squinting in the sun.

"Of course, I shouldn't say that we sent you away," the man spoke again. "I was but a young man at the time and not part of such a weighty decision. But our people, by one accord, did agree to it."

"But why?" Michael asked.

"For much the same reason as we sent the Lady Galifalia away," he responded. "To seed the world."

"And to catch a dragon, of course," the other now spoke. "That was our primary goal. May we enter?"

Aina and Michael wiped their faces on their sleeves, Aga sent for drink, and the five of them sat down where the council had been before.

"Allow us to introduce ourselves," one of the men began. "We are emissaries from the Valley in the Mountain. It is not a very enchanting, name, I admit, but it is what we have always called our home. It is a temperate fertile valley nestled at the feet of high, snow-capped peaks. It is quite a delightful place when you get to know it." He paused a moment. His smile was disarming. "I am Rugo and this is Millem. We received word, sent by our trusted friend and counselor Aga here, that Star had been tamed again. We have been traveling for nearly two moons."

Michael looked at Aga suspiciously. "How did you know more than two moons ago that I was going to tame Scorch?"

"I must admit that I jumped to some conclusions," Aga said with a shrug of his shoulders. "I acted the moment the rumor reached me that you had entered the fighting pits. Your arrival caused a lot of stir, and people were already talking about your potential. I just deduced what would happen next. It was only a guess, I know, but a well-founded one, wouldn't you agree?"

"And what if I hadn't succeeded?" Michael asked.

"Then they would have made the trip in vain," Aga said and smiled innocently. "So it was a good thing you came through."

"We have come to help with the ceremony," Rugo continued, "of settling Star into his new home. Of course, with you here, we will not have to stay very long. But we are here in case there are any issues to be clarified."

"Slow down," Michael said with a raised hand. "Who are you people?"

"As we said," Millem answered, "we are from the Valley in the Mountain. We serve King Radabinth as his emissaries."

"We are the remnant of the Dragon Keepers," Rugo added.

"You can talk with the dragon?" Michael asked astonished.

"No, only members of the royal house can do that," Rugo explained.

"So, are you telling me that I am of the royal house?"

"Look at the color of your skin. You are browner than the people living here. You do not descend from this folk." As if to prove his point, Rugo pulled up the sleeve of his tunic exposing his own brown arm.

"And can you understand the dragon's speech?" Millem asked.

"I can," Michael said.

"Then, yes, you are of the royal house."

"And Galifalia?"

"As we said, both of you were sent out into the world."

"But why?"

"As long as there are dragons, we need those who understand them. The time will come too soon when dragon lore is completely lost and dragons will disappear simply because no one understands them any longer. We are trying to forestall that day. Every generation a dragon, in this case Star, spends a period of time as a Luck Dragon, blessing the land of some happy, fortunate kingdom. Then there is the unavoidable period when he goes wild. We send someone who will be able to tame him. It is essential not to leave him wild for too long a time. Nothing good can come of it."

Millem continued, "Galifalia tamed Star in fulfillment of an ancient prophecy that renewed the elemental beings that benefit all of us. You, Michael, tamed the dragon when your time came. Your battle will be spoken of for generations. It has great meaning that instead of defeating the dragon, you were defeated, and then you tamed him. "

Michael's head swam trying to understand what they were telling him. He had to start with the riddle of his birth. "But why send me out as an orphan? And I've been told that Galifalia was one as well."

"We have not found a way to avoid it," Millem responded. "If a member of the royal house went out in the world with the intention of taming a dragon, it would most likely never happen. Something would get in the way. We have tried it and lost too many fine men and women. And the result is that the dragon remains wild for much too long."

"For some reason," Rugo added," it works best if you know nothing about what you have to accomplish. Your own natural, strong love for the dragon will attract you to him and will lead you to do what is right. It worked for the Lady Galifalia. It appears to have worked for you."

"Are you saying that Galifalia could also speak with Star?" Michael asked.

"Of course not," Rugo said. "She's a woman."

"Well, what's that supposed to mean?" Aina said, offended.

"You are related to Galifalia, are you not?" Millem asked.

"She was my grandmother," Aina said.

"And can you understand the dragon's speech?"

"Not a word," she admitted with a shake of her head.

"Yet you understand the dragon's heart, do you not?"

She hesitated before answering. "I feel a strong kinship with Star. But I thought it was because of my love for Michael."

"Even without Michael, you would feel that connection. The women of your royal house have the heart connection with dragons. The ability to speak with the dragon is carried through the mother's blood line and men connect with him through speech. It is strange, but we have grown to accept it."

"Is not yours the land that was plagued by the wild dragon?" Millem asked. When Aina silently nodded, he continued. "And what were your feelings about the dragon?"

Aina hesitated. She looked embarrassed, and finally stood up and paced. "I hated him," she admitted. "I wanted nothing more than to see him driven away."

"And yet?" Rugo prompted.

"I was fascinated by him," she admitted. A cascade of words followed. "I would have gone to fight him myself, if they had let me. I would sneak off to get a glimpse of him. I thought of him day and night. He stirred something in my heart I cannot explain. I was angry at him that he was so large and powerful and yet he only did things for himself, and never helped others. I started the warrior training so that those going off to fight him might have a chance and not just be offered as sacrifice. I began bringing food to the poor quarters of the town because I had to do the good that he wasn't doing. Oh, my, I never thought of this before. Everything I did was prompted by the dragon, because of the dragon. Isn't that the way everyone felt?"

"The king's reaction to the dragon was to become more ruthless, greedy and cruel," Aga pointed out. "You became more kind, caring and compassionate."

"Once," Michael recalled, "when we were talking about Scorch, you became angry and said that he just shouldn't be acting this way. I had no idea what you were talking about, but I think you were feeling the true nature of his heart."

"I am grateful for what you have told us," Aga said to the emissaries. "I have always wondered why Gali could not speak with Star. I had wondered if she had been a fluke and had not come from the Valley in the Mountain. I had never heard about this aspect before."

"Yet she was able to tame him, did she not?"

"Indeed, she did. Star was devoted to her all her life."

"She carried the connection with Star quite strongly. She was the daughter of the king and queen. Normally, we do not send out the children of the royal pair, and we much prefer to send boys out than girls. But she was born in a time when there were few other children, and those who were of the right age were sickly. It was a great sacrifice for the king and queen to send off their only child."

"My Lady Galifalia bore her royalty well," Aga said. "Much of what you are telling us I never knew. When I was given the boy to deliver to Gali, I was told very little and had to agree to much."

"The less the world knows about our workings, the more chance there is that the children we send can work out their destinies without interference. We leave it up to the nature of the dragon to bring things together."

"So let me get this straight," Aina said sitting up. "You are telling me that I am descended from the royal throne of the Dragon Keepers."

"If you are the granddaughter of the lady Galifalia, yes."

"And you are saying that Michael is also descended from the royal family."

"He has demonstrated to our satisfaction that he is. He is the child that we entrusted to Aga to bring to be raised by Galifalia. He is a distant relative to the queen, but without doubt of the royal house."

Aina turned to Michael with a broad smile. "Any more objections, Your Majesty?"

Michael ran his hand through his hair. He swallowed hard, trying to sort out his feelings. "When I had to leave the Dragon Compound, I went from exile to knight in the time it took to dress me in my new clothing. That was child's play compared to now going from knight to king. Star had trained me to fight, and I was ready for my new life. I have had no training to be a king."

"There is none," Aga said putting his arm around Michael. "Just as there is no training to becoming a father. You just do it, follow your heart and your good instincts, listen to the advice of others who have gone before you, and learn as you go. I want to recommend that you give both a good try." At this, everyone laughed.

"What is taking the refreshments so long?" Aina muttered. She stood and strode to the entrance, throwing aside the banners that made the makeshift door. She was astonished by what she saw. It looked like the whole army was collected there in one mass. Those standing around the door were looking rather sheepish. Colin stepped forward.

"Your Majesty, forgive us. We have been listening in to your conversation. They know," he said, gesturing to the assembled army behind him. "And they approve."

Michael came to stand beside Aina and took her hand. When the army saw them together, they erupted into uncontained cheering.

Epilogue

*A*ga, tell me something."

"That all depends on if I know the answer."

They had been sitting in silence some distance from the lights of the camp admiring the starry night.

"You have said you knew Galifalia as a young woman and joined her for awhile on what Mellifor called their great adventure. Years later you brought me as a babe to Nogardia. Just days ago you led Colin and his troops here to help us defeat Worrah. You appear old, yet everything you do reveals the strength and vigor with which you live your life."

"Well, life is much too interesting to be lived any other way. What were you wondering?"

Michael laughed. "Does this go hand in hand with being a wizard? How do you do it?"

Aga was silent a moment before answering. "What do you know about dragon tears?"

"As I related to you: They heal. They healed my broken body. As we speak they are healing the burnt and wasted land."

"You will have a wife younger than yourself. Does that not trouble you?"

Michael looked at the wizard with surprise. "Can you also read minds? Yes, it is this very thing that bothers me. I have spoken with Aina about this. She could choose a king suited to her own age, one who would stand strongly by her side as she grows old."

"You keep looking for excuses not to marry her," Aga said with a smile.

"I know it looks like that," he said abashed. "I just don't want to disappoint her."

"So, when you told Aina that you are more than ten years older than she is, what was her answer?"

"She did not respond with words. She took me in her arms and loved me with such a passion that I felt like twenty again."

"It won't be the last time that you feel younger. In fact, how have you been since Star healed you?"

"It's strange, but I have not felt this well for years. I know I'm still healing from my battle wounds, but down in my core, I feel strong and light, if that makes sense. I figured it came from the joy I've had finding Star again, and being able to openly express my love for Aina."

"Unless I am greatly mistaken, you will find that the increased strength and levity will be there for a long time to come. I've discovered that dragon tears bring more than healing. You will never have to worry about growing old before she does."

"I hope you are right," he said with a shake of his head.

"Come on," the wizard said, standing up. "Let's go see Star. Has he ever given you advice you could not use, even if you didn't understand it at the time?"

The two of them ambled across the fields and into a grove of trees. Star had taken to hiding from the many eyes that viewed him with a range of feelings, from wonder to fear to hostility. They had no trouble finding him, even in the dark. His coat shone as if the starry skies had descended to nestle in the branches of the trees. When they came upon him, Michael could feel the same peace and serenity emanating from him that he had known while living in the Dragon Compound. Star looked up and purred in his chime-like way.

"Star," Aga announced. "I bring you your young apprentice, burdened by many troubles."

Michael frowned. He had planned to frame it somewhat differently.

"Are you not happy?" Star asked, sounding surprised. "Haven't things turned out as you might have wished?"

"Far better than I could have imagined," Michael replied. "But—"

"You can't go back," Star said firmly.

"To Nogardia?" He was not sure what Star meant.

"Yes, you can't go back there, either. That life is finished."

"It's all so new to me," Michael said. "It's hard to imagine myself as king."

"Then don't bother imagining anything," Star suggested. "Be what you know yourself to be. Will you have any trouble being the queen's champion?"

"Not in the least. I have already gone to battle with you in her name."

"Then keep in mind that every true king is his queen's champion. He is her strength in the outer world. Be that for Aina. She will be your strength from within. You can trust that she will never fail you. It is a good arrangement."

"Will that be enough?"

"If you stop doubting it, yes. Now, tell me this, do you think you will have any trouble being the Dragon Master?"

Michael hesitated and did not respond.

"You can't go back," Star repeated firmly. "You will never be my scrub boy again. You can never return to being the dragon boy."

"I know," Michael said sadly.

"Don't worry," Star said lightly. "I'm sure they'll let you take me down to the river for a good scrubbing every once in awhile."

Michael laughed at his words.

"As it is, you'll have to teach the new scrub boys how to do it properly," Star continued. "You know I'm very particular."

"It's all so new," Michael sighed.

"Did I ever tell you about opening new doors in life?" Star asked.

"Yes," the knight admitted. "Repeatedly in my dreams."

"So you stand again at a threshold," Star said. "The only question is whether you are ready to walk through. Your old life is finished.

Leave it behind. Slough it off the same way I sloughed off my skin after our battle. There may indeed be portions of it that serve you, but you can never wear it as you did before. It's time to begin anew. We have come through a time of chaos, pain and distress. Now it is time for new beginnings. Instead of repeating the past, do the unexpected."

Michael shared Star's words with the wizard.

"I like the sound of that," Aga mused. "We could use some new beginnings, and even discover some new forms. Perhaps it is finally time to let go of some outworn practices. Who knows? With the help of a Luck Dragon, you just might manage to bring peace and prosperity into this land."

"With Star, I believe that even Gladur Nock can be changed," Michael pondered. "But how long can we expect it to last, with Worrah plotting from across our borders?"

Aga chuckled, "Not yet crowned, and already worried for his realm. Who can tell you how long peace will last, my king? No one can. Certainly not an aging wizard."

"No," Star agreed. "Not even a Luck Dragon." And the laughter of his chime-like voice filled the air.

Thus ends
The Dragon of Two Hearts

Book Two of
– The Star Trilogy –

About the Author

*R*aised in Los Angeles, Donald Samson spent the first twelve years of his adult life respectively in a Greek fishing village, a small German border town and finally in the mountains of Switzerland, healing from a mega-urban childhood.

Upon returning to the States, he took up the art of teaching young children. He was a Waldorf class teacher for nineteen years. He lives with his spirited wife, Claudia, two sons and sporadically obedient dog along the Front Range of the Rocky Mountains.

Mr. Samson has written plays for grades 3–7 and two plays for adults, one of which was a finalist in the Moondance Film Festival. He is the author of *The Dragon Boy*, Book One of The Star Trilogy. His other published works include two translations of Jakob Streit's biblical stories, *Journey to the Promised Land* and *We Will Build a Temple*. He was a contributing author to *Gazing into the Eyes of the Future, the Enactment of Saint Nicholas in the Waldorf School*. All four books are available from AWSNA Publications.

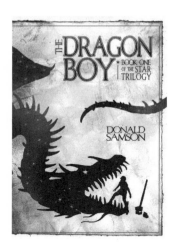

*R*ead the acclaimed first book of The Star Trilogy.

The Dragon Boy by Donald Samson is available from:

AWSNA Publications
publications@awsna.org
518-634-2222
or on order from your preferred bookstore.